THE PRICE OF PASSION

"If you report me to the authorities," Katerina said, her expression panicked, "my family will starve."

"You should have thought of that before," Drako said. "I would never send you to Newgate, and your fa~~~~ ~~~~ not starve. I do, however, demand rep~~~~

Katerina narrowed her ga~~~~ ~~~~ ~~~~ want?"

"I want all of you."

"I do not understand.

He smiled at her confusion. "I want you in my bed."

"I am a virtuous—"

"Do not deny you want me," Drako said, "and I want you as much as you want me."

His piercing blue eyes held hers captive. He stepped closer and offered his hand as if inviting her to dance.

"Follow your heart, Kat, not your head."

Katerina stared at him in indecision. Yes, she did want him. Where was the harm in one night of pleasure in a life filled with duty?

Books by Patricia Grasso

TO TAME A DUKE

TO TEMPT AN ANGEL

TO CHARM A PRINCE

TO CATCH A COUNTESS

TO LOVE A PRINCESS

SEDUCING THE PRINCE

PLEASURING THE PRINCE

TEMPTING THE PRINCE

ENTICING THE PRINCE

Published by Zebra Books

Ec...g
The Prince

PATRICIA
GRASSO

KT 0974205 0

Kensington Publishing Corp.
www.kensingtonbooks.com

Kensington Publishing Corp.
850 Third Avenue
New York, NY 10022

Copyright © 2008 by Patricia Grasso

All rights reserved. No part of this book may be reproduced
in any form or by any means without the prior written con-
sent of the Publisher, excepting brief quotes used in reviews.

If you purchased this book without a cover you should be
aware that this book is stolen property. It was reported as
"unsold and destroyed" to the Publisher and neither the
Author nor the Publisher has received any payment for this
"stripped book."

All Kensington titles, imprints, and distributed lines are
available at special quantity discounts for bulk purchases
for sales promotion, premiums, fund-raising, educational, or
institutional use.

Special book excerpts or customized printings can also be
created to fit specific needs. For details, write or phone the
office of the Kensington Special Sales Manager: Attn. Special
Sales Department. Kensington Publishing Corp., 850 Third
Avenue, New York, NY 10022. Phone: 1-800-221-2647.

Zebra and the Z logo Reg. U.S. Pat. & TM Off.

ISBN-13: 978-0-8217-8073-2
ISBN-10: 0-8217-8073-5

First Printing: November 2008
10 9 8 7 6 5 4 3 2 1

Printed in the United States of America

Chapter One

London, 1821

Anticipation strummed through her, sharpening her senses. She could almost hear the rhythmic pulsing of her surging blood.

Tonight the prince and she would rendezvous. She had waited five years for this moment and intended to savor every scintillating second of her evening. Scandal would explode like Vesuvius erupting, scorching society.

Katerina Garibaldi, the Contessa de Salerno, studied her image in the cheval mirror. A feline smile of satisfaction touched her lips, lifting the corners of her mouth. Excitement enhanced her beauty, her dark eyes gleaming like the priceless jewels she created.

Two delicate diamond buckle pendants—her own creation—clipped the gauzy straps of her violet gown. Diamond pins glittered in her black, upswept hairdo like stars sprinkled across the midnight sky. She wore a diamond cuff-bracelet on her right arm, and diamond fan earrings dangled from her earlobes, precluding the need for a necklace.

She wanted to dazzle the prince, not blind him.

From somewhere behind her, Katerina heard the humming of Nonna Strega, the widow she'd brought from Naples. The only other sound was the cicadas singing in the darkness of the garden below her window.

Katerina placed a dot of perfume above her upper lip. Inhaling her own jasmine scent heightened her awareness of herself when she stepped into society, a reminder to guard her expression and behavior and words.

The kohl lining her eyelids lent her a dramatic aura. Her gaze beckoned but never promised.

A lady should look her best when consorting with a prince. Lord, she felt like a princess in those fairy tales she told her daughter each evening.

Long, white gloves appeared in front of her. Katerina looked from the gloves to Nonna Strega. "No gloves tonight."

The older woman beamed with approval at Katerina. *"Bella, la Contessa."*

"Thank you, Nonna." Katerina smiled at her. "We speak English in England. Remember?"

"Si."

Once the woman had gone, Katerina crossed the chamber and opened the armoire's doors. She reached for the black, diamond-encrusted reticule. After slipping its gold links handle onto her left arm, Katerina walked down the corridor.

Her pace slowed as she neared her daughter's chamber. Should she enter or not? Seeing her daughter's sweet expression could change her plans for the evening, and she would never forgive herself if she missed this opportunity.

Katerina lifted her head high and rehearsed her grand entrance by floating with practiced poise down the stairs to the foyer. Her brother awaited her there, his dark gaze fixed on her graceful descent, but her sisters were nowhere in sight.

Her brother shoved his hands in his trouser pockets. "You are going through with this?"

"Hektor, do not attempt to dissuade me."

He shrugged. "Do what you must, Sister."

Katerina narrowed her dark, kohl-lined eyes on him. Something was definitely amiss. She had expected an argument but received indifference.

The majordomo opened the door. "Enjoy your evening, my lady."

"Thank you, Dudley."

Outside, Katerina paused before climbing into her coach. The sultry July evening reminded her of Naples. Returning to Italy would become impossible after tonight, regret at that tingeing her excitement.

Inverary House on Park Lane was a scant few blocks from her home in Trevor Square. Twenty minutes later, Katerina entered the duke's residence and climbed the stairs to the ballroom.

She had arrived purposely late. Her tardiness would whet the prince's desire.

A wave of uncertainty washed over her. There would be no returning to her old life once she went to the prince.

Katerina had never felt so desperately alone, not even on that long-ago night that had brought her to this moment. Her steps slowed. The nearer the ballroom, the more her confidence waned.

"Good evening, my lady," the duke's majordomo greeted her.

"Good evening, Tinker."

The man announced her arrival. "The Contessa de Salerno."

Katerina scanned the ballroom before joining the elite throng. She spotted her handsome quarry at the far end of the enormous chamber.

Summoning her courage, Katerina walked into the

crush of guests and wended her way slowly around the room. She ignored the greetings from friends and acquaintances, her intense focus fixed on her man. She did, however, spare a nod for her host and hostess like a young queen acknowledging her courtiers.

"Your Highness?"

The prince whirled around, the warmth of his relieved expression diminished by irritation. "Good evening, my lady." He bowed over her hand. "I despaired of seeing you this evening."

"Tonight is ours." Her voice was a throaty purr. "I brought you a gift."

His irritation vanished. "One of your priceless gems, my lady?"

Katerina opened her reticule and reached inside. In a flash of movement, she drew a pistol and pointed it at his head.

Several women screamed, drawing the crowd's attention. Guests began backing away out of the line of fire.

"What are you doing?" The prince appeared confused and shocked and frightened.

"Pulling this trigger will separate your royal head from your royal body," Katerina answered. Her smile was serene, but the hand holding the pistol shook like the palsy.

"You cannot be serious." His complexion had paled to a ghostly white. "What have I ever done—?"

"My name is Katerina *Pavlova* Garibaldi," she interrupted, noting his stunned recognition. "Justice has been delayed too long. Regrettably, I cannot execute you three times for the three lives you stole."

"You do not understand," the prince whined.

"Silence," Katerina snapped. "Die like a man instead of a weasel."

Without warning, a masculine hand materialized from

behind her, covering her hand on the pistol, but did not snatch it away. A husky voice spoke, a voice she'd grown to love. "Well-mannered ladies do not point pistols, darling."

Katerina kept her gaze on the prince and her hand on the pistol. "The coward deserves to die for his crimes against my family."

"His Highness *does* deserve punishment," the voice agreed, "but death by pistol is too quick and so messy."

"Do not deter me." Katerina steeled herself against her lover. "My fingers itch to finish what he started five years ago."

"Do you love me enough to listen before executing the prince?" His question was a husky whisper against her ear. "Speak."

"Do you trust me enough to lower the pistol while I speak?"

Katerina tightened her grip on the pistol, her finger on the trigger. *"No . . ."*

Two Months Earlier

The duchess's incessant matchmaking was pushing her perilously close to the edge of insanity. On the other hand, Roxanne Campbell's love of expensive jewels and her deep, deep pockets did encourage patience with the woman's meddling.

Katerina sat in her workshop overlooking the inner courtyard and put the finishing touches on the Duchess of Inverary's ring. She reached for another felt polishing stick and looked through the magnifier at the enormous emerald surrounded by baguette diamonds.

Hearing a blue jay's shriek, Katerina lifted her gaze to the blooming courtyard below the window. The first of

May in London was so much warmer than Moscow but positively frigid in comparison to Naples.

Oh, how she wished to return to Naples. Too bad, civil strife should vex that land of sunshine. The last she'd heard the Austrians had agreed to send soldiers to quell the rebellious rabble. Perhaps she could return to her beloved Naples once peace had been restored.

Katerina inhaled deeply, savoring spring's fresh scent. Lilacs and roses perfumed the air, mingling with her own jasmine fragrance. A gentle breeze teased the trees, their swishing leaves a comforting sound.

Her daughter's giggles from below brought a smile to Katerina's lips. Working as a team, Assunta and Concetta were wonderful nannies for Viveka. How fortunate that Nonna Strega had two able daughters.

"Her Grace has arrived."

Katerina looked over her shoulder at her brother. "You left her sitting alone?"

"Roksana and Ludmilla are entertaining her," Hektor said, referring to their sixteen-year-old twin sisters. "Do not keep our best client waiting."

"The last person to use the burnisher failed to clean and polish it." Katerina arched a dark brow at him. "I wonder who that was."

Hektor grinned, unrepentant. "I accept responsibility for my shortcomings." And then he disappeared out the door.

Katerina returned to her task, shining the emerald's facets. Perfection took time. The duchess could wait a moment or two.

Finally satisfied, Katerina placed the ring in one of two black boxes, the second containing a surprise for the duchess. Gifting one's wealthiest client with an occasional treat constituted good business. Her own father had given the czar many such treasures, and the czar had shown his appreciation by giving her father many commissions.

Brushing a stray wisp of ebony hair off her forehead, Katerina decided against freshening herself before meeting with the duchess. Betrothal and wedding rings for the duchess's stepdaughters awaited their finishing touches.

Imagine two of the duke's by-blows catching princes in marriage. That delicious thought heartened Katerina, even though the princes were Kazanovs.

Katerina left her workshop on Merlin's Way and strolled down the annex corridor connecting her workshop to her main residence on Lancelot Place. Pausing a moment, she watched her daughter singing to the nannies.

"Bravo." Katerina clapped for her daughter's performance.

Viveka looked up. "Mummy Zia, play with me."

"I will join you in a few minutes," Katerina called. "Can you wait?"

"I wait here." Viveka pointed at the ground.

Katerina continued on her way to the main house. Her daughter always made her smile. One day her daughter's father would pay for his crimes. She intended to honor the vow she had made five years earlier. Somehow.

Pausing outside the formal drawing room, Katerina smoothed her skirt and pasted a warm smile onto her face. Then she breezed into the room.

"Welcome to my humble home," Katerina greeted the duchess. "Your presence honors me."

"Good morning, Kat darling." The Duchess of Inverary gave her a dimpled smile and flicked a glance at her surroundings.

Decorated in shades of red and gilded mahogany, the drawing room screamed opulence. Red silk papered the walls, a crystal and gold chandelier hung overhead, thick carpets in jewel-colored designs hugged the polished wood floor. A gold clock, encrusted with diamonds, sat on the table.

"Hardly humble, darling."

Katerina sat on an upholstered chair near the duchess. "Roksana, please ask Nonna Strega to serve refreshments."

"Nonna is already on her way," her sister said.

"Your Grace." Ludmilla drew the woman's attention. "Did you know that *strega* means witch?"

"Thank you for that unsolicited information," Katerina said.

"Nonna is a witch?" the duchess asked.

"My daughter considers the woman a grandmother," Katerina explained. "Viveka's nannies are Nonna's daughters who refer to their mother as *strega*. When my daughter repeated their words, the pet name stuck."

"I see you consider your staff as family," the duchess said in obvious approval. "We Campbells feel the same about our dearest Tinker."

"I regret my inability to deliver your ring to Inverary House," Katerina said. "My irresponsible brother delayed its completion."

"Irresponsibility is a masculine trait," the duchess remarked.

The twins giggled at that.

"Go to the courtyard," Katerina dismissed her sisters, "and play with Viveka."

Still giggling, Roksana and Ludmilla left the drawing room. Nonna Strega arrived with a tray of refreshments.

"*Grazie*, Nonna. I will serve Her Grace."

Katerina lifted the teapot to pour the steaming brew. She passed the duchess the porcelain teacup and saucer before pouring her own.

"Nonna brews the tea with mint," Katerina said. "Please, help yourself to the anise cookies."

After sipping her tea, Katerina set the teacup and saucer down near the diamond-encrusted table clock. The piece reminded her of her late father who had designed it as a gift for the czar but died before presenting it.

Katerina reached for the small box and opened its lid. Baguette diamonds surrounded an octagonal, step-cut emerald set in platinum.

"Exquisite, *la contessa*." Pleasure gleamed in the duchess's eyes.

"The platinum strengthens the emerald's power to bring its owner love and money. The emerald, of course, comes from Cleopatra's mines."

The duchess gave her a dimpled smile. "I anticipate wearing the ring this evening."

Here it comes.

Katerina had known Roxanne Campbell would somehow turn their conversation to her Beltane Ball that evening. The duchess was trying to find her a husband. Again.

Ignoring the reference to the ball, Katerina offered the duchess a second box. "A gift to show my appreciation for welcoming me into Society."

"Darling, you did not need to reward me," the duchess said, reaching for the box.

Katerina smiled. "I *wanted* to create a special surprise for you."

"I adore special surprises," the duchess exclaimed, and lifted the lid.

Startling the eye, the brooch was a flower bouquet. White and colored diamonds, accompanied by emeralds, had been mounted in gold and platinum.

"I set the brooch *en tremblant*," Katerina told her. "The flowers will move when worn."

"How original, but I cannot accept—"

"If you do not accept my gift," Katerina interrupted, "you will hurt my feelings."

"Very well, I accept your gift." Another dimpled smile. "How will I ever repay your generosity?"

Forget about finding me a husband, Katerina thought. "Your friendship is my reward."

"I will wear the brooch tonight," the duchess announced. "The other ladies will expire from envy."

The Beltane Ball again.

"Did I mention the brooch is a replica from the Russian crown jewels?" Katerina nodded at the other woman's surprised expression. "My father created the original piece for Czar Alexander the First."

"I can hardly wait to tell Lady Althorpe," the duchess said. "You must promise to attend my ball tonight."

"I should work on those betrothal and wedding rings," Katerina hedged. "I promised Princes Stepan and Mikhail their rings would be finished no later than tomorrow."

"Finish Stepan's this afternoon and work on Mikhail's in the morning," the duchess said. "The other ladies will swarm you once they see this brooch."

The duchess was correct. Social gatherings provided business opportunities.

"Once you finish my stepdaughters' rings, I want you to make me a diamond ensemble," the duchess continued. "Magnus and I have made a bet. My wonderful husband believes his daughters have engaged in no sexual intimacies, but I know better."

Embarrassment stained Katerina's cheeks. Even worse, Hektor lounged in the doorway and smiled at the duchess's words.

"Kat darling, you blush like a virgin."

"If His Grace wins," Katerina changed the subject, "what does he get?"

"There is no chance of that happening," the duchess said, "but he requests a day of silence from me. Which is quite absurd since he only needs to await our next argument."

Katerina smiled at that.

"Let me tell you about Beltane," the duchess said. "The holiday celebrates lovers and fertility. We'll have a maypole queen, candied violets, and passion flower wine. All are special to this day. We will also be welcoming three of my nephew-in-law's cousins from Moscow—Princes Drako, Lykos, and Gunter Kazanov. Do you know them?"

Katerina lost her smile at the name *Drako* but managed to keep her expression blank. "I have never had the pleasure."

The Duchess of Inverary patted her hand. "I do believe Drako and you would suit."

Drako Kazanov. The one man she despised most in this world. The one man she had vowed revenge upon.

The duchess's voice intruded on her thoughts. "You must meet him before any ladies stake a claim. So very virile, you know, and wealthy beyond avarice. Money and virility is a powerful aphrodisiac."

Katerina glanced at her brother. Hektor was frowning at her, but she ignored him.

"Your Grace, I cannot refuse the opportunity to welcome a countryman to London."

"I excel at relationship strategies." The duchess gave her a conspiratorial wink. "Promise me you will dance with Drako."

"His Highness has not requested a dance, Your Grace."

The duchess's dimpled smile appeared. "Men want what eludes them. Adopt a cool but beckoning attitude."

Katerina stood to escort the duchess to the foyer. "Drako means dragon," she remarked.

"The dragon prince," the duchess echoed. "How deliciously dangerous."

Once the duchess had gone, Katerina faced her brother. "Tonight begins our revenge."

"You cannot know if Alina was fingering the prince or asking for his help," Hektor argued.

"Do not be ridiculous," Katerina said. "That man

destroyed our family. Alina, Ilya, and Papa . . . All dead within twenty-four hours."

"Dragons breathe fire," Hektor warned her, "and you may burn for your trouble."

Katerina gave her brother an ambiguous smile. "Even dragons die."

"Welcome to England, Your Highness."

"Thank you, Your Grace." Prince Drako Kazanov shook the older man's hand and sat in one of the upholstered chairs in front of the ducal desk. Stretching his long legs out, the prince appeared the perfect image of sleek sophistication, a man at ease with his richly appointed surroundings.

Magnus Campbell sat on a black leather chair behind an enormous oak desk. Mahogany bookcases had been built into the walls, and two black marble hearths supplied heat on chilly days. Indeed, the only touches of femininity were the duchess's portrait and a vase of fragrant lilacs.

Beyond the closed door sounded the muted voices of passing servants. The faint strains of music wafted through the air as the orchestra in the ballroom began playing.

Prince Rudolf Kazanov passed Drako a crystal glass of whisky and then raised his own in salute. "Welcome to London, Cousin."

"And to you, Cousin." Drako lifted his glass, returning the salute, and sipped the dark amber liquid, savoring its sharp taste. A bit too mild for him, though. He would have preferred vodka, a real man's drink.

"I'd give the Campbell fortune to live like my ancestors in the Highlands," the duke muttered, tugging at his cravat. "Bare-chested and wrapped in a plaid."

The older man's discomfort made Drako's own cravat feel snug. "What is a plaid?"

"A skirt," Rudolf answered.

The Duke of Inverary snapped his gaze to Prince Rudolf. "A plaid is *not* a skirt."

"I stand corrected, Your Grace." Rudolf sent Drako a sidelong smile. "A plaid *resembles* a skirt."

Drako grinned at their byplay. He could see that his cousin and the duke had formed a close friendship. And, if the rumors proved true, the Duke of Inverary was his cousin's natural father. Certainly, Fydor Kazanov had never behaved as a father should, not even to his undisputed sons—Cousins Viktor, Mikhail, and Stepan. Only Vladimir, the old man's heir, had received any loving attention.

Drako knew that he and his siblings had been lucky. Their own father had escaped the worst of the Kazanov traits. The truth was growing up Kazanov meant his father stood barely inside the normalcy line. If it hadn't been for marrying his mother, his father might have become another Fydor Kazanov.

"Where are your brothers?" the Duke of Inverary asked, changing the subject.

"Lykos and Gunter will arrive with Viktor and his wife," Drako answered. His piercing blue eyes, inherited from his mother, shone with easy humor. "Rudolf knew I would require a separation after traveling across Europe with my younger brothers and arranged for them to stay with Viktor. At least, until I find us a suitable residence."

"Could this be a permanent move?"

"Few things in life are permanent, Your Grace."

"Our vodka imports are doing well," Prince Rudolf said, changing the topic to business. "Unfortunately, the English commoners prefer gin because of the price."

"Perhaps we could export whisky to Russia," the duke suggested.

"Why would a man buy whisky when he can drink vodka?" Drako asked in genuine confusion.

Prince Rudolf chuckled. "I told you, Your Grace, my countrymen will never buy your whisky."

"Even Russian women prefer vodka," Drako added.

"Whisky is as fine a drink as vodka," Inverary said.

"Only if the man is a Scot," Rudolf replied.

"Did I mention the Kazanovs' newest venture?" Drako asked. Without waiting for the negative reply, he told them, "We made a fortune on our gold mines and precious gems investments. Baltic amber, Ukranian opals, Yakutian diamonds, Afghani emeralds and rubies."

"You should speak with the Contessa de Salerno," the duke said. "The countess will be interested in doing business with you. Roxie insists the woman is not only a master jeweler but a design genius."

A businesswoman? Drako had never heard anything so ridiculous. "A countess who owns her own business?"

"Not only is the Contessa de Salerno a master jeweler and design genius," Rudolf informed him, "but she is also your future bride. A match made in heaven, would you not say, Your Grace?"

"More likely, a match made in Inverary House," the duke grumbled.

"I beg your pardon?" Drako could not credit what he'd heard.

Feigned sympathy appeared on his cousin's face. "The Duchess of Inverary has found you a bride."

Drako flicked a glance at the duke. "I do not require a bride at this time."

"Your time is up, Cousin." Rudolf grinned, obviously enjoying himself. "Once the duchess decides, your bachelor days are done."

"Roxie wants everyone happily married," the duke added.

"Happily married is an oxymoron," Drako drawled.

"You may like the contessa," the duke said. "Tell him about her."

"Katerina Garibaldi is Italian by marriage but Russian by birth," Rudolf said.

"I may know her. What is her maiden name?"

"I asked her that question more than once," Rudolf answered. "Like an elusive butterfly, the countess evaded my query."

"The Queen of Naples gave her a letter of introduction," Inverary reminded him.

"The letter could have been forged," Rudolf said. "I suspect *la contessa* is not precisely what she appears, and, several weeks ago, I sent the Queen of Naples a letter of inquiry. An answer should soon be forthcoming, and then we will know for certain."

Drako smiled at the two men. A beautiful imposter, a master jeweler, a design genius. He loved a mystery almost as much as a challenge.

"The contessa supports a brother, two sisters, and a small daughter," the duke said. "Roxie noted the woman's home is filled with priceless objects."

"Beauty and wealth and talent?" Drako could not believe any woman could be so blessed. "The contessa must be much in demand."

Rudolf gave him a sidelong smile. "Yuri seems smitten."

"Yuri?" Drako sat up straight, the ashes of anger fanning into a tiny flame. "Yuri is in London?"

"Prince Yuri and Princess Anya are visiting their aunt and uncle," the duke told him. "You dislike the prince?"

"Yuri is a sniveling swine who creates irreparable damage wherever he goes," Drako answered.

Raisa, his slightly shallow and exceedingly naive fiancee, would still be living if she had never met Yuri. He had considered issuing a challenge at the time, but his brothers convinced him that Yuri was not worth a trip to the gallows. Vengeance did not bring the dead back to life.

"I would give you a word of caution," the duke said, drawing him from his thoughts. "You and your brothers should not find yourselves alone with any unmarried female, especially the Blond Brigade."

"A brigade?" Drako looked at his cousin.

"So dubbed by Mikhail," Rudolf explained, "the Blond Brigade are three she-wolves who will do *anything* to entice a prince into marriage."

"I will warn Lykos and Gunter," Drako said. "We will beware."

"Are there only the three of you?" the duke asked. "Or do you have other siblings?"

"We are nine brothers and three sisters."

The Duke of Inverary nodded with approval. "That is a healthy family."

Rudolf laughed. "If you knew his mother, you would say that is a miraculous family."

When the duke looked at him, Drako explained, "Father says Mother thinks fucking is an Asian city."

The three men laughed in easy camaraderie. The door opened, drawing their attention. They shot to their feet as the Duchess of Inverary crossed the room.

"Magnus darling, see the contessa's gift," the duchess said, pointing to the brooch.

"The contessa *gave* you that?" Inverary shook his head. "Why would she give you an expensive gift when you are willing to pay?"

"Katerina appreciates my friendship." The duchess gave Drako a dimpled smile. "Not only does tonight's ball welcome you to London but honors Beltane, a pagan holiday for lovers and fertility."

"Your Grace, if I could find a woman as beautiful as you," Drako said, bowing over her hand, "I would steal her in an instant and make her my bride."

"What a romantic idea," the duchess said, and then looked at her husband. "Our guests are arriving."

The Duke of Inverary offered his wife his arm and escorted her from the study. The two princes followed them out.

Drako gave his cousin a sidelong glance. "So, this contessa is beautiful?"

"Quite lovely."

"You sound like an Englishman." Drako lowered his voice so only his cousin heard his next words. "Would you care to place a small wager concerning the contessa?"

Prince Rudolf grinned. "I would never refuse the opportunity to take your money."

"Not only will I learn the contessa's maiden name," Drako said, "but I will win a place in her bed."

"No man in London has gone there yet."

Drako arched a dark brow at his cousin. "A thousand pounds?"

"You must be feeling insecure," Rudolf mocked him. "Two thousand pounds?"

Rudolf shook his head. "Five thousand pounds?"

Drako offered his hand. "Five thousand pounds, it is."

"Remember, Cousin, pride goes before a fall." Rudolf shook his hand. "Even you cannot perform miracles."

Chapter Two

"Do not announce me, Tinker."

The majordomo inclined his head. "As you wish, my lady."

Katerina paused for a long moment, perusing London's elite while she willed her quickening pulse to slow. Formally attired gentlemen provided a stark background for their ladies, gowned in their finest. Many wore jewels that she had designed.

Where is he? Katerina wondered. *Which of those men is the villain who destroyed my family? What will these aristocrats think when I unmask the monster?*

With the duchess's less than subtle nudging, Prince Drako Kazanov would seek her out, and Katerina had dressed to entice him. She wore a simple, low-cut emerald silk gown. Her jewels screamed immense wealth. Katerina wore a necklace of sixteen marquise-cut diamonds, square-cut emeralds serving as spacers. Wearing her late-sister's bandeau bracelet had been a stroke of genius. Panels of green enamel clover leaves and diamonds intersected with rectangular-cut emeralds.

The prince had given her sister the bracelet, and she

wanted to see his reaction. Or would he even recognize it? Perhaps the monster gave expensive trinkets to many women.

"I do hope you aren't trying to steal my job," Tinker whispered.

Katerina smiled at the majordomo. "You caught me daydreaming, sir."

"There are several unattached princes in attendance tonight," Tinker said. "I daresay, females dreaming of the unattainable fill the ballroom."

"My taste in gentlemen is more discerning than an appetizing title." Katerina lifted her head high and descended the stairs.

Skirting the dance floor, Katerina inhaled the ladies' mingling fragrances. She had touched her own jasmine scent above her upper lip lest others overwhelm her.

The orchestra was playing a waltz, the strains of violins transporting her across time and space to Moscow. Her father had enjoyed the violin, insisting its emotional tones inspired his creativity. Living in Italy had fostered her love of the opera, her designing of precious jewels was an obsession needing no inspiration.

"Contessa."

Katerina turned toward the voice and recognized the duchess's bosom crony. "Good evening, Lady Althorpe."

"I must tell you how much I admire the brooch you created for Her Grace," Lady Althorpe said. "Roxie told me you were an artistic genius. Lord Althorpe saw the piece and insisted I ask you to create a special trinket for me."

"Thank you for the praise." Attending the ball had already brought her a commission, possibly others before the evening ended. That pleased Katerina. "I look forward to assisting you."

"When may we consult?"

"At the moment I am finishing the rings for Her

Grace's stepdaughters," Katerina told her. "Shall we say one afternoon next week at your convenience?"

"Roxie has been asking for you." Lady Althorpe gave her a conspiratorial smile. "She wants to introduce you to a particular gentleman of the highest rank."

"If you will excuse me," Katerina said, "I will search for Her Grace. Until next week, my lady."

When Katerina turned to walk away, her gaze collided with an incredibly handsome gentleman standing a short distance from her. Tall and well-built, he wore his formal attire with casual ease.

Having caught her eye, the stranger proceeded to inspect her, slowly and insolently, as if he was considering purchasing her. His gaze touched her lips and caressed her cleavage, making her blush.

Katerina felt her cheeks heating. Never one to shrink from a challenge, Katerina returned his rude inspection from his angularly chiseled features to his torso and down his legs.

When she raised her gaze to his, the gentleman grinned and inclined his head in greeting. Katerina gave him an ambiguous smile and flicked a glance at the female admirers surrounding him, including the notorious Blond Brigade.

He rolled his eyes in apparent boredom. She arched a dark brow, conveying how little she sympathized with his plight, and then turned away.

Prince Yuri blocked her path. This prince was a good-looking blonde but not to her taste. The narcissistic boor considered himself irresistible. Any woman who loved Prince Yuri would find herself and the prince in love with the same person.

"Good evening, my lady." Yuri bowed over her hand. "I believe this waltz is ours."

Refusing his invitation would be rude. And that could harm her business.

"I believe you are correct, Your Highness."

Stepping onto the dance floor, Katerina and Yuri joined the couples swirling around the ballroom. She glanced at the hand holding hers and decided the prince was too soft and had never done a day's work in his pampered life.

"What an unusual bracelet," Yuri said, drawing her attention. "One of your creations?"

"My late husband purchased it from an estate."

Circling the ballroom in the prince's arms, Katerina let her gaze drift to the handsome stranger. The society maidens were still vying for his attention, but his gaze had fixed on her.

No, not her. He was staring at Yuri, the man's expression bordering on hatred.

Well, she could not fault his opinion of the prince. Yuri would never appear on her own list of favorite people.

"Will you ride with me tomorrow?" Yuri asked.

"Unfortunately, I must decline." Katerina assumed a look of regret. "I have a previous appointment."

Clearly, her refusal annoyed the prince. "I wondered if you would design me a pair of cufflinks?"

"I would be honored, Your Highness," Katerina said, as they left the dance floor. "Shall we say one afternoon next week?"

"Shall we say tomorrow?" Yuri countered.

"This waltz belongs to me," said a voice beside them.

"Good evening, Lord Gordon." Katerina waited until the prince walked out of earshot. "Thank you, Douglas, for rescuing me from that insufferable boor."

"I can recognize a damsel in distress," the Marquis of Huntly said, "but voicin' insults aboot royalty is naughty."

"Call me incorrigible," Katerina said, making him smile. When they stepped onto the dance floor, Katerina glanced at his hand. Douglas Gordon's hands were not soft like the prince's but still unblemished by manual work. A financial wizard, the Marquis of Huntly was a man with few opportunities for manual pursuits except, perhaps, golfing or gambling at White's Gentleman's Club or hunting in autumn. With his dark brown hair and gray eyes and pleasant expression, the Scottish marquis was handsome in the extreme. Many a society maiden would love to pass her life as his wife and help him spend his vast fortune.

"I wish to purchase my stepmother a special piece to commemorate her birthday next month," the marquis told her. "May I call upon ye to see yer designs?"

"I would love to design a piece for you," Katerina answered, "however, previous commitments have swamped me with work. Next week would be more convenient."

"Let us confer one afternoon next week." The marquis escorted her off the dance floor, steering her toward two older women. "Meeting Stepmama may inspire yer creativity."

The two older women noted their approach. One woman's expression was warm and the other's decidedly cool.

"I present the Contessa de Salerno," he introduced them. "Katerina, my stepmother and my aunt Cecelia."

"Roxanne Campbell has been trumpeting your genius," Aunt Cecelia said.

"I believe Her Grace exaggerates my talent."

"I do not approve of women working in the trades," Lady Gordon said.

The marquis laughed. "The contessa is an artist, not a tradeswoman."

"One person's art is another's trade," Katerina said. "If you will excuse me, I must greet my hostess."

Douglas walked beside her. When she looked at him, he said, "Prince Yuri will keep his distance if I accompany ye, and I want to apologize for my stepmother. She's pure English and canna help bein' difficult."

"You do not need to apologize," Katerina assured him. "Though I appreciate your concern, you need not protect me from Yuri. I will see you soon."

Leaving his side, Katerina headed in the duchess's direction. She knew Lady Gordon worried that her stepson would offer for a foreign widow with four dependents.

Katerina planned no romantic entanglements. At least, until she honored her vow of vengeance.

"Darling Kat," the Duchess of Inverary greeted her. "I wondered if you would change your mind about tonight."

"I always keep my promises, Your Grace." Katerina noted the dark-haired stranger dancing with one of the duchess's stepdaughters. "Is he your next victim?"

"In a manner of speaking, but that particular gentleman is much too sophisticated for my dearest Raven." The Duchess of Inverary gave her a dimpled smile. "Listen, darling, Drako is positively panting to meet you. Assume a cool but enticing attitude when you meet him. Ah, here he comes with my wonderful stepdaughter."

The duchess's words surprised Katerina. She snapped her gaze to the duke's youngest stepdaughter and the dark-haired man leaving the dance floor.

The closer the prince stepped, the more handsome he appeared, the faster her pulse beat. She had never considered the monster would appeal to her.

"Drako darling," the duchess introduced them, "I present my dear friend, Katerina Garibaldi, the Contessa de Salerno."

Prince Drako Kazanov gave Katerina his attention, a smile flirting with his chiseled lips. Good humor shone from his eyes.

Black hair. Piercing blue eyes. Magnificent muscles encased in formal attire tailored to his perfect physique.

Katerina knew she was in trouble. How could she dare even consider destroying the Lord's masterpiece of masculinity?

Prince Drako bowed over her hand. "I am pleased to meet the famously talented Contessa de Salerno."

For a moment, Katerina could not find her voice. His hand was not too soft. Simply perfection. Like the rest of him.

What a coil. The Lord should have made the monster as ugly outside as he was inside.

"Your Highness," she murmured, managing a polite smile.

"Her Grace tells me you hail from Moscow," the prince said, still holding her hand. "That we never met surprises me."

Steeling herself against him, Katerina disengaged her hand from his. "I knew my good luck would end sometime." And then she walked away.

Drako admired the gentle sway of her hips as she retreated. The contessa possessed many irresistible attributes. Beauty and talent. Intelligence and wit. Mystery and challenge.

Snatching her hand out of his did not deter him, merely added to her allure. If she stole a peek at him, the lady would be his eventually and, less important, so too would his cousin's five thousand pounds.

Look at me, Drako willed her, *and I will squander those five thousand pounds on you.*

The Contessa de Salerno paused to greet his cousins and their wives. While speaking, she turned her head and gave him a sidelong glance.

Well done, my Russian beauty. Drako inclined his head in her direction, enjoying her embarrassment at being caught. How long had it been since he had seen a sincere blush staining a lady's cheeks?

"I believe you are correct about the contessa suiting me,"

Drako said, looking at the duchess who was watching their byplay. "Choose the contessa for your May Queen."

"Kat could name another gentleman for her king," the duchess warned him.

Drako assumed an admonishing expression. "There is no chance of that happening."

"You arrogant devil."

"You adore arrogant devils," Drako teased her. "After all, you married one."

Her dimpled smile appeared. "I have lived to rue that day."

"You have loved every irritating moment."

Drako nodded at her and sauntered in the direction of his cousins, his gaze fixed on his quarry. Reaching their group, he stood beside the contessa. She pointedly ignored his presence.

"My lady," Prince Rudolf started introducing them, "I present my cousin—"

"We have met," Katerina interrupted, sparing no glance for the cousin.

"Have you met my brothers, Lykos and Gunter?" Drako asked her.

"Prince Rudolf introduced them," Katerina answered, still without looking at him.

"Is something wrong with my appearance?" Drako asked his cousins' wives.

"No, of course not," Princess Samantha answered.

Princess Regina wore a puzzled smile. "Why do you ask?"

Drako struggled against a smile. "The contessa refuses to look at me."

"There is nothing wrong with your appearance." Katerina rounded on him, her dark gaze colliding with his. "The Devil has the power to assume a pleasing shape."

"Thank you for the compliment." Laughter shone from his incredible blue eyes. "The Duchess of Inverary called me an arrogant devil."

That made her smile. "Her Grace is an excellent judge of character."

"Touche, la contessa."

"I have never seen anything as compelling as my aunt's brooch," Princess Samantha said.

"Actually, the brooch is a replica of a gift my father gave the czar." Katerina knew she had said too much as soon as the words slipped from her lips.

"Your father travels in the highest circles," Drako said. "Who is he?"

The prince was sharper than her wire-cutting snips.

"My father *did* travel in the highest circles," Katerina said. "He is deceased."

"Samantha, commission a piece for yourself," Prince Rudolf said, helping her evade his cousin's question.

"Mere gems do not interest me," Samantha told her husband. "I already possess the jewel in the Kazanov crown."

Prince Rudolf smiled. "Thank you, my love."

"A woman can never own too many jewels, a lady's insurance against life's rainy days," Katerina said. "Pearls accentuated by diamonds would embellish your classic beauty."

"What would embellish *my* classic beauty?" Drako asked, making his cousins and their wives laugh.

Katerina stared him full in the face and pretended to study his features. "A crucifix wrapped in wolfbane?"

Drako laughed, catching her with his easy humor. "My lady, may I have this dance?" When she opened her mouth to decline, he surprised her by saying, "Your jasmine fragrance symbolizes amiability so you cannot refuse me."

"I would enjoy dancing with you," Katerina lied, accepting his hand.

Stepping onto the dance floor, Drako and Katerina joined the other couples swirling in time to the music.

The prince placed his hand on her waist and drew her indiscreetly close. She tried to inch back, but he refused to let her retreat.

Katerina did not want to like him and fought the urge to lose herself in the music and the man, his skill and his sandalwood scent intoxicating her. She squelched that unwanted feeling and concentrated on the astounding fact that she was waltzing with her enemy.

"Your admirers appear unhappy with your choice of partners," Katerina said, observing the Blond Brigade's disgruntled expressions.

"And so are yours." Drako smiled at her. "You seem familiar."

"And so do you."

"What are you doing in England?" he asked.

Katerina gave him her sweetest smile. "Living."

"And where do you do that?"

"I live in a house"—He leveled an unamused look on her—"located on Lancelot Place in Trevor Square."

"What did you say your maiden name was?"

"I did not mention my maiden name." When he arched a brow at her, she asked, "Where is your princess?"

Drako dropped his gaze to her lips and, for one awful moment, she feared he might kiss her. "Alas, I am still searching for the appropriate woman to wear the title."

Katerina glanced at the Blond Brigade. "You are attracting many admiring candidates."

"I require a loving wife, not a greedy one." Drako escorted her off the dance floor as the music ended. "Besides, I prefer to do the chasing."

"What a novel idea."

"You are not searching for a wealthy husband?"

"I can take care of myself," she told him.

"Designing jewels like that bracelet?"

Katerina stiffened, though she managed to keep her

expression pleasantly blank. Had he recognized his gift to her sister?

Before she could think of a reply, Drako leaned close to whisper, "No man warming your bed makes for a cold existence."

"Excuse me, Your Highness." Katerina walked away, giving him no time to stop her.

Deciding to leave before succumbing to the powerful urge to vent her anger, Katerina wended her way through the crowd toward the door. She stopped short when a gentleman blocked her path.

"At the last ball, you promised me a second dance," Prince Yuri said.

Katerina forced herself to smile. Her business hinged on good public relations. "So I did, Your Highness, but—"

"No excuses, my lady."

Katerina accepted his hand and stepped onto the dance floor. At least, this prince kept a respectable distance between their bodies as they circled the ballroom.

"I must warn you to keep Drako Kazanov at bay," Prince Yuri said, his words for her ears only.

That got her attention. "What do you mean?"

"Beware Kazanov, for his reputation with women is legendary," Yuri said. "His fiancee committed suicide rather than marry him."

The music ended before Katerina could question him further. His remarks troubled her. What had Kazanov done that would make his fiancee suicidal? She supposed anything was possible. After all, he had shot her brother in the back.

Did Yuri know what had transpired five years earlier? If so, could he be persuaded to testify against Drako Kazanov in a court of law? No, that would only reveal her identity, ruin her thriving business, and put the prince on guard. She needed to exact her own justice.

Prince Yuri bowed over her hand in courtly manner. "Do not forget my cufflinks."

Wearing a troubled expression, Katerina glanced in Drako's direction and caught him watching her. And then another gentleman appeared in front of her.

"Dance with me?"

Katerina smiled at the Marquis of Huntly. She could hardly refuse a friend and prospective customer.

"Yes, Douglas, I will dance with you and then intend to end my evening."

The marquis escorted her onto the dance floor. She stepped into his arms, but her mind was on Drako Kazanov who was partnering Princess Anya, the worst of the Blond Brigade.

Why should the sight of Drako dancing with the blond witch trouble her? She despised him. Perhaps death came too quickly. Forty years of marriage to one of the Blond Brigade might be considered an appropriate torment. That idea made her lips twitch.

"What is so amusin'?" the marquis asked.

"My mind wandered to my daughter," Katerina said. "I apologize."

"At the risk of intrudin' in yer private business," he said, "I must warn ye aboot somethin'."

Another warning? Katerina tensed, her dark gaze fixing on his.

"Dinna trust those foreigners."

"Are you referring to Yuri and Drako?"

"Yes, indeed."

Katerina could not suppress her bubble of laughter, drawing the interested attention of other dancers. "My lord, *I* am a foreigner."

Douglas Gordon had the good grace to chuckle at himself. "Beautiful ladies are never considered foreigners."

"Thank you for the compliment," Katerina said, as the music ended, "but I know my limitations."

Keeping her gaze lowered to avoid eye contact and another invitation to dance, Katerina began her journey to the door again. She had gained several potential commissions and, more important, had seen the monster who had destroyed her family.

"I apologize for my inappropriate remark."

Katerina recognized the husky voice even before she lifted her gaze to Drako Kazanov. "Apology accepted."

When she moved to pass him, Drako said, "You do not sound forgiving."

"I did *not* forgive you," Katerina told him. "I accepted your apology."

"Please do not leave." Drako reached out and touched her arm, sending a hot shiver down her spine. "I must speak with you."

Katerina arched a perfectly shaped brow at him. "Speak, Your Highness."

Prince Drako drew her away from any potential eavesdroppers, the palm of his hand on the small of her back guiding her to a secluded alcove. Katerina noted several curious glances cast in their direction. If this man ruined her good reputation, she would kill him twice.

Whirling around to face him, Katerina felt overwhelmed. Standing against the wall, she needed to tilt her head back in order to look him in the eye.

"Beware of Prince Yuri," Drako warned her. "He is less than scrupulous, especially with women."

Katerina suppressed the urge to laugh in his face. Was this the proverbial pot calling the kettle black?

"I can handle Yuri," Katerina said. "How strange, Yuri felt compelled to warn me against you, Your Highness. Will you call him out for insulting you with disparaging comments?"

"I would never challenge a man for voicing an opinion," Drako said.

"And what if a man challenged you?" she asked, thinking of her deceased brother.

"I never allow others to goad me into rash action," he answered, "and a duel requires two participants."

"You would refuse to answer a challenge though some would name you a coward?"

"I assure you, my bloodthirsty countess, I am an expert marksman," Drako said, seeming amused by her questions. "A gentleman withstands outrageous slurs if the alternative means taking another's life."

Katerina stared into his piercing blue gaze, uncertain if he spoke sincerely. If the prince truly believed what he said, how could he have shot Ilya?

"I want to commission a special piece," Drako said when she remained silent. "I will supply the stones."

That surprised her. "You are interested in precious gems?"

Drako knew he had whetted her interest. "My brothers and I share ownership of several gem companies and mines in various countries." He lowered his voice to a husky whisper, "I own the Sancy."

"Le Grand Sancy?" Even her own father had spoken in awe of the fabled diamond.

Seigner de Sancy, the French ambassador in Constantinople, had purchased the fifty-five carat, pear-shaped diamond more than two hundred years earlier. The French king had persuaded Sancy to loan him the stone as security for raising money to pay his army. De Sancy entrusted the diamond to a messenger who was later found dead without the stone.

"The Sancy has been missing for two hundred years," Katerina said. "Where did you get it?"

"I enjoy many contacts across Europe and the East," Drako hedged. "I could be persuaded to allow you a peek."

Katerina flicked her tongue out to wet her lips, excitement surging through her. She recalled her father speaking about the fabled diamond and his wish to see the Sancy and other famous stones before he died.

The dragon prince was a devil who had gauged her weakness and was trying to entice her. To what end, though? His purpose eluded her.

"My daughter and my work fill my days," Katerina refused his offer, albeit with great reluctance. "However, I would be interested in purchasing stones if the price is right."

"We can discuss price when I view your designs," Drako said. "My invitation to see the Sancy stands if you change your mind."

"I may reconsider when time permits."

Katerina studied his chiseled features. She could see nothing of Viveka in the prince. True, the girl resembled her sister, but something felt wrong. Was Hektor correct? Could Alina have been calling for Prince Drako's help rather than blaming him for betraying her and their child?

Perhaps she would not kill him. After all, she would never wish to shoot an innocent man. Enticing him to love her and stealing the Sancy would suffice.

"Do you like what you see?" Drako asked, his voice intimately hoarse.

"I apologize for staring," Katerina said. "My mind had wandered to another time and place."

"Where were you?"

She gave him an ambiguous smile. "Moscow."

The orchestra stopped playing abruptly, drawing their attention, giving him no chance to question her. The Duke of Inverary held his arm up for everyone's attention.

"Ladies and gentlemen, my lovely wife informs me that the time has arrived to crown tonight's May Queen," the duke announced. "Roxie's choice is a relative newcomer

among us, an artistic genius, and a lovely young woman—
the Contessa de Salerno."

Katerina felt her heart sinking to her stomach, her composure slipping as the guests turned to look at her, hidden
in the alcove with the dragon prince. She had not anticipated this and disliked being caught off guard. The center
of attention was a dangerous place for her lest someone
discover her true identity. These people would shun her if
they knew the truth, and then her family would starve.

"Allow me, my lady." Drako took her hand in his to
lead her across the ballroom. "Their Graces are waiting
to crown you."

Katerina allowed the prince to escort her to the top of
the room but refused to meet anyone's gaze along the way.
With all eyes upon her, Katerina felt the ballroom was a
mile long.

Smiling, the Duke of Inverary set a hawthorn blossom
wreath on her head. "You must choose your king and then
share the Maypop cup."

"Maypop?"

"Passion flower wine."

Katerina glanced at Drako who now stood nearby with
his eldest cousin. Prince Yuri appeared arrogantly expectant
while Douglas smiled in amusement. His stepmother's eyes
were daggers, and the Blond Brigade—Anya, Lavinia,
Cynthia—was noticeably miserable. Katerina needed to
act with extreme care. She could not choose a married man
lest she offend his wife, nor could she choose most of the
eligible bachelors. She refused to demonstrate partiality
to any particular gentleman.

"I wish to welcome Prince Drako Kazanov to London
by choosing him as my king," she told the duke, her voice
no louder than a whisper.

"How gracious, my lady." The Duke of Inverary announced,

"Welcoming our newly arrived royals to England, the Contessa de Salerno has chosen Prince Drako Kazanov."

Needing no encouragement, Drako stepped forward and bowed over her hand. *"Grazie, la contessa.* Did you know this holiday celebrates sexual license?"

Katerina's lips turned up in a feline smile. "Did *you* know in the Romany culture the May King is sacrificed after mating with the Queen?"

"The Romany culture? Are you a bluestocking, my Russian gypsy?"

"I am no bluestocking, nor am I your anything."

Drako held the goblet of passion flower wine for Katerina. Then he sipped the wine before handing the duke the goblet.

Together, Drako and Katerina stepped onto the dance floor for their solitary waltz. The prince danced with the easy grace of a man who had waltzed a thousand times, weaving a spell around her, encouraging her to forget their audience.

When the music ended, Drako gently drew her close. "Thus with a kiss I die," he quoted Shakespeare, and planted a chaste kiss on her lips.

"You call *that* a kiss?" Prince Rudolf called, eliciting laughter from their audience.

Without warning, Drako yanked her against his body, his arms encircling her. One hand held the back of her head, the other on the small of her back pressing her against his muscular frame.

Drako claimed her in a smoldering kiss. His lips were warm and firm, first persuading and then demanding her surrender. He moved his mouth on hers, encouraging her to follow his lead. His sandalwood scent surrounded her, and his body heat seeped through her flimsy gown to warm her.

Powerless to resist, Katerina responded to his skill and

mastery. The world faded away, his lips on hers capturing her whole being. She wanted more. So much more.

And then muted noises sounded as if from a great distance away. Masculine chuckles and feminine giggles and embarrassed coughing yanked her back to reality like a dousing of cold water.

Breaking the kiss, Katerina stepped back a pace. She stared at his mouth, her expression stunned, shaken by her own response.

"I am still living," Drako teased her.

In a flash of movement, Katerina slapped him. Hard. So hard his head jerked to the side and their audience gasped.

Drako gave her a lopsided grin. *"Barely alive."*

Chapter Three

Hektor was going to give her grief.

Katerina eyed her brother across the dining table the next morning. After dragging the *Times* closer, he opened to the society gossip column and smiled. She suspected that his nonchalant attitude was feigned, and he had earlier read something in the newspaper.

"High society crowded the Duke of Inverary's annual Beltane Ball, a holiday celebrating lovers and spring's arrival," Hektor read, a smile lurking in his voice. "An Italian countess, the evening's May Queen, chose an eligible Russian prince as her consort. During their solitary waltz, the prince broke dozens of hopeful hearts by giving the countess a passionate kiss, which earned His Highness a stinging slap. Methinks the lady doth protest too much."

Katerina felt a blush heating her cheeks. "Thank you, Hektor. I must commend your vastly improved reading ability."

"You kissed a prince?" Roksana exclaimed.

"The prince kissed me."

"Are you going to marry him?" Ludmilla asked.

"If you marry him," Roksana asked, "will we become princesses, too?"

Katerina heard a muffled squawk of laughter from Dudley at the sideboard. No doubt, the servants' gossip would spread faster than the black plague.

"Mummy Zia, I want to be a princess," Viveka said.

Putting an arm around her daughter, Katerina planted a kiss on the crown of her blond head. "You are *my* princess, Viveka."

Katerina rose from her chair, saying, "I must polish those rings." Before disappearing out the door, she warned, "Do not tell anyone our last name."

"Do you want us to lie?" Hektor asked.

"Simply emulate the politicians," she answered. "Say, you cannot recall."

Her anger simmering, Katerina marched down the passageway connecting the house on Lancelot Place to the studio and forge on Merlin's Way. Prince Drako and the *Times* reporter were jeopardizing her good reputation. She had worked hard to make a new life for her family and herself and refused to risk her business, endangering her family, because the prince desired feminine diversion. If he needed a distraction, let him seek it elsewhere.

Inside her studio, Katerina donned her work apron and fingerless gloves. Then she took a felt polishing stick and the Flambeau girl's wedding band.

Katerina saw Drako's smiling image in the enormous diamond. How could she have known the prince was devilishly handsome? How could she have known her only enemy in the world would give her that sizzling kiss? How could she have known that kiss would become the evening's entertainment for hundreds of London's elite?

Her resolve failed her. Though her hatred had simmered for five long years, Katerina knew she could not kill Drako Kazanov. Hektor had been correct. Her sister calling for Drako did not prove that he was the man who had destroyed her family.

What about Ilya, though? Her impulsive older brother had rushed to challenge the man who had dishonored Alina and had taken a bullet in his back for his trouble.

Questions and doubts persisted. Who had dishonored and abandoned her sister? Who had murdered her brother, causing her father's heart attack?

Katerina resolved on less violent revenge. She would entice the prince to love her and then steal *Le Grand Sancy*.

If she learned he was an innocent man, she would return the diamond. If he proved guilty, then she would kill him.

Giving herself a mental shake, Katerina began polishing the diamond. And then she lost herself in her work as she always did.

"My lady?"

Katerina looked over her shoulder. "Yes, Dudley?"

"The princes have arrived."

"Princes?" she echoed, her mind still on the diamond.

"Princes Stepan, Mikhail, and Drako Kazanov."

Katerina looked at the workbench timepiece. Four hours had flown, and she had not changed her morning gown in preparation for clients.

So be it, she thought. Her shabby appearance would discourage the lecherous pain-in-the-arse prince.

"Serve refreshments," Katerina instructed the majordomo.

"Yes, my lady. How long shall I tell them to wait?"

She gave him a puzzled smile. "I will be walking directly behind you."

Dudley dropped his gaze to her morning gown and apron. His expression registered disapproval.

Katerina arched an ebony brow at him. "Do you detect something wrong with my appearance?"

The majordomo cleared his throat. "Well, His Highness is a wealthy, titled, eligible bachelor," Dudley answered, "and you are an eligible lady. I assumed—" He shrugged and turned away.

"What are your goals in life?" Katerina stopped him with her question.

"I pray for your happiness and—"

"Speak truthfully of *your* goals."

His lips twitched. "I pray for your happy marriage to a wealthy, exalted aristocrat."

Her dark gaze narrowed. "Why?"

"I yearn to announce London's elite entering your grand ballroom for society functions."

"I do not own a grand ballroom," Katerina reminded him.

"Obtaining a grand ballroom is easy once you have trapped a wealthy aristocrat into marriage," Dudley told her. "Imagine, a house filled with beautiful baby aristocrats—"

"My morning gown will suffice for today," Katerina interrupted, removing her gloves and apron. "If the prince thinks I am trying to attract his attention, he will lose interest in me, and that is not a winning strategy."

The majordomo brightened at her words. "My lady, your beauty is matched only by your shrewd intelligence."

"Thank you, Dudley, but do not forget my talent at creating jewels."

When she entered the formal drawing room, Katerina saw her brother and sisters chatting with Princes Stepan and Mikhail. Drako stood near the window overlooking the garden.

"Good afternoon, Your Highnesses." Katerina walked toward the Kazanov brothers, aware their cousin had turned at the sound of her voice.

The princes stood, as did her brother. Drako crossed the room and bowed over her hand.

"You are even more ravishing by daylight," Drako said, making her sisters giggle.

"You are too kind, Your Highness." Katerina shifted her gaze to her sisters. "Return to your studies now."

After they had gone, Katerina sat on the red upholstered settee and placed three jewel cases beside the Worcester porcelain tea service on the table.

Hektor resumed his place opposite her while Stepan and Mikhail sat on the sofa. Drako made himself comfortable beside her on the settee, his sandalwood scent sending her nerves into a near riot.

"I saw your daughter playing in the garden." Drako rested his arm across the back of the settee behind her. "Her blond hair surprised me. Does she take after her father?"

"Viveka resembles my deceased older sister." Katerina looked at the others. "How do you take your tea?"

"I will pour the tea," Drako said, "while you conduct your business."

That annoyed her. The devil was assuming the role of host, but she could not protest lest these princes and their wives find themselves another jeweler.

Katerina managed an insincere smile. "Thank you, Your Highness."

"Call me Drako," he said, reaching for the teapot.

"I would not feel comfortable doing—"

"I command you to call me Drako."

Katerina inclined her head, deferring to his preference. "Drako, then."

"Please excuse me," Hektor said, standing. "I have not read the morning *Times* today."

Drawing smiles from his cousins, Drako said, "Do not bypass the society gossip, Mister Hektor I-Cannot-Recall-My-Last-Name."

A hot blush stained Katerina's cheeks. Drako and Hektor had apparently enjoyed a revealing conversation.

"Yuri will be stopping here," Katerina reminded her brother. "Do you understand what I want?"

"I remember your instructions," Hektor assured her. "Though, my last name does escape me."

"What are your instructions regarding Yuri?" Drako asked.

"I never discuss my clients."

"I commend your discretion, my lady, now tell me what the problem is with Yuri." Drako gave her a boyishly charming smile. "We will not breathe a word to anyone else."

Katerina glanced at Stepan and Mikhail, who were waiting for her answer. "I follow the great bard's advice: Put not your faith in princes."

Drako set a steaming cup of tea on the table in front of her. "Poor Yuri."

Katerina ignored the tea. Instead, she reached for one of the black jewel cases and opened its lid.

"Your bride's wedding ring," she said, passing the case to Prince Stepan.

The wedding ring lay on a bed of black velvet. An enormous solitare diamond perched on a channel-set band of diamonds encased in platinum.

"Exquisite," Prince Stepan said.

"Superb craftsmanship," Prince Drako added.

"Craftswomanship," Katerina corrected him, making the three men smile. "And here is your bride's wedding gift."

The larger jewel case held a matching necklace, bracelet, and earrings. All three pieces had been created with oval-cut sapphires and diamonds set in platinum.

Katerina reached for her teacup and sipped the steaming brew while the princes admired her work. Relaxing back on the settee, Katerina felt the prince's arm on her shoulders and bolted upright away from the unwanted contact. She glanced at him, saying, "Help yourself to Nonna Strega's anise cookies."

He gave her a puzzled smile. "Grandmother Witch?"

"A pet name from her daughters, Viveka's nannies," Katerina explained. "Are you familiar with the Italian language?"

He shrugged. "I know a few words and phrases."

Stepan lifted his gaze from his bride's wedding gift. "The duchess is correct. You *are* a design genius."

"I do hope you are still complimentary when I send you my bill." Katerina reached for the last case.

The jewel case held a ring with a square-cut diamond set in platinum. Emeralds in the shape of leaves circled the enormous stone.

"I hope this pleases your betrothed," Katerina said, passing it to Mikhail. "Her Grace insisted a large diamond makes a statement"—the men chuckled at that—"and your bride has an interest in gardening."

"Belle will love it," Mikhail said.

"Your bride has not accepted your proposal," Stepan teased his brother.

Prince Mikhail gave him an unamused glance. "Belle will marry me, baby brother, and will be wearing this betrothal ring within days of your marriage."

"A simple scrolled wedding band will complement such an elaborate betrothal ring," Katerina said. "A butterfly brooch will make a spectacular wedding gift since flowers and butterflies are found in gardens. I thought yellow diamonds on gold to form the body and wings created in white diamonds, pink tourmalines, and amethysts. What do you say?"

"I say you are amazing," Mikhail answered.

Katerina inclined her head, accepting his compliment as her due. "I am expensive, too."

"Her Grace plans to announce our betrothal in the Friday *Times*," Mikhail said, "and I will present Belle her ring that morning."

"How can the duchess announce the betrothal," Stepan asked, "when the bride has not accepted your proposal?"

Mikhail rounded on his smirking brother. "Worry about your own wife, and leave mine to me."

"Friday is the day of Her Grace's Ladies Luncheon," Katerina remarked, leaning back and bolting upright again away from the prince's arm. She wished he would give her space. "Belle, of course, will wave her victory beneath the noses of the disappointed."

"More likely, the duchess will be waving the ring beneath those noses." Mikhail changed the subject then, asking, "How old is your daughter?"

"Viveka is five."

"Once Belle and I marry, my daughter Bess will be hosting a tea party for her cousins," Mikhail said. "We will send her an invitation."

"Viveka will love making friends her own age," Katerina said, wondering if Drako had instigated the invitation. "The company of adults can become tedious to an active child."

"Be certain to supply Viveka with a few tidbits of pretend gossip," Stepan told her. "The girls adore gossiping about make-believe society."

"I will think of something startling for Viveka to share with the girls," Drako said, his piercing blue gaze on the lady and a smile flirting with his lips. "Stolen kisses from a prince and all that."

"My lady?" Dudley entered the drawing room before Katerina could tell the prince to keep his distance from her daughter. "Excuse me, my lady, but the Marquis of Huntly requests an interview."

"Douglas?" Katerina could have sworn their appointment was the following week.

"Tell the Scotsman to come tomorrow," Drako instructed

the majordomo, earning himself a censorious look from his hostess.

Dudley looked from the prince to Katerina. "His Lordship insists on speaking with you."

Katerina looked at the princes and shrugged. "Send the marquis in here, Dudley."

A few minutes later, Douglas Gordon walked into the drawing room. He nodded at the Kazanov brothers but leveled an expression of supreme contempt on Drako.

"You are welcome, my lord," Katerina greeted him, fighting a smile at the marquis's reaction to the prince, "but I thought we scheduled our appointment for next week."

"I wanted to assure myself of yer welfare"—he shot Drako a pointed look—"after that tidbit in this mornin's *Times*."

"As you can see, the contessa is fine," Drako answered for her.

"No thanks to ye," the marquis muttered.

"Please be seated, Douglas," Katerina invited him. "Take a cup of tea with us."

"I do believe I will." The Marquis of Huntly dropped onto the sofa. "Are those sweet thin's Nonna Strega's anise cookies?"

"Help yourself," Katerina said, passing him the plate.

The Marquis of Huntly bit into a cookie and then rolled his eyes, indicating paradise. "Some day I'll steal Nonna away from ye, Kat, and then what will ye do?"

"I will weep a river most likely." Katerina watched Drako pour tea into a cup and slide it toward the marquis.

"I dinna want tea ye've touched," Huntly told him, illiciting smothered chuckles from the Kazanov brothers. "I dinna like ye." Then the marquis winked at Katerina, negating his childish statement.

Prince Drako narrowed his gaze on the Scotsman. "I

do not care much for you either, but I had the good grace to pour your tea."

"We Scots are na as refined as ye foreigners," Huntly said. "I apologize for hurtin' yer feelin's."

"My skin is thicker than that," Drako replied, irritation tingeing his voice.

"I'll pass on the tea," Huntly said, pausing to check his pocket watch. "I've made plans with Cousin Ross to practice our golfin', and then we'll be stoppin' for a whisky."

"Real men drink vodka," Drako said. "Whisky is for women."

The Marquis of Huntly turned a frosty gray gaze on the prince. "Will ye be golfin' on the Mall next Friday?"

Prince Drako glanced at his cousins, who nodded. "I will be there," he told the marquis.

Huntly smiled like a fox handed the key to the hen house. "I look forward to seein' ye golf." Then he looked at the Kazanov brothers, asking, "Do either of ye know anythin' aboot the Seven Doves Company?"

Prince Mikhail flicked a glance at his brother. "Why do you ask?"

"The owner is undercuttin' my prices," the marquis told them. "I tracked Wopsle down, but he deals with the Seven Doves through another agent—Alexander Puddles."

Prince Stepan laughed and held his hand up. "I am laughing at the man's name."

The marquis grinned. "Sounds like a dog, doesna it?"

Prince Mikhail reddened as if he, too, would explode into laughter. "I will ask around and let you know what I discover."

"Thank ye, Yer Highness." Douglas Gordon stood to leave, saying to Katerina, "I will see ye next week aboot that piece I want." And then he quit the chamber.

A moment after the marquis disappeared out the door,

the Kazanov brothers burst into uncontrollable laughter. Katerina looked at Drako, who shrugged his ignorance.

"Tell them," Mikhail gasped, regaining his ability to speak.

Prince Stepan slid his gaze from her to his cousin. "You must keep this in the strictest confidence."

"I promise," Katerina said.

Drako inclined his head. "You know I never tell tales."

"Bliss Flambeau is a mathematical genius," Prince Stepan began, "and the Flambeau sisters formed the Seven Doves Company to pauper their father."

"After Inverary acknowledged them," Mikhail continued, "Bliss turned the company's interests elsewhere thereby endangering Huntly's profits."

"Who is Wopsle?" Katerina asked.

"Wopsle is their business agent," Stepan answered, "but Alexander Blake has been dealing with Wopsle for Bliss because no one will work with a woman."

"Who is Alexander Puddles?" Drako asked.

"Puddles is the Flambeau dog," Mikhail answered, making them smile. "And, yes, I do believe the mastiff earned its name."

"I applaud their ingenuity," Katerina said. "I would never have guessed those sweet girls could be so deliciously devious."

"I believe the countess loves to see women besting men at their own games," Drako drawled.

Katerina ignored his comment. "What piece were you considering, Drako?"

"I want a dragon pendant on a gold chain," he answered.

"A dragon pendant for the dragon prince," she said. "Front view or side?"

Drako glanced down at his own body. "Side, I think, with slight modifications. I would not want to startle the ladies."

Katerina was not amused. "Full body or head only?"

"Full body, of course."

"Breathing fire or not?"

Drako grinned. "Breathing fire, definitely."

"Give me a week to design the sketches."

"I will give you anything you desire," Drako said, his voice seductively husky.

"Will you leave me alone?" Katerina countered, and then heard chuckles from their audience.

"Anything but that, my lady."

Before she could reply, Hektor entered the drawing room. Beside him walked Yuri.

Spying her guests, Prince Yuri's expression tightened into a pinch. "Good afternoon, my lady."

"Welcome to my home, Your Highness," Katerina greeted him, her smile polite. "Take tea with us."

"No, thank you." Prince Yuri ignored the three Kazanovs. "Another appointment requires my attention."

Apparently, Drako Kazanov was good for something, keeping Yuri at bay. The last time she designed him cufflinks, the prince had wasted the better part of an afternoon regaling her with stories about himself and fending off his questions about her personal life.

"Shall I sketch a few designs and send you a note when finished?" Katerina asked, aware the prince's gaze had drifted to Drako's arm on the settee behind her.

Prince Yuri nodded. "Please do."

"That sounds like an excellent idea," Hektor spoke up. "My sister will begin the actual work as soon as you settle your account for the last pair of cufflinks."

The prince's complexion mottled with embarrassed anger, and he turned to her. "Do you—?"

"I do apologize for my brother," Katerina interrupted, feigning appalled surprise, "but I know nothing about business dealings. After all, I am only a woman. Hektor is the man of the household and takes charge of monetary details." She forced a nervous giggle, gushing, "Goodness, I know nothing of numbers and such, but I do love spending money."

"I understand, dear lady." Yuri turned to Hektor, saying, "I must have misplaced the bill. Send me another." Without another word, the prince walked out of the drawing room.

"How did I do?" Hektor asked.

Katerina gave him a smile of approval. "Perfectly, brother. I see a glimmer of hope for you after all."

The Kazanov princes smiled with appreciation.

"Using a gentleman's bias against him is shrewd," Drako complimented her. "Poor Yuri could not hold his anger because you are, after all, merely a woman. You receive payment and retain his business."

"I have received no payment yet," Katerina said. "Yuri can be slippery, and I predict the possibility of his misplacing another bill for the cufflinks."

"Yuri is the prince of sponges," Hektor remarked.

"Though a prince, Yuri usually suffers from a lack of coin," Mikhail told them.

"I wish I could charge interest on outstanding balances," Katerina said, "but that could harm my business."

"*La contessa*, I believe the two of us would make a clever team," Drako said.

Katerina looked him straight in the eye. "I work alone."

The Kazanov princes stood to leave. Katerina and Drako walked down the hall together. Ahead of them walked Hektor between the Kazanov brothers.

"What is between you and the Scotsman?" Drako asked her. "He seemed familiar with your home."

"All my clients are familiar with my home," Katerina answered him.

"I am not prying," Drako said. "Humor me with an honest answer. *Please*."

The magical word *please* from an arrogant prince

worked a minor miracle. "Douglas Gordon is a client and a friend."

Drako nodded and dropped the subject. "Inverary has found a house for me and my brothers in Grosvenor Square. We will be moving this week."

"How convenient to live near your extended family," Katerina said, starting down the stairs. Too bad, three of her family had been destroyed, and the man beside her could well be the cause of their untimely deaths.

"I will escort you to Stepan's wedding," Drako told her.

"Are you asking or commanding?" Katerina said. "I do not require—"

"I would never presume to command you to accompany me," Drako interrupted. "The Duchess of Inverary suggested we attend together. You would never wish to offend Her Grace with her love of expensive jewels and deep pockets."

Katerina knew when she had been bested. The prince was correct. Ignoring the duchess's suggestion could hurt her business.

"I can see you are a formidable businessman," she remarked.

"Thank you, my lady."

"I was insulting you."

"How dare you."

Katerina laughed at his wit in spite of herself. And then she regretted softening her attitude.

Drako grasped her hand and bowed over it in courtly manner. "I knew I could make you smile."

After the door closed behind the princes, Katerina caught her majordomo smiling at her. "What is it, Dudley?"

"I must say, my lady, your strategy is excellent."

His comment confused her. "To what strategy do you refer?"

"Playing hard-to-get with His Highness." Dudley

passed her a sealed missive. "This arrived while you were conferring with the princes."

Katerina opened the note, its contents surprising her.

Consort with Prince Drako at your peril.

"Did Yuri leave this?" Katerina asked, passing Hektor the note.

"Prince Yuri was upstairs when it arrived," Dudley answered, peering over her brother's shoulder to read the note.

"Who delivered it?"

"I don't know," Dudley said. "I answered a knock on the door and found that lying on the doorstep."

"We should contact the constable," Hektor said, pocketing the note.

Katerina dismissed that with a wave of her hand. "Someone read the gossip in this morning's *Times* and decided to prank me."

Is this note a friendly warning that Drako Kazanov is dangerous? Katerina wondered. *Or is it a threat to keep my distance from him?*

Chapter Four

He hoped she had missed him.

Dressing for his cousin's wedding, Drako stood in front of the cheval mirror in his bedchamber and tied his cravat. He had left the countess alone for almost a week while he and his brothers settled into their Grosvenor Square town mansion.

Drako had sent Katerina a note specifying the time he would arrive to escort her to the wedding. The countess had replied that she would be ready.

What had he expected? A line of *X's* and *O's* scratched beneath her signature?

After slipping his arms into his topcoat, Drako inspected himself from all angles in the cheval mirror. He was a handsome, charming, wealthy prince. Of course, the countess had missed him.

Drako walked downstairs to the foyer. "Have my brothers gone?" he asked his newly acquired majordomo.

"Yes, Your Highness." Wilbur handed him a sealed missive. "This arrived for you."

Drako opened the note, containing an anonymous warning.

Stay away from the Contessa de Salerno.

Or else was implied but not stated.

"Who delivered this?" Drako asked.

"I found it on the doorstep when your brothers left," Wilbur told him.

"Leave it on my desk." Drako passed him the note.

"Yes, Your Highness."

Drako climbed into his coach for the short ride to Trevor Square. Apparently, Yuri was desperate for a wealthy wife and knew he could not win in a competition for the countess's affection.

The coach halted in Trevor Square. Without waiting for his man, Drako climbed out of the coach and banged the doorknocker.

The majordomo opened the door and stepped aside. "Good afternoon, Your Highness."

"Good afternoon, Dudley."

Hektor stood in the foyer and handed him a note. "Someone is threatening my sister unless she keeps her distance from you."

Drako read the note, his expression troubled. "Did you see the man who delivered this?" he asked the majordomo.

Dudley shook his head. "I found it on the doorstep."

"The same thing happened at my home only moments before I left," Drako told them.

"I think Kat should stay home today," Hektor said, his concern apparent, "but she considers this a prank."

"I will guard her with my life," Drako promised him.

"And who will protect me from you, Your Highness?"

Drako turned at the sound of her voice and watched her descending the stairs. The contessa was a woman worth the risk to his life.

A vision in a red silk gown, a barege silk shawl playing peek-a-boo with her cleavage. Her dark eyes beckoned him closer yet warned him not to touch.

No wonder Yuri harbored an interest in her. Not only was she beautiful but exceedingly wealthy. Her reticule alone must have cost a fortune. A lightweight linen pochette, the French floral pattern had been created in blood-red rubies, diamonds, and other fabulous stones. Framed by gold, the pochette fastened with intricately carved gold roses.

The lady wore no jewels except two. A diamond bandeau with a plume of invisibly set rubies accentuated her upswept ebony hair. A diamond and ruby dinner ring circled her right ring finger.

"My dear contessa, you stepped out of my fondest dream." Drako looped her hand through the crook of his arm.

"*Grazie*, Your Highness."

"I predict all the ladies will be commissioning jeweled headpieces after today."

"You have managed to guess my business strategy," she said.

Drako looked at Hektor. "Put that note in a safe place," he said. "I will be contacting the constable in the morning, and he will want to read it."

An hour later, Katerina sat beside Drako in St. Paul's Cathedral. She could not credit the ease of becoming a princess. The cleric spoke a few words, and—*voila*—a commoner, Miss Fancy Flambeau, became a princess.

Katerina wondered if the sender of those threatening notes was also in attendance. Prince Yuri had not bothered to mask his displeasure when she and the prince passed his pew, and the Blond Brigade had looked positively livid.

"Do you realize how fortunate you are?" Drako whispered. "Hundreds of prince-hungry maidens would love to stand beside me in church."

"We are sitting in a pew not standing at the altar," Katerina pointed out.

"I suppose I must work harder on my locations," Drako

quipped. "However, if I had to stand at that altar today, I would choose you to stand beside me."

Katerina gave him an ambiguous smile. "And tomorrow you would choose someone else."

When they arrived at Inverary House, the guests were milling around awaiting the formal receiving line. Tables for eight had been placed at one end of the enormous ballroom, reserving the opposite side for dancing. A small orchestra provided a soothing background for quiet conversations and muted laughter and air kisses.

Orange blossoms set against garlands of greenery decorated the ballroom. White roses and blue forget-me-nots posed inside crystal vases in the center of each table.

Katerina touched the prince's arm. "You will excuse me while I visit the withdrawing room?"

Drako nodded. "I will wait here for you."

Entering the withdrawing room, Katerina sensed the tense atmosphere. Then she heard a sneering voice, "Mikhail will never marry you."

Princess Anya had spoken. With the princess were the other two members of the Blond Brigade, Lavinia Smythe and Cynthia Clarke.

The object of the princess's disdain was a petite, ebony-haired woman gowned in ice-blue silk. Miss Belle Flambeau, no doubt.

"I hope I am not interrupting anything important," Katerina said, her smile insincere, deflecting attention from the Flambeau girl. "Trust me, Anya. Using the word *never* is a mistake."

"Yuri is angry with you," the princess told her.

"If your brother is upset," Katerina said, "only he can lighten his own mood. I am responsible for myself and my family."

"I do not like anyone upsetting Yuri." Princess Anya's expression pinched with angry contempt. "No one in Moscow has ever heard of you, and no true aristocrat labors for a living. Are you a real countess or an imposter?"

The blond witch's comment hit a little too close to home. The girl's poisonous tongue endangered her business, which, in turn, endangered her family. She had made a new life for herself and refused to let a spoiled twit ruin it.

"Your behavior, *child*, scarcely speaks well of royalty."

"A mere four years separate us," Anya countered, obviously insulted.

"Age and maturity are not necessarily connected," Katerina told her. "I have been married, given birth, and run a successful business. You, *little girl*, are a dandelion fluff carried on the breeze. Waiting, hoping, praying for fertilization."

"You will regret those words." Princess Anya brushed past her out of the withdrawing room, her blond cohorts directly behind her.

"You must be Belle Flambeau," Katerina said, turning to the ebony-haired woman.

"I am she." Miss Belle Flambeau appeared astonished by what had transpired.

"Do not let those blond bullies or their mamas intimidate you." Katerina gave her a warm smile. "Always deflect an insult by returning it to the sender."

Belle smiled. "You sound like my stepmother."

"Her Grace is the wisest of women." Katerina gestured toward the door. "Shall we present a united front by leaving together?"

Belle nodded. "Thank you, my lady."

"Call me Kat. All my friends do."

Drako and Katerina sat at a table with Prince Mikhail and Belle Flambeau. Prince Viktor and Princess Regina joined them as did Raven Flambeau and Alexander Blake.

Katerina could hardly believe that she was sitting with princes and princesses at a royal wedding. She felt like Cinderella at the ball. Her sister Alina would have gloried in this.

"I present my brother Viktor and his wife Regina," Prince Mikhail began the introductions. "Here are my cousin Drako and Katerina Garibaldi, the Contessa de Salerno."

"The contessa and I met in the withdrawing room," Belle said, and then finished the introductions by gesturing to the final two. "My sister Raven and Alexander Blake, the Marquis of Basildon."

The footmen began serving the wedding feast, the first course poached salmon in a pungent caper sauce. Belle Flambeau blanched at the plate in front of her. Either the girl disliked salmon, or she carried the prince's heir.

Katerina mentally rubbed her hands together. At first light in the morning, she would begin sketching the diamond ensemble for the duchess. Later, of course, would come Christening gifts. This year was looking exceptionally profitable, and the duchess had more stepdaughters to marry off.

"Alexander is an associate of London's famous constable, Amadeus Black," Belle said conversationally.

"Are you nearing an arrest in those Slasher murders?" Prince Viktor asked.

"We are investigating new clues," Alexander Blake answered.

"I planned to visit Amadeus Black tomorrow," Drako said, "but perhaps you can help us."

"Investigation is unnecessay," Katerina said.

Drako looked at her. "I will be the judge of that, Kat dear."

"What is the problem?" Alexander asked.

"Both the contessa and I received threatening notes this week," Drako answered, and then glanced at his cousins. "No chance of my note coming from a furious papa or an irate husband, I assure you, though I cannot speak for the contessa."

The gentlemen laughed. The ladies smiled. Except Katerina, who did not consider defiled maidens or fallen wives humorous.

"I will call upon you tomorrow," Alexander told Drako. "I would like to see those notes."

"Regina is a published author," Mikhail told Belle.

"I have never met an author," she said. "What kind of stories?"

Princess Regina smiled. "I write romances."

"I love romances," Belle said.

Raven Flambeau nodded. "So do I."

"I adore their happy endings," Katerina agreed. "Real life can sadden even the most optimistic among us."

"Some day Regina will write a real novel," Prince Viktor teased his wife.

The four gentlemen smiled. The four ladies did not.

"I was joking," Prince Viktor said, resting his arm across the back of his wife's chair.

"Do you see me laughing?"

"If I thought you had no talent," Viktor told her, "I would never have bought you a publishing company."

Princess Regina gave her husband a long look. "You would have done anything to marry me. You did want your son—"

"My love for you demanded I do whatever was needed to win your hand in marriage," Viktor interrupted, "and I have never experienced even one unhappy moment."

"You express the sweetest sentiments," Regina said.

Their teasing byplay heartened Katerina. Apparently, not all men were pigs, and true love did exist among aristocrats.

"Nothing says I-love-you better than a priceless jewel," Katerina said.

"Should not speaking the words be enough?" Viktor asked.

"Words will never be enough when you are sitting with

a shrewd businesswoman," Drako answered his cousin. "You know, Kat designs priceless jewelly creations."

"Drako is flattering me in the hope that I will discount my prices and save him a good deal of coin," Katerina said, making everyone smile.

The prince lifted her hand to his lips. "My darling contessa, you know my pockets are deep."

"Raven is an amateur sleuth," Alexander dropped into the conversation. "She is helping with the Slasher investigation."

"How do you help?" Katerina asked.

"I–I . . ." The girl appeared at a loss for words.

"Raven gets impressions from objects," her sister explained, "and sometimes she experiences visions."

Drako looked at Alexander. "Do you and the constable believe in such things?"

"The constable believes in whatever solves a crime," Alexander answered, "but I remain a skeptic."

Katerina slipped the ruby and diamond ring off her finger, passing it across the table. "What impression do you get of me?"

Raven Flambeau closed her eyes and held the ring between her hands for several long moments. When she opened them again, her violet gaze seemed to see into Katerina's soul.

"Revenge will not breathe life into the dead," Raven warned her.

Katerina's composure slipped, her expression stricken, but she recovered herself within seconds. "I will ponder your words."

"Upon whom are you seeking revenge?" Drako asked her.

You, Katerina thought but said, "The answer would surprise you."

"I hope not me."

Katerina gazed at him from beneath the thick fringe of her ebony lashes. "Have you trespassed against me?"

"Is that an invitation?" Drako asked, a smile lurking in his voice.

"You need not worry, Your Highness."

"And if I did trespass against you?" Drako rested his arm across the top of her chair, leaned close, and said in a husky voice, "Tell me, *la contessa*, what form your revenge would take."

"A poisoned dragon pendant, perhaps?"

"Ah, yes, the Italians do possess a special expertise with poisons."

"I am Russian by birth," Katerina corrected him, and then looked across the table at Belle Flambeau. "We have an author, a psychic, and a jeweler. How do you pass your time?"

"I save lives," Belle answered, silencing everyone. "Plants mostly."

"God blessed my sister with healing hands," Raven said. "The garden goddess promises minor miracles by restoring health."

"Are you a gardener or a healer?" Katerina asked her.

"Both."

"Do you believe in that nonsense?" Drako asked her.

"God blesses some souls with special gifts," Katerina answered. "So, yes, I do believe in such nonsense."

The footmen began clearing tables of the main course's remains. Other footmen served cheeses, fruit, coffee, tea, and cordials.

Hearing laughter from the table behind theirs, Katerina glanced over her shoulder and smiled to herself when she noted its occupants. The four remaining Flambeau sisters—Bliss, Blaze, Serena, Sophia—were seated with four bachelors—Princes Lykos and Gunter Kazanov, the

Marquis of Huntly, and the Marquis of Awe. Apparently, the Duchess of Inverary was planning ahead.

Katerina leaned close to the prince, whispering, "Look who sits behind us."

Drako flicked a glance in that direction. "The Duchess of Inverary is matchmaking," he said, his words reflecting her thoughts.

Katerina and Drako smiled at each other, one of their first sincere moments of camaraderie since being introduced. And then they eavesdropped on the other table's conversation.

"My father tells me you are a financial wizard and a business genius," Bliss Flambeau remarked to Huntly.

"I do verra well." Douglas Gordon's words were modest, but his tone sounded puffed with pride.

"Tell me about your businesses," said Bliss, the Flambeau's mathematical genius. "Papa compares your talent to King Midas's golden touch."

"I dinna want to bore ye with business dealin's," the marquis said.

"I love learning things I know nothing *aboot*,"— Bliss said, mimicking his accent. "I adore your Scots burr."

"Well, lass, ye've the accent to me," Douglas teased her. And then the marquis began introducing her to supply and demand and all the other laws of economics.

"I want to know about your particular dealings," Bliss said. "Papa has spoken so highly of you."

The Marquis of Huntly kept Bliss Flambeau entertained with stories of his business dealings. Whenever he paused, she encouraged him to keep speaking. He told her details of those he had won and those yet to be concluded.

Drako leaned close to Katerina. "Do most young men lose their wits when pretty females praise them?"

"All men lose their wits." She gave him a flirtatious smile. "No exceptions."

The orchestra played the first waltz for the bride, Fancy Flambeau, and groom, Prince Stepan, and the second for the bride and her father. Watching them, Katerina let her thoughts wander to her own father and bittersweet nostalgia, bordering on grief, washed over her. She would never dance with her father at her own wedding, nor would she ever see him again in this lifetime.

"Why is your expression sad?" Drako asked her.

"I miss my father," Katerina answered without thinking, her gaze fixed on the father and daughter swirling around the dance floor.

"I am sorry for your loss."

His words irritated her. "Spare me your condolences five years after the fact."

"Do you doubt my sincerity?" The prince sounded surprised.

Katerina rounded on him, her dark gaze crashing into his. "You do not have a sincere bone in your body."

"How can you say that?" Drako countered. "You do not know me well enough to make that judgment."

"I do not want to know you better."

Drako gave her a boyishly charming smile. "And that, *la contessa*, is a terrible lie."

Katerina realized if she wanted the prince to love her, giving her the opportunity to steal the Sancy, she should not alienate his interest in her. "I am sorry," she said, forcing herself to relax. "I should not have said that."

"I have experienced grief, too." Drako stood and offered her his hand. "Dancing with me will chase the shadows from your mind."

Katerina placed her hand in his and rose from her chair. "Will you slay my dragons?" she teased him.

"I will slay the monsters beneath your bed if you invite me into your bedchamber." Drako grinned at her frown. "As for the dragons, I refuse to commit suicide to please you."

The word *suicide* reminded Katerina what Yuri had told her about the prince's deceased fiancee. Somehow, the man and the gossip felt incongruous. Could Yuri have been lying? If so, why?

Stepping onto the dance floor, Drako and Katerina moved as one swirling around the ballroom. His touch, his smile, and his sandalwood scent conspired against her. An unfamiliar melting sensation warmed her belly, a pang of yearning surging through her. She needed to guard herself against the prince lest she end her days like poor Alina. Or the fiancee.

The waltz ended. The prince made to escort her back to their table, but she escaped his hold on her.

"You will excuse me," Katerina said. "Business demands I soothe Yuri's feathers."

"I will not excuse you," Drako said, "and you will not soothe that vulture's feathers."

"I beg your pardon?" Katerina said, surprised.

"You will give me, *your escort*, all your attention." The prince sounded more autocratic than a stubborn five year old.

Katerina gave him a long look, not quite comprehending. And then she dissolved into giggles, making the situation worse.

"At what are you laughing?" he demanded.

"You, of course."

"I am a prince."

"You are *a* prince but not *my* prince."

Katerina walked away and proceeded to dance with ten different men. She gave Yuri her second dance of the celebration because, though he was slippery with reimbursement, she did not want him floating stories about her to the ton. Prince Yuri was petty and mean-spirited and could create business problems.

"I warned you about Kazanov," Yuri said. "Why did you agree to be his escort?"

"With all due respect, Your Highness, my private life is my private business," Katerina answered. "To tell you the truth, the Duchess of Inverary insisted Prince Drako escort me, and Her Grace is my best client."

"I understand your motivation," Yuri said, his expression clearing, "but heed my warning and beware."

Katerina's third dance went to Douglas Gordon, the Marquis of Huntly, but her attention had fixed on Drako Kazanov. He leaned against a wall, his arms folded across his chest, his expression forbidding.

"Kazanov appears jealous of yer partnerin' me," the marquis remarked. "Wiggle yer fingers at him the next time we pass."

And she did.

Each time they swirled by Prince Drako, Katerina wiggled her fingers at him in greeting. His expression darkened like gathering storm clouds.

Katerina danced with Princes Lykos, Gunter, Viktor, Mikhail, and Rudolf as well as the Marquis of Awe, the Marquis of Basildon, and the Duke of Inverary. Prince Drako did not dance with any of his admirers.

"Kat darling, what a winning strategy," the Duchess of Inverary whispered. "Drako looks jealous."

Katerina refused to comment on the prince. "I saw your four stepdaughters sitting with four eligible bachelors," she remarked. "Are you matchmaking, Your Grace?"

"Maidens and bachelors are like flowers." The older woman's dimpled smile appeared. "I plant them in the same box and pray a couple will take root, entwining their stems around each other."

"And what kind of flower am I?" Katerina asked, amused.

"Rare and exotic."

Katerina smiled. "Thank you, Your Grace."

"May I have this dance, *la contessa*?"

Katerina recognized Drako's voice before she turned to him. Apparently, he had decided anger was not a winning strategy.

"I would enjoy that," she murmured, placing her hand in his.

They stepped onto the dance floor, joining the other couples. Katerina noted the unhappy expressions on the faces of the prince's admirers, especially the blond bullies.

"Some day I will be *your* prince," Drako said, drawing her attention from the sidelines.

"You will need to stand beside me in church for that," Katerina said, her smile teasing.

His piercing blue gaze held hers captive. "You do not need to tell me what I already know."

Katerina missed a step, which brought a smile to his chiseled lips. "Are you—?"

"I know what I am doing," Drako interrupted. "Pay close attention to the dance lest you crush my toes."

Katerina said nothing, too surprised by what he had implied. Loosely implied, albeit.

"Silence becomes you," Drako teased her.

The waltz ended. Thankfully, since Katerina still could not find her voice or a witty reply.

"The bride and groom have left," Drako said, guiding her off the dance floor. "We should make our escape now."

"Where are we going?" Katerina asked, unable to keep the alarm out of her voice.

"I am taking you home," Drako answered, slanting her a smile. "I must rise early tomorrow to learn this golfing in order to beat that Scotsman at his own game."

Alexander Blake, the Marquis of Basildon, walked with them downstairs to the foyer. When the marquis started down the street, Drako called, "Do you need a ride?"

"Thank you," Alexander answered, "but my grandfather's home is only a few doors away."

"You walked here instead of taking your coach?" Katerina quipped. "What will society say?"

"My reputation is ruined, and I will never be received in the best drawing rooms." Blake nodded at Drako. "I will call upon you tomorrow afternoon."

When Drako gestured to his coachman, parked across the street, Katerina said, "We can walk to him."

"I will carry you," Drako said, lifting her into his arms before she could protest, and stepping into Park Lane.

Suddenly, a coach materialized from nowhere and careened down the street. It headed directly at them, the horses out of control.

"Watch out." Alexander Blake moved into action, yanking Drako back in time to save their lives but not their formal attire. All three landed in the dirt, and the coach disappeared in the direction of Cumberland Gate.

"Thank you for saving us." Drako helped Katerina up, asking, "Are you injured?"

"I am fine, but my gown is ruined."

Drako and Blake smiled at each other. Their condescending attitude irritated Katerina, but she managed to refrain from commenting on it. After all, the Marquis of Basildon had saved her life.

"What a freakish accident," she said.

"That was no accident," Alexander Blake told them. "The driver steered his coach at you."

"I told you the threats were no prank," Drako said.

"Who would want me dead?" she asked.

"Apparently, the same person who wants me dead."

Within minutes, the prince's man halted the coach beside them. Alexander opened the door, and Drako lifted Katerina inside.

"I will meet you at the contessa's at two o'clock tomorrow," Alexander told Drako. "Raven will accompany me."

Twenty minutes later, Drako escorted Katerina into her Trevor Square mansion. He nodded at the majordomo and reminded her, "Do not forget that Alexander and Raven will want to read your note. Two o'clock sharp."

"I wish you had remained silent about that," Katerina said. "A prank and a freakish accident do not prove attempted murder."

"I will not ignore any danger to you."

"Perhaps the greatest danger comes from you," she said.

"I worry for your safety and would never endanger you in any way." Drako gave her an easy smile. "I am harmless."

"Dragons do breathe fire." Without another word, Katerina left him standing there and climbed the stairs. One satisfying glance over her shoulder told him the sway of her hips was almost as frustrating as her chilly attitude.

Katerina knew one thing for certain. The Kazanov prince was untrustworthy. If he discovered the truth about her, Drako would ruin her reputation and her business.

Chapter Five

His little witch was pushing him closer and closer toward the edge of insanity.

Alexander Blake, the Marquis of Basildon, stood in his bedchamber at his grandfather's, the Duke of Essex, and scraped the dark stubbles off his face. His thoughts had fixed on Miss Raven Flambeau instead of concentrating on the sharp blade skimming his skin.

The beautiful, maddening brat had sat beside him at her sister's wedding feast and then danced with almost every bachelor in attendance. Lately, he could not predict her behavior, and that was frustrating him. Where was the sweet girl he had known all his life?

"Ouch." Alexander dropped the blade and reached for a handkerchief, pressing it against his chin. "Damn her," he muttered. "This is her fault."

One moment the charming minx looked at him with true warmth. In the next instant, she could freeze him more effectively than a blast from the north wind in winter. His skepticism, of course, did not help their budding relationship, but he refused to feign a belief in her psychic abilities just to soothe her ego.

His grandfather was correct, though. Roxanne Campbell

was tutoring her stepdaughters in vixen wiles designed to torment a man. Raven appeared an apt pupil.

Because of the rift between his grandfather and his late father, Alexander had lived his entire life in Soho Square next door to the Flambeau sisters. He had always considered Raven a baby sister and failed to notice her growing into a young woman who harbored a fondness for him.

Appearing at his door one night to profess her love, Raven had caught him off guard, and he had behaved badly. Very badly. He winced when he recalled his less than sensitive reaction that night, insisting she was too young for love. Now he regretted those words.

Their lives had changed dramatically since then. He had reconciled with his grandfather and accepted the title Marquis of Basildon, the Duke of Essex's heir.

Meanwhile, the Duke of Inverary had acknowledged his seven Flambeau daughters and moved them into his Park Lane mansion, his duchess determined to secure the most auspicious marriages for them as befitting a duke's daughters. Roxanne Campbell was winning at the marriage stakes. The eldest daughter married her Russian prince and the second oldest was considering an offer from her own Russian prince. The exalted titles were merely icing on the cake of the vast Kazanov wealth.

And now the Kazanovs' three royal cousins had dropped into London society. That gave Alexander pause and put a frown on his face. What if Roxanne Campbell decided that Raven should marry a prince instead of a marquis? Perhaps he should hurry the betrothal process along.

After tying his cravat, Alexander donned his topcoat and inspected himself in the cheval mirror. He was no prince, but he was tall and well built. Nobody would lose their lunch at the sight of his face.

If she played her cards right, Miss Raven Flambeau would become his marchioness and then his duchess after his grandfather passed. On the other hand, maybe *he* would be the lucky one if she married him. Life would never be dull with Raven.

Alexander smiled as he walked down the hallway to the stairs. He had not bothered to send her a note about visiting the Contessa de Salerno. If she had true psychic ability, Raven would know what he intended.

And then Alexander sobered. Someone was trying to kill the prince, the countess, or both. Murder was no laughing matter.

Alexander had no doubt that the anonymous sender of those notes was a member of society. He had an idea to flush the culprit out, but neither Raven nor the countess would enjoy their roles in his charade.

Twigs, his grandfather's elderly majordomo, was loitering in the foyer and opened the front door for him. "Have a good afternoon, my lord."

"Thank you, Twigs."

"We will miss you."

Alexander smiled at the old man. "I will be returning after I've rid London of its criminal element."

"That relieves my mind," Twigs said.

"Are you relieved that I will return?" Alexander asked. "Or rid London of its criminals?"

"Both, my lord."

Alexander paused outside the mansion to instruct his driver to park in front of Inverary House and then strolled down the street. The flower fragrances from Hyde Park wafted across Park Lane, and he inhaled deeply of springtime's scents.

Life was much pleasanter on Park Lane than Soho Square, an enclave of French emigres who had escaped the Terror thirty years earlier. No matter in which era one lived, immense wealth guaranteed an easier existence.

"Good afternoon, my lord," the Inverary majordomo

greeted him, stepping aside to allow him entrance. "We have been expecting you."

"Thank you, Tinker."

Raven Flambeau sat in a highbacked chair, a white bonnet with pink ribbons on her lap. She looked innocent in her pale pink gown, but her pouting courtesan lips and beckoning violet eyes and touch-me plump breasts gave proof to her passionate nature. Good God, he ached just looking at her.

"You are late," she greeted him.

Alexander lifted his gaze and caught her smug smile. Did she know what he had been thinking?

Raven passed the majordomo her bonnet. "Hide this," she said. "If my stepmother asks, you saw me wearing the bonnet."

Tinker's lips twitched. "You can rely on my discretion."

Alexander guided her out the door, saying, "We are visiting the Contessa de Salerno."

"Yes, I know," Raven said in a long-suffering voice. "Please do not ask how I know."

Alexander heard the majordomo's muffled squawk of laughter. He glanced over his shoulder, but the door was already closing.

How would he survive forty years of marriage with her? How could he survive all those years without her?

The ride from Park Lane to Trevor Square was short and comfortable in his grandfather's coach, its seats fashioned from the softest leather. Raven leaned back, the perfect picture of delicate femininity, no evidence of her hoydenish ways apparent.

"Leaving your oh-so-proper bonnet at home could ruin your reputation and send your stepmama into a swoon," Alexander teased her.

"If God had wanted us to wear bonnets, He would not have given us hair to cover our heads," Raven told him. "I want to feel the breeze in my hair on a day as glorious as today. You won't tell, will you?"

Alexander grinned at the innocence of her question. "My lips are locked forever."

Raven gave him an easy smile, reminding him of the old days before he had spurned her love. "You danced with a dozen men yesterday."

"Fifteen, actually, but only one dance per gentleman." She lost her smile, assuming her cool demeanor. "I love dancing and, as they say, variety is the spice of life."

"Sometimes bland is better than spice," he said.

The coach halted in Trevor Square, allowing them no opportunity for further conversation. The contessa's majordomo opened the door.

"The Marquis of Basildon," Alexander introduced himself, handing the man his card. "Miss Raven Flambeau."

"Her Ladyship is expecting you," the man said, closing the door behind them. "Please follow me."

The majordomo led them upstairs to the drawing room, where not only the prince and the contessa awaited them but also a young man. Both men stood when Raven walked into the room.

"Thank you, Dudley," the contessa said. "Please close the door on the way out."

"Yes, my lady."

Alexander looked at the man. "No interruptions, Dudley."

"Yes, my lord." Dudley looked at his mistress, asking, "Shall I pour the tea?"

"I will pour the tea," the contessa said.

"Very good, my lady." Dudley left the drawing room.

"Nonna Strega brews the tea with mint." The contessa lifted the teapot and poured the steaming liquid into delicate china cups. Without glancing over her shoulder, she called, "Tightly, Dudley."

The drawing room door clicked shut.

"Alexander and Raven, I present my brother Hektor," the contessa introduced them.

Ignoring Alexander, Hektor bowed over Raven's hand. "I do hope you are not married or otherwise attached."

Raven gave him a warm smile. "Not formally, no."

"The lady is unofficially betrothed," Alexander said, a pang of jealousy shooting through him.

"The most beautiful women are always taken." Hektor bowed over her hand again. "May we meet again, my lady." Then he left the drawing room.

Raven smiled to herself. The door did not click shut behind the brother, and she suspected the majordomo was eavesdropping in the hallway. Tinker eavesdropped all the time and knew absolutely everything that happened inside Inverary House.

"I wear no ring," Raven said, sitting on the sofa. "Ergo, I am a free agent."

"Ergo?" Alexander sat in a highbacked chair and lifted the teacup to his lips. "Isn't that in the snail family?"

Raven's violet gaze narrowed on him. His teacup developed a hairline crack, leaking tea droplets on his trousers.

"I will pay for the damage," Alexander told the contessa, setting the cup on its saucer.

Arrogant swine, Raven thought and turned away from him, her gaze crashing into the contessa's and the prince's. Both were watching them with great interest.

Though irritated with Alexander, Raven managed her sweetest smile. Her gaze scanned the drawing room, noting the shades of red and gilded mahogany, its opulence rivaling Inverary House's formal drawing room. Artfully arranged red roses posed inside white and gold fine porcelain vases while myriad flower fragrances wafted into the room through the open window along with a child's giggles.

"My daughter is playing in the garden," the contessa said, seeing where her gaze had drifted.

"She sounds delightful," Raven replied.

Prince Drako passed Alexander the two missives and then sat beside the contessa, lifting his arm to rest it on the back of the settee behind her. Raven noted the contessa inching away from his body.

"The handwriting is different, but that means nothing," Alexander said, reading the notes. "He could have disguised his handwriting on both."

"Or she," Raven corrected him, making the prince and the contessa smile.

Alexander passed her the notes. Raven read them and placed both on her lap, the palm of a hand on each. Closing her eyes, she leaned back against the sofa and relaxed.

Several silent moments passed. Her breathing evened while her mind cleared of the mundane.

And then her mind's eye opened, heavy mist swirling in front of her. Two openings formed in the mist. She saw two parchments and two hands holding quills, and then the mist holes closed.

Raven opened her eyes and looked from Alexander to Drako to Katerina. "I saw two hands writing on parchment."

"Did you see a face?" Alexander pressed her.

"I said"—irritation tinged her voice—"I saw two hands writing on parchment."

When Alexander ran a hand down his face, Raven smiled inwardly at his frustration. Her almost-betrothed was a cement block, no more perceptive than a cobblestone.

"What kind of hands?" Alexander tried again.

"Human." Raven heard the countess giggle and the prince chuckle.

"*Raven.*" Alexander's voice held a warning note.

"I saw a cloud of mist which had two holes," Raven told him. "A right hand appeared inside each hole, one a man's and the other a woman's. I believe two people, working separately and unaware of each other, wrote the notes."

"How do you—?"

"I know because I know," Raven interrupted, leveling a displeased look on him.

"What does this mean?" the contessa asked.

"I believe she means someone is trying to kill you," Drako answered, "and someone else is trying to kill me. Is that correct?"

Raven nodded. "Yes."

"Which of us was targeted last night?" Drako asked.

"Both."

"That is too incredible," Alexander remarked. "What are the chances—?"

Raven rounded on him. "Did you ever hear of killing two birds with one stone?"

Alexander grinned. "You are too amazing for words."

"Are you insulting me?"

"I was complimenting you."

Her expression cleared. "Thank you, Alex. I believe that is a first."

"We know the birds," Alexander said, turning to the prince. "Now we need to find the stone."

"No, we need to find the hands that hired the stone," Raven corrected him.

Alexander winked at her. "Good thinking, Brat."

"Do you have hartshorn?" Raven asked the contessa. "Two compliments make me dizzy."

"Very funny." Alexander looked at the prince, saying, "I have formulated a plan to catch the culprit—"

"Culprits," Raven corrected him.

"Excuse me, culprits," Alexander amended. "Protecting my birds is of utmost importance."

"I can take care of myself," Drako told him, "and my brothers and cousins will help." He looked at the contessa, adding, "Kat needs either Hektor or me whenever she leaves the house."

"I am perfectly capable—"

"You will not leave this house unless accompanied by me or your brother," Drako interrupted. "If need be, I will post guards around you."

The contessa rolled her eyes but acquiesced to their wishes. "I will only venture out when accompanied by Hektor or you"—the prince smiled at that—"or some other trustworthy gentleman."

The prince lost his smile.

Raven swallowed a bubble of laughter. As her stepmother had said, the contessa was a brilliant strategist.

"Since His Highness has been paying particular attention to the contessa," Raven said, "I think every society maiden and young widow must be considered suspect."

"Your thoughts mirror mine," Alexander told her with a smile of approval. "I need your help flushing the guilty out by spying."

Raven brightened at his needing her help. "That sounds exciting. What do I do?"

"Befriend the Blond Brigade."

"What?"

"Make friends with those blondes who are privy to all the gossip," Alexander repeated himself.

"Those three will not befriend me," Raven argued. "Besides, they have been cruel to my sisters."

"All you need to do is converse with them at social functions," Alexander said. "Gossip together, and listen to what they say. If necessary, I will ask Bliss or Sophia or Serena."

"How about Blaze?" Raven asked, her smile mischievous.

Alexander grinned. "Blaze would sooner strangle the three and be done with it."

"I will need to explain the situation to my sisters," Raven said.

"Tell no one."

"I don't understand."

"You cannot tell your family," Alexander said.

"They will think I betrayed them," Raven argued.

"The blondes are silly, shallow creatures," Alexander explained, "but they are not stupid. If your family feigns anger, they will know. Do you want to help save two lives or not?"

"Sometimes in life we must consort with those we dislike," the contessa said.

Her head throbbing with tension, Raven wished she had stayed home. Alex did not need to live in Inverary House with an outraged family. On the other hand, she could not refuse his request to help.

"I will do it," she agreed, albeit reluctantly.

"Thank you," Alexander said. "Meanwhile, I will befriend those gentlemen who have shown an interest in the contessa."

"Prince Yuri and I have despised each other since boyhood," Drako told him. "Pay close attention to him."

"I did not know that," Katerina said.

"You do not know me very well." Drako winked at her. "Yet."

"People who act rashly make mistakes," Alexander continued. "We need to entice the culprits into rash action, which means your relationship must become fodder for gossips. You and Drako will need to spend time together."

"What?" Katerina exclaimed.

"Sometimes in life we must consort with those we dislike," Drako echoed her own words.

Katerina rounded on him. "Did you send those threats in order to spend time with me?"

Drako laughed in her face. "Kat darling, I need not resort to devious methods."

"How much time do we need to spend together?"

Katerina asked Alexander. "My work and my daughter keep me busy."

"Take rides in Hyde Park, attend the opera, dance more than twice at balls," Alexander answered. "In short, transform yourselves into fodder for the gossips."

"What happens to my reputation?" Katerina asked, disheartened by his advice.

"Your reputation will survive," Drako assured her. "Who knows? We may even end by standing at the altar."

His words did not reassure her. Marry the scoundrel who had destroyed her family? Definitely not. True, she was beginning to doubt his guilt, but she could never love or marry the prince unless she knew the whole truth.

"We must be leaving now," Alexander said, standing. "I will ask Amadeus Black if he can spare any men to keep an eye on you but, I assure you, the runners will be invisible. I want to see any threatening notes you receive."

Raven stood when he did. "Thank you for your hospitality."

Alexander offered Raven his arm. "Shall we take a spin in Hyde Park before you begin your charade?"

"I would like that very much."

Katerina started to rise to escort them downstairs, but Alexander gestured for her to sit. "We can see ourselves out."

Once they had gone, Drako resumed his seat beside Katerina. His smile was pure satisfaction. "I think I will enjoy our togetherness."

The prince was much too close for her peace of mind. His heat and his sandalwood scent weakened her defenses. Steeling herself against him, Katerina said, "With all these empty seats in my drawing room, you do not need to crowd my person."

"Crowding is cozy," Drako said. "I like cozy."

Katerina decided to discuss practical matters. "How do you want to pass our time together?"

Drako chuckled. "My darling Kat, you do not want hear my honest answer."

"Oh." Katerina felt an embarrassed blush heating h cheeks.

"You blush like a virgin," he teased her, "and I ado blushing women."

"There cannot be many women who remain blushin virgins in your vicinity," she countered.

"I am no seducer of women," Drako defended himsel "We will start with the opera tomorrow evening, I think Properly chaparoned, of course. Now let me see th dragon sketch."

Katerina opened her sketch book. The etching was full-body, long-jawed dragon's profile, its open mout shooting a tongue of flames. Two ears sat on top of it head, four triangular scales running from the back of it head down its neck. Its body lengthened and thickene into a tail that curled up.

"This will make a fine piece to pass down the genera tions," Drako said, his gaze on the dragon. "What stones do you suggest?"

"Gold, of course, for the whole frame," Katerina an swered. "Diamonds for the head, tail, feet, and ears as well as placed between sapphire body scales. The head scales should be emeralds, a ruby eye, and an amber and gold tongue."

"I will supply the stones," Drako said. "You know, my invitation to see the Sancy still stands."

Now the prince lived in his own mansion, Katerina thought, viewing the Sancy meant learning where he kept it. Which would make stealing it easier.

She did not want to appear too eager, though. "If I change my mind, I will let you know."

"Let us walk in the garden," Drako said, standing. "I would like to meet your daughter."

Katerina was instantly suspicious. "Why?"

"The day is fair," he answered, "and your daughter sounds wonderful. I like children."

"You do not have any children," she said.

"I have never married," he said, "but I lived my life with eight brothers and three sisters, all younger."

"I do not think meeting Viveka is a good idea," Katerina hedged, desperate to keep the two apart.

"I wish her no harm." His blue gaze narrowed on her. "What do you fear?"

"I fear nothing," she lied.

Drako gestured toward the door. "Then let us walk in the garden."

The inner courtyard was a garden of tranquility. There were a small gazebo, a bubbling fountain, a stone path that meandered past lilac and rose bushes, green shrubbery, lawns, and flower beds.

"Viveka," Katerina called. "Come here."

The five year old whirled around at the sound of her mother's voice. A sunshine smile lit her small face.

"Mummy Zia!" The girl dashed toward them, not bothering with the meandering stone path. Reaching them, she wrapped her arms around her mother. "Will you play with me?"

"I want you to meet my friend," Katerina said. "Make a curtsey to Prince Drako."

Viveka did not bother with the curtsey. Instead, she looked up at him, asking, "Are you a real prince like the ones in the stories?"

Drako crouched down, eye level with the girl. "Yes, I am a real prince." Then he took her tiny hand in his and kissed it in courtly manner, making her giggle.

"That tickles," Viveka said. "I like tickles. Where is your crown?"

"I never wear my crown when the sun shines," he answered. "It makes me hot."

His kindness to her daughter touched Katerina, but she could not relax. Disturbing thoughts nagged her that this man could be Viveka's father. What would she do if he learned their true identities?

"Who is this?" Drako asked, shifting his gaze to the doll in her hand.

"Lady Alina," Viveka answered.

Katerina froze, almost afraid to breathe. She had not known Viveka named her new dolly for Alina. Guilt ripped through her when she realized she had not given Viveka much attention in recent days. Commissions that fed and clothed and sheltered her daughter had kept her busy.

"Alina is a pretty name," Drako said, standing. "I knew a beautiful lady named Alina a long time ago." He offered the child his hand. "Shall we sit in the gazebo?"

Katerina was surprised when her daughter gave the prince her hand. Viveka was shy with strangers, especially men.

"Are you coming?" Drako called over his shoulder.

"Yes." Katerina followed them to the gazebo but wished the visit would end.

"I would invite you to a princess tea party," Drako was saying when Katerina joined them. "Do you like tea parties?"

"I love tea parties," Viveka answered. "What is a princess tea party?"

"A tea party for princesses."

"I am not a princess."

"You are my princess," Drako told her, "and I will give you a crown to wear."

"Mummy Zia, I want to go to the princess tea party."

"Of course, you may attend the tea party." Katerina managed a smile for her daughter, but fear quickened her pulse. Drako Kazanov was a danger to her daughter and to her own peace of mind. "We need to wait for the invitation, though."

"I want a pink dress for the party," Viveka announced.

Drako chuckled. "Your daughter is a typical female, I see." He looked at the girl, saying, "Drako means dragon. I am known as the dragon prince, and your mother is making me a jeweled dragon."

"You are a prince, not a dragon. Dragons are monsters."

"Do you see the pearls your mother is wearing?"

Viveka looked at her mother. "Yes."

"When dragons fight in heaven, they make raindrops fall into the ocean," Drako told her. "The oysters who live beneath the water swallow the dragon raindrops, and pearls are born."

Viveka clapped her hands, bringing a smile to his lips.

"I must be leaving," Drako said, standing. "Your mother has work to do, but I will see you again." He bowed over Viveka's hand and then Katerina's. "I will send you a note about tomorrow evening." Then he turned and walked toward the mansion, leaving mother and daughter sitting in the gazebo.

Katerina felt her pulse slowing with every step Drako took away from them. She hoped the prince was satisfied with his conquest of her daughter. She wondered if the Alina he had once known was her sister. She prayed his limited knowledge of the Italian language did not include the word *zia*.

Midnight. Hushed silence beneath a clear sky. A full moon shone overhead, casting eerie shapes in light and shadow.

A solitary coach traveled eastbound on the Strand, the horses' hooves and the wheels breaking the night's stillness. Passing Ludgate and Cannon Streets, the coach turned onto Bishopgate and halted in front of Dirty Dick's.

Baron Edward "Crazy Eddie" Shores climbed out of his coach and walked into the tavern. He paused inside the door to orient himself and scanned the crowded room for his man. Smoke hung in the air as did the smell of gin and unwashed bodies.

Spotting his man in a dark corner, Crazy Eddie wended his way through the crowd and dropped into the chair opposite his minion. "My friends are displeased by your failure, Scratchy."

"'Twas the other gent what saved 'em, guv," Scratchy defended himself. "I'll get it right next time."

"The targets will be on guard," Eddie told him. "Watch them for a few days to note their habits. Take them down separately, and no carriages this time."

Scratchy looked confused. "But, guv, how can I watch two people at the same time if'n they ain't together?"

Crazy Eddie suffered the awful feeling that he'd picked the wrong man for the job. "Could you get a friend to help?"

"Well, there's me brother Itchy."

Crazy Eddie leaned forward and grinned. "Scratchy and Itchy?"

Scratchy chuckled. "'Twas me mum what called us that cuz we was always bringin' home the lice."

"Get Itchy to help," Crazy Eddie said, sitting back away from the man. "For God's sake, do not use a pistol in a crowd. Only the targets drop. Understand?"

Scratchy bobbed his head.

"Make sure Itchy understands."

Scratchy bobbed his head again.

"If the opportunity arises while watching them, take it," Crazy Eddie ordered. "Don't hesitate."

"Will do, guv."

Crazy Eddie tossed four sovereigns on the table and stood to leave. "Get yourself and Itchy a couple of bottles of gin and women for tonight."

"Thank ya, guv." Scratchy grinned, scooping the sovereigns. "Me and me brother won't let ya down, guv."

Chapter Six

The Contessa de Salerno was a beautiful enigma.

Prince Drako sat behind his desk in his rented Grosvenor Square mansion and pondered the pleasure of solving her puzzle, learning her secrets. The five thousand pound bet with his cousin did not matter. What did the money matter when he had met the most compelling woman?

He ought to cancel the wager and give his cousin the five thousand. Except, Rudolf would enjoy teasing him about developing a fondness for the woman.

The sound of leaves swishing in the breeze outside his open window caught Drako's attention. He glanced over his shoulder. The sun had broken through the clouds, the air clean after the morning rain.

Drako returned to his gem company accounts, lifting the quill and dipping its point in the ink. Again, his thoughts wandered to the Contessa de Salerno and the guest he was expecting within moments, the contessa's brother.

Hektor could not be older than eighteen or nineteen, and young men were notoriously loose-lipped. In spite of his loyalty to his sister, squeezing him for information should be relatively easy. Much easier than focusing on his ledgers.

As instructed, his majordomo had set a tray on his desk. There were a bottle of Kazanov vodka, small glasses, and a zakooska consisting of pickled herring, Swiss cheese, and dark pumpernickel squares. The vodka would loosen the boy's tongue, and he could not serve 100 percent proof without the proper accompanying food.

"Mister Hektor has arrived," Wilbur announced.

"Send him in." Drako stood and circled the oak desk to greet his visitor.

Hektor walked into the office, his expression a mixture of suspicion and amusement.

"Welcome to my home." Drako shook the younger man's hand. "Please sit."

Hektor dropped into the black leather chair in front of the desk. Perching on the desk's edge, Drako poured vodka into two small glasses and handed him one.

"To Mother Russia." Drako raised his glass in salute and then belted the drink down in one gulp.

Hektor did the same. He shivered as the liquid fire burned a path to his stomach.

Drako gestured to the tray. "Help yourself."

"No, thank you, Your Highness," Hektor refused. "I prefer you tell me what this concerns."

This might not be as easy as he had thought. "My cousin imports vodka," Drako said. "I will tell him to send you a case."

Hektor narrowed his dark gaze on the prince. "Why?"

"That look in your eye reminds me of your sister," Drako said, hoping his smile encouraged camaraderie. "I want to commission six crystal tiaras, but do not tell Kat."

Hektor relaxed. "May I ask the reason you need six tiaras?"

"My cousin's daughter will be inviting Viveka to a princess tea party," Drako answered, "and I promised her a tiara. Since the five princesses do not own crowns, I decided to commission them."

"That is a generous gesture."

Drako shrugged. "As the oldest of twelve, I know the importance of little things to children."

Hektor studied him for a moment and then cleared his throat. "What are your intentions toward my sister?"

"With your help, I intend to protect her from those assassins," Drako answered, "and I promise not to ruin her reputation. Now tell me about her late husband."

Drako watched Hektor shift uncomfortably in his chair. Had he touched a sensitive subject? Kat was close-mouthed about her late husband, too.

"What do you want to know?" Hektor asked.

"Did your sister love him?"

"I suppose so. She married him."

"How did he die?"

"He stopped breathing."

Drako grinned. "Accident or illness or what?"

"Garibaldi caught a fever," Hektor said. "His lungs filled and quit on him."

"Was he as handsome and charming as I?"

Hektor laughed at that. "Garibaldi was charming, I suppose. Dark-haired and swarthy like most Italians. His son by his first wife inherited the title and estates. When civil unrest broke out, Katerina moved us out of harm's way."

"I see." Drako did see that two dark-haired parents had produced a blond daughter. Not impossible, but unlikely. The puzzle was growing more complex. "Another vodka?"

Hektor shook his head.

"Why did Kat fear me meeting Viveka?" Drako asked.

Hektor shifted in his chair again. "My sister never introduces Viveka to clients. Call her overly protective."

"Surely, I am more than just a client."

"Are you?" Hektor countered. "My sister has never spoken to me about you."

Except to warn you against telling anyone your last name, Drako thought.

Hektor knew how to keep his mouth shut, hedging around facts, divulging little. Squeezing more information from him today would be impossible.

A knock on the door drew Drako's attention. "Enter."

Wilbur walked into the room. "His Highness, Prince—"

Rudolf brushed past the majordomo. "I am family," he told the majordomo. "Do not be so stuffy, man."

"I apologize for doing my job," Wilbur said.

Rudolf smiled. "I forgive you."

"Thank you, Your Highness." The majordomo left the room.

"Rudolf, I present Kat's brother Hektor," Drako introduced them. "Send the contessa a case of vodka, cousin, and bill me."

Hektor turned to Drako. "Give me a few days on those tiaras." And then he made his escape.

Rudolf poured himself a shot of vodka, dropped into the leather chair, and gulped it down in one swig. "What was the boy saying about tiaras?"

Drako walked around the desk to sit down. "Viveka will be invited to the next tea party, and the girls need tiaras to wear."

"You do love children," Rudolf said. "Why do you not sire a few?"

"I need a wife first."

"Did that tree house you built for your brothers collapse yet?"

"Nothing collapses when I build it," Drako informed him. "The tree house awaits the next generation."

"You missed your calling as a carpenter."

"Thank you, cousin, but princing pays better than woodworking."

"Did you see that downpour this morning?" Rudolf asked. "Viktor and I went to Bond Street, but both our wives had engaged our drivers. Viktor could not locate a place for the coach outside Marcello's, and in complete frustration, said, 'Lord, help me find a place near the shop and I will never drink or gamble again.'

"At that moment, old Lord Witherspoon exited Marcello's and his coach pulled out. Viktor looked heavenward, saying, 'Never mind, Lord, I found one myself.'"

Drako shouted with laughter. "You are lying, cousin."

"Yes, I am." Rudolf grew serious. "Tell me about the attempted murder."

"There is not much to tell. Someone tried to run us down," Drako said. "Alexander Blake saved our lives and is now investigating."

"You can depend on me and my brothers to help." Rudolf reached into his pocket and tossed a folded parchment on the desk.

Drako looked at the parchment and then lifted his gaze to his cousin, making no move to read it. He raised his brows in a silent question.

"The Queen of Naples says there is no Contessa de Salerno," Rudolf told him. "She has never met or heard of Katerina Garibaldi."

"The contessa is an imposter," Drako murmured. "How interesting."

"What are you going to do?"

Drako lifted the parchment and, without reading it, locked it in his desk. "I will do nothing, and neither will you."

Rudolf looked surprised. "You could threaten her into revealing her real name and win five thousand pounds."

"The wager is cancelled," Drako told him, "and I will pay the five thousand pounds."

"I do not need you to give me money," Rudolf said. "I want to win it."

Drako smiled at that. "There will be other wagers, cousin. Kat's ruse is not harming anyone. She is a puzzle I will enjoy solving piece by lovely piece. Do not tell anyone about the queen's letter."

"I will keep the secret." Rudolf burst into sudden laughter. "You love her, cousin."

Drako ignored the comment and the laughter. "Have you ever met anyone whose parents had black hair but the child was blond?"

Rudolf was silent for a moment. "Blaze Flambeau has red hair, but I understand His Grace's aunt was a redhead. Why?"

"Kat has black hair and, according to her brother, so did her late husband," Drako answered. "Yesterday, I met her blond daughter."

"The girl may have inherited the color from an ancestor."

"Viveka called Kat her Mummy Zia," Drako added. "*Zia* is Italian for *aunt*."

Katerina looped the rope of pearls around her neck, the lustrous stones reminding her of the gentleman waiting for her in the foyer.

Dragon raindrops transformed into priceless gems. The prince had made dragons into whimsical creatures, but she knew better. Dragons breathe fire and kill without effort or remorse.

Which was Drako Kazanov? The whimsical creature who gave humans pearls? Or the fire-breathing monster of lore?

Doubts dogged her days and her nights. She was beginning to like him, hoping the prince was as innocent as her brother thought, but unable to bring herself to trust him.

Katerina took a final peek at herself in the cheval mirror. She had definitely dressed to entice.

Her subdued black gown with its rounded, low-cut bodice showed her cleavage to best advantage. The dark color provided a stark background for her perfect pearls, their luminosity hopefully attracting new commissions.

Katerina dotted her jasmine scent above her upper lip. Then she grabbed her diamond-encrusted reticule, its contents having kept her grounded in reality since fleeing Moscow.

Poised at the top of the stairs, Katerina waited until the prince sensed her presence and turned around. Only then did she begin her graceful descent, the appreciative gleam in his eyes making her glad she had dressed to entice.

Prince Drako bowed over her hand. "My dear contessa, you look ravishing."

"Thank you, Your Highness."

Dudley opened the door. "Have a good evening."

Sitting beside him in the coach, Katerina flicked the prince a sidelong glance. His strong profile attracted her as no other man ever had. And that worried her. What if she developed a fondness for him, and then he proved guilty of destroying her family? What if she reached that point and could not exact the revenge she had vowed at her father's grave?

"I will take you home directly after the opera," Drako was saying, "and then go alone to the Althorpe ball. Those gossipmongers who see us at the opera will know there is no scandal brewing, and your reputation will remain untarnished."

"How thoughtful of you." Katerina wondered at his reluctance to escort her to the Althorpe ball. Was he thinking of her reputation? Or his own evening's enjoyment?

"I have changed my mind," Katerina announced. "I wish to see *Le Grand Sancy*."

"I will make your wish come true," Drako said.

Their driver steered the coach into the line that had formed on Bow Street near the Royal Opera House. By unspoken agreement, Drako and Katerina resigned themselves to waiting inside the coach instead of disembarking and walking the short distance.

"Do you still miss him?"

Katerina looked at the prince, confused by his question. "Who?"

"Your late husband."

"Time heals all wounds, as they say."

"How did Garibaldi die?" Drako asked her.

"He stopped breathing," Katerina said, sounding like her brother, stalling for time to think of a plausible untimely demise.

Drako smiled. "What caused the breathing to stop?"

"Why do you ask?"

"Idle curiosity."

"My husband broke his neck when a horse threw him," Katerina told him.

"Sudden deaths are the most difficult to accept."

"Yes." Was the prince thinking of his suicidal fiancee?

"I have not seen your late husband's portrait," Drako said. "Describe him."

Katerina ignored the question as their coach halted in front of the opera house. "Here we are."

Drako climbed out first and then assisted her. "Rudolf and Samantha will be waiting in the box."

Looping her hand through the crook of his arm, Drako escorted her into the lobby. They drew stares from a few, especially Yuri and Anya, but did not pause to speak to anyone.

"Good evening, Your Highnesses," Katerina greeted their chaparones.

"We want no formalities tonight," Prince Rudolf

said, helping her into her chair. "You must call us Rudolf and Samantha."

Katerina noted the many lorgnettes turning in their direction. The raised fans came next as society whispered about their attending the opera together. Though she felt conspicuous, Katerina maintained a bland expression and ignored the stares.

Mozart's romantic opera, *Le Nozze di Figaro* (*The Marriage of Figaro*), was sung that night. The romances and hilarious mistaken identities hit the right chord for Katerina. She did not think she could have borne a tragedy.

Katerina hoped her companions did not want to socialize in the lobby during intermission. The center of attention was not the best place for her, and she preferred blending into society's background, a much safer place for a woman in her position.

When the curtain closed for intermission, Rudolf and Drako left the opera box for the lobby, but Samantha elected to remain there.

"I dislike all that shallow posturing in the lobby," Samantha told her. "I can never tell who is sincere or not."

"I agree with you," Katerina said, relieved to remain in the opera box.

That a princess would feel insecure surprised Katerina, but she understood the woman's feelings. Real or feigned, society smiled at one another, and discerning the difference between the two proved impossible.

Business demanded Katerina speak to both the sincere and insincere in order to gain commissions, and she envied Samantha the financial security that had given her the freedom not to socialize.

"My husband and my children are my most prized possessions," Samantha said, "and I care not a whit for anyone's approval."

"Indeed, you are lucky in your family," Katerina said.

"You must have felt the same about your late husband," Samantha said. "I would be devastated if Rudolf passed away at a young age. When the time comes, I hope I pass first. Though, my aunt insists men should die first because women can live as happily without the men as long as the ladies enjoy financial security."

"I hope to marry again while still young enough to mother more children," Katerina told her.

"Drako seems smitten."

Katerina was saved replying by Prince Yuri, who stepped into their opera box. "I expect you ladies are enjoying the performance."

"Good evening, Your Highness," Samantha greeted him.

"There is no need for formalities between equals," Yuri said, and then looked at Katerina.

"I am enjoying tonight's performance, Your Highness," she said. "If only real life could be so light-hearted."

"Yes, indeed."

Katerina noted that Yuri did not consider a countess his equal.

"Will you be attending the Althorpe ball later?" Yuri asked.

Now Katerina appreciated Drako's decision to go alone to the Althorpes. "Regrettably, no. I plan to go home."

Speculation appeared in Yuri's eyes. She knew he was wondering if Drako would be going home with her.

Rudolf and Drako returned as Yuri was leaving. Katerina caught Drako's expression before he masked his feelings. Contempt had replaced affability. The prince's dislike of Yuri seemed more than schoolboy rivalry carried into adulthood.

At opera's end, Katerina turned to Samantha. "I will see you at your aunt's Ladies Luncheon."

During the coach ride home, Katerina decided to probe

into the prince's past. After all, he had probed into hers on their way to the opera.

"Did you ever come close to offering marriage?" Katerina asked him.

"I was engaged once."

Katerina hid her surprise at his answer. She had expected him to lie.

"What happened?"

"Raisa died before we could marry," he answered.

"How unfortunate." Katerina assumed an appropriate look of sympathy. "I am sorry for your loss." She hesitated asking precisely how the woman had met her untimely end.

"In case you are wondering," Drako said, lifting his arm to rest on the back of the seat behind her, "Raisa suffered an accident, a fatal fall."

"You must have been hurting terribly."

"Ours would not have been a love match," Drako admitted, "but I did care for her. Grief devastated her family, and for that I was sorry."

"Were you there?" she asked. "I mean, when Raisa suffered her accident."

"Unfortunately, I had been traveling for several months on business."

Katerina wondered if his extended absence could have affected his fiancee to such a drastic extent. The prince was becoming a puzzle. She did not trust arrogant, self-serving Yuri but could not take the giant leap of trusting Drako either.

"Here we are."

Katerina glanced out the coach's window. "This is not my home."

"This is my home." Drako climbed out of the coach and turned to assist her. "You wanted to see the Sancy."

She hesitated.

"Seeing the Sancy will take five minutes," he assured her. "I promise to behave myself."

Katerina placed her hand in his and stepped down, suffering the uncanny feeling that walking into his home would change her life forever. Perhaps the feeling was pure whimsey since she had never visited a gentleman's home before. Katerina required gentlemen clients to come to her home for their jewels, or if delivery was required, she sent her brother.

A woman needed to guard her reputation with extreme vigilance. If she ruined her reputation, she chanced ruining her business. Which kept her family fed, clothed, and sheltered.

Curiosity got the better of Katerina. She did not hide her inspection of the foyer, which appeared much the same as her own and others belonging to the upper class. Had she really expected a prince's foyer to be paved with gold?

"We will be leaving again in five minutes," Drako told his frowning majordomo.

"Explaining yourself to your man surprises me," Katerina whispered, walking beside him up the stairs.

"I am protecting you from gossiping servants," Drako told her. "Servants in one household gossip with others."

"Thank you."

The prince's office contained the usual paraphernalia of the wealthy. Walls of books, high-arched windows allowing light, leather chairs, and an enormous oak desk lent the room a masculine atmosphere.

"Your home is lovely."

"If I remain in London," Drako said, "I will purchase my own home and send to Moscow for my belongings."

"Leave the door open, please."

"Leave the door open while I unlock the Sancy?"

"The door stays open," Katerina said, "or I will leave without seeing the Sancy."

"Very well." Drako sat behind the desk and lifted keys from an unlocked top right drawer. One key unlocked the bottom desk drawer and the other the strongbox inside. Removing a leather pouch from the box, he lifted a folded cloth from inside.

"Too bad, you cannot see it by daylight." Drako unfolded the cloth and passed her the stone.

Katerina stared at the fabled diamond, resting comfortably in the palm of her hand. Her nerves rioted at this once in a lifetime opportunity.

The fabled *Le Grand Sancy* was a fifty-five carat, pear-shaped diamond of fiery brilliance. Most believed the Sancy was the first diamond cut and polished with symmetrical facets.

Katerina could see the reason men murdered and died to possess it. And yet—The legend itself was larger than the stone's reality. In the end, the diamond was merely a lifeless stone. No mind, no heart, no soul.

"Truly God's handiwork," Katerina said, passing it to the prince. "I wish my father could have seen it."

Drako stuffed the Sancy into its leather pouch and locked it in the strongbox. That went into the locked bottom drawer. He tossed the keys into the unlocked top drawer.

Watching him, Katerina could scarcely credit his cavalier handling of the legendary diamond. The prince was asking for someone to steal it. She was no thief but would steal it at the first opportunity. If he proved innocent of wrongdoing to her family, she would return the stone along with a lecture on carelessly leaving those keys around.

"Our five minutes have expired," Drako said, circling the desk. "Let us leave before Wilbur suffers a stroke from a brewing scandal."

Downstairs, Drako paused to speak to his majordomo.

"After delivering the countess home, I will be meeting my brothers at the Althorpe ball, but there is no need to wait up. We have keys."

"Thank you, Your Highness."

Sitting beside the prince in the coach, Katerina turned to him with a smile. "Were you assuring your man that we were not intending to create a scandal?"

"You are a fast learner, my lady."

Dudley opened the door when they reached the Trevor Square mansion. Drako stepped into the foyer, nodded at the majordomo, and bowed over her hand.

"I enjoyed your company this evening," Drako said, "and I will be escorting you to the duchess's Ladies Luncheon this week. Good night."

"You may lock the house," Katerina instructed Dudley. "Has my brother retired?"

"I believe he is in the parlor."

Katerina walked upstairs to the family parlor, one of her favorite rooms in the house, second only to her studio. The parlor was cozy and comfortable, its muted colors a balm to the eyes when compared to the formal drawing room's ornate luxury. Her clientele loved opulence that screamed success, and success bred success.

"What are you doing?" Katerina asked, walking into the room.

"Practicing my sketches." Hektor passed her several papers. "What do you think?"

Katerina perused the tiara sketches. "I like the third."

"Do you think it suitable for a grand lady?"

"A princess would wear the third tiara." Katerina passed him the sketches. "I saw *Le Grand Sancy*."

Hektor snapped his gaze to hers. "Have you been drinking?"

"Drako owns the Sancy and let me see it," she told him. "I saw where he stashes the key and plan to steal it."

"Are you serious?" Concern etched across her brother's expression. "Do you want to live in Newgate Prison?"

"Drako will never catch me," Katerina assured him. "If he proves innocent, I will return the diamond."

Katerina left the parlor and started up the stairs to her bedchamber. Her thoughts wandered to the prince and his delight in showing her the Sancy. And then she realized he had not tried to kiss her good night. That put a frown on her face. She did not actually want to kiss him, but his failure to try to steal a kiss bothered her.

Meanwhile, Prince Drako sat in his coach making its way through London to the Althorpe mansion. He had been tempted to steal a kiss, and restraining himself had been difficult. If he alienated her, she would refuse his escort and protection, and their plan would fail. They needed to be seen together to entice the culprits into rash action, but he felt responsible for keeping her reputation above gossip.

And then there was the fact of her and her brother's discrepancies in answering his questions. Apparently, the Queen of Naples had not been mistaken. There was no Contessa de Salerno. Which left him wondering who Katerina was.

"His Highness, Prince Drako Kazanov," the Althorpe majordomo announced him.

Drako descended the stairs into the ballroom. He caught several people from the opera eyeing him, noting the countess's absence. Taking her home had been a sterling idea.

Spotting Alexander Blake, Drako headed in his direction. "Good evening," he greeted the other man.

"Are you unaccompanied tonight?" Alexander asked him.

"Kat and I attended the opera earlier," Drako answered. "We are walking a fine line between togetherness and saving her good reputation."

"If you are considering golfing on the Mall later this week," Alexander said, "then I would advise you against it."

The image of Douglas Gordon's smug smile rose in his mind's eye. "Pride prevents me from following that particular advice."

"I suspected you would not be deterred." Alexander sighed. "I dislike the game, but we will be golfing together."

"How is Miss Flambeau progressing?" Drako asked.

"We just arrived." Alexander flicked a hand in her direction. "Raven believes taking them on one at a time is best. Cynthia Clarke appears headed for the ladies withdrawing room, and I am ordered to dance with one of the others to keep her busy."

"You need my help," Drako said. "I will dance with the other."

"We make a good team, Your Highness."

"I prefer my team of the female persuasion," Drako said. "That assures my captaincy."

"The contessa does not seem amenable to following orders." Alexander grinned and walked away.

"He is correct about that," Drako muttered to himself. Spotting his quarry, he walked in the opposite direction and hoped his dancing would not be reported in the society gossip column.

Chapter Seven

Divide and conquer, Raven thought, trailing behind the blonde. The trio would become suspicious if she attempted befriending all three at the same time. Catching each alone, she could drop a simple grain of flattery into her target's mind without the others noticing and sending them into high alert.

Raven walked into the ladies withdrawing room. Thankfully, the evening was young, and the female guests had not started visiting the withdrawing room to freshen themselves or rest. The only woman in the room was the blonde, who gave her a quick sidelong glance and no greeting.

"Good evening, Lady Cynthia." Raven opened her reticule and reached for her handkerchief. She gently patted her brow as if that had been her purpose in going there.

Cynthia Clarke looked surprised at the greeting. After a second's hesitation, she said, "Good evening, Miss Flambeau."

There was no hint of sarcasm or hostility in the girl's tone. Most likely, too much of a coward without her friends standing beside her.

Raven returned her handkerchief to the reticule and

turned to leave, her gaze resting directly on the blonde for the first time since entering. "Pardon me, Lady Cynthia, but you are wearing pink in place of your customary white."

A disgruntled expression appeared on the girl's face. "Am I required to wear white?"

Ah, yes. There was the hostility.

"My compliments on your choice," Raven said, her smile sugary. "The pink accentuates your lovely complexion."

The blonde's mouth dropped open, and surprise momentarily stole her wits. "Why—I . . ." A tiny smile touched her lips. "Thank you, Raven. I admire your gown's shade of blue."

Raven knew the blond trio deemed her own birth on the wrong side of the blanket as irrefutable proof of her ignorance in taste and social skills. Therefore, a bit of self-effacement should evoke a touch of sympathy.

"Thank you, Cynthia." Raven gave her a conspiratorial smile as if confessing a grievous sin. "Your compliment belongs to my stepmama who chose it for me."

"The Lord blessed Her Grace with impeccable taste," Cynthia said, her smile widening. "You are wise to listen to her."

"I will certainly pass your compliment along to her," Raven said, aware that female socialites sought to please her stepmother.

The girl's smile grew. "Please do."

"Enjoy your evening." Raven walked out of the withdrawing room feeling sickened by her own sweetness.

One down and two to go. Raven harbored no illusions about Anya and Lavinia. Cynthia Clarke was a follower and easier to sway than the others would prove.

Though her gait was gracefully meandering, Raven felt as if she were marching into battle. Entering the ballroom, she spied the Russians—Anya, Yuri, and their aunt Princess

Lieven—speaking with her father and stepmother. At least, Anya would temper her tongue in front of an audience.

"Good evening, Your Highnesses," Raven greeted them.

Princess Lieven smiled at her, and Prince Yuri bowed over her hand. Princess Anya gave her a sullen look.

Raven ignored the blonde's unspoken hostility. "What an interesting shade of green, Anya, and so complimentary with your blond hair."

The Russian princess seemed taken aback. "Thank you, Raven. The color's correct name is spring green, willow green being last year's shade."

Raven managed a smile. "I am learning new and interesting things every day."

"Your gown is lovely, too," Anya said. "I imagine you needed Her Grace to advise you on style and color."

The Lord giveth a compliment, Raven thought, *and the Lord taketh away.*

Raven felt the urge to backhand the blond twit to repay her backhanded compliment. Instead, she said, "My wonderful stepmother has been a wealth of useful information."

When the Russians moved on, the Duchess of Inverary leaned close, saying, "Raven dearest, you are learning to play the game."

"The game is sending my stomach into revolt," Raven admitted, making her father chuckle.

"Do not ever change," the duke said. "Society needs ladies like you." He turned to his wife. "Roxie, I am wandering to the card room."

"I will wander with you, my love," the duchess said, "for here is Alexander wanting Raven to dance."

Alexander Blake stood there, smiling and offering his hand. "My lady, may I have this dance?"

Stepping onto the dance floor, Raven whispered, "My thoughts are not ladylike."

"How were your overtures received?" Alexander asked, as they began moving in the rhythm of the waltz.

"As expected, Cynthia proved relatively easy," Raven answered, "but Anya gave me a backhanded insult."

"Let us take care of Lavinia together." Alexander inclined his head in the Smythes' direction where Prince Drako Kazanov was engaged in conversation. "Drako offered to help. As soon as you drop your compliment, he will deflect Lavinia's nastiness by inviting her to dance."

"God bless the prince."

His hand on the small of her back, Alexander guided her off the dance floor. They circled the ballroom slowly, pausing to greet and speak with others along the way.

"Good evening, Your Highness, Ladies Prudence and Lavinia," Alexander greeted them. "You remember Miss Raven Flambeau."

"Roxanne Campbell's stepdaughter," Prudence Smythe said. Her expression seemed pinched as if something sharp was sticking into her unmentionables.

"Good evening, Blake and Miss Flambeau," the prince greeted them.

Lavinia Smythe said nothing, no flicker of acknowledgment.

A direct assault of friendliness would not work on this blonde, Raven decided. Instead, she turned to the mother who wore a classic strand of pearls adorned with a diamond clasp.

"What an exquisite necklace, Lady Smythe. I admire it greatly."

Prudence Smythe lifted her hand to touch the necklace. "My daughter's most recent birthday gift to me."

"Well, Lavinia has superb taste and obviously holds you in the highest regard," Raven said.

The woman's pinched expression eased. Slightly. "My

Lavinia has inherited her late sister's grace and flair, one of society's great ladies in the making."

Raven smiled and nodded. She wished society did not frown on public puking.

"Lady Lavinia, will you honor me with this dance?" Prince Drako asked.

As the blonde placed her hand in the prince's, Raven turned to Alexander. "I would speak with my stepmother."

"I believe she and your father went into the card room," Alexander told her. "I will escort you there."

"Enjoy your evening, Lady Smythe." Raven accepted Alexander's arm and, as they walked away, whispered, "My head is pounding, and I want to go home."

Alexander grinned. "Let's find your parents and tell them I will escort you to Inverary House."

Mother and daughter sat in the foyer and waited for Drako to arrive. Katerina had accepted his escort to the duchess's Ladies Luncheon while Viveka wanted to see the dragon prince again. The prince's note had stated that he had something for the little girl.

Anticipation and ambivalence mixed inside Katerina at the prospect of seeing the prince after a four day absence. Their evening at the opera had not been mentioned in the *Times* gossip column, which meant her reputation remained intact. However, the prince's dances with the blond bullies had been mentioned, and Katerina did not think highly of a man who could escort one lady to the opera and then dance until dawn with the blond trio.

She could not be jealous. Could she? No, that was too absurd even to consider.

Katerina decided to return to her cooly polite demeanor on the ride to Inverary House. They could pass those few minutes discussing the plan to unmask the culprits threatening their lives.

"Where is the prince, Mummy Zia?"

Katerina smiled at her daughter's impatience. "Prince Drako will arrive in a few minutes."

Viveka stood and crossed the foyer to the majordomo. "Dudley, are you a prince?"

"I am a prince among majordomos," Dudley answered.

"What is that?"

"The majordomo is the man in charge of the whole household," Dudley told her. "I meet all the visitors first."

Viveka sent her mother a reproving look. "I never meet any visitors, just the dragon prince."

"Only majordomos are allowed to open the door for visitors," Dudley said. "Little girls play in the garden."

"What do little boys do?"

"Little boys cause trouble."

Katerina laughed at the same moment the doorknocker banged. Viveka rushed back to her seat beside her mother while Dudley opened the door.

"Good afternoon, Your Highness."

"Good afternoon, Dudley." Drako stepped inside the foyer and then, in courtly manner, bowed over Viveka's and Katerina's hands. "Two beautiful ladies. What a lucky prince I am."

"I am a princess, not a lady," Viveka said.

"I stand corrected."

"What does that mean?"

"I made a big mistake," Drako said. "You look pretty in pink."

Viveka smiled. "I know."

Drako turned to her mother. "And you look pretty in purple."

"The gown is violet whisper, not purple."

"Oops, I made two mistakes." Drako reached into his pocket for a paper. "Viveka, this is for you."

"I do not know reading," Viveka said, lifting the paper out of his hand. "What is it?"

"You are invited to the princess tea party."

Viveka clapped her hands, her eyes gleaming with excitement. "Where is my crown?"

"Viveka." Her mother's voice held a warning note. "Mind your manners."

"You cannot attend the tea party without a princely escort," Drako told her. "I will bring your crown that day, and I am inviting you and your mother on our own private outing the day after tomorrow."

Viveka stared up at him. "What is an outing?"

"We are riding through the park, buying candy at the sweet shop, and visiting the Tower Menagerie," Drako told her.

"Candy?" Viveka clapped her hands again. Then, "What is men-jury?"

"The Tower Menagerie is where the wild animals live," Drako explained, "but the animals live in cages. We can see them, but they cannot touch us."

Katerina lost her placid expression, displeased with his unexpected and unwanted invitation. She did not want her daughter endangered, nor did she appreciate his strategy which forced her to accept.

"Shall we leave, my lady?"

"Yes, Your Highness." Katerina stood, her smile cold. "I am ready."

Drako bowed over Viveka's hand again, making her giggle. Katerina planted a kiss on her daughter's cheek.

Dudley opened the door. "Enjoy your day, my lady."

Katerina sat in silence inside the coach. She kept her gaze fixed on the view outside the window.

"Is something wrong?"

"You should not have extended the outing invitation in front of Viveka," Katerina said, rounding on him. "You force me to accept or disappoint her, and I do not want my daughter endangered."

"Relax, Kat." Drako stretched his long legs out. "There is no danger in a simple outing."

"Unseen danger lurks all around us," she told him, making a sweeping gesture with her arm. "I am responsible for her safety."

"I can protect her." Drako said nothing more for a long moment, his gaze dropping to her necklace, the only jewelry she wore. "What an interesting piece."

Katerina rolled her eyes at the change of topics. She counted to ten and then added another ten for good measure.

A source of pride, Katerina considered this particular necklace one of her masterpieces. While living in Naples, she had purchased an unusually large and oddly shaped harlequin opal, her task was displaying the thirty-two carat stone without diminishing its distinctive beauty and shape. She had created a one-of-a-kind pendant on a polished gold chain accentuated with hundreds of tiny diamonds.

"Thank you, Your Highness." Katerina told herself the prince had no children and did not realize one never offered a child anything without consulting with the parent first. "I have been doing my inventory and discovered a surplus of opals. Wearing this necklace may bring me a few commissions for opal jewelry."

Drako laughed. "My darling contessa, I never appreciated a woman's shrewdness until I met you."

"Thank you, Drako."

"Actually, I was insulting you."

Katerina heard the teasing smile in his voice and echoed his own words to her. "In that case, how dare you."

Drako grinned. Katerina smiled. They shared a rare laugh together.

"Your dancing with the ladies at the Althorpe ball did not help our scheme to unmask the guilty," Katerina said, "and do not tell me you were sacrificing yourself for my reputation."

"Ah, I wondered if you had read that tidbit in the *Times*." Drako arched a dark brow at her, his incredible blue eyes seeming to see into her heart. "You sound like a jealous woman, darling. Could you be developing a fondness for me?"

Katerina tried to regain the upper hand. "I was thinking of Alexander Blake's plan."

"For your information, Raven Flambeau wanted to separate the blondes," Drako told her. "Blake and I kept two busy while she befriended the third."

"I see." Katerina wished she had kept her mouth shut. She did sound like a jealous woman, and nothing could be further from the truth. *She hoped.*

At Inverary House, Drako escorted her into the foyer. "Stay here until I return," he told her. "Do not accept a ride from any lady who offers."

"You do not believe a lady—?"

"We do not know anything yet," he interrupted. "Take no risks."

Scheduled each year on the day the gentlemen golfed on Pall Mall, the Duchess of Inverary's Annual Ladies Luncheon was one of society's most exclusive invitations and limited to one hundred guests. There were three categories represented. First came the duchess's cronies and other ladies of some importance like Princess Lieven, the Russian ambassador's wife. Second were matrons like the duchess's nieces and the Kazanov princes' wives, followed by the young unmarrieds. An invitation one year did not necessarily guarantee an invitation the next.

Katerina supposed she should feel honored to have received one, giving her the opportunity to catch more commissions, but she disliked society events in general. Without their gentlemen's civilizing presence, the ladies could deteriorate into unladylike behavior. No one could be more ruthlessly waspish than a woman when there were no men to witness the transgression.

She could not relax around these women. She was not like them. She would never be one of them.

These women would shun her if they knew her true identity and what she was. Except the duchess, of course, who was sweet in a mercenary sort of way.

"The ladies are gathering in the ballroom," an Inverary footman told her.

"Thank you, sir."

Two violinists played background music while one hundred ladies milled about greeting and gossiping with friends. At the opposite end of the ballroom stood the un-crowned queen of society surveying her ladies-in-waiting.

The Duchess of Inverary looked regal in a red gown and dripped diamonds. Several diamond rings adorned her fingers, diamonds by the yard draped her neck, and diamond cuffs circled her wrists. Her sparkling brilliance was almost blinding.

Katerina smiled with genuine pleasure. She had created all the jewels the duchess wore. The woman had style, the red gown grabbing the eye first and the fiery diamonds keeping the eye fixed on her.

Most women dressed for other women, and the duchess was no exception. Men only noticed when the bill arrived.

"Good afternoon, Your Grace." Katerina's gaze drifted to the two women standing beside the duchess. "Lady Althorpe. Lady Smythe."

"Kat darling, I am so relieved you could accept my invitation," the duchess gushed. "Did you read the morning

Times? Prince Mikhail and my dearest Belle are officially betrothed, and the ring you created is exquisite."

"I am glad you approve," Katerina said, "and I thank you for the invitation."

The Duchess of Inverary was purposely standing with Lady Smythe to rub the other woman's spiteful nose in the betrothal announcement. The duchess would make a formidable enemy.

"Belle, come here," the Duchess of Inverary called, spying her stepdaughter walking into the ballroom. "Thank the contessa for creating your exquisite betrothal ring."

"Thank you, my lady," Belle said. "Your creation is all that a bride could want and then some."

"The pleasure was mine."

The Duchess of Inverary held her stepdaughter's hand up so those in their immediate vicinity could see it. The square-cut diamond had been set in platinum, emeralds in the shape of leaves circling the enormous stone.

Insult is an art form, Katerina told herself. The duchess is baiting Prudence Smythe, Prince Mikhail's former mother-in-law who had sought a match between the prince and her youngest daughter. She was probably hoping the woman would snipe at the ring, thereby allowing her to pounce. Figuratively, of course.

Prudence Smythe looked as if she had sat on a tack. "A betrothal ring does not make a marriage," the woman said. "Mikhail may change his mind yet."

The Flambeau girl paled at that.

"Swallow your tongue," Katerina scolded, a smile softening her words.

A couple of the Flambeau sisters giggled at that. With them stood a young woman, no more than fifteen or sixteen, who had glorious mahogany hair as well as intriguing eyes, one blue and one green.

"Who is this young miss?" Prudence Smythe asked.

"You have not met Tulip," the Duchess of Inverary said. "How remiss of me. Tulip is the Duke of Essex's granddaughter, sister of the Marquis of Basildon."

"I didn't know Bart had a granddaughter," the woman said, her gaze shrieking the word *bastard*.

Katerina recognized the malicious gleam in the woman's eyes. She had seen that exact look leveled at herself many times. The blond bully's mother would swoon if she knew that three women in her vicinity—Belle, Tulip, and herself—had been born on the wrong side of the blanket.

The girl had pluck, though. Tulip lifted her nose into the air and drawled in a good imitation of the duchess, "You cannot possibly know all the insider *on-dits*."

Prudence Smythe narrowed her gaze on the girl. "She inherited Bart's temperament, I see. If you will excuse me." And then she walked away.

"You show remarkable promise," the duchess told the girl. "I predict you will become one of society's great ladies."

"That is a title to which I do not aspire," Tulip said, affecting a cultured tone.

Katerina laughed at the girl.

"Being the queen of society affords a woman great freedom," the duchess told her.

Tulip smiled at her mentor. "I may reconsider my aspirations."

"Please excuse me while you are doing that," Katerina interjected. "I would freshen myself before lunch."

Katerina left the ballroom and headed for the ladies withdrawing room. Perhaps the luncheon would not go as badly as she had expected.

She could, after all, fade into the background. Unlike Belle Flambeau, she was not betrothed to a prince all the unmarrieds had chased, nor had any gossip appeared in the *Times* regarding her attending the opera with Drako.

Katerina smiled to herself. She could relax and enjoy a

luncheon without worry that any lady would take a verbal shot at her. The ladies had other targets in mind.

And then Katerina walked into the ladies withdrawing room, coming face to face with the Blond Brigade and Raven. All conversation ceased when they spied her. Definitely not a good sign.

"You should have treated Yuri kinder," Princess Anya said, rounding on her. "There is no prince in your future now."

Katerina had no idea to what the girl was referring. She felt like she had arrived at the opera during the third act.

"Yuri danced twice with both Cynthia and Lavinia at the Althorpe ball," Anya continued, "and all three of us danced with Prince Drako." The princess turned to Raven, saying, "Tell the contessa what you told us."

"I am sorry for hurting your feelings," Raven said, sounding unrepentent, "but I heard Prince Rudolf telling my father that Prince Drako believes lonely, young widows make an easy target for gentlemen's advances."

Katerina felt sorry for Raven. Her mouth spewed venom while her gaze begged forgiveness.

"Well, darlings," Katerina drawled, imitating the duchess, "Princess Samantha told me Drako despises insipid blondes. Reminds him of his former fiancee, I suppose."

Lavinia Smythe whirled toward the princess. "You never told me Drako had been engaged."

"I did not know." Princess Anya turned to Katerina. "You are lying."

"If you do not believe me," Katerina said, "then ask your aunt." Instead of insulting the blondes, Katerina bonded them to Raven with an insult. "I love the gown, Raven, but that shade of yellow makes your complexion sallow." At that, Katerina turned away but heard snatches of their conversation before she walked out the door.

"You do not look sallow," Cynthia Clarke said.

"And the gown is the latest style," Lavinia added.

"Sit with us for the luncheon," Anya invited her.

"I would love to sit with you," Raven accepted.

That poor, self-sacrificing girl, Katerina thought. She shuddered to think how the food would taste sharing a table with those revolting three.

Katerina found her place, relieved and pleased with the duchess's choice of her companions. Princesses Regina and Samantha as well as three of the Flambeau sisters—Belle, Bliss, Blaze—sat at the table.

"Tell us about your scare the night of Stepan's wedding," Princess Regina said, as the footmen began serving.

Katerina dismissed the other woman's concern with a wave of her hand. "That was a freakish accident, easily avoidable."

"Are you certain?" Princess Samantha asked. "My husband seemed concerned."

"We consulted the constables who concluded it was an accident." Katerina looked at Belle across the table. "Thank you for inviting my Viveka to the tea party. You cannot imagine how excited she is."

"You are welcome," Belle said. "Bess is beside herself with anticipation since she never hosted a tea party before."

The conversation turned to other diverse topics reflecting the women's various interests. The mothers discussed children and babies, Katerina explained how she created jewels from idea to sketch to finished product, Belle offered advice on flowers and gardening, Blaze spoke about thoroughbred racing since her father had gifted her with a horse, and Bliss asked questions about the business end of jewelry design.

Katerina flicked an occasional glance at the table where Raven sat with the blondes. With a smile frozen on her face, the poor girl sat among enemies and looked miserable.

"Raven is a traitor," Blaze grumbled to her twin.

Bliss pursed her lips and nodded in agreement. "We

should kick her out of our company and take her share of the profits."

"Sisters, be a little understanding," Belle said. "Raven is the youngest and perhaps needs acceptance."

Listening to them, Katerina could see the reason Prince Mikhail loved Belle Flambeau. Her kindness in the face of adversity spoke well of her.

"My fingers itch to slap her," Blaze said, casting a sour glance at the other table.

"Circumstances are not always what they appear," Katerina cautioned the girl. "Perhaps your sister is sitting with them to squelch any rumors the witches are brewing against Belle."

"Well, I will never speak to her again," Bliss announced.

"Neither will I," Blaze agreed.

Once the main luncheon ended, the ladies drifted to the formal drawing room where coffee, tea, and desserts would be served. Friends gravitated toward friends. Older women boasted about their grandchildren, young matrons discussed babies and exchanged housekeeping advice, and the younger unmarrieds congregated near one of the white marble hearths.

Katerina sent up a prayer of thanks that she was not considered an unmarried, who always seemed to be competing against each other. She supposed they were competing in a general sense since the number of available, wealthy, gentlemen was finite. Avoiding that fray, she sat with Princesses Regina and Samantha while the duchess and several older women sat nearby.

She wished Belle Flambeau had sat with them instead of allowing her sisters to drag her along with them. The gentle sister lacked the emotional stamina to deal with the unmarrieds' spite.

"Kat dearest, how remiss of me not to admire your unique necklace," the Duchess of Inverary drawled.

"You have had other concerns on your mind today," Katerina said, and flashed the Smythe woman a glance. "Most especially your stepdaughter's betrothal to Prince Mikhail."

"Advancing age sometimes distracts people," Lady Smythe interjected.

"No matter how old I am, Pru," the Duchess of Inverary said, "you will always be older." The duchess smiled at Katerina, saying, "I would like you to make me a few pieces in opal and diamond."

"I would love to accommodate you," Katerina said, "but this particular necklace is one of a kind. Opals, however, are similar to diamonds in that they coordinate well with a variety of shades."

"Is the necklace one of your creations?" Lady Smythe asked her. "A gift from your late husband? Or a lover perhaps?"

Several women gasped at that last question. Unwilling to allow her good reputation to be smeared, Katerina rounded on the older woman.

"I am a virtuous widow," she said, "and you possess the tongue of an adder."

"An adder is a venomous snake," the duchess added.

"V-e-n-o-m-o-u-s," Princess Regina spelled the word, making her sister-in-law giggle. "Venomous means poisonous."

Prudence Smythe opened her mouth to reply, but a loud gasp from the unmarrieds drew their attention. Belle Flambeau bolted out of her chair and now stood in front of Lavinia Smythe.

"Bitch," the gentle Flambeau girl said, eliciting another shocked gasp and smothered laughter from her sisters.

"Breeding does tell," Prudence Smythe said into the silence.

Belle Flambeau rounded on their group, her gaze on

the elder Smythe. "Like daughter, like mother. Baby bitch and Mama bitch."

The Flambeau sisters erupted into wild applause. Except Raven.

"Belle, these ladies are our guests," Raven said, though not unkindly.

Blaze Flambeau, the volatile redhead, leaped to her sister's defense. "Raven, go to hell with your new friends but watch your back. Those blondes would eat their own young."

Lifting her nose into the air, Belle Flambeau left the drawing room. Blaze Flambeau fell into step with her sister, casting one furious look over her shoulder before disappearing out the door.

A stunned silence reigned in the drawing room for several long moments.

In growing misery, Katerina had watched the altercation. She was grateful that Raven had assumed the role but knew from experience how difficult life was when sisters argued. Alina had despised her from their initial meeting, and Katerina had lived with her sister's hatred from that first day at the age of five until her sister's death in childbirth.

Though she knew what Raven was feeling, she'd had only one hostile sister. Enduring the hostility of six sisters was six times the misery.

Guilt consumed Katerina, and she wished she had stayed home. How could she ever repay the Flambeau girl's sacrifice?

"How delicious," the Duchess of Inverary drawled, breaking the stunned silence. "This year's luncheon will be discussed for the next twelve months."

Chapter Eight

He hoped the Marquis of Huntly had fallen ill and would be unable to participate in the golfing. Nothing serious enough to cause death, of course. He did not wish the other man any real harm. A debilitating hangover would suffice.

Drako stepped out of his coach at the far end of Pall Mall, where the men were gathering, and reached for his golf bag. Its sparkling cleanliness shrieked the embarrassing fact that he had never played before today.

Though his cousin had explained the game and demonstrated the rudiments of play, Drako felt doubtful of today's outcome. He suspected that the game was not as easy as his cousin made it sound. Knowing the rules and executing them were two different tasks.

For some unknown reason, Drako needed to beat the marquis. He did not care if he scored near the bottom but wanted the marquis dead last.

Seeing Prince Yuri among the gathered men, Drako amended his wishes. He wanted to trounce the other prince, too.

Drako hooked his golf bag over his shoulder and began walking toward the men, where several waiters from

White's Gentlemen's Club were serving drinks and snacks. Though the Mall and St. James's Street had been cleared in preparation for the day's event, faint whiffs of horse dung teased his nose.

Katerina is the lucky one, Drako thought. She sat safely inside Inverary House and enjoyed a genteel luncheon, followed by tea and pleasantries with the other ladies. Refusing to be named a coward, he needed to defend his manhood by participating in a silly game on a public street or risk his kin teasing him until the day he died. Losing to every man present was infinitely better than not showing up at all.

Drako spotted Alexander Blake hurrying toward him and smiled a greeting. At the other man's wave, he stopped walking and waited for him to approach.

"I want to speak privately before we join the others," Alexander said.

Drako nodded. "I dropped Kat at Inverary House and will escort her home later."

"Golfing on the Mall is by far the safer event today," Alexander said, smiling. "After the betrothal announcement this morning, the cats will unsheath their claws."

"A civilized luncheon followed by pleasantries seems like an easy day," Drako said.

"You think so?" Alexander's smile grew into a grin. "Those so-called ladies are more vicious than wild cats. I predict few pleasantries today and hope Raven can survive the storm."

"Well, I would prefer lunch to golfing any day," Drako said, illiciting a chuckle from Blake. "At least, I know how to eat."

"We've been placed into groups of four," Alexander told him. "I invited Baron Edward Shores to golf with us. Eddie walks the line between legal and illegal vices and knows the underworld scuttlebutt. I may learn something about the situation."

"Who is the fourth player?"

"The Marquis of Huntly insisted on joining our group."
The day would be worse than he had thought.

Drako glanced toward the gathered gentlemen and
spotted the marquis, who wore a predatory smile directed
at him. "Have you ever golfed with the marquis?"

"I dislike golfing." Alexander shook his head. "My
hobby is catching criminals."

"Do you know anything about Huntly's golf game?"

"I did overhear your cousin arguing against his joining
our group," Alexander answered. "Rudolf said the match
would be between a dinosaur and a mouse."

So much for wishes, Drako thought. "I suppose I am the
mouse."

"Rudolf did mention that you and your brothers had
never played the game," Alexander replied, "but that fact
did not prevent him from trying to coax the gents into
wagering whether the dinosaur or the mouse would win.
Unfortunately, nobody was willing to place his money
on the mouse."

Drako and Alexander walked toward the gentlemen
who were now standing with their game partners. Drako
did not know all the men, though some he recognized
from operas and balls.

The Duke of Inverary, the Russian ambassador, Rudolf,
and Yuri comprised the first group. Drako assumed
Rudolf was planning to keep Yuri and him separated.

"Welcome to the annual London Golf Match," the Duke
of Essex called to the assembly. "This damn cane prevents
me from playing again this year, but I will await the
winner at White's."

The Marquis of Huntly sidled up to Drako while the first
players approached the tee. "I canna wait to see ye golfin'."

Hearing the smile in the other man's voice, Drako looked
at him and then dropped his gaze. "You are wearing a skirt."

"'Tis my lucky plaid," Huntly said, as he looked at Alexander.

"You doomed yourself to failure by insisting on this group," Drako told him. "Blake dislikes the game, and I have never played in my life."

"There's all kinds of winnin'," the marquis said. "Ye canna be that bad, dragon man."

"Prince," Drako corrected him. "Dragon prince, not man."

A gentleman approached them as the next group prepared to tee off, and Alexander introduced him. "Your Highness, I present Baron Shores."

"Most call me Eddie," the baron said, smiling. "Some call me Crazy Eddie."

"Crazy Eddie?" Drako echoed. "You look sane and pleasant."

"I'm smiling because I heard you were a worse golfer than I," Eddie said, making the other two men chuckle.

Drako wished he had stayed home. He disliked losing, especially in public, and knew he was out of his league in the golfing game.

Watching the groups tee off, Drako pointed down Pall Mall, asking, "What are those flags?"

"Those flags mark the cups," Huntly answered.

"What cups?"

Even Crazy Eddie laughed at that.

"The cups are the holes," Huntly told him. "Ye do know yer supposed to hit the ball into the holes in the fewest strokes possible?"

"That much I know." Drako was not only irritated with himself but also his cousin. Rudolf was a joker and had failed to mention a few of the important specifics of the game.

"What is the news around town?" Drako heard Blake asking Eddie.

"That depends," the baron answered.

"That depends on what I want to know?" Alexander asked. "Or that depends on if you want Amadeus Black to leave you to your businesses?"

Crazy Eddie smiled. "Both, I guess."

"Do you know anything about the threats to Prince Drako and the Contessa de Salerno?"

"I have heard nothing," Eddie answered. "I'll let you know if I do."

"Amadeus would appreciate your cooperation," Alexander said, and dropped the subject.

"Ye and Kat are in danger?" Huntly asked, his voice low so none could hear.

"I am in more imminent danger of losing this game," Drako answered.

And then it was their group's turn to tee off.

Drako stepped to the tee and set the feather-stuffed leather ball on it. After drawing a club from his bag, he gripped it using the overlapping method his cousin had taught him.

"Ye dinna have the correct club," Huntly said. "Ye've grabbed the putter when ye need a driver."

Embarrassed, Drako could have throttled his cousin. The incorrigible prankster had insisted the smaller club worked best for distances.

The Scotsman stepped closer, lifting the putter out of his hand, and offered him his own club. "My driver will bring ye luck."

Drako smiled and took the other man's driver. "Thank you."

"I'll watch yer back while yer playin'," Huntly whispered. "You are not such a bad fellow after all."

"I dinna know if ye've just insulted or complimented me," the Scotsman said. "Keep yer left arm straight but not stiff. Ye ken?"

Drako nodded and turned back to the tee. He touched

the face of the club to the ball without hitting it as he lined his shot up.

"Keep yer head down and eyes on the ball," Huntly instructed him. "Yer left hip bears yer weight, and when ye hit the ball, swing in an arc. Dinna fail to follow through, yer left heel keepin' ye balanced."

Wham! Drako hit the ball. It sailed through the air and landed halfway to the first flag.

"That wasna too bad, dragon man," Huntly called. "Ye couldna have done it without me, of course."

Alexander Blake teed off next, followed by Crazy Eddie. Neither man played very well but knew what to do. Huntly tee'd off last. The ball landed near the first flag.

"Ross and I can take ye to Blackheath to practice," Huntly told Drako, as they were walking down the Mall to take their next shots.

"I am uncertain if I like the game," Drako said, "but I appreciate your offer."

Huntly smiled. "Ye dinna like losin', dragon man."

"Public humiliation is decidedly unappealing," Drako said.

"And what are yer intentions toward the countess?" Huntly asked. "I willna tell a soul."

Drako stopped walking. "What business is that of yours?"

"I like the lass," Huntly said. "Kat is honest, virtuous, and concerned with her family obligations. She doesna dish dirt like the other ladies, and I wouldna care to see her hurt."

"I will not hurt her," Drako told him.

"Well, ye may not mean to hurt her," Huntly said, "but, as they say, good intentions pave the road to hell."

"I said, I will not hurt her." Drako did not bother to mask his irritation.

Huntly held his hand up. "I'll take yer word on it, then."

The game traveled the length of Pall Mall, rounding the

corner onto St. James's Street. Golf balls flew past Brook's and Boodle's and Crockford's. The final flag stood near White's, the refuge of London's aristocratic males.

Alexander Blake walked in the direction of his ball. Beside him, the Marquis of Huntly was advising him which club to play.

Drako stood beside the baron and watched them. He flipped his ball into the air and caught it while waiting for the outcome of Blake's final shot.

"So, Eddie, tell me how you earned your nickname," Drako said, his ball slipping out of his grasp. He leaned down to retrieve it.

Whoosh! An arrow whizzed past where he had stood only a second earlier.

Crazy Eddie shrieked in pain, an arrow sticking out of his upper arm. Instead of ducking for cover, Drako rushed to help the baron.

"I'm stuck," Eddie screamed, grabbing his arm. "The stupid bastard hit me."

Golfing ceased. The gentlemen still in play dropped their clubs and ran down St. James's Street toward them. Those who had completed the course dashed out of White's to see what was happening.

"Do not touch the arrow," Drako warned Eddie, kneeling beside him. "Inverary's physician will remove it."

By that time, the Marquis of Huntly and Alexander Blake were kneeling on the other side of the fallen man. The three men exchanged glances, their gazes saying that Drako had been the intended target. By unspoken agreement, they lifted the baron to carry him into White's. Inside the lobby, the three gingerly placed him on a couch.

Dr. Elliott, the duke's personal physician, had been recruited to attend the event in case of injury. "Someone fetch me two bottles of whisky and a sharp knife," he ordered, and then studied his patient's arm.

"You aren't going to amputate, are you?" Eddie cried. "How will I gamble without my arm?"

"Calm down, young man," Dr. Elliott said. "I plan to cut your sleeve before removing the arrow lest the wound fester into something worse."

"I want that arrow for evidence," Alexander Blake said.

The whisky and the knife arrived at the same time. The physician uncapped one bottle of whisky and placed it in Eddie's left hand.

"Take a few swigs," the physician said. "The whisky will calm you."

"Can you tell me who would want you dead?" Alexander asked.

In the act of lifting the whisky bottle to his mouth, Eddie paused and sent Blake a reproving look. "How many hours do you have to listen?"

All the gentlemen laughed at that. Even Alexander Blake smiled.

Drako watched the physician cut the baron's sleeve and part the edges. Then he reached into his bag for the bandages.

"I am going to remove the arrow and press a cloth on the arm to staunch the bleeding," Dr. Elliott told his patient. "Then I will pour whisky on the wound to prevent festering."

"Will that hurt?" Eddie asked.

"Not as much as walking through life with an arrow stuck in your arm." Dr. Elliott chuckled at his own joke. "A few of you gents hold him down."

With strong and steady hands, Dr. Elliott yanked the arrow out of Eddie's arm. Blood flowed from the wound before the physician pressed a cloth on it.

Drako turned his back on the sight, his stomach rolling with nausea, and crossed to the opposite side of the room. Dropping into a leather chair, he leaned over so his forehead touched his thighs.

Take deep breaths, Drako told himself, accustomed to his lifelong reaction to blood. At the age of ten, he had witnessed a child run down by a coach. Blood, broken bones, shrieks of pain, cries of grief. Whenever he saw blood, that day came racing back to him. *Inhale and exhale. Inhale and exhale. Inhale and—*

"That arrow was aimin' for ye," Huntly said.

Drako did not bother to look up. "I know."

"Are ye ill, dragon man?"

"Seeing blood sickens my stomach."

"What can I do for ye?"

"Vodka," Drako said. "I need vodka, Scotsman."

"That could be a problem in this establishment," Huntly told him.

"Rudolf stocked the bar."

"I'll return in a minute."

All seemed quiet across the room where the physician was stitching Crazy Eddie. And then he heard Blake's voice, saying, "Go home and rest, Eddie. Come to Constable Black's office later to give us a statement."

"That is unnecessary," Eddie balked. "I didn't—"

"Trust me," Alexander interrupted. "You do not want Constable Black looking for you."

"I'll be there."

A small glass containing clear liquid appeared in front of Drako, who clutched it like a drowning man. He gulped it in one swig and shuddered as it burned a path to his stomach.

"Do not tell anyone about my stomach," Drako said, "or I will need to kill you."

"Yer secret is safe with me, dragon man." Huntly grinned. "Ye didna place last. That dubious honor belongs to yer cousin Stepan cuz he's been lyin' abed with his bride all week. Ah, here comes yer cousin. Ross and I will watch yer back whenever possible." The Scotsman nodded at Prince Rudolf and walked away.

"You still suffer that peculiar affliction?"

"Every man has a weakness," Drako said. "Mine produces nausea when I see bleeding."

"You may have lost the game," Rudolf said, "but you made Huntly a friend."

"The Scotsman likes me because I golf poorly," Drako said. "A silly game if you ask me."

An hour later, calm had been restored inside White's. The golfers sat around tables drinking, gossiping, and heckling each other about the game. The men's favorite target was Prince Stepan who had won the previous year but placed dead last this day. The management had already advised the players—including the illustrious Dukes of Inverary and Essex—they would not be allowed in the dining room unless properly attired.

Drako sat with his brothers and cousins as well as Huntly and his cousin, the Marquis of Awe. Letting the conversation swirl around him, Drako worried about Katerina and himself, the danger becoming all too real after the day's close call.

Pouring himself another vodka, Drako downed it in one gulp. Should he cancel the trip to the Tower Menagerie or not? He did not want to disappoint Viveka, nor did he relish trying to explain the reason he was canceling their outing. Which meant he needed to keep silent about the arrow incident.

Drako reached for the bottle of vodka and realized it was empty. He stood and crossed the room to the deserted bar. "Is the bar still open?" he asked the bartender.

"Your Highness," the man drawled, "this bar has been open for more than a hundred years."

A chuckle beside him told Drako that Prince Yuri

stood there. "I want another vodka," he told the bartender, ignoring the other prince. With bottle in hand, Drako turned to walk away.

"Are you giving me the cut?" Prince Yuri asked him.

Drako shifted his gaze to the prince. "What do you want?"

"I wondered if you had bedded her."

That statement confused Drako. The royal swine could not be asking what he was thinking. "I beg your pardon?"

"I am referring to the Contessa de Salerno," Yuri said, his smile malicious. "You usually take my leavings."

With his free hand, Drako grabbed the prince by the front of his shirt and yanked him within an inch of his face. "I should have killed you years ago."

All conversations in the room ceased. All gazes swiveled to the two princes. All waited for what would happen next.

"As I recall," Yuri said, seemingly unruffled, "you dislike the sight of blood."

"I will make an exception in your case, swine." Drako released him, shoving him away as if he was an unclean abomination.

"Swine?" Prince Yuri's voice rose in anger.

The listening gentlemen chuckled at that.

Prince Yuri shifted his gaze to the smiling men, his complexion mottling with fury. "My honor demands you meet me at dawn."

"You have no honor," Drako told him, "and I do not relish a bullet in my spine."

The listening men gasped at the slur.

"Take that back," Yuri shouted.

Drako shook his head slowly, purposely fixing a smile on his lips designed to infuriate the other prince. "A man cannot take back the truth."

When he turned to walk away, Yuri struck him. Caught off guard, Drako crashed into the bar. The bottle of vodka slipped from his hand, splattering vodka and shattered glass across the floor.

Drako reacted in an instant. He grabbed Yuri with one hand and returned the blow with the other, hitting the prince's face dead-center. Then Drako tossed Yuri several feet into a table, sending its occupants scurrying out of harm's way.

"My tooth," Yuri shrieked, lying on top of the upset table. "I swallowed my front tooth."

"Consult Dr. Elliott and send me the bill." Drako walked away, crossing the room to the door. Outside the club, he gestured his driver to bring the coach around.

Two steps behind him was the Marquis of Huntly. "Yer head doesna contain much in the way of brains, dragon man," the marquis said. "Someone tried to kill ye today, and tonight ye walk aboot alone."

Drako shrugged. "If I stayed inside, I would have killed him."

"I ken ye and Yuri share a hostile history," Huntly said, "but consider how the contessa would feel if the arrow had hit its mark."

"What do you mean?"

"The lass is sweet on ye."

Drako smiled and then wished he hadn't. His cheek-bone throbbed, and his eye was beginning to swell. Even his knuckles hurt. "How can you tell?"

"When I was dancin' with her at the weddin'," Huntly answered, "her attention focused on ye, not me. Mark my words, dragon man. One look at yer bruises will have her cooin' in sympathy."

The coach halted beside them. Gesturing his driver to stay where he was, Drako opened the door. "I never considered that."

"Ye'll chase her until she catches ye." Huntly chuckled

at his own wit. Then he grew serious, adding, "Mind what I said about her feelin's cuz I wouldna want to harm ye."

Drako leaned back and closed his eyes as the coach started moving. He had lived thirty-three years but, until tonight, had never struck another person. It felt . . . *good*. He should have slugged Yuri years ago and, if the opportunity presented itself, he would do it again.

The coach halted in front of Inverary House, and his driver opened the door. He could not go inside. His bruises would alarm any ladies who lingered after the luncheon.

"Tell the majordomo to fetch the Contessa de Salerno," he instructed his man. "I will wait here."

Several moments passed, and then Katerina appeared. She climbed into the coach, her mouth dropping open at his swollen and blackening eye. "I thought *I* had endured a bad day," she exclaimed, her soft fingertips reaching to touch his brow. "What happened?"

"Yuri hit me," Drako said, "and I returned the favor."

"Oh, you poor man," Katerina said. "A damp cloth will lessen the pain. You poor, poor man."

She was cooing.

Drako would have smiled if his face didn't hurt so much. "My eye and cheekbone throb. I would appreciate a damp cloth."

Katerina sat back beside him and slipped her hand into his. "Trust me, you will feel better in a while."

Ten minutes later, Katerina led Drako into her Trevor Square mansion. "Dudley, bring a cool, damp linen to the dining room," she instructed.

"Yes, my lady." Dudley looked at Drako. "I do hope the other gent is in worse shape."

"I knocked Prince Yuri's front tooth down his throat," Drako told him, unable to keep the satisfaction out of his voice.

"Good for you, Your Highness."

"You knocked his front tooth out?" Katerina dissolved into giggles. "I can hardly wait to see his gaping smile."

"I told him to send me the bill." Drako smiled through his pain. "You are a bloodthirsty wench, Kat."

"I cannot deny my Romany blood," she said, and then froze as if she realized she had said too much.

Drako knew that she had spoken truthfully but pretended that she had been joking. "Leaving Russia does not make one a gypsy. Though, I do not believe there is anything wrong with being a gypsy."

"Most people of your ilk would not agree with you," Katerina said, leading him down the corridor to the dining room.

"What is my ilk?" he asked, admiring the sway of her hips.

"An arrogant aristocrat."

"Oh, *that* ilk."

If she had gypsy blood in her veins, then he would not have met her in Moscow. She would never have been accepted into society or been invited to the same social functions. He held no prejudices against Romany bloodlines and tried to recall any scandals he'd heard about a Russian aristocrat marrying a gypsy. From where did she inherit her gypsy blood, mother or father?

Five minutes later, Drako sat at the dining table and held a damp linen to his eye. "I dislike golfing," he said, "and, considering what happened afterwards, wished that I could have attended the luncheon."

"How strange, I was wishing that I could have golfed instead of dealing with those witches," Katerina told him. "I feel very badly about Raven."

Drako lifted the linen from his eye and looked at her. "What happened?"

"The blondes targeted Belle," Katerina answered, "and

Belle called Prudence and Lavinia Smythe a mama bitch and a baby bitch."

Drako shouted with laughter. "Ouch, ouch, ouch."

"I am sorry for making you laugh," Katerina apologized, and then giggled. "Relating what happened is funnier than experiencing it."

"How does Raven enter into this?" he asked her.

"She reminded her sister the blondes were their guests," Katerina answered, "and the Flambeau sisters turned on her. I could feel the tension in the house even after the guests left. Only Her Grace seemed unaffected by the furor, deeming her guests would be discussing the luncheon for a long, long time."

"Only the Duchess of Inverary could make that statement without losing friends." Drako stared at her a moment, trying to think of a way they could pass more time together. An idea popped into his mind, and he gave voice to it. "I noticed Viveka does not have a tree house, and I would like to make her one."

"A tree house?"

"A tree house is—"

"I know what a tree house is," she said. "If she wants a tree house, I can afford to—"

"I was not offering to purchase her a tree house," Drako said. "I was offering to make her one. My tree houses are built to last for generations and will never collapse."

Katerina looked astounded. "*You* build tree houses?"

"I possess many talents you will enjoy exploring," Drako said.

His suggestive statement seemed to fly right past her. Which was unusual for a woman of her sophistication.

"I built my younger brothers a tree house," he added, "and the tree house is waiting for the next generation. Not all princes are useless, you know."

"I will consider it and let you know," Katerina said, after several silent moments.

Drako placed the linen on the table and stood to leave.

"Would you care to stay for supper?" Katerina invited him.

Her invitation surprised him. This was the first time she had wanted him around. Maybe the Marquis of Huntly was correct about a woman's sympathy. Appearing too eager would not do, though.

"I appreciate your invitation," Drako said, "but my face hurts. Will you ask me again when I feel better?"

"You will stay for supper after our trip to the Tower Menagerie," Katerina said, rising to escort him to the foyer. "I will not take *no* for an answer."

Reaching the foyer, Drako leaned close to whisper against her ear, "I was planning to steal a kiss, but Dudley's presence is foiling my plans."

"Oh, my," Dudley exclaimed, already hurrying down the hallway. "I forgot my kettle on the stove."

"Do you think Dudley heard me?" Drako asked, smiling.

"If I were a gambler," Katerina said, giving him a flirtatious smile, "I would wager no fewer than four staff are sitting in the kitchen and capable of lifting the kettle off the stove."

They stared into each other's eyes, their smiles dying slowly as physical awareness leaped to life. Drako's gaze slid to her mouth. Unable to resist, he lowered his head, and his lips touched hers in a gentle kiss.

Drako inhaled her jasmine scent. She was soft and sweet and sensuous.

He cupped the back of her head, holding her steady, deepening their kiss. She slid her arms up his chest to entwine his neck and returned his kiss in kind.

Drako yearned to see her naked, feel her breasts rubbing against his bare chest. And that thought made him end the kiss.

The time was not ripe. He wanted to persuade her into his bed, not frighten her away.

Drako stepped back a pace and smiled at the color rising on her cheeks. She blushed like a nervous virgin.

"I am sorry," Katerina said. "Your injury—"

"Your kiss is worth the pain." Drako lifted her hands to his lips. "Until the day after tomorrow, my lady."

Chapter Nine

Several miles east of Trevor Square stood the Central Criminal Court Building. Alexander Blake paced back and forth inside a small office while awaiting the arrival of Baron Edward "Crazy Eddie" Shores for his interview. Watching him were Constable Amadeus Black and his assistant Barney, chief of the constable's runners.

A legend in London, Amadeus Black enjoyed a fierce reputation for catching the most cunning criminals. Society's elite paid him vast sums of money for his celebrated investigatory services. The city of London paid him a civil servant's paltry fee when faced with a particularly puzzling or gruesome crime.

Standing over six feet tall, the constable cut an imposing figure in his customary conservative black attire. Even the most hardened criminals cringed at the mention of his name, and Alexander admired him greatly.

"How was the golfing?" Amadeus asked, perched on the edge of his desk.

"Besides the fact that I witnessed an attempted murder," Alexander answered, and stopped pacing, "I can honestly say I like the game enough to play once a year."

Both Amadeus and Barney chuckled at that.

"I tried golfing one time," Barney told them, "but I couldn't hit the damn ball."

"Nothing is ever as easy as it appears," Amadeus remarked.

"Crazy Eddie knows something," Alexander said. "He screamed that the stupid bastard hit him."

Amadeus looked at Barney. "Wait unseen outside the building and follow Eddie when he leaves. Schedule the runners to monitor the baron around the clock. I want to know where he goes and who he sees."

"I understand." Barney left the office.

"I assume you consulted Miss Flambeau," Amadeus said.

"Raven believes two entities are involved but unaware of each other."

"An interesting concept and quite possible."

"I've assigned Raven the task of befriending the Blond Brigade," Alexander said. "Those witches are privy to the juiciest gossip."

A knock heralded the baron's arrival. Alexander opened the door and stepped aside, ushering the baron into the office.

"Baron Shores," Amadeus greeted him, "please be seated."

It was a command, not a request. The baron sat where directed.

"I am relieved you survived your ordeal," Amadeus said. "Tell me what happened."

Eddie shifted uncomfortably in his chair, as did most people the constable questioned. "I was standing on St. James's Street with Prince Drako," Eddie said, staring the constable in the eye. "The prince was flipping his golf ball into the air. When it slipped through his fingers, he bent to retrieve it. That's when I felt a sharp pain in my arm and saw the arrow."

"Truly terrifying," Amadeus said. "How does the arm feel now?"

"The wound pains me," Eddie answered, "but I am fine otherwise."

"Do you think the prince was the assassin's target?"

The baron's gaze skittered away, and he shifted in his chair. "That could prove true, I suppose."

Amadeus was silent, waiting for the baron to look at him again. When he did, Amadeus said, "I know you have underworld contacts." He held his hand up when the baron opened his mouth to speak. "Do not bother to deny it. I want you to keep your ears to the ground and report to me if you learn anything."

Crazy Eddie looked relieved. "I can do that for you."

Amadeus gestured to the door. "I thank you for visiting me so promptly."

Eddie stood, a nervous chuckle escaping him. "No sane man relishes the thought of London's famous constable looking for him."

Amadeus turned to Alexander as soon as the door clicked shut behind the baron. "You are correct. Eddie knows something."

Alexander checked his pocket watch and slung his golf bag over his shoulder. "I may call upon Raven to see if she heard any gossip."

Outside the Criminal Court Building, Alexander climbed into his grandfather's coach for the ride to Park Lane. He felt certain she'd had an easier day. After Belle married her prince, he and Raven could officially become betrothed. The duchess, of course, would insist on a spectacular ring for her stepdaughter and a lavish society event to celebrate their betrothal. He hoped this trouble with the prince and the contessa would be resolved by that time.

The coach halted in front of his grandfather's Park Lane mansion. Alexander grabbed his golf bag, climbed down, and then noticed the cloaked figure sitting on the front steps.

Raven.

Alexander dropped the golf bag and sat beside her. "How was the Ladies Luncheon?"

Raven burst into tears, sobbing as if her heart had broken and would never mend. Alexander put his arm around her and drew her close, planting a kiss on the side of her head.

"Tell me about it."

"B–B–Blaze called me a traitor," Raven sobbed, "and Bliss wants to kick me out of the Seven Doves. Sophia and Serena slammed the bedchamber door in my face. Even Belle prefers to wait a few days before speaking to me."

"Good job, Raven."

"Good job?"

"You played your role convincingly," Alexander said. "That means their anger appeared sincere."

"My sisters hate me," Raven told him, a catch of emotion in her throat. "Their anger *is* sincere."

Do not laugh, Alexander told himself. *If you laugh, she will never forgive you.*

Alexander took his handkerchief from his pocket and wiped her tears. Then he placed the handkerchief in her hand, saying, "Blow your nose."

And Raven did, several unladylike honking sounds. After a couple of sniffles and a dainty dab at her nose, she offered him the handkerchief.

Alexander gave her a rueful grin. "You keep it."

Raven smiled at that, though her lips quivered with her struggle to hold back her tears.

Alexander suppressed the urge to yank her into his arms and kiss her into a daze, making her forget her sisters. She had gone from surrogate baby sister to desirable woman in a short time. They would conduct their relationship with perfect timing along the way. Taking advantage of her need for comfort would not do, and the front steps of his grandfather's Park Lane mansion was definitely not the place for a passionate kiss.

Rising from the steps, Alexander offered her his hand, which she accepted with a wobbly smile and stood. He put his arm around her shoulder and drew her against his muscular frame. They strolled down Park Lane to her father's house.

Alexander tilted her chin up. "Consider how sorry your sisters will feel when they learn the truth."

"You are correct *for once*," Raven said, regaining her fighting spirit. "I will make them grovel for their mistrust."

He loved her.

Or did he?

Sitting in his Grosvenor Square office, Prince Drako leaned back in his chair and closed his eyes. He conjured the contessa's image as she had looked the previous evening when they had shared a laugh about Yuri's missing tooth. How could he be sure he loved Katerina when he had never loved another woman?

True, Raisa and he had been engaged, and he had cared for her. Theirs had not been a love match, though.

Deciding the time to marry had arrived, he had proposed to her, and Raisa had wanted to be a princess. Perhaps their lack of a shared love had left her susceptible to Yuri's lies. Once she had succumbed to his false charm, the swine had tossed her aside.

If only he had warned her about Yuri or not traveled so extensively for his businesses. Life was filled with if-onlys. He refused to allow any if-only to ruin his chance with the contessa.

Katerina was an amazing woman and equal to him

in every way. Lovely, intelligent, and shrewd. A strong woman who could take care of herself and her family.

She did not need him. She did want him, though.

Drako rubbed his eye and dropped his hand at the twinge of pain. He had winced at his own reflection this morning while shaving.

His thoughts turned to his lifelong nemesis. Yuri had hated him since their school days. The closer his relationship with the contessa, the more imminent the danger from Yuri.

The swine would target her simply because of him. On the other hand, Katerina was a wealthy widow, and Yuri was perpetually short of funds.

A knock on the door drew his attention. "Enter."

Wilbur walked into the office. "Mister Hektor requests an interview, Your Highness."

"Send him here." Drako rose from his chair and crossed the office to greet his guest at the door. He shook the younger man's hand, led him across the room to a leather chair, and then circled the desk to drop into his own chair.

Hektor stared at him for a moment. "What happened to your eye?"

"Yuri's fist caught me off guard after yesterday's golfing," Drako answered. "I returned the favor by knocking his front tooth down his throat. Literally."

Hektor grinned. "He will find the tooth somewhere."

Drako smiled, his gaze dropping to the man's satchel. "You finished the tiaras?"

Opening the satchel, Hektor removed a cloth-covered tiara. He repeated that five more times until a row sat across the desk. Then he unfolded the cloth from one tiara.

"Good job." Drako inspected the tiara. Created in white gold, crystals lit the tiara's fleur-de-lis motif.

"I used gold because platinum is more costly," Hektor said, "and silver tarnishes easily."

"We would not want the princesses wearing tarnished tiaras."

"All the tiaras are exactly the same," Hektor said. "That prevents arguments between the princesses."

"I see your sister's shrewdness in you," Drako said. "Did you inherit your Romany blood from your mother or father?"

Caught off guard, Hektor looked startled. "What?"

"Last night Kat mentioned her Romany blood," Drako said, "and I wondered from which parent."

"Our mother was Romany, not Russian," Hektor answered, his expression clearing. He reached into his satchel again, removing a black box, and placed it on the prince's desk. "Kat finished your commission this morning."

Drako opened the box and lifted the dragon pendant hanging from a heavy gold chain. The dragon's profile was a blaze of sapphires and emeralds lit by glittering diamonds. It had a ruby eye and a fiery tongue of amber and gold.

"Your sister's genius amazes me," Drako said, staring at the dragon. "Are you capable of producing this?"

"Kat is teaching me what she learned from our father," Hektor answered, "but God blessed her with extraordinary vision. My sister is a prime example of the student surpassing the teacher."

Drako poured vodka into two small glasses, passing one to Hektor. He lifted his glass, saying, "I salute your sister's vision and talent."

Hektor raised his glass in salute to his sister and belted the vodka down. Then he set the empty glass on the desk, gesturing that one was enough.

"How much do I owe you for the tiaras?" Drako asked.

"Sixty pounds total."

"And the dragon pendant and chain?"

"One thousand pounds."

Surprised by the piddling amount, Drako looked from Hektor to the jeweled pendant. "This piece is worth much more than one thousand pounds."

"You supplied the stones," Hektor reminded him, "and Kat waived her fee, only charging you for the gold."

"How much would it cost otherwise?"

Hektor stared at the pendant and then shrugged. "Fifty thousand pounds, perhaps."

"I will pay the fifty thousand," Drako insisted, "or I will never commission another piece."

Opening his desk drawer to draft a bank note, Drako saw the letter from the Queen of Naples. If he showed the letter to Katerina, she would bluff her way out of telling the truth, but her inexperienced brother might be persuaded to give him information.

Drako wrote the bank note and passed it to Hektor. Unfolding the letter, he placed it on the desk, saying, "We must discuss this important complication discovered by my cousin."

Reading the letter, Hektor shifted in his chair, his complexion paling. "The Queen of Naples does not remember my sister."

"Your sister is an imposter." Drako locked the queen's letter in his desk again. "I want you as an ally, Hektor. Even more important, I want you as a brother-in-law."

The younger man looked stunned. "Why?"

I love her, Drako thought and knew it was true. He could not imagine a life without the contessa beside him. However, he was not going to open his heart to her brother.

"I will marry her, no matter who she is."

"Does Kat know?"

"You know the answer to that," Drako said. "Your mother was a Romany, and your father designed the czar priceless jewels. What is your last name?"

Hektor shifted in his chair again, his expression pensive

as if mulling something over in his mind. His loyalty to his sister conflicted with something else, something Drako did not understand.

"Kat will tell you what she wants you to know," Hektor said, "but her logic is faulty. Though, I do believe she is experiencing doubts. On the other hand, I must do whatever possible to keep her out of Newgate Prison."

That caught Drako's curiosity. "Tell me what you can without betraying her trust."

"Kat wanted to kill you when she heard you were in London," Hektor told him. "My logic and her doubts have settled her mind on stealing *Le Grand Sancy*."

Drako stared at him in silence, unable to credit what he had heard. "Why did she want to kill me?"

"My sister harbors a grudge against you."

"What grudge can she harbor against a man she recently met?"

"You will need to ask her."

Drako ran a hand through his hair. For obvious reasons, he could not ask the contessa the reason for her grudge. Asking the brother different questions might give him more information.

"Do you hold a grudge against me?"

Hektor shook his head. "I doubt you are guilty of what she believes. My sister is no thief and will return the Sancy once you prove innocent."

Drako was hopelessly confused. He could not defend himself against invisible charges. After pouring another vodka for Hektor and himself, he rose from his chair to stand at the window, ordering, "Do not speak while I think about this."

Closing his eyes to the manicured garden, Drako pulled the pieces of the contessa puzzle from his mind and tried to fit them together. There was a woman of Romany blood, an expatriate from Moscow, pretending to be an

Italian contessa. She was a master jeweler and design genius whose father had created priceless jewels for the czar. There was a five-year-old daughter who called her Mummy Zia. *Aunt.* The little girl had a doll named Alina, which had surprised the mother who had quickly masked the emotion.

An idea popped into his mind, an idea almost too absurd to consider. The Romany blood had confused him, but all families had their secrets.

Drako rounded on Hektor. "I commend your loyalty, but I need to ask you a question. Nod or shake your head. Is your last name Pavlova?"

Now Hektor looked surprised. "Are you guilty?"

"I have never harmed anyone except Yuri yesterday," Drako assured him. "Is your name Pavlova?"

Hektor nodded.

Drako smiled, knowing the younger man was an ally. "I will not ask the reason for the grudge. Your sister will tell me. Now, I want you to make me a wedding ring."

"For what?"

"I am going to trap your sister into marriage," Drako told him. "Only then will she forget about killing the man who harmed her family."

"Do you know the villain's identity?" Hektor asked.

Drako ignored the question. "I need Kat to steal the Sancy on the day of my choice."

Hektor laughed. "How do you plan to arrange that?"

"I will entice her into making her move four days from today," Drako answered, "but you must promise to escort her to my house in case those assassins are watching her."

Hektor nodded. "I can do that."

"Take notes on the wedding ring," Drako said, passing him parchment and quill. I want a wide band of yellow gold inscribed with *Ot dushi*. Inside the band I want *Ot dushi* translated into English *from my soul*."

The sentiment made Hektor smile. Looking up from his notes, he said, "Welcome to the Pavlova family, Your Highness."

Drako reached across the desk and shook the younger man's hand. "Welcome to the Kazanov family."

Once Hektor had gone, Drako went looking for his brothers and found them lunching in the dining room. With a flick of his hand, he sent Wilbur from the room.

"You will go out of town four days from today," Drako told them, "and you will be gone for two days."

Prince Lykos raised his dark brows. "Where are we going?"

"What is this about?" Prince Gunter asked.

"This concerns seduction and marriage," Drako answered.

The two younger princes smiled. "Whose seduction?" Lykos asked.

"And whose marriage?" Gunter finished.

"We are your brothers," Lykos said.

"You can trust us," Gunter added.

Drako looked from one brother to the other. "Can you keep a secret?" He smiled when they nodded in unison. "I have chosen a bride and plan to trap her into marriage. Her identity will remain secret until she accepts my proposal."

"Would not life be simpler if you offered for her?" Lykos asked.

Gunter nodded in agreement. "Why do you need to trap the lady into marriage?"

"The lady is strong-willed," Drako answered, "and she may not accept unless I give her no choice."

"I think he is referring to the Contessa de Salerno," Lykos told his younger brother.

Gunter grinned. "I think so, too."

After lunching with his brothers, Drako searched for his majordomo and found him in the foyer. He lifted the day's invitations from the silver tray on the table and casually flipped through them. A reception at the Russian embassy, the Kenwood ball, the Wakefield ball, and the Winchester ball.

"Wilbur, I would speak with you in my office," Drako said, tossing the invitations on the silver tray.

"Yes, Your Highness." The majordomo followed him up the stairs and into his office.

"Take a seat," Drako said, circling his desk.

Wilbur looked surprised. "You want me to sit, Your Highness?"

Drako gestured to the leather chair in front of his desk. The majordomo sat.

"My brothers will be traveling out of town four days from today," Drako told him, "and they will be gone for two days. I am giving the household staff two paid holidays and traveling expenses to visit friends and relatives. I need the house empty for those two days. Do you understand?"

"Yes, Your Highness." Wilbur looked thoroughly confused and then suspicious. "Forgive my impertinence, Your Highness, but—" The majordomo hesitated momentarily. "Does this concern possible illegalities?"

Drako gave the man a reassuring smile. "This concerns immorality only."

The gown needs jewels.

Katerina inspected herself in the cheval mirror a final time. She wore a blue silk day dress with a modest neckline and short, puffed sleeves. Around her shoulders, she wrapped a white cashmere shawl bordered with blue flowers and carried a pagoda parasol instead of a bonnet.

Grimacing at her lack of jewels, Katerina concluded that sapphires or aquamarines would have complemented the gown. However, she did not want to attract attention to herself, especially from thieves loitering at the Tower Menagerie.

Katerina walked down the corridor to her daughter's bedchamber. She had grave misgivings about taking her daughter out in public and hoped the prince was correct about their safety. A carriage accident or attempt at the Tower would be the most opportune moments for the villains to make their move.

Viveka's bedchamber was empty. Excitement had sent her daughter to the foyer.

Drako and Viveka were awaiting her in the foyer. When the prince turned to watch her descending the stairs, the appreciative look in his gaze gave her a feeling of satisfaction.

"Good afternoon, my lady," he greeted her.

"Good afternoon, Your Highness." Katerina turned to her daughter. "Are you ready for your outing?"

Viveka nodded and slipped her hand into the prince's, a trusting gesture not lost on her. Katerina raised her gaze to Drako's, but he merely smiled.

Katerina could see no resemblance between them and again doubted that Drako had sired Viveka. If only she could be certain. Lifting a white bonnet with pink ribbons from the table, she tried to set the bonnet on her daughter's head.

Viveka brushed her hand away. "No bonnet, Mummy Zia."

Silently counting to ten, Katerina held onto her patience. The bonnet was a recurring argument between them. "Little girls always wear bonnets."

"I am a big girl."

Prince Drako and Dudley chuckled.

Katerina shifted her gaze to the men. "Do not encourage her."

"Where is your bonnet, Mummy Zia?"

Viveka looked like Alina but acted like Katerina. Though she was proud of her daughter's intelligence,

Katerina did not appreciate having that intelligence turned on her.

"I brought my parasol," Katerina said.

"I will carry a parasol, too," Viveka told her.

"You do not own a parasol. Shall I buy you one?"

Viveka smiled. "Yes, Mummy Zia."

Katerina assumed a disappointed expression and turned to Drako. "I am sorry, Your Highness, but we must postpone our outing until I purchase Viveka a parasol."

"I will wear the bonnet today," Viveka said, "and carry the parasol next time."

Ignoring the men's smiles, Katerina placed the bonnet on her daughter's blond head and tied the pink ribbons under her chin. She turned to the prince, saying, "We are ready now."

Drako looked at Viveka. "You look beautiful in your bonnet."

She smiled at him. "I know."

Dudley opened the door, saying, "Enjoy your afternoon."

Outside, Drako assisted Katerina into the carriage and then lifted Viveka up. He climbed inside, closed the door, and sat opposite mother and daughter.

"I decided on a closed carriage and driver for safety's sake," Drako said. "The Tower is located in a rough section of London."

The ride to Hyde Park was short even with the weekday traffic. Leaving Trevor Square, the driver turned onto Knightsbridge and entered the park through the Edinburgh Gate.

Inside Hyde Park, the city seemed far away. Elm, oak, and birch trees bloomed here. Dark green shrubbery as well as primary-and pastel-colored flowers accentuated the trees and the grass.

Society in their finest rode here to see and be seen. They passed four young ladies in a carriage, the Blond

Brigade and Raven Flambeau. Recognizing the prince and his companions, the ladies leaned close to gossip. In the distance, Prince Yuri reined his horse away when he spied the Kazanov carriage.

"We are fueling the gossipmongers," Drako said.

Katerina said nothing, uncomfortable with her position. She could not afford a tainted reputation.

"Mummy Zia, you are not using your parasol," Viveka said.

"Thank you for reminding me, sweeting." Katerina smiled at her daughter. "I do not need a parasol inside the carriage."

"By the way, I cannot escort you to the Winchester ball," Drako told her. "My brothers and I will be leaving town that day to inspect thoroughbreds at various places and will be gone for a couple of days. I am even giving my staff two paid holidays to visit relatives and friends in our absence. For safety's sake, I want you to remain home while I am gone."

"No escort will give me a good excuse to stay home and work."

An empty house was incredibly good luck. Stealing the Sancy would be easy, no risk of getting caught.

"Are you enjoying yourself, sweeting?"

Viveka tore her gaze from the park's activity and nodded at her mother. She looked at the prince, asking, "Do you have a daddy?"

Her question surprised Katerina. She had never considered that her daughter thought about daddies.

"My daddy lives far away," Drako answered.

"I have an Uncle Hektor and a fairy godfather," Viveka told him.

Katerina and Drako exchanged smiling glances. "Who is your fairy godfather?" the prince asked.

"Dudley is my fairy godfather," Viveka answered. "Dudley

said little boys have fairy godmothers, and little girls have fairy godfathers."

"When your mummy marries again," Drako said, "you will get a new daddy but still keep your fairy godfather."

Listening to him, Katerina could not envision this man abandoning his pregnant paramour and their unborn child. Her sister Alina must have been trying to tell her something other than the cad's identity. Still, her sister calling his name was the only thread of evidence she had.

Thinking about the worst twenty-four hours of her life was giving her a headache. She would put that aside for today and enjoy the afternoon with her daughter.

Katerina listened to her daughter chattering about the following week's tea party but peeked at the prince. He was a fine figure of a man with his strong, masculine profile and black hair accentuated by his piercing blue eyes. Women would be vying for his attention even had he not been born a wealthy prince.

Leaving Hyde Park, their driver turned the carriage onto Piccadilly and then Bond Street. When the coach halted in front of a small shop at the end of the street, Drako climbed down first and then assisted Viveka and Katerina.

Katerina felt secure and content. Holding their hands, Viveka walked between them. Passing pedestrians would believe they were a happy family.

The sweet shop was painted pristine white with pink trim, the perfect background for their products. White shelves held rows of glass jars filled with enticing confections. There were lollipops in more than a dozen colors and flavors, twists of barley sugar, gobstoppers that changed color when sucked. Another shelf held jars of nougats, Wellington sticks, and Nelson's balls. There were jars of walnut, orange, and lemon creams as well as a variety of taffy and fudge.

Viveka looked awed, her blue eyes large with wonder. She turned in a circle for the full, spectacular view.

Katerina could not remember being that young and innocent. Oh, she had once been five years old but doubted her life had been as carefree as her daughter's.

Unexpected tears welled up, but Katerina blinked them back and suppressed her bittersweet memories. She had vowed on the day of Viveka's birth that the babe would live with loving approval and unconditional acceptance and never want for anything.

She had kept her promise. That gave her more satisfaction than any jewel creation.

"What would you like, princess?" Drako was asking Viveka.

"The prince means you may choose three different sweets," Katerina interjected, "if you promise to save some for tomorrow."

Drako gave her a sheepish grin. "I should have known that since I am the oldest of twelve."

Viveka inspected every shelf, pausing to study the contents of its jars. "I want a lollipop."

The shopkeeper grabbed a sheaf of paper and twisted it into a candy holder. "Which flavor do you want?"

"She needs one of each flavor," Drako answered.

Katerina rolled her eyes. "Your Highness, Viveka cannot possibly eat—"

"She will eat one lollipop a day for"—Drako glanced at the row of jars—"for twenty days and decide which are her favorites to select on our next visit. What is next, princess?"

Viveka placed a finger across her lips while pondering her second choice. "A gobstopper."

"Give her seven," Drako instructed the shopkeeper, and then looked at Katerina. "She will eat only one a day."

"I promise," Viveka said. "I would like taffy."

"Give her a sample of each," Drako said, inspecting the jars of taffy. "Is that Russian taffy?"

"Yes, it is."

"What is Russian?" Viveka asked.

Drako sent Katerina a reproving glance, which made her squirm mentally. Why should she have passed the Russian culture to a child who would never live there? She had only lived in Moscow from the age of five to eighteen and had never felt accepted. Only her parents had cherished her, especially the father she had first met at the age of five. The Romany blood was stronger in her than in her brother and sisters. After wandering for the first five years of her life, nowhere felt like home.

"Viveka has never lived in Russia," Katerina defended herself.

"Her Russian blood is her heritage." Drako crouched down, eye level with the girl. "Russia is our homeland, where your mother and I were born. Do you understand?"

Viveka nodded, but her expression mirrored her confusion.

"You will understand when you are older." Drako stood and asked Katerina, "What candy would you like?"

"Nothing, thank you."

"Give me a sampling of everything," Drako instructed the shopkeeper.

"Your Highness—" Katerina began.

"The sweets are for me," Drako interrupted, "and I do not like sharing."

Viveka giggled. "I do not like sharing either."

Laden with their purchases, they climbed into the waiting carriage. Now Drako sat on the other side of Viveka, their candy parcels covering the seat opposite. Staring at the sheafs of paper, Katerina thought they had purchased enough candy to open their own shop. Thankfully, her brother and sisters would eat much of it.

The Tower was located in east London, a seedier section

of the city. Their coach traveled down the Strand through the weekday traffic and turned onto Tower Hill Road.

The menagerie was housed in the Lion Tower, a semicircular bastion outside the Middle Tower at the castle's entrance. With Viveka walking between them, Katerina and Drako followed the crowd. Seeing the roughness of the spectators, Katerina tightened her grip on her daughter's hand and kept her parasol unopened to use as a weapon if needed.

Their first stop was the thirty-foot anaconda. The South American aquatic boa made Katerina nervous, and she looked down at her daughter's pale face.

"Viveka is afraid," she whispered to the prince.

Drako lifted her into his arms. "Is that better?"

Viveka nodded.

"Do you know how the snake eats his food?" he asked the girl.

"Do not tell us," Katerina ordered him. "You will give her nightmares, especially after she devours all that candy."

Katerina kept alert to the crowd jostling them as they wandered to the second exhibit, a ten-foot alligator from America. Chuneelah, the Indian elephant, came next, followed by Old Martin, a brown bear.

"Where are the lions?" Viveka asked.

"I am sorry, princess," Drako answered, "but there are no lions in residence. When the lady lion died, her husband lion died of a broken heart."

"How do you know this?" Katerina asked.

"Rudolf told me."

The next exhibit was the nine-foot-tall grizzly bear, easily one thousand pounds. The grizzly was watching the crowd watching him.

With Viveka in his arms, Drako squeezed through the crowd, who made way for him. Katerina followed, albeit reluctantly. In the midst of a rough crowd was not where she wanted to be.

Jostled from behind, Katerina felt herself sliding toward the grizzly. She lifted her unopened parasol like a sword at the same moment the grizzly made a grab for her.

With his free hand, Drako yanked Katerina to safety, and they moved away from the caged bear and the crowd. Frightened, Viveka burst into tears.

"Mummy is safe," Drako soothed the child.

"I slipped, sweeting," Katerina said, "but I am uninjured. The bear caught my parasol. I think he dislikes bonnets, too."

Viveka gave a watery chuckle and then rested her head on the prince's shoulder.

Returning to the carriage, Katerina climbed inside and lifted her daughter onto her lap. When the girl calmed, Katerina caught the prince's gaze over her daughter's head and whispered, "Someone pushed me."

Chapter Ten

Thank God, I was not born a blonde.

That thought kept running through Raven's mind as the foursome rode in the Clarke coach along Rotten Row. Cynthia Clarke sat beside her, Princess Anya and Lavinia Smythe on the opposite seat.

Raven felt herself slipping nearer the edge of screaming hysteria. All their conversations centered on which unfashionable ladies were wearing last season's colors and endless speculations on next season's colors and styles. Apparently, mankind's survival depended upon hemlines going up or down.

While staying alert to any hint of conspiracy, Raven devised a system to filter their drivel out. If she gave them a vacuous smile at appropriate moments, the blondes believed she was listening.

An uneasy truce marked the Blond Brigade's relationship, rather then a true friendship. They were an alliance of entities who shared a common goal—winning an offer of marriage from a wealthy aristocrat, preferably a prince.

Each exhibited a different attitude toward her. Cynthia Clarke seemed sincerely friendly while Princess Anya was condescending. Lavinia Smythe was coldly tolerant of their befriending her.

"What do you think, Raven?" Cynthia Clarke asked.

Raven gave the blonde a vacuous smile. "Sorry, I missed what you said."

"You were daydreaming of your handsome marquis," Cynthia teased her. "If the contessa could develop a fondness for Yuri, then the three of us could marry a Kazanov prince."

"Prince Drako has developed a fondness for the contessa," Raven said, "but that still leaves three eligible princes."

"Yuri wants the wealthy contessa," Princess Anya said. "Cynthia and Lavinia do not have enough money to attract him. If the contessa could marry Yuri, then I could marry Drako."

"*I* want Drako," Lavinia said. "You can marry one of the others."

"All the Kazanov princes are handsome and wealthy," Raven interjected.

"I do not care about handsome," Anya said. "I want the heir."

Lavinia rounded on her. "So do I."

"Why are you arguing?" Cynthia asked. "The Contessa de Salerno has attracted Prince Drako."

Princess Anya could not be silenced, though. "Lavinia, you cannot expect to marry Prince Drako because Prince Mikhail has defected to Belle Flambeau."

"We will see about that," Lavinia Smythe said, the smugness of her smile meant to infuriate.

Princess Anya narrowed her gaze on the other woman. "Are you threatening me? If so—"

"*Anya.*" Cynthia Clarke's voice held a warning note.

Raven mentally shook her head. This alliance could easily deteriorate into a blond civil war. Perhaps she should encourage a rift between them and inadvertently learn their secrets.

Cynthia prevented more skirmishes by changing the subject. "Your stepmother told my mother that Alexander Blake and you are unofficially betrothed."

Raven shrugged. "I suppose you could say that."

"You will become a marchioness and then a duchess," Princess Anya said, "but that is absolutely fantastic for a young lady from your background."

Enough is enough, Raven decided, her gaze on the princess frigid. "To what background do you refer?"

Princess Anya gave her a condescending smile. "I merely meant, a lady without benefit of a society upbringing."

"Perhaps the society upbringing is a hindrance," Raven countered. "Three of the seven Flambeau sisters have received offers from two princes and a future duke."

"Goodness, I never considered that," Cynthia said. "You should be giving us advice."

"Be quiet," Anya snapped.

Lavinia Smythe gave Cynthia a sour glance but remained silent. When the coach halted in front of the Smythe residence, Lavinia climbed down without a word of farewell to her friends.

"Do not let Lavinia bother you," Princess Anya said to Raven. "Mikhail's forthcoming marriage to your sister upsets her."

Once the coach had delivered Anya to her residence, Cynthia smiled at Raven. "Do not let either of them annoy you. Anya believes she is better than we are because she is a princess."

"Do not worry about my feelings," Raven told her. "I inherited my father's thick skin."

"You are so fortunate to have won Blake's heart," Cynthia said. "I wish a gentleman would look at me the way he looks at you. Why, I would not care a whit if he was only an earl or a baron."

Raven swallowed a laugh. She assumed Cynthia believed herself magnanimous to forgo a prince or duke for love's sake.

"What if the man was a merchant or a carpenter?" Raven asked her.

Cynthia shrugged. "Love could tempt me, I suppose. Mama would keel over, which could be fun to watch."

Unexpectedly, Raven felt guilty about spying on the other girl. She suspected Lady Clarke was pushing her daughter.

Then Raven steeled herself against her soft feelings. She had a job to do, a task that had put her at odds with her sisters, and Cynthia Clarke was the weak link in the trio.

"I overheard my stepmother telling Lady Althorpe that the contessa had received a threatening note," Raven said, her gaze on the other girl.

"Really?" Cynthia exclaimed in surprise.

Genuine surprise or feigned?

"What is the contessa doing about it?"

"Lady Althorpe asked that same question," Raven answered, and placed a finger across her lips as if trying to remember. "Mmm, I believe Her Grace said that Amadeus Black is investigating."

"Constable Black?"

The blonde's fear was genuine. Which meant Cynthia knew something about the threats.

The Clarke carriage halted in front of Inverary House before Raven could reply. The coachman opened the door, and Raven moved to step down.

Cynthia caught her arm, asking, "You will keep me informed?"

The blonde definitely knew something, but Raven

could not believe she was involved. "Keep you informed about what?"

"I want you to let me know how the contessa is faring," Cynthia said, her expression genuinely concerned.

"I will let you know if I hear anything."

Raven climbed out of the coach and squelched the urge to dash down Park Lane to Alexander's grandfather's. The afternoon was ageing, and when her parents planned an evening out, they insisted on a late luncheon with their daughters.

Her father considered family meals a unifying activity, but his family togetherness had fallen on deaf ears since she had befriended the blondes. Meals had become the most stressful times of her days recently.

Hurrying into the dining room, Raven slipped into the closest vacant chair. At one end of the rectangular, mahogany table presided the duchess while the duke sat at the other end. Serena sat in the chair beside hers and beyond that was Sophia. Blaze, Bliss, and Belle sat on the opposite side of the table. A furtive movement beneath the table told her that Puddles loitered there for handouts.

"Sorry for my tardiness," Raven murmured, flicking her stepmother a sheepish smile.

Her sisters had been chatting. Now their conversation died, a strained silence hanging like a storm cloud over the table.

A footman set a plate containing braised beef and a vegetable medley in front of Raven. Another footman stood ready with a pitcher and ladle.

"Thank you, but I do not care for any sauce," Raven refused it, sending him retreating to the sideboard.

"Dearest, were you riding in Hyde Park?" the duchess asked.

Raven nodded. "Today's weather was perfect for an open carriage."

"Glorious sunshine," Blaze murmured, lifting her crystal glass of lemon barley water to her lips. "All that blond brilliance inside the carriage must have blinded the riders on Rotten Row."

Raven stared at her sister. The crystal glass developed a hairline crack, dripping lemon barley water onto her lap.

Blaze set her glass on the table and glared at her. Raven glared back.

Serena stood abruptly, drawing her attention. Her sister lifted her plate and walked down the length of the table to another chair.

Her own sister refused to sit beside her? That hurt.

Raven flicked a glance at a smirking Blaze and swallowed the tears that threatened. Her sisters would be sorry when they learned the truth, and Blaze would grovel more than the others if she wanted forgiveness.

Looking down the table at Belle, Raven asked, "How are the wedding plans?"

Her sister smiled. "Her Grace has charge of those."

"Are you planning a report for your new friends?" Blaze asked her.

"Enough." The duke banged his fist on the table, startling everyone. "I will not countenance civil war in my own home."

"Magnus darling," the duchess said, "do not allow girlish squabbles to upset you."

"I never realized daughters could be more difficult than sons," the duke muttered.

The Duchess Of Inverary gave her husband a dimpled smile. "Sons use their fists and then forget the grievance while daughters use their tongues and harbor grudges."

"Perhaps daughters should use their fists and be done with it."

"Darling, using fists would be unladylike."

No one dared speak a word after their father's outburst.

Raven knew her sister would not cease her verbal assault, though.

Puddles, the mastiff, emerged from under the other side of the table. Blaze leaned close to her dog and stared into its eyes in silent communication.

Circling the table, Puddles stood beside her chair. The mastiff growled low in its throat and bared its fangs.

Raven caught her sister's eye and lifted a piece of braised beef off her plate. She offered it to Puddles who wagged his tail and gently lifted it from her fingers.

"Traitor dog," Blaze muttered.

"I told you that dog was not eating with us," the duke said, his voice stern.

Blaze turned an innocent expression on him. "I didn't know Puddles was under the table, Papa." She looked across the table. "This is your fault. You and your new friends always cause trouble."

Raven had suffered enough. "I did nothing but offer a kind word," she exclaimed, bolting out of her chair and tossing her napkin down. "You know nothing of kindness because you never needed a friend." Childhood bitterness welled up and spilled onto her sisters. "You and Bliss always had each other, as did Serena and Sophia. Even Fancy and Belle shared their innermost secrets. I was the youngest and the odd one out, no matter which duo I attached myself to."

With those parting words, Raven marched out of the dining room, leaving stunned silence in her wake. Reaching the foyer, Raven walked out the front door instead of going upstairs.

Already regretting her outburst, Raven walked down Park Lane to Alexander's grandfather's mansion. She needed to calm herself, and now was a good time to speak with Alex about her carriage ride.

The door opened as she started up the stairs, and

Alexander appeared. "What are you doing here?" he asked. "Have you learned something?"

"I fought with my sisters at lunch," Raven answered. "This morning I rode with the blondes in Hyde Park, and I'm getting definite hunches about their involvement."

"Good girl," Alexander said. "I received a request from the prince to go to the contessa's. There was another assassination attempt today. Would you like to accompany me?"

Raven flicked a glance in the direction of Inverary House. "I would love to accompany you."

Thank God for lollipops, gobstoppers, and siblings.

Katerina wrapped the last lollipop in a linen and placed it behind the rosebush in her garden. Looking over her shoulder, she asked, "Are the gobstoppers hidden?"

Hektor smiled. "Yes."

"Did you note where I placed the lollipops?"

"Duly noted."

"You are in charge of the treasure hunt," Katerina said, "while I am conferring with Alexander Blake. Whatever Viveka finds, she can eat this week. What Roksana and Ludmilla find will be eaten next week and the week after that."

"I understand."

Katerina walked down the garden path and entered the house. Her sisters and her daughter waited inside the doorway.

"Were you peeking?"

Viveka shook her head. "I tried to peek, but Roksana said no cheating."

"Do whatever Uncle Hektor says." Katerina touched her daughter's blond head. "Enjoy your hunt, sweeting."

Roksana opened the door, and with a whoop of excitement, Viveka dashed outside. "Uncle Hektor, where did Mummy Zia hide the candy?"

Hektor laughed. "You must hunt for the treasure yourself. No cheating."

Katerina walked down the corridor, passing through the foyer, and then up the stairs. Prince Drako, Alexander Blake, and Raven Flambeau awaited her in the formal drawing room.

Alexander Blake stood when she entered the room. Watching the treasure hunt from the window, Prince Drako crossed the drawing room toward her. They met in the middle of the Persian carpet, and he escorted her to the upholstered settee.

"Are you starting a new business?" Raven asked, her gaze on the mountain of candy on the gilded mahogany table.

"His Highness could not control himself on our excursion to the sweet shop," Katerina said with a smile. "Please help yourself."

"I believe I will indulge myself," Raven said, reaching for a Wellington stick. She sucked daintily on the sweet stick.

Katerina suppressed her laughter at the marquis's strangled expression as he watched his almost-betrothed sucking on the stick. She flicked a glance at the prince beside her. He appeared close to laughter, too.

"How goes the spying?" Katerina asked.

Raven stopped sucking. "The blondes are more an uneasy alliance than true friends. A common enemy draws them together, any woman who endangers their schemes to trap a prince into marriage." She looked at the prince. "Anya and Lavinia were arguing about who would get you."

Prince Drako rolled his eyes. "I have given neither woman any encouragement in that direction."

"The blondes believe if the contessa could develop a fondness for Yuri," Raven said, "each of them could marry the prince of her dreams. I suggested if Lavinia or Cynthia could develop a fondness for Yuri, the result would be the same. Unfortunately, Yuri requires more wealth than the Smythes or the Clarkes possess."

"Yuri lost most of his inherited wealth a few years ago," Drako told them. "His lack of business savvy keeps him on the brink of bankruptcy."

"How do you know this?" Katerina asked.

"Moscow society is as small as London's," Drako answered.

Katerina knew nothing about Moscow society. Her Romany mother and her artisan father—albeit the czar's jeweler—had meant that she would never have been accepted. Her sister's thinking otherwise was a tragic miscalculation.

"I apologize for creating problems between you and your sisters," Katerina told Raven. "I hope your situation has improved since the ladies luncheon."

"The situation is worse," Raven admitted, "but I intend to make them grovel for my forgiveness when the truth is revealed."

Katerina felt guilty for causing a problem for the Flambeau sisters. Alina's hatred had broken her heart. How much worse for sisters who had previously been devoted to each other.

"Sisters should never argue." Katerina looked at Alexander Blake. "Can another way of gathering information be found?"

"Absolutely not," Raven said, drawing her attention again. "Cynthia knows something. When I mentioned your threatening note, Cynthia seemed frightened by the prospect of Constable Black investigating."

"What happened today?" Alexander asked.

"A crowd had gathered near the bear's cage," Katerina answered, "and Drako made a path for us to the front. I felt hands shoving me toward the grizzly. Only Drako and my parasol saved my life."

"You saw nothing?"

Katerina shook her head. "I do not believe Drako is being targeted since the blondes would not want him harmed. No one knew he would be escorting me to Fancy Flambeau's wedding."

"Raven was correct about two separate entities," Alexander said, glancing at his almost-betrothed. "The arrow at the golf match was aimed at him."

"Arrow at the golf match?" Katerina echoed, confused.

"You didn't tell her about the assassination attempt?" Raven exclaimed.

"Baron Shores took an arrow meant for the prince," Alexander said. "The baron suffered a flesh wound only, but what he said leads me to believe he knows something. We instructed our runners to follow the baron everywhere."

Katerina turned her head to stare at the prince, her dark gaze accusing. Someone had shot an arrow at him, and still he had taken them to the menagerie.

"I can explain," Drako said.

"Perhaps you should have explained *before* you endangered my daughter."

"I suggest you remain in seclusion for a few days," Alexander Blake said, standing to leave.

Raven stood when he did. "We will see you at Belle's wedding."

"Don't bother to see us out." Alexander hurried Raven out of the room.

Standing when Raven did, Drako walked across the drawing room to watch the treasure hunt in the garden. Katerina rose from the settee and glared at his back, too angry to approach him.

"How dare you endanger my daughter and me," she said. "Especially my daughter. You are the most appallingly irresponsible excuse for a—"

Drako whirled around to face her, cutting off her intended

tirade. "You are correct," he agreed, shoving his hands into his trouser pockets. "I apologize for my thoughtlessness."

Katerina did not know what to say. His apology had effectively stolen her bluster.

"I meant to avoid disappointing Viveka, not endanger her," Drako said, crossing the room to stand in front of her.

That the prince was admitting his mistake and apologizing surprised her. "You should have given me the choice of canceling our outing," she said finally.

"I realize that now," he said. "Think about forgiving me while I am out of town."

"I will consider it but I make no promises."

"Thank you, my lady." Drako bowed over her hand, his voice a husky whisper. "I look forward to our reunion."

Thank God, the blinking idiots could not hit the broad side of a barn.

If the moron brothers had been better marksmen, he would be dead instead of nursing a painful wound.

Cursing himself for hiring the simpletons, Crazy Eddie climbed out of his coach in front of Dirty Dick's and opened the tavern's door. Heavy smoke assaulted him, escaping through the open portal like a fog bank rising off the Thames.

Crazy Eddie stepped inside the tavern and paused, scanning the crowd for his men. The room reeked of gin and unwashed bodies. Drunken conversation and women's shrill laughter bounced off the walls, making him wish his business dealings did not require him to frequent such establishments.

Spotting the brothers, Crazy Eddie wended his way through the crowd to the table in a dark corner. At least, the idiots knew enough not to sit where their conversation could be overheard. Though, he doubted the heavy-drinking patrons would remember anything in the morning.

No sooner had Eddie slipped into the chair opposite the brothers when a buxom tavern wench approached the table. "What'll it be, guv?"

Eddie eyed her enormous breasts and generous cleavage. "I'll take you, puss."

The woman laughed. "D'ye think ya man enough to handle the likes of me?"

"I can handle you," Eddie answered, perusing her ample charms. He winked at her, adding, "Or die trying."

She laughed again.

"What's your name, puss?"

"My name is Marianne," she answered, "but my friends call me Randy."

"Are you randy?"

"I have my moments."

Crazy Eddie smiled. "Bring us a bottle of gin and two glasses."

"I wished I knowed how ta charm the girls like that," Scratchy said, as the woman walked away.

"Me, too," Itchy agreed.

"Money helps," Eddie told them. "We'll speak after the gin comes."

When the woman returned with the gin and glasses, Eddie handed her the money and then produced a shiny, gold sovereign. Wearing a wicked smile, he slipped the coin in the deep crevice between her breasts.

"Keep that close to your heart, puss."

"I'll do that, guv."

Eddie set the glasses in front of the brothers and poured the gin. Treating his agents kindly—even the hopelessly incompetent—made for good business.

His smile vanished. "You damn near killed me," he said, his voice low. "I told you not to shoot into a crowd."

Scratchy looked confused. "I used an arrow, not a pistol."

"You are not Robin Hood." Eddie rolled his eyes at the man's stupidity. "Do not shoot anything into a crowd."

"Can we push in a crowd?" Itchy asked.

Eddie looked at the brother, wondering if Scratchy was the brighter of the two. "What do you mean?"

"I followed the woman to the Tower and pushed her at the bear," Itchy answered, "but that prince bloke saved her."

Scratchy chuckled. "The bear only got the parasol."

"Your failures displease my friends," Eddie warned them. "Lay low for a week and try again. Take them down separately. That means, do nothing if they are together. Do you understand?"

Both brothers bobbed their heads.

Eddie rose from his chair and tossed a few sovereigns on the table. "Get yourselves a couple of women to pass the time."

"We thankee, m'lord," Scratchy said, scooping the sovereigns.

"Indeed, we do, m'lord," Itchy added.

"Enjoy yourselves." Crazy Eddie walked away, certain the brothers would need more than money to attract any woman. At least, he need not fear suffering another near-fatal accident at their incompetent hands for the next week.

Chapter Eleven

What will the prince do when he discovers the Sancy missing?

Wearing a bedrobe, Katerina stood at her bedchamber window and gazed at the garden, shrouded in darkness. She smiled to herself, imagining his expression when he realized the diamond had been stolen.

Unfortunately, she could not be present to see his face, only content herself with the knowledge that she had finally taken her revenge. That is, if she did not get caught.

And if the prince proved innocent? She would return his diamond and resume her search for the real villain's identity.

Katerina turned away from the window. Night had fallen, the household slept, the moment had arrived. Vengeance would be hers.

Removing the robe, Katerina tossed it on the bed and grabbed the old black cap. She crossed to the cheval mirror and donned the cap, tucking her black hair inside.

Katerina inspected her reflection and decided she could pass for a boy. Luckily, she had found her brother's boyhood clothing in a trunk. She wore tight black breeches and a black shirt which she left loose. No one could ever mistake her derriere for a boy's flat arse.

Satisfied with her disguise, Katerina opened the armoire's doors. She reached for her jeweler's tools and added them to the contents of her black reticule.

Katerina crossed to the door and gasped in surprise. Her brother was leaning against the doorjamb.

Hektor looked at her attire. "Are you going somewhere?"

A determined glint appeared in her dark eyes. "Do not deter me from my duty."

"I want to speak with you." Hektor placed a hand on her shoulder and forced her back into the chamber. He closed the door and leaned against it. "Are you certain about this?"

"Let me pass," Katerina ordered, "or I will go out the window."

"Walking alone at this hour is dangerous," he said. "I will drive you to Grosvenor Square."

Katerina shook her head. "I do not want you involved."

"Jake has the coach waiting on Merlin's Way," Hektor said. "I told him I was sneaking out to meet a lady and did not require a driver."

Katerina stood in silent indecision for a moment. "Very well, you may drive me."

"Wait here for a few minutes," Hektor said, turning to leave, "and then sneak outside."

Katerina slipped out of her bedchamber five minutes later. She hurried down the corridor to her studio. Another flight down brought her to the forge and the exit onto Merlin's Way.

Stepping outside, Katerina paused to get her bearings. The night held an eerie atmosphere. The moon shone overhead, yet a creeping fog off the Thames swirled around her ankles.

"Are you having second thoughts?"

Katerina moved then, her brother's voice breaking the spell. Climbing onto the coach, she suffered the unmistakeable feeling of breeches ripping.

"I just split the damn breeches," Katerina said, dropping onto the seat beside him. "My posterior is bigger than yours was at twelve."

"Thankfully, the evening is mild," Hektor said, "so you will not catch a draft."

That made Katerina smile. The humor in the situation slowed her pulse, and she felt that tonight would end well.

Hektor drove one block and turned right onto Knightsbridge Road. "What will you do with the Sancy?"

"I will keep it safe until I know if Drako is innocent or guilty."

"How do you propose to discover his innocence or guilt?" Hektor asked, steering the coach onto Park Lane. "If he is innocent, how will you return the Sancy?"

Katerina felt her irritation rising. Her brother was asking questions she could not answer. She had not considered the logistics of returning the diamond, only taking it.

"Well?"

"I do not know."

"Perhaps you should consider the endgame before beginning play." The coach entered Upper Grosvenor Street, a mere two blocks from Grosvenor Square and the prince's mansion. "Neither Alina nor Ilya would have risked prison for you."

"I am doing this for Papa," Katerina said.

Hektor halted the coach in front of the prince's mansion, dark and silent. "How will you get inside?"

"I brought my needle file to pick the lock." Katerina moved to climb out of the coach, but her brother touched her arm.

When she looked at him, Hektor warned, "Beware, Kat. Dragons are dangerous creatures."

"The dragon has left his lair," Katerina said, gesturing to the dark mansion. "I do not want you seen in this vicinity. Go home and make sure Dudley sees you for an alibi."

Katerina climbed out of the coach. She cast her brother a confident smile, ignoring the niggling feeling of impending doom, and turned toward the mansion.

On silent feet, Katerina hurried to the front door. She needed to get inside quickly lest one of the prince's neighbors, his own Kazanov cousins, return from a late night out.

Katerina stood in the shadows and rummaged blindly in her reticule. Her fingers touched the needle file, and she lifted it out.

Crouching in front of the door, Katerina stuck the needle file into the lock, but the door opened without her help. The last person to leave had forgotten to lock the door.

Serves the prince right for leaving his home unattended.

She had always insisted that several staff guard her own mansion so someone was always in residence. Once he discovered the Sancy missing, the prince would employ the same security.

Katerina stood and gave her brother a thumbs-up. Stepping inside the foyer, she closed the door behind her and threw the bolt. She wanted no thieves entering the house in her wake.

Leaning against the door, Katerina stowed the needle file into her reticule, pausing to let her eyes become accustomed to the dark. If only she could have lit a candle.

Katerina felt her pulse quickening, excitement mounting and mingling with trepidation. She could almost hear her blood surging through her body.

And then doubt assaulted her, catching her by surprise. Was she doing the right thing? Stealing was wrong, but she had sworn at her father's grave to avenge the injustice inflicted upon her family.

Katerina gave herself a mental shake. Summoning her courage, she crossed the foyer to the stairs and tripped on the bottom step. She grabbed the bannister to keep from falling.

With both hands on the bannister, Katerina climbed the stairs slowly. She paused on the second floor landing. The prince's office was the third door on the right.

Katerina placed the palm of her hand against the wall and groped her way down the corridor. She reached the office door and stepped inside, closing it behind her.

Someone had failed to close the drapes behind the desk. Ribbons of moonlight streamed into the room, precluding the need to hug the walls.

"Ouch." Katerina banged her knee on the desk as she circled it. Then she dropped into the prince's chair.

Opening the unlocked top drawer, Katerina reached inside and found the two keys. She tried the first key, but the lock would not budge. Then she tried the second key. Success.

Katerina placed the strongbox on the desk in front of her. She unlocked it without any trouble and lifted the pouch. It felt empty. In disbelief, she reached inside the empty pouch.

"Damn, damn, damn," she cursed.

"Looking for the Sancy?"

Katerina screamed, one hand flying up to ward off an attack, the other clutching her chest as if to slow her racing heart. And then the identity of the voice's owner slammed into her.

The dragon prince had caught her.

Why hadn't she heeded her brother's warning? How could she talk her way out of this?

Prince Drako lit a night candle and stared at her frightened expression. He perched on the edge of the desk, his muscled thigh so close she could have touched it. A smile flirted with his lips as she inched away.

"You said you were going out of town," Katerina accused him, opting for the offensive position.

Drako did smile then. "I lied."

He had her where he wanted her. Getting her there was the easy part. Persuading her into his bed without alienating her affections would prove the more difficult task.

"How did you know?" Katerina demanded.

Drako ignored her question. He had won the upper hand and refused to relinquish it. "Do you have anything to say in your defense?"

Stalling for time, Katerina flicked her tongue out to lick her lips. Her expression cleared, and when she answered, her voice was intimately throaty.

"I noticed your lax security," she said, "and decided to teach you a lesson. Better that I *borrow* the diamond than a common thief steal it. Do you not agree?"

Drako smiled, his expression softening. She was a good liar. He would give her that.

"No harm done, then?"

Without a word, Drako reached out and opened the desk's top drawer. He unfolded a parchment on the desk in front of her.

Katerina looked from the parchment to him. "I assume you want me to read this."

He dragged the candle closer, giving her more light. "Please do."

Drako studied her face as she read the letter from the Queen of Naples. Her complexion paled, her expression became stricken. To his immense fascination, she schooled her features into a blank expression.

Katerina raised her dark gaze to his. "Drako, darling," she drawled, "you cannot expect a queen to remember every lowly countess."

The remark made him smile. Her innocent look combined with audacious lies amazed him. She could have fooled him if he didn't know the truth.

"You are an imposter and a thief," Drako said, his caressing voice at odds with his words.

"I am no thief," she defended herself. "I planned to return the diamond. Eventually."

"You planned to steal the Sancy and then return it?" Drako chuckled at her folly. "Why would you do that?"

Katerina could not answer lest she reveal her true identity. "Your lax security—"

"I want the truth, *Katerina Pavlova*."

Surprise widened her eyes, and her mouth dropped open. Her stunned expression gave him a certain amount of satisfaction.

"I am not the villain who destroyed your family," Drako told her before she could utter a word. "Nor am I your niece's father."

"Viveka is my—"

"Niece," he interrupted. "*Zia* means aunt. Though, I do admire your responsibility to your family. No other woman of my acquaintance would have shouldered the enormous burden of a family's survival. You have succeeded where many men would have failed."

All pretense gone, Katerina locked her dark gaze on his. "Alina called your name on her deathbed."

"I told Alina to call upon me if she ever needed my help," Drako said.

"Did you love my sister?"

"I hardly knew her."

"Why would you offer to help?"

"Alina was painfully out of her league," Drako said. "I felt sorry for her." He rose from his perch on the desk to tower over her. "I was traveling abroad and learned what had happened upon my return. I visited the Pavlova residence, but you had disappeared."

"I believe you." Katerina closed her eyes, relieved the man she loved had proven innocent. And then she smiled without guile. "I will be leaving now."

"I do not think so." Drako placed his hands on her

shoulders and gently forced her to sit again. "Besides misjudging me without any evidence, there is the matter of your attempting to steal my diamond."

"If you report me to the authorities," Katerina said, her expression panicked, "my family will starve."

"You should have thought of that before," Drako said. "I would never send you to Newgate, and your family will not starve. I do, however, demand reparation."

Katerina narrowed her gaze on him. "How much do you want?"

"I want all of you."

"I do not understand."

He smiled at her confusion. "I want you in my bed."

"I am a virtuous—"

"Do not deny you want me," Drako said, "and I want you as much as you want me."

His piercing blue eyes held hers captive. He stepped closer and offered his hand as if inviting her to dance.

"Follow your heart, Kat, not your head."

Katerina stared at him in indecision. Yes, she did want him. Where was the harm in one night of pleasure in a life filled with duty?

She placed her hand in his hand. His fingers closed around her hand and gave it a gentle squeeze, telling her without words that he would never give her cause to distrust him.

Drako slid his gaze down her body. "What, in God's name, are you wearing?"

"My brother's oldest clothing." She gave him a rueful smile. "I split the backside on my way here."

"Your breeches are enticing me beyond endurance." Holding her hand, Drako turned to leave the office. "Come with me, princess."

With an uncertain step, Katerina walked into his

bedchamber. Moonlight cast the chamber in deep shadows and dimly lit furniture shapes.

Her gaze fixed on the bed. Katerina did not know what she had expected, but the bed appeared ordinary. On the other hand, she had never stood in a gentleman's bedchamber before. Excepting her brother's, of course.

Drako lit the night candle on the bedside table and turned toward her, no triumph or gloating in his tender expression. He surprised her by plucking the cap off her head and tossing it aside. Her ebony mane cascaded around her, falling almost to her waist.

"I love your hair." Drako inched closer and lifted the long, ebony strands, rubbing them between his fingers and then inhaling her scent. "Silky and sweet and seductive."

Katerina did not know how to respond. For five years, she had feigned sophistication, but the truth was she had never been so intimately close to a man. While most women her age had already married and given birth, she had been building her jewelry design business to support her dependents.

Pretending to be a sophisticated widow, Katerina had assumed the persona of a come-hither but do-not-touch flirt. She had none of the finer qualities of a true lady. No breeding, no inherited wealth, no genteel accomplishments.

Katerina was an imposter in more ways than one. No one knew that better than she. And now this man would discover her secrets.

Drako drew her against his muscular body, his arms encircling her, his blue gaze holding hers captive. "I hope your trembling means you desire me," he said, his voice husky.

"I–I . . ." Katerina hesitated, sighed, and then confessed, "I have never done this before."

He dropped his arms, stepping back a pace, and frowned at her. "You are not a widow?" He sounded surprised.

Katerina shook her head. "Duty demanded I never marry."

His expression softened. "You chose to sacrifice your own happiness for your niece."

"I chose nothing," Katerina said. "Circumstances thrust my fate on me. Explaining my daughter's existence and my virginity would have proved impossible."

"I think difficult but not impossible," Drako said, and noted her innocent confusion. "Some ladies pretend a virginity they do not possess. You could have feigned carnal knowledge."

"I would not have risked my daughter's future for momentary pleasure," she told him.

Drako hesitated, torn between his desire and his conscience. Desire won. He would deal with his conscience later though he was not insensitive to her fear and the fact that he would be taking her virginity. Her first, her last, her only lover.

The prince turned and walked away, leaving Katerina to wonder if her virginity had changed his mind. She had always assumed that gentlemen prized virginity. Or did they only value innocence in their intended wives?

Was Drako thinking about his deceased fiancee? Was he concerned that taking her virginity would make her suicidal?

No man would ever send her over that edge. Her strong Romany blood would incite her to kill him, not herself.

She was here. She was willing. And she wanted him.

Drako turned around, a dram of vodka in his hand. "Drink this."

Relief surged through Katerina. She wanted him, and his failure to defer to her virginity meant she had no choice about bedding him without benefit of marriage. Technically, she was not behaving immorally.

Lifting the glass from his hand, Katerina belted the vodka down in one gulp like a true Russian and then coughed as the liquid fire burned a path to her belly. After setting the glass on the table, she met his gaze and said, "I am ready."

"You are not going to the gallows."

Drako traced a finger down her cheek. He dipped his head, his mouth claiming hers in a long, slow kiss. And Katerina responded, accepting his kiss, returning it in kind.

Gently grasping her upper arms, Drako forced her to sit on the edge of the bed. "I will undress your beautiful body now," he said, kneeling in front of her. "Do not feel any maidenly embarrassment."

Easier said than done, Katerina thought. She had never bared herself for any man.

Ignoring her doubtful expression, Drako removed her shoes and then rolled the hose down her legs. He massaged her right calf and foot, pressing a kiss on it before moving to lavish the same attention on her left foot.

Katerina closed her eyes. She did not know if his hands or the vodka were relaxing her.

Drako lifted his gaze to hers as he set her left foot down. Reaching for her, he unbuttoned her shirt slowly, exposing her creamy skin inch by inch and then sliding the shirt off her shoulders, baring her breasts.

"Exquisite," he murmured, staring at her breasts with their pink-tipped peaks.

Drako leaned close, but instead of touching her breasts, he pressed his mouth on hers. Only their lips touched. Placing the palm of his hand against her cheek, he felt her heat.

"Do not blush," he whispered, pleased by her innocence.

Drako reached for the waist of her too-tight breeches and peeled them down her body. After slipping her feet free, he tossed them over his shoulder and leaned close to inhale her scent.

"I love your fragrance."

"Jasmine?"

"The jasmine is lovely," he answered, "but nothing compares with the essence of Kat."

His blue gaze holding hers captive, Drako stood and removed his shirt. He smiled when she snapped her eyes shut.

"Your modesty pleases me but not tonight," Drako said, amusement in his voice. "If you look at me, princess, I will leave my breeches for the moment."

Katerina opened her eyes, her breath catching in her throat. His chest was sleek, well-toned muscles with a light matting of black hair.

Drako reached for the jewelry case on the bedside table and removed the dragon pendant. He slipped the heavy gold chain over her head, the blazing dragon pendant falling to the valley between her breasts.

"The dragon marks you as mine," he told her.

His words sent a ripple of excitement coursing through her body. She felt a melting sensation in her lower regions, and her breasts ached for his touch.

Drako took her hand, urging her off the bed, and led her across the chamber to the window. Moonlight illuminated her nakedness and the glittering pendant between her breasts.

"Wishes do come true," he said. "I have passed many nights imagining you standing in the moonlight wearing only my dragon pendant."

Drako wrapped his arms around her, their bare chests touching. The coarse black hair on his chest teased her sensitive breasts, her nipples hardening in arousal.

"Kiss me," Katerina whispered, lifting her face to his, looping her arms around his neck.

Drako needed no second invitation. One of his hands held the back of her head, the other cupped her buttocks.

Their kiss was long and langorous. She clung to him,

losing herself in him. The world faded away, his lips becoming her whole universe.

Without taking his mouth from hers, Drako lifted her into his arms and carried her across the chamber. Gingerly, he placed her on the bed.

"Douse the light," she whispered.

"No, princess, I want to watch you while we make love."

Katerina closed her eyes when he started to remove his trousers. She felt the mattress dip with his extra weight.

Silence. No movement.

Katerina opened her eyes. Drako was leaning over her, a smile on his lips.

He lowered his mouth to hers, savoring her taste like the finest wine. His tongue flicked across the crease of her lips, which parted for him, allowing him entrance to the sweetness beyond.

"I want to touch you."

She shivered in response. "And I want to touch you."

"You honor me with your virginity." Drako kissed her again. "Tonight belongs to you, Kat."

Drako glided his fingertips across her lips to her flushed cheek to the curve of her ear. He pressed a gentle kiss on her forehead, running his fingers down the slender column of her neck and through silken strands of her hair.

Sliding his hands down her arm, Drako held her hand and then lifted it to his mouth to kiss. His lips traveled up her inner arm to the base of her throat.

Katerina closed her eyes. She felt relaxed but excited, floating on a cloud but butterflies winging inside her belly. Hot and shivery at the same time, her nerves tingled in a sensual riot.

"Open your eyes." When she did, Drako said, "Watch my hands on your body."

Katerina trembled at his words, knowing his gaze never

left hers while his hands roamed her body. She watched his fingers glide down her body to her navel. On the return journey, his hand lingered to caress the smooth skin around her breasts, making her squirm with need. His lips followed his hand, caressing her breasts.

"So enticing," he whispered, and kissed her breasts. He cupped them in his hands and gently suckled her nipples.

Katerina thought she would die from the pleasure. Her lower regions throbbed, and the throbbing became more insistent as he licked and suckled each of her nipples.

Without taking his lips from her nipples, Drako shifted his hand to caress the natural curve of her hip and then the smooth skin of her belly, making circular motions between her belly and the valley between her thighs.

Katerina moved with him. She leaned into the palm of his hand, now caressing her belly and then massaging her thighs and buttocks. When he turned her in his arms, Katerina clung to him as if she never wanted to let go.

Their lips met in a devouring kiss, each trying to steal the other's soul. Her hips moved in the waving motion of a woman held in desire's thrall.

Drako slid the palm of his hand down her body to slip between her thighs. His hand was slow, his touch gentle, his lips on hers persuasive.

"I am going to prepare you to receive me," he told her. "There is nothing to fear, only pleasure awaiting you. Do you trust me?"

Her eyes were glazed, her expression dazed with desire. "Yes," she breathed.

Drako slid one long finger inside her, whispering, "You are wet for me." After a moment, he slid a second finger inside her and began a slow, rhythmic stroking.

Spreading her legs, Drako knelt between them and positioned himself. He kissed her and moved forward in one powerful but kind thrust.

Katerina cried out against his lips.

"No more pain, princess," Drako promised, remaining motionless to let her become accustomed to him filling her. "Only pleasure from this moment on."

He kissed her again and began moving in long, slow strokes, building her pleasureable tension.

Innocence vanished and instinct surfaced. Katerina wrapped her legs around his waist, meeting his thrusts, her hips beckoning him deeper, urging him in an ancient mating dance.

Drako grinded himself against her body, and his thrusts became shorter and faster. She met each thrust with one of her own.

Taking her by surprise, Katerina cried out as tremors of pleasure shook her body. She clung to him, her intimate contractions sending him over the edge of ecstasy.

Drako fell against her, his seed spilling deep inside her trembling body.

Both lay still for long moments. Drako fell to the side, taking her with him. His arms circled her, holding her close against his body, her head resting upon his chest.

Silence. The only sound was their labored breathing as they floated from heavenly pleasure to earthly reality.

"What do you think, princess?"

Katerina sighed. "Can we do it again?"

"Soon, my love." Drako reached over to snuff the night candle. "My body needs to recover first."

Silence again.

"Drako?"

"Hmmm?"

"Who destroyed my family?"

Good God, the woman had a mind like a steel trap. She could not let go of that dangerous thought.

"Sleep now, princess." Drako dropped a kiss on the top of her head. "Your revenge will wait until morning."

Katerina snuggled into him, her hand in his. She was too tired to argue and promptly fell into a deep, dreamless sleep.

Holding her close, Drako felt her breathing evenly and knew she slept. He would need to ponder her vengeance and how to coax her out of it. Revenge had a nasty habit of turning on its owner. He had plans for the woman in his arms and not one of them included watching her hang for murder at the gallows.

Chapter Twelve

Boom. Boom. Boom.

Drako surfaced from a deep, dreamless sleep. The woman in his arms still slept, lying on her side facing the windows. His body pressed against her backside, one arm circling her, his hand cupping a warm breast.

He smiled drowsily. One morning he would awaken her by slipping his shaft inside her while she slept. Not today, though.

Opening his eyes, Drako noted the early hour. The sun had not risen though night's darkest hours had passed. What had awakened him?

Boom! Boom! Boom!

The noise carried in the predawn silence, disturbing his woman who stirred and then settled into sleep again. Drako realized someone was banging on his front door. If he ignored it, the intruder would go away.

Boom. Boom. Boom.

The banging grew louder, more insistent, mirroring the intruder's impatience. When his woman stirred again, Drako pressed a kiss on the side of her neck and then slid out of bed.

Slipping into his robe, Drako glanced toward the

bed and saw her watching him. "I will return in a few minutes," he said, his voice husky. "Go back to sleep."

Drako closed the bedcurtains and headed for the door. He hurried down the corridor to the stairs, cursing the idiot who had broken their peaceful sleep.

Boom! Boom! Boom!

"Who is it?" Drako demanded, before unlocking the door.

"Hektor Pavlova, you lying bastard."

Drako opened the door and ducked the younger man's fist. Hektor rushed inside, but Drako grabbed him before he reached the stairs and shoved him against the wall.

"Where is my sister?" Hektor demanded, flicking a glance at the stairs.

"Lower your voice," Drako ordered. "Kat is sleeping in my bed." He ducked another fist aimed toward his face.

"You promised not to dishonor her."

"I want to marry her," Drako said, his words calming the younger man. "Kat cannot return home until tonight lest someone sees her and ruins her reputation. I will escort her home after dark."

"How can I trust you?" Hektor asked. "You may be planning to lie abed with her all day and then forget your promises."

"If you wait here *in silence*," Drako said, "I can prove my intentions are honorable."

Hektor stared into his eyes for several long moments. Finally, he nodded.

Cursing all brothers, Drako climbed the stairs to his chamber. He parted the curtains and sat on the edge of the bed.

"Rudolf is waiting for papers in the foyer," he lied. "If you value your reputation, do not leave this bed."

Katerina yawned. "Why does he need papers at this hour?"

"Rudolf rises early to breakfast with his children."

That lie brought a soft smile to her lips. "What a good father."

Drako gave her a quick kiss and pulled the curtains shut. Walking down one flight, he grabbed the pouch he had left on his desk as well as her reticule.

Gaining the foyer, Drako noted his future brother-in-law's forbidding expression. "Keep this safe," he said, passing him the pouch.

Hektor opened it and reached inside. His dark eyes, so much like his sister's, widened when he saw the enormous diamond in his hand.

"Behold, *Le Grand Sancy*."

"You are giving me the Sancy?"

"Temporarily. You will return it when I marry your sister."

"Are you insane?"

"Some say love is a form of insanity." Drako dropped his gaze to the pouch, adding, "Do not lose your sister's wedding gift."

"Has Kat accepted?"

"I have not proposed yet."

"What if she refuses?" Hektor asked.

Drako gave the younger man an affronted look. "I am a wealthy, handsome, charming prince. There is no chance of her refusing, and if she does, you may keep the diamond."

"Kat is not like other women," Hektor said, shaking his head.

"That is one of her most endearing qualities." Drako opened the door. "Do not mention you were here, and do not lose the diamond."

Hektor grinned and left.

Drako bolted the door. He could enjoy his guest in absolute privacy all day. There was something good to be said for being born a commoner, who could run naked through his own house without fear of upsetting the servants.

Entering his chamber, Drako set the reticule on the dresser and crossed the room. He opened the bedcurtain to sit on the edge of the bed.

Katerina gave him a lazy smile. Lifting her hand, she touched the skin on his chest exposed between the sides of the robe.

"Has Rudolf gone?"

Drako lifted her hand to his lips. "Yes."

"I must leave, too."

"I will escort you home tonight," Drako told her. "Else you could be seen on the street."

"My work—"

"—will wait until tomorrow," Drako interrupted. "Since we are awake"—he planted a kiss on her mouth—"I will heat water. While you are washing, I will cook breakfast."

That surprised Katerina. "You can cook?"

"I possess many talents of which you are unaware."

Her smile was feline. "I am aware of your most important talents."

Drako grinned and gave her a quick kiss. Grabbing a shirt from his armoire, he tossed it across the bed. "Wear this. I will bring the water."

Katerina lay in the prince's bed, an expression of contentment on her face. She had not felt this relaxed in years. Forever.

The prince was not what she had expected. Handsome and charming, yes. A fantastic lover. A wicked sense of humor. Sensible. Surprising in many ways, too. Who would have expected a cooking prince? On the other hand, she had not tasted his culinary creations.

In her mind's eye, Katerina replayed their intimate activities of the previous night. Feeling herself getting hot and weak, she had no doubt they would pass the day in his bed. She liked his hands on her body.

Drako knows who destroyed my family. That thought stepped from the shadows.

Before this day ended, she would learn the villain's identity. She would remain in London, but knowing the man's identity would prove invaluable in the event an opportunity presented itself.

Drako walked into the chamber and poured the heated water in the basin. He tossed a linen in her general direction. "Come to the kitchen," he said. "I am making you a surprise."

After he'd gone, Katerina rose from the bed. Every muscle ached and her legs trembled, reminding her of the previous night.

And then Katerina noticed the dried blood droplets on the sheet. Her virgin's blood. Embarrassment heated her whole body.

Katerina washed and then reached for the prince's shirt, lifting it to her nose. Inhaling his sandalwood scent made her legs weak. His fragrance was seductive and profoundly masculine.

Katerina giggled when she slipped his shirt on. It fell almost to her knees. She rolled its sleeves and left the bedchamber in search of the kitchen.

Drako was standing at the stove when she appeared. He glanced over his shoulder and gave her a devastating smile.

"What are you cooking?" Katerina felt suddenly shy.

"Blini," Drako answered, referring to the small Russian pancakes.

"How can I help?"

He gestured toward the table. "Eat the blini on your plate."

Katerina sat at the table. She looked at the blini and burst into giggles. Strategically positioned blueberries formed a smiling face on her blini.

"Do you like my artwork?" Drako asked over his shoulder.

"You are incredibly talented."

"On rainy days I entertained my eleven brothers and sisters," Drako told her. "They considered eating in the kitchen a treat."

Drako set a platter of stacked blinis on the table beside a bowl of blueberries. He poured steaming coffee into two cups and joined her.

After pushing the blueberries aside, Katerina tasted the blini. Browned to perfection, the pancake was light and fluffy with no hint of grease. She speared a blueberry with her fork, saying, "Delicious. My compliments to the chef."

"Thank you, princess." Drako downed a piece of blini topped with blueberries. "Without caviar or smoked fish, I improvised with blueberries."

Katerina chewed daintily on another piece of blini and then speared two blueberries. "Who destroyed my family?"

"The hour is too early for serious conversation," Drako told her.

Katerina narrowed her gaze on him. Was he stalling? She would not press him now but would learn what she wanted before leaving.

"Who do you think wants us dead?"

Drako waved her question away with his fork. "Serious conversations will give us indigestion."

Katerina popped two blueberries into her mouth. "What would you like to discuss?"

"I want to know all about you," he answered.

"Such as?"

He pointed his fork at her plate. "Why are you eating the blini and the blueberries separately?"

His question confused her. "What do you mean?"

"First you eat the blini," he said, "and then you eat the blueberry."

"So?"

"So, princess, the blini and the blueberry taste scrumptious together," he said. "Try it."

"I like to eat my food separately." Katerina popped a piece of blini into her mouth. After eating it, she poised her fork over a blueberry. "Many people eat their food separately."

Catching her eye, Drako stabbed a blueberry and a piece of blini. He ate them together with gusto.

"Because I eat my food separately does not mean I am wrong," Katerina insisted.

Drako shrugged. "If you say so."

"I *do* say so." Were they actually arguing about the best way to eat blini and blueberries?

"How old are you?" Drako asked, changing the subject.

"I am twenty-three years," she answered. "And you?"

"Thirty-three years, which means I have ten years more experience eating blinis and blueberries," he said, making her smile. "What is your favorite food?"

"I love whatever Nonna Strega cooks or bakes," Katerina answered. "And yours?"

"I love the taste of you," Drako answered without hesitation.

Katerina blushed, making him smile. "I refuse to discuss intimacies at the table." Engaging in intimate activities and discussing those intimacies were vastly different.

Drako grinned. She sounded so damn prudish. "What is your favorite color?"

"Diamonds," she answered, her smile impish, looking heartwrenchingly young. "And yours?"

Drako paused as if considering. "Whatever you wear is my favorite color."

Katerina rolled her eyes. The prince sounded like a practiced seducer.

"Which lucky gentleman gave you your first kiss?" he asked her.

Katerina blushed, her answer surprising him. "You did."

"*I* did?" Drako stared at her for a long moment. "Why did you wait so long?"

"I have never allowed liberties with my person," Katerina said, her tone prim, "and, as I recall, you stole the kiss without my permission."

Drako marveled that he had been destined to be her first in everything. Her last and her only, too. "So our Beltane Ball kiss was your first?"

"That is what I said."

"I believe you."

Insecurity caught Katerina and gave her a shake. "Did I kiss incorrectly?"

"Darling, you were exquisite," Drako assured her. "That is, you performed remarkably well for a beginner with natural ability. There are many kinds of kisses, you know, and I intend to teach you every one of them. Shall we retire to our bedchamber?"

Katerina hesitated. "We should clean breakfast away first."

"I pay servants to clean my messes," Drako said. "If you insist, though, we will do it later. I cannot wait to begin your instruction."

Rising from his chair, Drako circled the table and offered her his hand. The corners of her lips turning up in a smile, Katerina placed her hand in his, and they left the kitchen.

"I must tell you something," Katerina said, walking into the bedchamber.

Drako cocked a dark brow at her. "Yes, princess?"

"I saw blood on the sheets," she said, a crimson blush staining her cheeks.

"All virgins bleed," Drako said, struggling against a smile. "You are a normal woman."

Katerina worried her bottom lip. "What will we do about the blood on the sheet?"

"My servants will wash it."

"Servants gossip," Katerina said, "and I do not want yours to see my virgin's blood."

"My servants will not know the blood's source." Drako opened the armoire, grabbed a blanket, and covered the tell-tale stains. Then he unbuttoned her shirt, slipping it off her shoulders to reveal her naked body. "You still blush like a virgin."

Drako dropped onto the bed beside her, drawing her into his embrace. "A caress is—"

"You were supposed to teach me the various kisses," Katerina reminded him.

"We must discuss caresses first."

Katerina stared into his piercing blue gaze, her expression concerned. "I do not touch correctly, either?"

"Darling, there is no right or wrong in lovemaking," he said. "A caress is a kiss with fingertips, fingers, knuckles, or palms of your hands."

"Fingertips." Drako ran a fingertip across her nipples.

Katerina moaned at the sensation, her nipples beading into instant arousal.

"Finger." Drako slid one long finger down the valley between her breasts and stroked their rounded undersides.

Katerina squirmed, moving her body to entice his fingers to her nipples.

"Knuckles." Drako glided the weathered skin of his knuckles back and forth across her belly.

Katerina smiled, enjoying the sensation of his roughness against her softness.

"Palm of hand." Drako slipped the palm of his hand down the outside of her thigh and then up the sensitive inside.

Katerina responded instinctively, trying to clasp his hand between her thighs.

"The kisses for this morning's lesson are the magic kiss, the desperate kiss, and the forever kiss," Drako said, his hand escaping her clasping thighs. "You must remember, my dear contessa, making love is a journey, not a destination."

Using his index finger, Drako caressed her lips. His lips followed his finger, his tongue penetrating her mouth. At the same time, he used his finger to caress around her mouth.

And Katerina responded. She returned his kiss in kind, sans the finger.

"That was the magic kiss," Drako told her. His lips left hers and caressed her face—sliding across her cheek to her temples, forehead, and down her cheek to her neck. He kissed every inch of her flesh from her face to her toes.

Katerina squirmed, her body tingling wherever his lips touched.

"That was the desperate kiss," Drako whispered, his mouth returning to hers. "And now the forever kiss." He hugged her close, his hands caressing her tenderly, his mouth on hers for long, sweet moments.

"Take me," she whispered on a sigh.

Her invitation was irresistible.

His lips never leaving hers, Drako spread her legs with his own and entered her in one swift thrust. Katerina followed his lead, her body meeting his every thrust and grind.

Reaching a shared paradise, Drako and Katerina floated back to reality. He fell to her side and pulled her close, reluctant to part with her body.

Drako opened his eyes, his gaze focusing on her reticule where he had placed it on the dresser. "What *do* ladies carry in their reticules?" he asked, a smile in his voice.

"Most ladies carry nothing of consequence," Katerina answered, "but my reticule holds items that keep me sane. Shall I show you?"

The corners of his lips turned up. "I will live on tenter-hooks until you do."

Leaning over him, Katerina gave him a quick kiss and then rose from the bed like Venus rising from the sea. She retrieved the reticule and sat beside him on the bed.

Katerina reached inside it for the first item. "A gold sovereign for emergencies," she said, setting it aside. Next came an embroidered handkerchief. "This belonged to my mother."

Drako took the handkerchief and ran a finger across the embroidery. "I assume you never use this for its intended purpose."

Katerina shook her head and, reaching into her bag again, produced a delicate gold chain with a Neapolitan devil's horn. "And this protects me from the evil eye."

"I thank the Neapolitans for keeping you safe," Drako said.

Next came two small vials, one holding water and the other dirt. "Holy water from Saint Basil's Cathedral," Katerina explained, "and this holds Moscow dirt."

Drako noted the cloud of sadness in her eyes. Escaping from Russia, she had needed to take a piece of home with her.

"My father's gold timepiece reminds me to live in the moment," she said, "and this jeweled compass tells me where I am and where I am going."

"No pistol or knife?" he teased her.

Katerina grew serious. After replacing her belongings into the reticule, she lifted her dark gaze to his. "You know who destroyed my family."

"Live in the moment, princess, not the past," Drako said, running a finger down her cheek. "Besides, I have already taken revenge for you."

"What do you mean?" she asked. "Is he dead?"

"Darling, *poor* is much worse than dead," Drako answered. "Yours was not the first family he destroyed, but I paupered the bastard to insure no others became his victims. Now he lives on his family's largesse without funds to attract another starry-eyed innocent."

His advice and his revenge did not sit well with Katerina. He would not be so cavalier or lenient if his own family had suffered.

"If I told you his name," Drako added, "you would race off to Moscow, and I want you here with me."

"His punishment does not fit the crime."

"If we killed him, then we would be no better than he."

Katerina could not accept that. She had promised her father at his grave that she would take revenge. Letting it go for the moment, Katerina determined to find a way to learn what she wanted.

Leaning over him, Katerina brushed her nipples against his chest. Her lips touched his. "Let us live in the moment."

And they did. Morning aged into afternoon, its shadows lengthening until dusk.

Early evening, those moments when society had finished its daytime activities and had gone home to prepare for night's activities. Halting the phaeton in front of the Trevor Square town house, Drako climbed down and then assisted Katerina.

"Ooops." Katerina laughed, her hat falling off and her tight breeches splitting even more when she bent to pick up the hat.

Drako threw his arm around her shoulder and yanked her against his body. "Do not worry about the breeches," he whispered. "I know you possess a delightful arse."

The door swung open, revealing her majordomo. "Welcome home, my lady," he greeted her. "Your Highness."

"Dudley, will you wait outside with my phaeton?" Drako asked. "I want a private word with the countess."

"Of course, Your Highness." Dudley stepped outside and closed the door, leaving it open a crack.

"Tightly, Dudley," Katerina called, and the door clicked shut. She looked at the prince. "What did you want to discuss?"

Drako stepped closer and, lifting her hand, kissed both palms. "My darling contessa, will you marry me?"

Katerina's expression registered surprise, and then she smiled, a decidedly feline smile. "Yes, Drako, I will marry you"—she placed a finger across his lips—"as soon as you identify the villain who destroyed my family."

Midnight. Twinkling stars shone in the black sky, the moon waned, and a ground fog swirled around, creeping stealthily up the banks of the Thames.

A coach halted in front of Dirty Dick's Tavern. Baron Edward "Crazy Eddie" Shores climbed down but paused before entering the establishment, steeling himself against the noise, the smoke, and the smells of London's lower class.

Eddie opened the door and stepped inside, pausing a moment, his gaze scanning the crowd through the haze of smoke. His associates sat in a dark corner at the other end of the room, and he wended his way through the crowd of familiar faces. Same stinking patrons, different night.

"How goes it?" Eddie said, dropping into the chair.

"We got news for ya," Scratchy said, his voice low.

"We been watchin' the prince and the lady," Itchy added, and then chuckled. "She ain't no fine lady neither."

That drew Eddie's interested gaze. "What do you mean?"

"I seen this boy breakin' into the prince's place last night," Scratchy said, "and the lad passed all night and all day there. After dark, the prince and the boy come outside and drive off in a coach."

"I was standin' across the street from that lady's house," Itchy continued the story. "I seen the prince and the boy climb outa the coach, but the lad's hat fell off. The lad was no boy, but that lady in disguise."

"How interesting," Eddie said. "And then what happened?"

The brothers looked at each other blankly, confused by the question. "Nothin' happened," Itchy answered. "They walked inside the house, and I never saw them agin. That butler bloke came outside and saw me so I slipped away."

Eddie looked from one brother to the other. "Was anyone else in the streets?"

Scratchy and Itchy shook their heads in unison.

"You didn't try to take them down?"

"Oh, no." Scratchy chuckled as if relieved. "We done just like ya said. Don't take them down together."

Eddie ran a hand down his face. "You did exactly what I told you." He couldn't decide which brother was stupider, but knew he could not change his instructions now. Nor could he hire anyone else. The more people knew, the easier for the secret to become known.

He stood then and tossed them a couple of sovereigns. "I'll be in touch. Keep up the good work."

Strolling toward the door, Crazy Eddie smiled to himself. That Russian prince was getting what, according to rumor, no man in London had got from the countess. He could hardly wait to share this news with his client, who would not be pleased.

Chapter Thirteen

Leaning against the window sill, Alexander Blake glanced at Constable Amadeus Black sitting at his desk in the Central Criminal Court Building. Alexander checked the time on his pocket watch and then let his gaze drift around the tiny office.

The room reflected the constable. Tidy and stark, Amadeus always wore black which lent his tall frame an imposing, no-nonsense aura. The room was free of dust, unlike the prosecutor's who refused to clean his own office.

Only the size of the office and the man were incongruous. The room was tiny by any standards, the constable stood over six feet, and his legendary cunning in apprehending the guilty was immeasurable.

Alexander checked his pocket watch again, five minutes until noon. "What time did Barney say?"

"Are you pressed for time?" Amadeus asked.

"I am consulting with the Contessa de Salerno about Raven's betrothal ring," Alexander answered.

"Ah, I understand," Amadeus said. "Prosecutor Lowing was complaining about the cost of using the runners to watch suspects in that particular case, but I told him the prince was paying out of his own pocket for their services."

"Drako Kazanov can afford the price of protecting the contessa," Alexander said, "and, I dare say, the man seems smitten."

"How does the contessa feel about the prince?"

Alexander shrugged. "I believe she has the prince jumping through hoops like a dog."

That put a smile on the constable's face. Very few people had ever seen the constable's somber expression break into a smile.

The door swung open. Barney walked into the office, nodded at both men, and dropped into the chair in front of the desk.

"Eddie Shores met at Dirty Dick's with two brothers commonly called Scratchy and Itchy," Barney told them. "The brothers are not known for their sharp intellect."

Alexander smiled. "If they're our men, no wonder they hit Eddie instead of the prince."

"I want Scratchy and Itchy followed," Amadeus said. "If Eddie consults with any other undesirables, I want runners watching them. Disregard the baron's usual society cronies, though."

"Drako and Yuri have a hostile history," Alexander said, "and the Blond Brigade wants to catch Drako in marriage."

Amadeus nodded. "Tail those four, too."

Barney looked confused. "What is a Blond Brigade?"

"Princess Anya, Lavinia Smythe, and Cynthia Clarke are the blondes," Alexander answered.

"Do you actually suspect cultured young ladies would conspire to commit murder?" Barney asked.

"Nothing surprises me," Amadeus answered, "and nobody is above suspicion."

Alexander checked his pocket watch again and then heard Amadeus say, "You can leave now."

With a nod to both men, Alexander hurried away. He walked out of the Criminal Court Building, and before climbing into his grandfather's coach, instructed the driver, "Lancelot Place in Trevor Square."

Alexander relaxed on the soft leather seat. The ride across town was not long but slowed by the weekday traffic. His thoughts drifted to his almost betrothed. Was Raven riding in Hyde Park with the blondes? Or was she arguing with one of her sisters?

Shopping, Alexander decided. Since signing the betrothal contract was scheduled for the next day, Raven was shopping for a new gown to make herself beautiful for him.

When the coach halted in front of the contessa's residence, Alexander opened the door and climbed down without waiting for his coachman's assistance. "I am not my grandfather," he told the surprised driver. "I am capable of getting out of a coach without help."

"Yes, my lord."

Alexander hurried up the few steps and, using the knocker, banged on the door. "Hello, Dudley."

"Good afternoon, my lord." Dudley stepped aside to allow him entrance. "My lady is expecting you."

Following the majordomo up the stairs, Alexander walked into the opulent formal drawing room. Only the mountain of candy from his previous visit was missing.

"Good afternoon, Alex," Katerina greeted him, sitting on the red settee. "Make yourself comfortable."

Alexander sat in a highbacked chair and accepted the cup of tea she passed him. "I want you to make Raven a betrothal ring."

"Congratulations, my lord." Katerina smiled. "What did you have in mind?"

Alexander shrugged. He knew nothing about jewelry. A ring was a ring, wasn't it?

"A classic setting, I suppose."

"Classic encompasses many styles," Katerina told him.

"I prefer my creations reflect the wearer of the jewel. Tell me about Raven."

Alexander grinned. "Do you mean other than her alleged otherworldly talents? She has no hobbies that I know of."

"When you conjure her in your mind," Katerina asked, "what do you see or feel?"

"Raven reminds me of fire and ice," he answered.

Katerina nodded. "A concrete image." Staring into the dark hearth, she placed a finger across her lips as if considering a weighty problem.

"What is wrong with a simple betrothal ring?"

The contessa looked at him as if he had suddenly turned purple. "There is nothing simple about a woman's betrothal ring," she told him. "A simple diamond in a classic setting is for the unimaginative. If the ring is unique, Raven will appreciate that you cherish her."

"I suppose you are correct," Alexander said, "but I never considered the gravity of choosing a betrothal ring."

"Prince Mikhail gave Belle Flambeau a ring shaped like a flower because of her gardening interest," Katerina said, "and your ring must be unique to Raven."

"How expensive is unique?"

"Unique or simple, my creations are expensive," Katerina said, "but I insist on a discounted price because of the help you have given Drako and me in this other matter."

"I do not require a discounted price," Alexander said. "I can afford the best, and Raven and I are doing what we love."

"Discounted will still be expensive," Katerina assured him, "but foregoing my usual fee will make me feel better about the trouble my predicament has caused between Raven and her sisters."

Alexander nodded in understanding. "What do you suggest?"

"I own a rare star ruby—the fire—and would use it as

the centerpiece surrounded by diamonds—the ice—in a classic setting," she answered. "Legend says the star ruby will darken to a blood red if anything threatens its owner."

"Raven will love it."

"I will prepare a sketch for your approval, of course."

"I do not need to see any sketch," Alexander said, standing to leave. "I trust your judgment."

"I thank you for your confidence in me." The contessa stood when he did to escort him downstairs to the foyer. "Will you and Raven be attending the Wakefield ball tonight?"

"We will be there," Alexander answered. "Properly chaparoned by her father and stepmother, of course."

"Do you consider my brother a suitable bodyguard-escort?" she asked, as they reached the foyer.

"Hektor?" Alexander gave her a puzzled look. "Hektor is a fine choice, but aren't you attending with the prince?"

Katerina smiled at him. "His Highness and I are not in accord at the moment."

Reeling from the refusal of his marriage proposal, Drako had closeted himself in his office to think about his next move. He lifted a small glass to his lips and swallowed the vodka in one gulp. Leaning back in his chair, Drako propped his legs on his desk and pondered his future princess. The problem was getting her to the altar without revealing the villain's identity.

A knock on the door drew his attention. "Enter."

Prince Rudolf walked into the office and sat in the chair in front of the desk. His gaze focused on the bottle of vodka and the empty glass. Then he arched a brow at Drako. "You are drinking rather early in the day, cousin."

Drako poured another shot of vodka and raising his

glass in a toast said. "I salute women." He belted the liquid down in one gulp.

Rudolf chuckled. "Are you toasting all women or one in particular?"

"The Contessa de Salerno is tormenting me," Drako admitted, albeit reluctantly.

"Our little imposter is giving you a problem?" Rudolf teased. "Blackmail her into bed."

"I did."

His cousin's expression registered surprise. "Where were you these past two days? I heard you gave your household two paid holidays along with instructions to visit relatives."

"I was lying in my bed with the contessa," Drako said. "By the way, I told her you rise at dawn every morning to breakfast with your children. If she mentions it, cover for me."

"Is that the problem?" Rudolf asked.

Drako could not mask his frustration. "The problem is I proposed marriage, and she refused me."

Rudolf burst into laughter. "I have never heard of any woman who refused a prince's marriage proposal. Perhaps you should have bedded her after the vows had been spoken."

"I do not find you amusing," Drako told him. "Kat will marry me if I reveal the identity of the man who caused the deaths of her father, sister, and brother."

Rudolf shrugged. "Tell her what she wants."

"She wants to kill the bastard," Drako said, "and I refuse to see her hang on the gallows." He rubbed his forehead, trying to soothe the beginnings of a headache. "I gave Hektor *Le Grand Sancy* and told him to keep it until I married his sister."

"You, cousin, are an idiot." Now Rudolf poured himself

a vodka and downed it in one gulp. "Why did you give her brother the diamond?"

"I needed to prove my intentions were honorable."

"Which concerns you more," Rudolf asked, "the loss of the bride or the loss of the diamond?"

"I want to marry her," Drako answered without hesitation.

"Get her pregnant," Rudolf said, "and the contessa will be running down the aisle to the altar."

"What an excellent idea." Drako grinned at the thought and rose from his chair, feeling more hopeful at that moment than he had since escorting the contessa home. "I am going to visit her."

Rudolf stood when he did. "Do you plan to impregnate her this afternoon?"

"The contessa could be carrying my child already," Drako replied, as they walked down the stairs to the foyer.

"Too bad, you canceled our bet."

"Never mention that bet again," Drako warned his cousin.

Drako commandeered the coach his brothers had ordered brought around for their own use. Relaxing on the soft leather seat, he let his thoughts wander to Katerina. What mood would he find her in? Would she blush when she saw him? Most likely. She did blush like a virgin.

He needed to get her into bed in order to get her with child. Once she carried his child, she would marry him, and he could even reveal the villain's identity. Katerina was a woman who would always put her child before her revenge.

And then another, more disturbing thought occurred to him. After giving him her virginity, she would not consider allowing another man into her bed. Would she?

Definitely not, Drako told himself. He had needed to use coercion. No other man with designs on her would be successful. More important, Katerina was a virtuous woman. In fact, he had never met another woman who possessed her heart and determination.

When the coach halted on Lancelot Place, Drako climbed out and hurried up the stairs. He grabbed the doorknocker, giving it several hard bangs against the wood.

"Good afternoon, Your Highness," Dudley greeted him with a smile.

"Good afternoon, Dudley." Drako walked into the foyer. "Is your mistress home?"

"Her Ladyship is working in her studio," Dudley answered. "Please come with me to the drawing room, and I will fetch her for you."

The two men walked up the stairs together. When they reached the second floor, the majordomo turned right to get to the annex corridor while the prince turned left and headed for the drawing room.

Drako smiled at its slightly overstated opulence. His darling contessa was such a fraud. The drawing room's decor reflected what her clients expected to see, not her own personality. A woman who thought nothing of eating breakfast in a kitchen while wearing a man's shirt would not feel comfortable in this drawing room. He could guarantee the only time his contessa sat in this room was when guests arrived.

Wandering across the room, Drako gazed out the window overlooking the garden. Viveka was playing with her darkhaired nannies. She carried her doll, Alina, named for her natural mother.

For an intelligent woman, Katerina had not bothered listening to her own common sense regarding the girl's father. Blond children did not usually have darkhaired fathers like himself. There were always exceptions, of course, and the girl's mother had been a blonde.

"Good afternoon, Your Highness."

Drako turned away from the window to see Katerina breezing into the room. Crossing the distance between them, Drako cocked a brow at her use of his title. "So formal a greeting, my love?"

Her dark gaze devoured him, beckoning him close. She folded her arms across her chest, telling him without words to keep his distance.

That did not bother him, though. Her stance emphasized her bosom. In his mind's eye, he conjured her flawless breasts with their dusky pink nipples.

Drako gestured to the settee. "Let us sit and discuss a matter of importance."

"I was designing Raven Flambeau's betrothal ring when you interrupted me," she said, standing her ground.

Interrupted? Drako thought. She considers me an interruption?

Suppressing his irritation, Drako said, "I came to ask you to reconsider my marriage proposal."

"I did not refuse your proposal." Dropping her gaze to the jeweled clock on the gilded mahogany table, Katerina seemed to steel herself against him. "I will marry you after you reveal the villain's identity."

Drako narrowed his gaze on her. The stubborn little witch. Why, she was even more stubborn than . . . than he was.

"We will engage in no physical intimacies, either," Katerina told him.

"Have you considered the possible consequences of our passion?" When she paled, Drako felt a sense of satisfaction as if he had gained control again. He would have admired her pluck if she had not been refusing him.

"I pray that is not the case," she said, "since I dislike the idea of our first child born out of wedlock."

"No child of mine will enter this world outside the bond of marriage." Drako counted to twenty to calm himself and then added another ten count. He forced his voice to a moderate tone, asking, "Are we still engaged for the Wakefield ball tonight?"

"I am so sorry, Your Highness," Katerina apologized, "but I have arranged for another escort."

"Who?"

Her smile was decidedly feline. "I cannot reveal his identity much the same as you—"

"Kat." His voice held a warning note.

She was annoying him on purpose, trying to goad him into telling her what she wanted to know. The misguided minx seemed to think that two could not play the same game.

"Very well, my lady." Drako gave her a devastating smile. "Are you still accompanying me to the Flambeau wedding?"

She was frowning at him, a suspicious glint in her dark eyes. "Yes, Your Highness."

"Save me a dance at the ball tonight." Drako nodded in farewell and, without a backward glance, left the drawing room.

Walking down the stairs to the foyer, Drako wondered if his cousin could tell him how to impregnate a woman without bedding her. He doubted even Rudolf could help him there.

She wanted him. Badly. He could read it in her gaze. All he needed to do was entice her.

Hektor Pavlova and Dudley were talking in the foyer. Seeing them gave him an idea.

"Hektor, I would speak privately with you," Drako said. "Outside would be best."

"Of course, Your Highness."

Dudley opened the door for them. "Have yourself a good afternoon, Your Highness."

"Thank you, Dudley."

Drako stood beside Hektor on the top step outside. "Your sister is behaving badly, and I need your help."

Hektor gave him an I-told-you-so smile. "What problem is she creating?"

"Kat accepted my proposal," Drako answered, "but refuses to marry me until I reveal the villain's identity."

"Do you want me to speak to her on your behalf?" Hektor asked.

"No, I want access to her bedchamber," Drako said baldly. "If I impregnate her, she will marry me without stipulation."

Hektor stared at him in silence, reluctance etching across his expression. "And what if she will not agree to marry you without stipulation?"

Drako ignored that question, did not want even to consider it. "If I reveal the villain's identity, she will end on the gallows."

"You are correct about that," Hektor agreed, "but I do not want to know when you are bedding my sister. Besides, I am not always available to—"

"I can help you," Dudley whispered, drawing their attention. "I was not eavesdropping, merely overheard by accident."

"Dudley is the master of the front door," Hektor said. smiling. "No one enters without his permission."

Drako beckoned the majordomo outside, saying, "Close the door tightly behind you." When the man did as ordered, he said, "I know you have the contessa's well-being at heart."

The majordomo looked him straight in the eye. "My help has a price."

"How much do you want?"

"My loyalty cannot be bought with money," Dudley informed him, his expression affronted. "I want a grand ballroom where I can announce London's elite as they arrive for an exclusive evening as the guests of the contessa and her aristocratic husband."

"If the contessa marries me, I will give you London's biggest, grandest ballroom." Drako grinned at the man. "Is there anything else?"

"I want a dozen baby princes and princesses," Dudley added. "I yearn to announce all those christenings, birthdays, come-outs, and weddings."

Drako glanced at Hektor, who was rolling his eyes. Then he looked at the majordomo and said, "I cannot promise you a dozen. Only God can do that. Do we have a deal?"

"Yes, Your Highness." The majordomo grabbed his hand and shook it. "Indeed, we have a deal." Then he retreated inside, closing the door tightly this time.

Drako looked at his future brother-in-law. "Do you know who is escorting your sister to tonight's ball?"

"I am."

Relief surged through Drako. "Be sure to guard her well." Then he started down the steps to the coach.

"Your Highness?"

Drako turned around.

"You did not ask about the Sancy."

"I do not care about the Sancy," Drako said. "The diamond is a stone without heart or soul."

Duty before desire, Katerina told herself. She had almost weakened that afternoon and accepted the prince's proposal without stipulation. The sight of her father's jeweled clock had reminded her of her duty. Graveside promises took precedence over her own happiness.

She needed the prince to reveal the villain's identity. Enticing him out of his stubborn silence had been her intention when deciding her outfit for the evening, a gown bolder than anything she had ever worn in public.

The black gown was strapless with a daringly low-cut

bodice, its silk clinging to every curve. Diamond florets sparkled in her ebony, upswept hairdo, and around her neck dangled the startling opal and diamond necklace she had worn to the ladies luncheon. No earrings, no bracelet, no rings.

Covering her more interesting endowments, Katerina wrapped a black lace shawl around her shoulders, intending to discard it in her coach. She carried her black, jeweled reticule containing the items that kept her grounded in reality.

A satisfied smile touched her lips when she inspected herself in the cheval mirror. If the prince had desired her in boy's breeches, he would be panting like a lovesick dog once he saw her tonight.

The other ladies would be gowned in summer pastels. Her stark black, accessorized by the opal and diamonds, would make her stand out in the crowd like a bejeweled bird of prey set down in a cage of twittering canaries.

Katerina walked down the stairs where her escort awaited her. She smiled, thinking her brother appeared more handsome in his formal attire than she had expected. He was a grown man now, no longer the boy she had whisked out of Russia.

"You look spectacular," Katerina said, reaching the foyer.

Hektor placed a finger between his neck and his shirt. "Then I look better than I feel."

Dudley opened the door. "Enjoy your evening."

"Thank you, Dudley." Katerina walked out the door in front of her brother.

"I have already made other plans," Hektor told the majordomo, and followed her outside to their coach.

The Wakefields lived in Berkeley Square, a short distance from the prince's residence in Grosvenor Square. Though the ride was short, the line to disembark in front of the mansion was long.

Katerina had avoided Hektor all day, sending him a message via Dudley regarding the time to leave this evening. She had hoped to evade his questions about where she had been for a night and a day.

"We have not spoken since I dropped you at the prince's," Hektor remarked. "How did that go?"

"Finding the Sancy took a while because he had moved the stone to a different location," Katerina lied. "I walked home slowly, sticking to the shadows."

"Did the prince mention the Sancy when he visited today?"

"Here we are," Katerina said, relieved that their arrival helped her evade his question. "Tell no one your last name."

Their coachman opened the door. Hektor climbed out first and then offered her his hand. Discarding her shawl on the leather seat, Katerina accepted her brother's hand and stepped out of the coach.

"I gather you are planning to torment the prince tonight," Hektor remarked, his gaze on her low-cut bodice.

Katerina feigned innocence. "I do not know what you mean, brother."

Hektor escorted her inside, following the other guests up the stairs to the ballroom. When they reached the front of the line, her brother leaned close to the Wakefield majordomo to give him their names.

Katerina scanned the gathered crowd. The Marquis of Huntly was dancing with Miss Bliss Flambeau. Prince Yuri stood with a group of gentlemen on the opposite side of the ballroom. Prince Drako was already crossing the room to greet them.

"The Contessa de Salerno," the Wakefield majordomo announced. "Lord Hektor."

"I hope elevating my social status does not upset you," Hektor whispered.

Katerina gave her brother a sidelong smile. "I elevated myself when we moved to England."

Prince Drako waited at the bottom of the stairs, a smile touching his chiseled lips, his blue gaze fixed on her bodice. "You are ravishing this evening, *la contessa,*" he said. "Did you not realize wearing clothing was required?"

When her brother chuckled, Drako said, "Good evening, *Lord* Hektor." He looked at Katerina again. "Your choice of escorts pleases me."

"My intent was not to please you," Katerina told him.

"Yes, I know," Drako said, looping her hand through the crook of his arm. "Your intent was to cause me worry."

"I did not think you capable of worry," Katerina said, circling the dance floor with him. She glanced over her shoulder to be certain her brother was following.

The Duke and Duchess of Inverary stood with Prince Rudolf and Princess Samantha as well as Drako's brothers, Princes Lykos and Gunter. Alexander Blake and Raven Flambeau were waltzing together.

"Kat darling, you look especially lovely tonight," the duchess greeted her. "I admire your panache."

"And I admire yours," Katerina returned the compliment, the older woman having chosen a ruby gown for the evening. As expected, most of the other ladies wore summer pastels. She gestured Hektor forward. "You remember my brother."

"I could never forget any man as handsome as Hektor," the duchess said, her dimples appearing. "If only I were ten years younger."

The Duke of Inverary coughed, earning himself a censorious glance from his wife. The duke shook her brother's hand. "Good to meet you, young man."

"Your Highnesses, I present my brother Hektor," Katerina introduced him to the others. "Prince Rudolf, Drako's cousin, and Princess Samantha. Here are Drako's brothers, Princes Lykos and Gunter."

Hektor did her proud. He bowed over the princess's hand and shook hands with the princes.

"We were wandering to the card room," Prince Lykos said to Hektor.

"Would you care to join us?" Prince Gunter asked.

"I would love to join you," Hektor answered, and then glanced at his sister. "I will see you later."

Katerina suffered the feeling that this scenario had been planned in advance. "Do not lose the family silver, dear brother."

"I expect to win," he said.

"Every man expects to win," she warned, "but few men do."

"Drako darling, don't you agree that our dearest Kat is an Original?" the duchess asked.

"Kat is an Incomparable." Drako dropped his gaze to her generous cleavage, adding, "Our dearest contessa has more panache than clothing this evening."

"You are making her blush, you devil," the duchess said. "All the other young matrons are so attired."

"All the other ladies are not"—Drako caught himself before saying the other ladies were not his intended bride—"are not as enticing as the contessa." He turned to Katerina, offering his hand. "Dance with me?"

"I would love to dance with you." Katerina placed her hand in his.

Drako led her onto the dance floor and drew her into his arms. Joining the other couples, they swirled around the ballroom to the strains of the waltz.

"I have never seen you in black," Drako said.

"I am mourning what might have been," Katerina replied. When he laughed, she warned, "Do not make a scene."

He smiled. "I defer to your wishes, of course."

When the music ended, they returned to the Inverary group. Alexander Blake and Raven Flambeau joined them there.

"The contessa has a bodyguard tonight," Alexander said to Drako. "I think you should follow her lead."

"My brothers are more than willing to sacrifice their lives for mine," Drako said.

"Good evening, my lady."

Katerina turned to see Prince Yuri, accompanied by his sister and his aunt. "May I have this dance?"

"Yes, Your Highness."

Katerina felt Drako's gaze on her as she followed the prince onto the dance floor. She stepped into his arms. "I heard you lost a tooth," she remarked. "I could make you a gold tooth."

Yuri smiled without showing his teeth. "Perhaps I will call upon you."

The Marquis of Huntly claimed her next dance. "The prince seems smitten," he said.

"To which prince do you refer?" she asked, her dark gaze gleaming with mischief.

Huntly grinned. "Ye missed an outstandin' fight after the golfin' match."

"So I heard."

Waltzing past the Inverary group, Katerina wiggled her fingers at Drako. He inclined his head in acknowledgment, his smile benign as if knowing she was trying to irritate him.

When the music ended, the Marquis of Huntly escorted Katerina to the Inverary group. He bowed over her hand, saying, "Dancin' with you, my lady, is like dancin' with a dream."

"You are too kind, my lord."

Drako touched her hand. "Will you honor me with the next dance?"

"I am sorry, Your Highness," Katerina answered, "but I need a rest. If you will excuse me?" At that, she walked away, skirting the dance floor on her route to the ladies withdrawing room.

Katerina could feel the prince's blue gaze on her, but sheer willpower kept her from glancing back. Thankfully, the ladies withdrawing room was deserted, the hour too early for the ladies to feel the need to escape.

After freshening herself, Katerina perched on a chair. She wanted the prince to realize without a doubt that she was avoiding him.

Drako was nowhere in sight when she did return to the ballroom thirty minutes later. Scanning the dance floor as she circled it, Katerina saw the prince's brothers partnering two of the Flambeau sisters, and her own brother was speaking with Alexander Blake in the midst of the Inverary group.

Katerina sidled up to the duchess, her curiosity gaining the upper hand. "Do you know where Prince Drako has gone?"

"Ah, Kat, you are developing a fondness for our handsome import." The Duchess of Inverary gave her a dimpled smile. "I believe darling Drako has left the ball. Brokenhearted by your refusal to dance with him, I might add."

That surprised Katerina. "Alone?"

The duchess gave her a knowing smile. "Apparently."

The streets of London could be dangerous, Katerina thought, becoming alarmed. What a reckless risk for him to have taken. He needed a bodyguard as much as she. Perhaps, even more.

Katerina wandered to her brother's side, whispering, "I want to go home now."

"Of course." Hektor turned to Alexander Blake. "If you will excuse me? The queen has spoken."

Katerina and Hektor circled the dance floor in the

direction of the stairs. Both stopped short when a man stepped in front of them.

"You cannot leave," Prince Yuri said. "I want another dance."

"Not now Yuri," Katerina snapped, her thoughts on Drako's safety.

Hektor chuckled as they walked around the surprised Russian. "You were not very polite."

Giving her brother a sidelong glance, Katerina said nothing. Her mind had fixed on Drako's welfare. She hoped his coachman was armed and prepared to protect him.

Reaching their home, Katerina climbed the stairs to her bedchamber. Without bothering to light the night candle, she removed her jewels and set them on the bedside table beside her reticule. Next she slipped the gown off and finally her undergarments.

Strong hands grabbed her from behind, yanking her back against a muscular frame. One hand held her imprisoned, and the other covered her mouth, preventing her scream.

"Your body or your life," a husky voice whispered against her ear.

Katerina relaxed, the intruder's sandalwood scent revealing his identity. "How did you get in here?"

She could hear the smile in his voice when he answered, "I flew on wings of love."

Chapter Fourteen

Whirling around, Katerina entwined her arms around his neck and drew his face toward hers. She pressed her naked body against his fully clothed frame. Their kiss smoldered and melted into another. And then another.

"I feared for your safety," she whispered against his lips.

"No one has ever spoken more treasured words to me." Drako scooped her into his arms and carried her to bed.

He paused for a moment to gaze at her lying unashamedly naked to his view. She held out her arms in invitation.

"Patience, my love," Drako said. "I must discard my clothing."

His gaze on hers, Drako unfastened his shirt and tossed it aside. He dropped his trousers and stood there wearing only his black silk drawers.

Katerina slid her gaze from his face to his shoulders and muscled chest. Her gaze slipped lower to his tapered waist and—

"Do you like what you see?" Drako asked, a smile in his voice.

"I *love* what I see." Katerina held her arms out again. "Come to me."

Drako crossed the short distance between them. Instead

of joining her, he pulled her off the bed, yanking her into his arms, their naked bodies touching from chest to thighs. He kissed her desperately, pouring all his love into that single, stirring kiss.

His lips left hers to brush her cheek and down the delicate column of her throat while one hand held her against his frame and the other roamed her body, caressing every inch of her flesh. Her skin felt like the finest silk, and her jasmine scent intoxicated his senses. She was all the woman any man could ever want.

Drako dropped to his knees in front of her, his lips worshipping her belly, his hands caressing her sweetly rounded buttocks. Gently, he forced her to sit on the edge of the bed and buried his face between her breasts, inhaling her seductive scent. He kissed her breasts and licked her aroused nipples while she caressed the back of his head and neck.

Drako parted her legs and knelt between them. His hand drifted lower and lower, brushing his lips across the sensitive flesh between her navel and her nether regions. And then he crouched lower, his tongue flicking up and down her intimate crevice.

"What are you doing?" Katerina exclaimed, panicking, pushing against his shoulders.

"Trust me, love." When she stilled, Drako tongued and kissed the vulnerable spot between her thighs.

Katerina clung to him now, pulling him closer and closer. When she cried out in pleasure, he pushed her down on the bed and, looping her legs over his shoulders, entered her in one powerful thrust.

He rode her fiercely, their mating a wild frenzy. She cried out again, and he joined her in paradise, filling her with his hot seed.

They lay together, their breathing labored. For a long time, they held each other close, trying to prolong the moment.

"I did not know people did that," she whispered.

"You are unschooled in many of life's pleasures." Drako lifted his head and planted a kiss on her lips. "All work and no play has made the contessa a dull girl."

"You think I am dull?"

"My passion has energized your life," he teased her. "So, you are no longer a dull girl."

Katerina turned her head to kiss his shoulder. "You need to go home now."

"My home is wherever you are."

"Requiring your coachman to wait outside all night is cruel," she said.

"I am paying him an exorbitant salary to wait," he replied. "However, I am a merciful man and will tell him to go home and return at dawn."

"Go home now," Katerina said. "I do not want to set a bad example for my daughter."

"What if we were married?"

"We are not married," she said. "My household will lose respect for me if I allow you to pass the night in my bed."

"I would never wish to distress your household." He rose from the bed, moaning, "Oh, that I were a poor, common man."

When she started to rise, Drako gestured to her to stay where she was. "I can find my own way out."

Katerina fell back on the pillows, asleep before he had finished dressing. Drako stared at her for long moments and dropped a light kiss on her forehead. With any luck, they would be married before summer's end.

Raven Flambeau dressed in a hurry the next morning, her thoughts on Alexander and their betrothal signing scheduled for that evening. Signing the betrothal agreement would set the tone for their married life together, and she intended to be his equal partner, no matter how radical the idea.

Until her recent move into her father's and stepmother's home, Raven and her sisters had led independent lives though sheltered as befitting a duke's daughters. She had formed a plan to put Alexander and his grumpy grandfather, the Duke of Essex, in their places.

Alexander had better lose his outspoken skepticism since children sometimes inherited psychic gifts. She refused to allow any husband of hers to behave insensitively to their children. At least, her own papa kept an open mind about the existence of psychic abilities.

Leaving her bedchamber, Raven figured she had enough time for breakfast before Cynthia Clarke arrived for their Bond Street outing. She grimaced, thinking there was more than enough time to argue with her sisters. Having delayed going downstairs, she hoped some of her sisters had gone their separate ways.

Raven walked into the dining room. Apparently, luck was not with her that morning. Her father, her stepmother, and all her sisters were still breakfasting.

"Good morning," she called a general greeting, and headed for the sideboard. "Good morning, Tinker."

"And a good morning to you, Miss Raven," the majordomo returned her greeting. "Would you care for tea or coffee this morning?"

"Coffee, please." Taking a plate, Raven helped herself to a spoonful of scrambled eggs, a thin slice of ham, and a scone. She turned around and walked to a chair close to her father, the opposite end of the table from her sister Blaze.

The duke chuckled, reading the *Times*. "Listen to this, Roxie," he said to his wife. "Disguised as a boy, a woman was seen leaving the home of a foreign prince early one evening after passing nearly twenty-four hours alone in his company. This reporter smells a scandal brewing."

"Magnus dear, that is inappropriate for breakfasting with your daughters," the duchess said.

The Duke of Inverary looked down the length of the table at her. "Someone wrote it in the *Times*."

"I understand, dearest." The duchess's dimples appeared. "What a delicious tidbit. I wonder the woman's identity."

The Flambeau sisters laughed. So did the duke. All of them knew the duchess was seriously addicted to juicy gossip.

"Belle, I scheduled the fitting for your wedding gown this afternoon," the duchess reminded her.

Belle blushed. "I could never forget my wedding gown."

The duchess shifted her gaze to Blaze, sitting beside Belle. "What are your plans for today?"

"Papa is taking me to see thoroughbreds," Blaze answered. "He said I could choose my own future champion."

The duchess glanced at her husband and then at the girl. "How do you know which horse will become a champion?"

"Horses never lie," Blaze answered. "I will ask them."

"I see." The duchess turned to Bliss, Blaze's twin. "And your plans, my dear?"

"I am meeting with Wopsle, the Seven Doves business agent," Bliss told her.

The duchess looked at her husband. "I thought Wopsle refused to work with a female."

"Papa persuaded him otherwise," Bliss answered for her father.

"I know how persuasive your father is," the duchess said. "And you, Sophia?"

"I am painting this morning," she answered. "Blount from the Bond Street Gallery is coming to see my work."

"Painting is so messy," the duchess remarked. "How does Blount know about your painting?"

"Papa told him how talented I am."

The Duchess of Inverary arched a brow at her husband, who concentrated on the sausage in his plate. "Serena dear, do you have special plans for today?"

"Bishop is coming to hear my singing and flute playing," the girl answered.

"Bishop, the opera director?" The duchess could not keep the surprise out of her voice.

Serena nodded. "Bishop is interested in a new voice, especially one who plays the flute, for the starring role in *The Maid of Milan*."

The duchess gave her stepdaughter a horrified look. "You cannot aspire to an opera career like Fancy? How will we find you a suitable husband?"

The Duke of Inverary cleared his throat. "If Serena wins the role, I will provide her with bodyguards to and from the opera house, and she promises not to make a career of it."

"With her talent and your persuasiveness, I daresay Serena will win the role," the duchess said, her expression less than pleased. "Raven, you must be engaged in a normal young lady's activities."

"We are all normal young ladies," Blaze insisted, and then glanced down the table at Raven. "Excepting one, of course."

"Yes, you are normal young ladies," the duchess said, "but you are strange, normal young ladies."

"I am going shopping today in preparation for this evening," Raven said, and almost burst into laughter when her stepmother visibly relaxed in her chair.

"You purchased your gown already," the duchess said, searching for more details.

"I need a particular accoutrement for the signing," Raven said.

"On advice from your papa?"

Raven gave her an ambiguous smile. "The best advice on gentlemen comes from you."

"Thank you, dearest. I don't understand what you need to purchase, though."

"You will understand when you see what I buy," Raven said.

"You should buy a blond wig," Blaze said. "Then you can look like your new friends."

"Perhaps you should purchase a wig to hide your revolting red hair." Raven smiled, noting her sister's complexion matched her red hair.

"I will not listen to my daughters arguing at the breakfast table," the Duke of Inverary intervened, his voice stern. "My God, the indigestion will kill me."

"I am sorry, Papa," Raven said.

"Sorry," Blaze mumbled.

Thirty minutes later, Raven sat beside Cynthia Clarke inside the Clarke coach for the short ride to Bond Street. Princess Anya and Lavinia Smythe were not accompanying them on the shopping excursion.

"The marquis and you will be signing your betrothal contract tonight," Cynthia said, and then sighed. "When his grandfather passes, you will become his duchess."

Raven gave the blonde a sidelong glance. "Yes."

"Anya and Lavinia stayed home because they're jealous," Cynthia said.

"Jealous of me?" Raven smiled at that, thinking the blondes were too vain to feel jealous of any other woman.

"They're jealous in a general sense," Cynthia explained. "You have found a handsome, wealthy title to marry. The marquis's grandfather is as wealthy as your father."

"I did not find the marquis," Raven drawled. "The marquis found me."

"You sound like the duchess," Cynthia said.

The two women looked at each other and laughed.

Raven decided that Cynthia Clarke wasn't so obnoxiously snobby after all. Too bad this blonde was a follower, who had followed the example of the wrong young ladies. She didn't doubt that the poor girl's mother had pushed her into that unusual friendship.

"Do you think a suitable gentleman will ever offer for me?" Cynthia asked.

"Love will find you," Raven assured her, "when you least expect it."

"I do hope so."

"Here we are."

The coach halted in front of Webb's Jewelers on Bond Street. The driver opened the door and helped them down.

"Are you purchasing the marquis a gift?" Cynthia asked, as they entered the shop.

"I want to buy my father a birthday gift," Raven lied, unwilling to share the real reason. "Unfortunately, my pin money cannot afford the Contessa de Salerno's prices."

"That will change as soon as you marry the marquis," Cynthia told her. "You will be able to afford a treasure chest of jewels then. Please offer His Grace my felicitations on his birthday."

"I will definitely extend your best wishes," Raven said. "There it is."

"What?"

Raven stopped at one of the jewelry cases. She pointed at a magnifying glass, its long handle encrusted with semi-precious stones. "I want that," she told the proprietor.

"Yes, my lady," the man said, reaching for the magnifier.

"I am merely a miss, not a lady."

"She is a miss now," Cynthia spoke up, "but she will become a marchioness through marriage."

"Best wishes on your good fortune," the proprietor said, passing her the magnifier for a closer look.

Raven gave the man an impish smile. "The marquis is the one who enjoys good fortune."

The man returned her smile. "Spoken like a true marchioness."

"I will take this," Raven said, handing him the magnifier. "A red velvet pouch will do for the wrapping."

"Does His Grace use a magnifier?" Cynthia asked her.

"Papa's eyesight is beginning to fail," Raven lied. "Advancing age, you know."

"Mama uses a magnifier for her needlework," Cynthia told her. "Her age is advancing, too."

"Advancing age is no picnic." Raven paid for her purchase. "Our own ages are advancing, too."

Leaving the shop, the two women enjoyed a short ride through Hyde Park. Cynthia shared gossip, overheard from her mother, about each passing gentleman and lady. Raven could not help but wonder what was said about her and her sisters.

"Did you read this morning's *Times*?" Cynthia asked, as the coach left the park to drop her home.

"I have not read the newspaper today," Raven answered.

"Really, Raven, you must read the society gossip daily," Cynthia said. "Everyone does. How else will you know the latest happenings?"

"My own life concerns me more than anyone else's," Raven said. "What appeared in today's society gossip?"

"A noblewoman, disguised as a boy, was seen leaving a foreign prince's residence after passing almost a whole day in his company," Cynthia told her. "Mama said the woman is no lady. I wonder if we know them."

Raven had a good idea who the two might be but would never share her thoughts with anyone. "Speculation could ruin an innocent woman's reputation."

"I suppose you are correct," Cynthia agreed. "Is there any news about the constable's investigation?"

Raven looked at her. "What investigation?"

"Isn't Constable Black investigating the threatening note sent to the Contessa de Salerno?"

Raven heard the change of tone in the other girl's voice, the need for information. "The note was no mere threat. There was an assassination attempt, too."

Cynthia gasped. "I never heard about that."

"Very hush-hush." Raven touched the blonde's arm and knew the girl's surprise was feigned.

"The contessa looked healthy at the Wakefield ball," Cynthia said.

"Thank a merciful God for that." Raven gave her a side-long glance and leaned close to whisper, "Someone tried to kill Prince Drako at the golfing match on Pall Mall."

"What?" Cynthia cried. "Are you certain?"

This time the blonde's surprise was genuine. Apparently, her theory about killing two birds with one stone was correct.

"Alex is Constable Black's associate," Raven reminded her.

The Clarke coach halted in front of Inverary House just as the Duke of Inverary and Blaze were exiting on their way to see thoroughbreds. Raven smiled as the Clarke coachman helped her down.

"Good afternoon, Your Grace," Cynthia called from the coach's window, her voice sugary sweet. "Best wishes for your birthday."

Raven covered her mouth with one hand, trying to stifle the bubble of laughter threatening to escape. Her sister Blaze stared at Cynthia as if she had sprouted a second head.

"Thank you, young lady." The Duke of Inverary's face remained expressionless, his long years navigating society as natural as breathing. "I appreciate your thought."

Cynthia gave him a sweet smile. "I was sorry to hear about your eyesight, Your Grace."

The duke looked bewildered, his experience momentarily failing him. "Thank you, young lady."

Raven climbed the front steps as the Clarke coach started moving. She glanced over her shoulder and caught her sister shaking her head. Blaze was muttering to herself, the only word audible being *blondes*.

Putting the final touches on her appearance that evening, Raven crossed her bedchamber to stand in front of the cheval mirror for one last peek at her reflection. She had decided on the demure look, as befitting a virgin bride, to throw the Blakes off guard before the fireworks began.

Her pale pink gown sported a modestly scooped neckline, its embroidered white flowers circling the high waist and scalloped hemline. She had brushed her ebony hair back, braided and knotted at the nape of her neck, a hairpin shaped like a sprig of baby's breath adorned the braided knot.

Raven looped the fireworks inside the red velvet pouch over her left wrist. Fashionably late by twenty minutes, she walked down one flight to her father's office.

After taking a deep breath, Raven reached out to tap on the door but changed her mind at the last minute. If she planned to control the proceedings, she needed to start before entering. Without seeking permission to enter, she opened the door and breezed into the office.

"Good evening," she called a greeting.

Her father sat behind his desk while her stepmother perched on a nearby chair. The Duke of Essex occupied one of the three chairs positioned in front of the desk.

Alexander stood and crossed the room to meet her. When he smiled and bowed over her hand, Raven almost felt guilty about what she planned. *Almost.*

Raven made herself comfortable on the chair and

then gave the Duke of Essex her sweetest smile. "Good evening, Your Grace."

The old codger grunted in reply. "You're late, young lady."

"My name is Raven," she said, and heard Alexander's muffled chuckle.

Her father cleared his throat. "The Blakes have already signed the betrothal contract. We need your signature only."

"Of course, Papa." Raven reached for the document but ignored the offered quill. Reaching into her red velvet pouch, she produced the magnifier. "I must read it first."

"Reading is unnecessary," the Duke of Essex told her. "Your father's barrister wrote the contract."

"My sister Bliss insists I should never sign anything I haven't read."

The old man's gaze fixed on the magnifier. "Is there a problem with your eyesight?"

"The magnifier is for reading the fine print," Raven said. "My sister Bliss says the devil lives in the fine print."

Lifting the magnifier, Raven read every word in the document. Slowly.

Halfway through, Raven peeked at her audience. Her father and Alexander looked amused, her stepmother apprehensive as if she feared a deal breaker. The Duke of Essex appeared irritated by her display of female stubborness.

Raven read the last word and looked at her father. "I require several changes."

"The contract is standard except for the amounts of money," Alexander told her.

"Nevertheless, I require changes." Raven placed the unsigned document on her father's desk.

Alexander sighed. "Tell us what you want, sweetheart."

"I want a June wedding, not December."

"It is too late," the duchess said. "Your sister's wedding

is scheduled for the first day of June. We would need to rush the arrangements."

"Your stepmother needs a rest after planning both Fancy's and Belle's wedding," her father added.

"I am willing to wait until next June," Raven said.

"I am *not* willing." The Duke of Essex banged his cane on the floor. "I cannot live forever, and next June means an added year before I can hold my great-grandson."

"Only the good die young," Raven said. "Think of it as an incentive to live."

"I agree to a wedding next June." Alexander smiled at his grandfather.

The Duke of Inverary lifted the quill to make the necessary change in the betrothal contract.

"Congratulations, Alex. You have managed to find a bride as contrary as yourself," his grandfather said. "I can already hear the sounds of crashing crockery."

"I am not a commodity," Raven told her father. "There will be no dowry, but you may give us a gift."

Her father shrugged. "I agree."

"So do I," Alexander said. "Your value to me is not monetary."

"You cannot think beyond what happens between the sheets," the Duke of Essex said. "I do *not* agree. See here, Miss—"

"Raven is marrying me," Alexander interrupted. "What you want does not matter."

"The chit is behaving this way on purpose," Essex complained.

"My name is Raven, not chit."

"Grandfather, let me handle my own betrothal," Alexander said. "Unless you do not want to see your great-grandson?"

"Bah, do what you want."

Again, the Duke of Inverary adjusted the betrothal contract.

Raven looked at her father. "I retain ownership and control of any assets I bring into the marriage."

"Now see here," the Duke of Essex exploded.

"In the event of my early demise," Raven talked over the blustering duke, "my assets pass to my children. If I die without issue, the assets I share with my sisters revert to them."

"This is outrageous," Essex exclaimed.

Raven peered at Alexander. He was smiling as if amused by her antics.

"I agree to this, too."

"A wise choice." The Duke of Inverary amended the contract again.

"Anything else, sweetheart?"

Raven gave Alexander a winsome smile and then told her father, "If Alex proves unfaithful, I can divorce him and keep the children."

Alexander lost his good humor. "I agree if the same stipulation holds true for her."

"I would never be unfaithful."

"And neither would I."

"Your sister Tulip is proof that your father wandered," Raven reminded him.

"And you, sweetheart, are proof that your father—"

The Duke of Inverary coughed, drawing the younger man's attention.

"I apologize, Your Grace."

"I want faithfulness written into the contract," Raven insisted.

"So do I," Alexander snapped.

The Duke of Essex burst into laughter, drawing everyone's surprised attention. "The chit has spunk," the old duke said. "I see a dozen strong sons carrying my bloodline into the future."

Raven curled her lip at the old man. Leaning close to her father's desk, she signed the betrothal contract.

No sooner had she dropped the quill when Tinker arrived with a celebratory bottle of champagne. He popped the cork, filled the flutes, and left the office.

"How does Tinker always know the right moment to appear?" Alexander asked.

Raven looked at him. "Tinker eavesdrops."

Alexander grinned. "He sounds like my grandfather's Twigs."

While the two dukes and the duchess congratulated themselves on making an outstanding match, Raven whispered to Alexander, "We must speak privately."

Alexander cocked a brow at her. "Another stipulation?"

Her lips twitched. "No."

"Come." Alexander stood and held his hand out.

"I spoke with Cynthia Clarke today," Raven said, when they stood in the privacy of the corridor. "She was genuinely surprised that someone had tried to kill Prince Drako."

"And the contessa's brush with possible death?"

"Cynthia feigned surprise," Raven answered. "I am correct about killing two birds with one stone."

"So it would seem," Alexander said. "The runners are watching the Blond Brigade, too. How goes it with your sisters?"

Raven shrugged. "Blaze has begun muttering to herself about blondes."

"Kat."

A voice in the distance called her name. She surfaced from the depths of sleep, but her eyelids were too heavy.

"Do not sleep on the sofa," the voice told her. "Go to bed."

Katerina opened her eyes, focusing on her brother sitting at the writing desk in the family parlor. "I was resting my eyes."

Hektor smiled at that. "Do you usually snore when resting your eyes?"

"I do not snore." She was awake now.

"If you say so." Hektor returned to his sketching.

Katerina stared at his back, hating the wait for something that never happened. Especially, when that something was worrying her.

Avoiding her brother all day, Katerina had worried about his reading that nasty tidbit in the morning *Times*. She should have mentioned it herself and dealt with his reaction ten hours earlier.

No one could know she was the disguised woman seen leaving the prince's residence. Except her brother.

During the day, Hektor had popped up wherever she had been in the house but had not mentioned the gossip. Perhaps he hadn't read the newspaper that morning. She could not be so lucky.

"I caught you napping in your workshop this afternoon," Hektor said, and then chuckled. "You were snoring and drooling."

"I do *not* drool or snore." Katerina recalled feeling tired, dizzy, and slightly nauseous. She had put her head down for a moment. When she'd opened her eyes, she had lost an hour and gained a stiff neck. Stress and work were taking their toll on her body.

"You retired relatively early last night," Hektor remarked. "Are you ill?"

Yes, she had retired early, but the prince's lovemaking had kept her awake. "I have been working hard to finish all the commissions in a timely manner."

"I would like to see the Sancy."

His request sent Katerina into action. She rose from the sofa, yawned, and stretched. "I am going to bed."

Leaving the parlor, Katerina walked down the hallway toward the stairs but stopped short. Was Hektor laughing in the parlor?

She started up the stairs, her thoughts turning to Drako. Where was he that evening? Were his brothers watching out for his safety? Which gown could she wear to the Flambeau wedding that would entice him into revealing what she needed to know?

Gaining her chamber, Katerina undressed and tossed her discarded clothing across the bench at the foot of her bed. She extinguished the night candle and crawled naked into bed, too tired to don her shift.

Katerina closed her eyes and almost immediately succumbed to sleep. A feathery-light caress on her breasts brought a smile to her lips. This dream was much pleasanter than the nightmare of reliving the worst day of her life. Happy dreams that seemed real were the most enjoyable.

She opened her eyes. Leaning over her, Drako lay beside her in the bed. His skillful hand on her breast teased its sensitive tip into arousal.

"You are not dreaming." Drako nuzzled the side of her neck. "I am real, princess."

"How did you get in here?" she whispered.

"Stone walls cannot keep love outside, my sweet."

With silken fingertips, Katerina caressed his cheek and then glided the palm of her hand down his neck and across the breadth of his shoulders, feeling his strength. She entwined her left arm around his neck and slowly pulled his face toward hers.

Their lips met in a long, langorous kiss. He lay across her, their warm, naked flesh touching, his dark chest hair teasing her nipples.

Katerina poured all her emotion into the kiss, telling

him without words of her love for him. Pressing him back on the bed, she hovered over him for a moment and planted tiny kisses down his neck to his chest.

She smiled when he moaned, and her lips continued their sensual descent of his muscular body. His stomach muscles quivered as she brushed her lips across his belly. She slid her lips lower, and he moaned again, telling her of the pleasure she was giving him.

Katerina reached for his erect shaft, holding him in her fingers, eliciting another moan from him. She flicked her tongue down and then up his stiff manhood and then sucked its head gently.

Drako growled and, without warning, yanked her up to position her on top of him. Then he lowered her, piercing her slowly, filling her until their groins met.

"Ride me, princess." His voice was a husky whisper.

And Katerina did. She moved back and forth, tentatively at first, gradually increasing the tempo.

Drako and Katerina reached paradise together, their cries mingling, until they floated back to the reality of her bedchamber. She rested her head against his chest, his arms wrapping around her body.

"Where did you learn that?" Drako asked.

"You taught me."

"I never—"

"Your actions last night taught me what to do." She raised herself up to look into his eyes. "Do you doubt my morals?"

"No doubts, my love," he assured her.

Katerina relaxed against his chest again. Silence reigned for several long moments while she decided to give him the benefit of the doubt whether to believe his assurance or not.

"Did you read the morning's *Times*?" she asked.

He grunted. "Rudolf told me about it."

"How could anyone have recognized me?"

"Someone is watching us."

"Then you must leave immediately," Katerina said, sitting up. "I do not relish the idea of being named in that nasty reporter's gossip."

"Do not be cruel," Drako said. "I doubt I can walk at the moment."

"Hektor is suspicious."

Drako narrowed his gaze on her. "What do you mean?"

"He has been stalking me around the house all day and catching me napping on the job," she answered. "Tonight he wanted to see the Sancy. Perhaps you should loan it to me lest he catch me in a lie."

"You put me off long enough," Drako said. "Putting your brother off should be easy. Why were you napping?"

"Our nightly trysts tire me."

The tiredness stems from sharing midnight intimacies, Katerina told herself, unwilling to consider anything else. The only other alternative was too scandalous to consider.

Chapter Fifteen

The prince was sneaking into the contessa's house at night. Perhaps bedchamber would more aptly describe his nocturnal destination.

Baron Eddie Shores relaxed back on the leather seat inside his coach as it traveled Knightsbridge Road toward Hyde Park Corner. He smiled with contentment. Learning other people's secrets always proved lucrative. Maybe he should forget his current project and blackmail Drako Kazanov. He would bet his last shilling the Russian prince would pay any amount to protect the countess.

The coach halted in front of The Guinea on Bruton Place off Berkeley Square. Servants from the great mansions frequented the tavern, the location of his weekly meeting with his client's representative.

Eddie climbed out of the coach and walked into the tavern, scanning the room for his contact. The tavern's decorative scheme of plain timber and brownish-yellow plaster lacked personality. When one walked into Dirty Dick's, its seedy ambiance hit the customer like an avalanche. Apparently, bad ambiance was better than no ambiance, which seemed suitable for the colorless people serving the wealthy.

Spotting his contact sitting alone on the far side of the room, Eddie walked around the crowded tables. His contact was of average height with dark hair and eyes, his angular features marked him as Polish or Russian as did his heavily accented English.

Eddie knew better than to assume the man's employer was Polish or Russian. Amateurs sometimes believed they could fool professionals like himself. The contact could be representing an English aristocrat or even an American.

Sitting down opposite the man, Eddie shook his head when he gestured to the bottle of gin. Then Eddie asked the same question he always asked when they rendezvoused, knowing he would receive the same answer.

"What is your name?" Eddie asked, enjoying the irritated expression on the man's face.

"That is unimportant to our business," he answered in his accented English.

"What is your employer's name?"

"That is also unimportant."

Eddie smiled. "I like to know with whom I do business."

The man did not return his smile. "Your lack of progress displeases my employer."

Eddie did not like the man's attitude and decided not to sell him Prince Drako's nocturnal secret. "Tell your employer that delicate matters take time for successful completion."

"If the deed is not done soon," the man said, "my employer will go elsewhere."

"Is that so?" Eddie did not take kindly to threats. "Tell your employer that going elsewhere cuts both ways."

"What does that mean?"

"Certain persons would appreciate knowing your employer's plans," Eddie answered, issuing his own threat.

"You can prove nothing." The man stood and looked down at him. "Complete the task."

At that, the man quit the tavern. Eddie rose from his seat and walked outside, noting the man's direction.

"Follow that bloke at a discreet distance," Eddie instructed his driver before climbing into the coach.

Thirty minutes later, Eddie watched the man enter a mansion on Knightsbridge near the Rutland Gate. If he wasn't mistaken, the mansion was the Russian ambassador's residence.

Which person inside the ambassador's circle did the boor represent? Or was the supercilious servant acting on behalf of the ambassador himself? Did the ambassador, his family, and his staff enjoy diplomatic immunity?

If caught, the Russians would simply pack their bags and go home. He would go to the gallows.

Murder for hire was a risky business. He would concentrate on simple vices from now on—harmless activities like drinking, gambling, whoring.

Eddie needed to do two things. First, he would speak to the brothers. Then he would watch the ambassador's residence during the day to discover the man's identity.

"Take me to Dirty Dick's," Eddie instructed his driver.

His man turned the coach in a U and drove toward Hyde Park Corner and Piccadilly. The Strand would take them across town to Bishopgate.

The coach halted in front of Dirty Dick's. Eddie climbed down, hoping the brothers were there. He was in no mood to search for the blockheads.

Stale smoke and body odors and shrill laughter greeted him inside the tavern. Knowing some things never changed comforted him.

Seeing the brothers at a table across the room, Eddie joined them there. "Listen carefully," he said. "We are changing the plan."

"What'll it be, luv?"

Eddie turned his head and recognized the buxom Randy from a previous visit. "And if I said *you*?"

Randy laughed. "You flatter me, guv."

"Good answer, puss." Eddie winked at her. "Bring my boys another bottle of whatever they're drinking."

Randy walked away, shouting to the bartender. "Another bottle of swill, Dickie."

"What's the plan?" Scratchy asked.

Eddie looked around and lowered his voice. "Do *not* kill anyone. Watch them and report their activities to me."

"What if'n we catch'em alone like?" Itchy asked.

"Do nothing except watch." Eddie ran a hand down his face and looked from one brother to the other. "Do you understand?"

"How long do we watch'em?" Itchy asked.

"Until I say stop." Eddie rose from the table and tossed a few pounds on the table for the swill the brothers were drinking.

Early afternoon the following day, Eddie hid in his coach on the opposite side of the road from the Russian ambassador's residence. He had arrived at the hour when callers would be visiting. After seeing his man opening the door for guests, Eddie knew the man was the ambassador's majordomo. A man in that household position answered only to the ambassador and his family. He could think of no reason the ambassador or his wife would want to harm Kazanov or the countess. Prince Yuri shared a hostile history with Drako Kazanov, but why would he want the countess eliminated?

Eddie needed time to consider this. Certain authorities would relish the information, but he was unwilling to share his knowledge yet. Perhaps he could find a way to turn a profit.

* * *

Her menses were late.

Anxiety awakened Katerina on the morning of the Flambeau wedding. Not only had her menses failed to appear, but she was also tired and dizzy and—

Katerina leaped out of bed and dashed for the chamber pot. Dropping to her knees, she gagged dryly.

Someone knocked on the bedchamber door.

Katerina did not want anyone to see her like this. "Do not—"

Hektor opened the door and hurried across the chamber. Crouching down, he put a steadying arm around her. "You cannot attend the wedding in this condition. Shall I send the prince your regrets?"

Katerina would have shaken her head if she hadn't been so nauseous. "Society will gossip if I do not attend."

Hektor helped her across the room to sit on the edge of the bed. "No one will gossip if you are ill."

"I will feel better in a while," Katerina said, holding her hand up against further argument.

"Like yesterday and the day before?" Hektor asked. "When will you tell Drako about the babe?"

Stifling a groan, Katerina lifted her gaze to Hektor's. When had he gone from baby brother to keeper?

"Drako did not destroy our family," she said, "but he knows the villain's identity."

"I never doubted his innocence," Hektor replied. "I warned you about fire-breathing dragons."

"Thank you for reminding me that you told me so," Katerina snapped. "Drako proposed marriage, but I insisted I would only marry him after he revealed the man's identity."

"Take my advice, Sister. Reconsider his proposal."

"I need to know who destroyed our family."

"No one destroyed our family," Hektor said, shaking his head. "Alina's social-climbing and Ilya's hot temper brought their downfalls. Papa had a weak heart which would have killed him eventually."

Katerina said nothing. She knew the truth in what he was saying, but she had made a graveside promise. How could she live with herself if she did not follow through?

"Let it go, Sister," Hektor said, "or risk ruining your own life. The prince needs a legitimate heir. If you carry a boy, your son will not thank you for tossing his birthright away. You, of all people, should understand—"

"I will consider your advice," Katerina interrupted, and sighed, too weary to argue.

"Suitable brides for a prince fill London society," Hektor warned, turning to leave. "Do not take too long to consider my advice."

Alone again, Katerina slid her hand to her belly. Forgetting her graveside promise felt like a betrayal of her father, but refusing the prince's proposal was certainly a betrayal of her baby.

What a damn coil. She needed to find a way to exact her revenge without her baby suffering the consequences. Her task seemed impossible.

Katerina lay back on the bed and glanced toward the window. A gentle breeze flirted with the sheer, lace curtains. Brilliant sunshine, a summer's breeze, and sweet flower fragrances promised an ideal day for a wedding.

Drako had not visited her the previous night. Where had he gone? Had he attended the opera with another woman? How many young ladies, more suitable than she, had waltzed with him at various balls?

Katerina moaned and rolled over, turning her back on the glorious day outside her window. She didn't feel like celebrating a wedding or the perfect summer day. She yearned to pull the coverlet over her head, escaping the reality of her situation. Even the worst day of her life had not brought her so low. She supposed her growing baby was playing havoc with her emotions as well as her body.

The door opened. Carrying a tray, Nonna Strega walked into the room.

"Mangia, la contessa." Nonna Strega set the tray containing dry, toasted bread and black tea on the bedside table.

"We speak English in England," Katerina corrected her. "Remember?"

"Si, eat for the *bambino,"* Nonna said, gesturing to the tray. "You feel better."

Katerina groaned at her words. Did the whole household know about her predicament?

"I will eat." Katerina gestured Nonna out of the room. The last thing she wanted was an audience to her retching.

Leaning against the headboard, Katerina ate the dry toast in tiny bites and then sipped her tea. Surprisingly, she did feel better and ready to face the world again. Almost.

Katerina pondered the problem of what to wear to the wedding. Since the siren red had not enticed the prince to reveal what he knew, she would try blushing pink and a modest neckline, accessorized with classic pearls and diamonds. Nothing too ostentatious, though. The perfect look for an expectant mother.

Ten minutes after the appointed time for the prince's arrival, Katerina walked down the stairs to the foyer where he awaited her. Her heart ached at the sight of him, so compellingly handsome in his formal attire.

"You are lovelier than summer's freshest blossom," Drako murmured, bowing over her hand. "You seem a trifle pale, though."

"I am quite well," Katerina assured him. "Working to complete my commissions in a timely manner has deprived me of sleep."

"Slow your pace," Drako advised, escorting her out the door. "An illness will keep you from finishing anything."

"I am certain you are correct."

"If you are agreeing with me," he teased her, "then you are definitely ill."

Thirty minutes later, Drako escorted her down the center aisle of St. Paul's Cathedral. Katerina felt dozens of speculative gazes on them and worried that society suspected her of being the woman seen leaving a prince's residence. They slipped into a pew directly behind the groom's brothers.

Her mind wandering during the ceremony, Katerina told herself she should never have succumbed to the prince's charms nor engaged in physical intimacies. She had been so carefully circumspect for five long years but, in the end, had fared no better than Alina or even her own mother.

Bedding the prince had not inspired him to reveal what he knew. If she was honest, she had bedded him because she loved him and thought she could steal a few moments of happiness in a life filled with hard work and worry that someone would discover her true identity. Either her baby or her graveside promise would pay the consequence of her foolish pleasure.

"I cannot decide which look I prefer," Drako whispered. "Your seductive red or virginal pink."

Katerina gave him a sidelong glance, her lips twitching into a smile.

"Both gowns incite me to ravishment," he added.

Katerina giggled. She blushed when the Kazanov princes turned around to look at her.

"We could be standing at the altar together," Drako whispered.

"Tell me the villain's identity," Katerina said, "and I will gladly stand beside you there."

And then Katerina saw in her mind's eye the disturbing image of Drako standing in front of the clergy and speaking solemn vows with another bride. The emotional pain was almost physical, and she placed the palm of her hand against her chest.

"Are you ill?" he asked.

Heartache, she thought but whispered, "Heartburn."

An hour later, Drako and Katerina followed the other wedding guests into Inverary House. Katerina could not shake the feeling that people were watching them and speculating about their relationship. From there, her thoughts veered to her brother's advice and the best way to inform the prince of his impending fatherhood.

Like the eldest Flambeau sister's wedding, the head table had been placed at one end of the grand ballroom while violinists played background music at the opposite side. The guest tables sat in the middle with a portion of the space reserved for dancing. Garlands of blue forget-me-nots decorated the ballroom, and the heady perfume of red, white, and yellow roses scented the air.

"If you will excuse me," Katerina whispered, "I need to visit the withdrawing room."

Katerina walked away, hoping the withdrawing room would be deserted at this early hour. Her stomach was queasy, and she needed to muster her strength before assuming her placid, public mask.

Entering the withdrawing room, Katerina decided that luck was running against her that day. The Blond Brigade stood there, giving her the impression they had been waiting for her appearance. She did not have the strength to deal with these three witches today.

Lavinia Smythe rounded on her. "Have you read the *Times* recently?"

Without giving her time to reply, Princess Anya asked,

"Are you the woman who was seen leaving a prince's residence?"

Well, that was certainly forthright. No maidenly coyness or subtle sophistication there.

Katerina managed a smile. "Are you referring to the woman disguised as a boy?"

"Are you the woman?"

Struggling against her nausea, Katerina kept her face an expressionless mask. "I doubt I could pass as a boy," she said, glancing at her own bosom, "but none of you would have a problem with that particular disguise."

Anya and Lavinia looked distinctly unhappy with her answer, but Cynthia prevented their trading insults by asking, "Did Prince Drako receive a death threat?"

"No threat," Katerina answered, turning to leave. "Someone tried to kill him at the Gentlemen's Golfing Day."

Waiting for her in the hallway, Drako offered her his arm, "Is something wrong?"

"The Blond Brigade accused me of being the woman seen leaving your house," Katerina answered. "Their rampant gossip will pauper my business before year's end."

"Marry me," Drako said, "and live wealthy."

"I plan to marry for love, not money."

"Does one preclude the other?"

"No, Your Highness." Katerina gave him an inscrutable smile. "Loving a wealthy man is much easier than loving a poor man."

Seated at their assigned table were Prince Viktor, Princess Regina, Alexander Blake, and Raven Flambeau. Prince Stepan and Princess Fancy had exchanged positions with Prince Mikhail and Belle Flambeau, who now sat as husband and wife at the head table.

"My lady, I believe you met my wife at our wedding," Prince Stepan said.

"I enjoyed your opera performances," Katerina said. "Will you return to singing?"

"I retired from the stage for the joys of motherhood," Fancy answered.

"I cannot imagine my baby brother as someone's father," Prince Viktor said, making everyone smile.

The Inverary footmen began serving the wedding feast. Oyster soup arrived, accompanied by caviar and tiny slices of toast.

Katerina looked at the oysters swimming in the broth and felt nauseous. Glancing at Fancy, she noted the other woman's pallor and hoped nobody noticed her suffering the same malady as the prince's pregnant wife.

"Oops." Moving the caviar away from his wife, Stepan said, "Our baby dislikes the sight of caviar."

Everyone smiled at that.

Drako leaned close to her, asking in a soft voice, "Is something wrong?"

"Hunger eludes me," Katerina said, managing a smile.

The meal's second course of roasted chicken and vegetable medley was easier to handle. She could take her time cutting the poultry, taste a tiny piece, and move the vegetables around. Her plate would appear as if she had eaten her fill.

Katerina listened to the men's conversations as if from a great distance. They discussed vodka and rare gem businesses, the cost of opera productions, and London's crime rate. Sneaking peeks at the prince, she wondered if their child would resemble him.

Katerina knew she needed to tell him about her pregnancy and her past. What if Drako revoked his marriage proposal once he learned the whole truth about her? Perhaps Hektor was correct, and she should not wait before accepting the prince's offer of marriage.

Aware that everyone at the table was smiling at her,

Katerina felt her panic rising. She had no idea what had been said.

"Is that not correct?" Drako asked her.

"I am sorry," she apologized, feeling a blush heating her cheeks. "My mind had wandered."

"I said, you would like to charge interest on delinquent accounts," Drako told her.

Katerina nodded. "I consider accruing interest an incentive to paying bills in a timely manner."

"My sister Bliss will appreciate that idea," Fancy said. "She is the family's mathematical genius."

"Where did your mind wander?" Drako asked her.

"I was thinking about Viveka," Katerina lied. "Wearing the tiara, my daughter has been parading around the house."

"Viveka is practicing for the tea party." Drako looked at his cousins. "I commissioned tiaras for the tea party Bess is hostessing."

"Did you commission one for me?" Stepan asked, making everyone smile. "I always attend the tea parties."

"I refuse to purchase a grown man a tiara."

Prince Viktor turned to Alexander Blake. "Have you and the constable rid London of its criminals?"

"The crime business is booming," Alexander answered. "I wish I had a pound for every crime committed in this town."

The Inverary footmen cleared the remains of dinner. Several musicians joined the violinists, creating a small orchestra for dancing. The wedding guests began circulating from table to table, socializing with friends and enemies.

Katerina rose from her chair, telling the prince, "I need to refresh myself and will return in a few minutes."

"I will walk with you." Raven Flambeau stood when she did and fell into step beside her. "Have you received any more threatening notes?"

"Thankfully, no."

"I believe the Blond Brigade is involved somehow," Raven told her. "Unable to mask her thoughts, Cynthia Clarke is easy to read."

Desperation swelled within Katerina's breast. She needed to know what the immediate future held for her.

Katerina touched Raven's arm, asking, "Will you tell me my future?"

"I am not a fortune teller," Raven answered. "I merely get impressions from objects and people."

Slipping her diamond and pearl dinner ring off her finger, Katerina offered it to the other woman. "Please, tell me what impressions you receive."

"Come with me." Raven escorted her to the duke's office, closing the door behind them. Sitting in one of the chairs, she took the ring and closed her eyes. "I see you at a misty crossroads, troubled by which road to travel. Neither leads to inner peace. Walk straight ahead, and a middle road will open if you set limits."

"What do you mean?" Katerina asked.

"I do not necessarily understand the meaning of my impressions." Raven passed her the ring. "You will be an excellent mother."

Katerina kept her composure. There was no way this girl could know she was carrying the prince's baby. "I am an excellent mother already."

"I meant *again*."

On their way back to the ballroom, they found Drako and Alexander loitering in the corridor near the ladies withdrawing room. Both men seemed surprised to see them walking down the hallway.

"I am ready for my dance," Katerina said, hoping to distract the prince.

"Then you shall have your dance," Drako told her, escorting her to the ballroom. "Where did you go?"

"I consulted with Raven."

"About what?"

"We consulted about private female matters," Katerina answered. "Dance with me?"

"Your wish is my command, my lady."

"Chivalry has not died."

Katerina stepped into his arms for their waltz, feeling as if she belonged there. She had never seemed to belong anywhere in her entire life, except when she stood with the prince's arms around her. Perhaps her changing body made her emotionally sensitive. Katerina wished she knew an older, experienced matron with whom she could trust her secret.

"You are preoccupied." It was a statement, not a question.

"I am considering your proposal." That seemed to satisfy him.

Katerina danced next with the Marquis of Huntly. Douglas Gordon escorted her onto the dance floor, and they began swirling around the ballroom with the other couples.

"Ye seem a bit pale today, lass," the marquis said, "though ye look as lovely as ever."

"I have been feeling under the eaves this week," Katerina said. "Luckily, nothing serious."

Huntly held her gaze captive, a slight smile flirting with his lips. "So, do ye want to guess the identity of the prince and the disguised lady?"

Katerina felt the blood rushing to her face. "I–I . . . No, thank you."

"Ye've guilt written across yer face," Huntly told her. "I dinna think ye possess the constitution for subterfuge, lass."

"You seem smitten with Bliss Flambeau," Katerina remarked, ignoring his comment.

"Miss Flambeau is an excellent conversationalist."

In her mind, Katerina replaced the word *conversationalist*

with *listener*. All men shared a common flaw. If the female listened to the male, she was undoubtedly an excellent conversationalist. Apparently, Bliss Flambeau realized this and was using it to her own advantage.

At music's end, Huntly escorted her off the dance floor and bowed over her hand, saying, "I'll be stoppin' by durin' the week to see those sketches ye made for my stepmother's birthday present."

"I will look forward to your visit." Katerina turned to walk away and found her path blocked. "Good to see you, Your Highness."

"I believe this is our dance," Prince Yuri said.

Katerina inclined her head, accepting his offered hand. She stepped onto the dance floor, feeling uncomfortable with his nearness.

"You should have heeded my warning about Kazanov," Yuri said, as soon as they began swirling around the ballroom. "I know you are the disguised woman seen leaving the prince's residence."

"You cannot know something that never happened," Katerina parried, struggling against the urge to knock his other front tooth down his throat. "Such speculation can hurt the innocent."

"I apologize if I accuse you falsely." His smile was smug. "Kazanov sent his late fiancee over the brink into suicide."

"The woman suffered a fatal fall," Katerina defended Drako.

"Leaping from a third-floor window can hardly be called an accidental fall," Yuri said.

That bit of information caught Katerina off guard. Drako had not told her the whole truth, but perhaps he did not want to malign the dead.

When she remained silent, Yuri continued, "The other

night at White's I heard Prince Rudolf talking about the bet he and Drako made."

That confused Katerina. "Bet?"

"Drako and Rudolf wagered whether or not he would get into your bed."

Katerina stopped dancing, stepping away from him. "You go too far, Yuri."

"I apologize." He did not sound remorseful. "I would like to call upon you concerning a gold tooth replacement."

"Find yourself another jeweler." Katerina turned away, but his voice stopped her.

"I could ruin your business."

"You could ruin my business," Katerina said, rounding on him, "but then I would need to kill you."

That made him smile. "Are you threatening me?"

"Consider it a promise." Katerina walked off the dance floor, leaving him standing alone.

If she questioned him, Drako would lie. Instead, Katerina approached Prince Rudolf who stood with the Duke of Inverary.

"A lovely wedding, Your Grace," Katerina greeted the duke before turning to the prince. "Your Highness, may I have this dance?"

"I would love to dance with you." Rudolf escorted her onto the dance floor.

Pretending to enjoy the music, Katerina remained silent while they circled the ballroom. Finally, she said, "Tell me about your bet with Drako."

Prince Rudolf missed a step. "Bet?"

"Your bet about his visiting my"—Katerina hesitated— "my bed."

"A joke between cousins means nothing, my lady."

"Ah, but the joke was at my expense."

"We meant no harm," Rudolf said. "Forgive us, please."

"I will consider your plea." When the music ended,

Katerina said, "I must find Huntly to arrange an appointment. Please excuse me."

Katerina circled the ballroom and spied the Marquis of Huntly speaking with his cousin, the Marquis of Awe. Pasting a bright smile on her face, she approached the two Highlanders. "Douglas, I wonder if I may presume upon our friendship to borrow your coach."

"I dinna mind ye borrowin' it," Huntly said. "Why do ye need it, if ye dinna mind me askin'?"

"I dinna mind at all," Katerina mimicked his accent, making the two Scotsmen smile. "I want to go home."

Huntly looked puzzled. "What aboot Kazanov?"

"The prince and I are not in accord," she answered, "and I do mind you asking the reason."

"Fair enough, lass. Come along, and I'll see ye to my coach."

Huntly escorted her out of the ballroom and downstairs to the foyer. He sent an Inverary footman to instruct his driver to bring the coach around.

"Drive the countess to Trevor Square and then return here." Huntly turned to her, asking, "When Kazanov asks for ye, what shall I tell him?"

"Tell him to go to hell."

Chapter Sixteen

"Darling, you have tasted forbidden fruit."

"Well said, Your Grace." Drako gave the Duchess of Inverary his most charming smile, wondering how she could possibly know such private details. "Did I mention how ravishingly beautiful you look in red?"

Her dimpled smile appeared. "No, Your Highness, you failed to mention that."

"How remiss of me."

"I will forgive you if you walk with me," the duchess said, looping her arm through his. "Let us enjoy a private conversation."

"I cannot think of any woman with whom I would prefer to walk," Drako said, escorting her around the perimeter of the dance floor.

"Except our dearest Kat, you flattering devil." Arm in arm, Prince Drako Kazanov and the Duchess of Inverary left the crowded grand ballroom and strolled down the second-floor corridor. "I knew the two of you would suit."

"You, Your Grace, are a relationship genius."

"Yes, I know." The duchess gave him her dimpled smile. "I do hope you are offering her marriage."

"Kat refused my proposal."

"She did what?"

Drako grinned at the rare sight of the Duchess of Inverary caught off guard, her expression a mingling of horror and surprise. "She cannot marry me until settling a certain personal problem which defies solving."

"What unholy problem could prevent her from marrying a prince?" the duchess asked.

"When her father died," Drako told her, "Kat made a graveside promise and feels obligated to honor his memory."

"The promise did not preclude her marrying her first husband," the duchess said. "Why is marrying you different?"

Drako inclined his head, deciding the duchess was infinitely more cunning than he had thought. "Kat knows I possess the information that will make her graveside promise possible."

"Tell her what she wants."

"Doing that would cause even more problems."

"*You* solve her problem, darling, and then marry her."

Drako grinned. "A simplistic view, Your Grace, but a sterling idea."

"All my relationship ideas are sterling," the duchess said. "Except the gold and platinum ones, of course."

By unspoken agreement, the prince and the duchess strolled back to the ballroom. Though they smiled and nodded at several guests, no one dared to intrude on their private conversation.

"I would adore helping to plan my dear Kat's wedding," the duchess told him. "I have been trying to find her a husband since the day I made her acquaintance."

"How fortunate she resisted your matchmaking until I arrived on the scene," Drako said, and then leaned close. "How did you know the countess and I . . . ?"

Though he left the rest of his words unspoken, the Duchess of Inverary knew what he was asking. "A well-loved woman glows," she answered. "Remind me another day to explain the reason my dearest Magnus gifted me with this fabulous diamond ensemble which, by the way, Kat designed."

"My countess is truly a design genius," Drako said, eyeing the priceless diamonds. He escorted the duchess to her husband's side and bowed over her hand. "I thank you for your advice, Your Grace."

Drako walked away. Circling the ballroom, he scanned the crowd for his countess. When he'd last glimpsed her from a distance, she had been waltzing with Huntly, but he did not see her anywhere now. Thinking she may have retired to the withdrawing room, Drako walked toward the ballroom's exit where he spied Huntly and Rudolf speaking.

"Have either of you seen Kat?" he asked.

Huntly grinned. "Well, dragon man, I've a feelin' a snake slithered into yer paradise."

"What do you mean?"

"Yer lady insisted on borrowin' my coach and goin' home alone," the Scotsman answered.

That puzzled Drako. They had not argued, and she had seemed in good spirits if slightly preoccupied. "Did she say anything?"

"Kat told me to tell ye to go to hell."

"She heard about our wager," Rudolf said, "but I never told her."

"Who else knew?"

Rudolf shrugged. "I saw her dancing with Yuri."

"*Sukin syn*," Drako muttered.

"What did the dragon man say?" Huntly asked Rudolf.

"He said *son of a bitch*."

Without another word, Drako marched out of the ballroom. He instructed a footman to call for his coach.

What a damn setback, Drako thought while he waited. He would kill the person who had squealed about the stupid bet. For God's sake, he had canceled the wager almost as soon as he'd met her. How could Yuri have known about it? His own brothers did not know. Or did they? Had his cousins and his brothers been discussing it somewhere within earshot of Yuri?

Reaching Trevor Square, Drako climbed out of the coach and hurried up the mansion's stairs. He grabbed the knocker and banged on the door, the sound demanding entrance.

"Do not answer the door," Drako heard Katerina's voice inside the foyer.

"Yes, my lady," the majordomo replied.

"This is Prince Drako Kazanov." He banged the knocker against the door again. "I command you to open this door."

"Dudley, if you open the door," Katerina said, "I will terminate your employment."

"Kat." Drako heard the brother's voice.

"Mind your own business, Hektor." Katerina sounded close to the door when she said, "I do not want to speak to you, Drako. Go home."

"Kat, let me explain about—"

"Your actions speak for you, Your Highness."

Drako ran his hand down his face. He would never have imagined pleading his case on a public street while his coachman pretended deafness. Explaining himself through a closed door would not work, never mind the humiliation of listening servants. He needed to get inside.

"Hektor, are you there?" he called. "Open the door."

"Do not move, brother," Katerina ordered.

"What is all this shouting?" one of the sisters asked.

"What is happening?" the other sister demanded.

God have mercy, Drako thought, *now the sisters were listening in the foyer, too.* He should have charged an admission fee.

"Roksana and Ludmilla, return to your chambers,"

Katerina ordered, her tone angry and touchingly distraught at the same time.

"We want to stay."

"You always send us upstairs at the most exciting times."

"Do what Kat says," Hektor ordered.

"I hate you."

"We hate *her*, too."

At that, Katerina burst into tears. The sound of her sobs wrenched his heart. He had not intended to ignite a family feud.

Drako pounded his fist on the door. "Roksana and Ludmilla, do not disrespect your sister."

"They did not mean it," Hektor was comforting a sobbing Katerina. "Go upstairs with Nonna Strega, and I will handle the prince."

The sound of Katerina's weeping faded away. Then silence.

Drako heard the lock being thrown, and the door opened to reveal Hektor. Beyond him stood Dudley, ashen-faced from the unexpected uproar.

"I must speak with your sister," Drako told the younger man.

"Come with me," Hektor said, gesturing him inside. "Dudley, do not worry about your employment. I opened the door, and she cannot terminate her own brother."

Hektor led Drako upstairs to the family parlor and closed the door behind them. "Please, sit down."

"I must speak with Kat."

"If Kat agrees, you can speak to her after we talk."

Drako inclined his head and sat on the upholstered settee. Hektor sat on the highbacked chair opposite him.

"What happened at the wedding?"

For a brief moment, Drako considered diluting the truth but realized that lying would not help his cause. He had inadvertently hurt the woman he loved and needed the brother's support to rectify the situation.

"Before the duchess's Beltane Ball, my cousin Rudolf told me about a beautiful contessa originally from Moscow," Drako began. "This contessa not only seemed to have secrets but had rejected all male overtures. I wagered five thousand pounds that I would learn her secrets and find a place in her bed."

Hektor looked displeased. "I hope there is more to this story, or I may be forced to call you out."

"I met Kat that night," Drako continued. "I swear I canceled the wager soon after I met your sister."

"Only a man in love would give another a fifty-five carat diamond to prove his honorable intentions," Hektor said. "Who knew about this wager?"

"Until tonight, I thought the wager a secret between cousins," Drako answered, "but Yuri must have overheard Rudolf mention it to his brothers."

"What has Yuri to do with this?"

"I suspect Yuri mentioned it to Kat at the wedding," Drako answered, "and when I leave here, I will be returning to the wedding to speak with him."

Hektor grinned. "Do not earn yourself a trip to the gallows."

"Yuri is a weasel who frightens easily," Drako assured him. "Besides, I dislike the sight of blood."

"You must pretend ignorance about what I am going to tell you," Hektor said. "My sister will tell you in her own time. Do I have your word?"

Drako nodded. "I will keep your confidence."

"Brace yourself, Your Highness," Hektor said. "Kat is pregnant."

She was carrying his baby? Drako bolted off the settee.

"Sit down, Your Highness." Hektor stood when he did. "Please let me finish."

Looking as shaken as he felt, Drako dropped onto the settee, and then he grinned. He was going to be a father. He and Kat would share a child.

"I must tell you about my sister's background which, I suspect, has colored her whole life," Hektor said. "My sister is a bastard who never met her father until she was five."

That revelation did not shock Drako. "Her illegitimacy means nothing to me."

"Illegitimacy means a great deal to Kat," Hektor said. "Our Romany mother had an affair with our married father, but he did not know of Kat's existence until she was five. His first wife had died by that time. Father married Mother who delivered me within the first year of marriage and died delivering Roksana and Ludmilla two years later.

"Alina and Ilya, his first wife's children, despised Kat as the proof of their father's infidelity. They considered father's talent creating jewels as a stepping stone in their social-climbing."

"Her younger sisters professing their hatred made her weep," Drako remarked, "but they probably consider her a surrogate mother."

"Kat is the only mother they have ever known," Hektor agreed. "My sister shared our father's passion and talent for creating incredible beauty from stones and metal. The two of them passed long hours in his studio, which fostered even more jealousy and hatred.

"I once told you that Kat is a perfect example of the student surpassing the teacher." Hektor paused, as if considering his next words. "Kat is not the woman the world sees. Striving for perfection is my sister's Holy Grail because she believes exceeding others' expectations will bring her acceptance."

"You love her very much," Drako said, digesting the younger man's words. "She has been fortunate in her brother."

"Thank you," Hektor said, "but I have been lucky in my sister."

"If Alina and Ilya despised her," Drako asked, "what motivates her need for revenge?"

"She wants justice for our father," Hektor answered. "His weak heart could not endure the untimely deaths of his two oldest children."

"I want to speak with her tonight," Drako said.

"I cannot promise she will agree," Hektor said, standing. "I will try but not force her."

After Hektor had gone, Drako rose from the settee and wandered around the parlor. He could have kicked himself for making that stupid wager with his cousin, even in jest.

His lady was hurting. Yuri, her sisters, and he had sapped her strength that night. Temporarily, he hoped. Possible loss of reputation was always felt more keenly by those with shadowy origins. He needed to convince her of his respect and love.

Upstairs in her bedchamber, Katerina sat brushing her hair. With Nonna Strega hovering over her like a mother hen, she had changed into her nightshift and bedrobe. Her jewels had been locked away, her face freshly scrubbed. Only her red-rimmed eyes and nauseous stomach marked the evening's emotional upset.

She was tired, weary of the responsibility of caring for dependents, of guarding every word and action, of smiling at people she disliked. Her bed had never looked more inviting. Hiding beneath the coverlet for the rest of her life held a certain appeal at the moment.

The remembrance of what she and the prince had done in her bed kept her from doing that. She should have banished him from her chamber that first night. Each time she glanced at the bed, the thought of him popped into her mind.

She was a fraud in more ways than one. Not only had she assumed a title but also the respectability of a properly born lady. The prince would not wish to marry her if he knew the whole truth.

And then there was the problem of Yuri, threatening to ruin her reputation and business. How would she feed her family if she lost her reputation and no one commissioned her jewels?

A knock on the door drew her attention and her dismay. She was in no mood for visitors.

The door opened slowly, and Roksana peered into the chamber. "Can we speak with you?"

Katerina gave her sister a wobbly smile. "Of course, you are welcome in my chamber."

Looking shame-faced and contrite, Roksana and Ludmilla walked into the room. The sisters hesitated and glanced at each other.

"We did not mean what we said," Ludmilla spoke up.

"We apologize for making you cry," Roksana added.

"I forgive you," Katerina said, looking from one sister to the other. "I do understand your frustration, but there are some things personal and private."

Ludmilla nodded. "I never saw you weeping before."

"Neither did I," Roksana said.

"I can assure you there have been many times I have wished to weep and wail," Katerina told them. "Surrendering to the urge would have disturbed the whole household."

"Do you love the prince?" Roksana asked.

"Yes, I love the prince." Katerina surprised herself with her open admission.

"Will you marry him?" Ludmilla asked.

"I have not decided whether to accept his offer or not,"

Katerina answered. "When I decide, you will be the second to know."

"Who will be the first?" Roksana asked.

"The prince will be the first to know, of course."

The sixteen year olds giggled at that, and Katerina wondered if she had ever been as carefree as her sisters. She doubted it. All those years of deflecting her older siblings' hatred had robbed her of a light heart.

Another knock on the door drew their attention. "May I come inside?" Hektor called, walking into the room. He looked at Katerina and then at each of his younger sisters. "I assume all is forgiven."

"We are sorry," Roksana apologized.

Ludmilla nodded. "We did not mean what we said."

"I forgive you," Hektor told them. "If I ask to speak privately with Kat, will you relapse into anger?"

"No relapses," Roksana answered.

Ludmilla moved with her sister toward the door. "Speak away, dear brother."

Once her sisters had gone, Katerina asked, "Did Drako leave?"

"No."

"Did you tell him about the baby?"

"*You* are going to tell him about the baby," Hektor said.

"Where is he?"

"His Highness is waiting in the parlor."

"You put him in the family parlor?" Katerina turned away. "I do not want to speak with him tonight."

"The prince is worried and needs to explain the wager," Hektor said. "Listen to his apology, and tell him about the baby."

Katerina did not want to face him that night, especially because her emotional reaction positively screamed her tender feelings for him. "He can apologize tomorrow."

"Good God, Kat, have pity on the man," Hektor exclaimed. "He loves you."

"Drako *wants* me," Katerina corrected him. "An ocean of difference lies between wanting and loving."

"Sister, your childhood is blinding you to the man's love." Hektor dropped onto the edge of the bed. "I went to his residence the morning after you broke into his house. The prince gave me the Sancy to prove his honorable intentions."

That caught her by surprise. "He gave you the Sancy?"

"Drako told me to keep it safe until he married you," Hektor said.

"What if we never marry?"

Hektor shrugged. "I assume the Sancy is mine."

"Then you should applaud my refusal to speak with him."

"I prefer a happy sister to a fifty-five carat diamond," Hektor told her.

Katerina smiled. "Thank you for that."

"Accord the prince the respect of listening to his apology," Hektor said. "You need not forgive him."

"Give me the Sancy," Katerina said, "and I will speak with him."

"Will you accept his marriage offer?"

"I am returning his property and listening."

"Wait here," Hektor said, standing. "I will fetch it from my secret hiding place."

"Where is that?"

"If I told you"—Hektor winked at her—"my hiding place would be no secret."

Downstairs, Drako paced back and forth across the parlor. He had almost given up hope when he heard a noise behind him.

Katerina stood inside the parlor doorway. With her ebony hair hanging loose to her waist, Katerina wore a simple bedrobe wrapped tightly around her.

No woman had ever looked more beautiful.

"Thank you for seeing me." Drako crossed the parlor to her. "Shall we sit on the settee?"

"I prefer standing."

Drako realized regaining ground with her was not going to be easy. Her brother had persuaded her to see him, but she was in no mood to listen. "Please?"

Katerina held his gaze for a brief moment and then nodded. Instead of the settee, she crossed the parlor to perch on the edge of the highbacked chair.

Drako knelt on one bended knee in front of her, preventing flight, and grasped her hands in his before she could protest. "I am sorry for upsetting you," he apologized. "The wager was a jest between cousins and canceled once I had met you."

"A man who wagers about crawling into a woman's bed is crass in the extreme," Katerina said, her tone frigid.

"All men are crass to one degree or another," Drako said, "but I swear we outgrow it."

"My brother is not crass."

"Hektor hides his crassness," Drako said, and felt a glimmer of hope when her lips twitched into a ghost of a smile. "Brothers are not allowed to show their crassness in front of sisters."

"I do not want to see you for a while," she told him.

"Do not lie," he said. "You *do* want to see me."

"Yuri suspects I am the disguised woman seen leaving your house," Katerina said. "His suspicions can ruin my reputation and business."

"The *Times* did not name the prince in question," Drako reminded her. "Yuri is angling for a reaction."

Katerina reached into her pocket and produced the velvet pouch containing the Sancy. "This belongs to you," she said, holding it out to him. "A soulless stone cannot replace my virtue."

"Darling, you are dearer to my heart than a hundred million Sancys," Drako said, refusing the velvet pouch. "Consider the diamond a wedding gift."

"I cannot accept your proposal." Katerina hesitated for a brief second and added, "At this time."

Drako narrowed his blue gaze on her. "Why?"

Katerina looked away and took a deep breath, seeming to fortify herself. "You do not know me."

"I know you better than you know yourself."

"You insufferable, conceited, arrogant—"

"I am all those things," Drako interrupted, "but I know myself, what I want and what I need. *You.*"

"I am a bastard," she whispered.

"Bastardy means nothing to me," he assured her, and then realized it was the wrong thing to say.

"Being born a bastard matters to me," Katerina said, the ice returning to her tone.

"I understand," Drako said, trying to regain lost ground. "I understand because bastardy matters to Cousin Rudolf."

Katerina looked confused. "Prince Rudolf?"

"Cousin Rudolf is a bastard and did not enjoy the luxury of being raised by the biological father who loved him," he told her.

"Rudolf is a prince."

"Fydor Kazanov was too proud to acknowledge he had married a woman carrying another man's child," Drako said. "No man can control his origins, Kat. Your being born outside the bonds of marriage cannot diminish the woman you are."

"You would consider marrying a bastard?"

"You would consider marrying a minor prince?" he teased her.

"I will consider it," she relented. "I will inform you of my decision when it is made."

"Thank you, my love." Drako kissed the palms of her

hands and then stood, knowing he had won that night's battle but would win no more concessions. "Sleep well, my love. I promise Yuri will never bother you again."

"What are you planning?" She looked worried.

"I am not planning a walk to the gallows to hang for a swine like Yuri."

Drako left the parlor and descended the stairs to the foyer where her brother waited. "Remain home tomorrow to receive a lumber delivery," he ordered the younger man. "We will be building Viveka's tree house. I have already drafted the plans."

"We?"

"If she sees me in the courtyard every day," Drako said, "Kat will be unable to resist me."

"You think my sister cannot resist a prince?"

Drako grinned. "I think your sister cannot resist the man she loves."

The sound of his future brother-in-law's laughter followed him outside. "Inverary House," he called to his driver.

Climbing into his coach, Drako lost his charming smile. He planned to confront his old nemesis and persuade him to cease harassing Kat, without spilling the swine's blood.

Fifteen minutes later, the coach halted in front of Inverary House. Drako leaped out, calling to his driver, "Wait here. I will be leaving again in ten minutes."

Drako nodded at the duke's footmen and hurried upstairs to the second floor. Reluctant to ruin his cousin's wedding, he decided to ask someone to send Yuri outside.

Walking into the ballroom, Drako spied Rudolf and Alexander Blake speaking. He sidled up to them and said in a low voice, "I need a private word with Yuri and want you to send him outside."

Rudolf gave him a knowing smile. Alexander Blake looked suspicious.

"The pig upset Kat by accusing her of being the woman

seen leaving a prince's residence," Drako explained, "and I intend to persuade him to cease harassing her."

"Killing him would be easier," Rudolf said. "I can arrange an untimely accident."

"I did not hear that," Alexander said, and then looked at Drako. "Calm down before you speak with him."

"If Yuri threatened Raven's reputation," Drako asked, "would you calm down?"

"No, I would ask Rudolf to arrange an untimely accident," Alexander answered, making them smile. "I will bring Yuri outside but intend to witness this conversation."

"I will tag along, too," Rudolf said. "I love a good fight."

Drako left the ballroom and nodded to the footmen in the foyer again. Outside, he began pacing back and forth in front of the mansion and hoped the swine did not refuse the request.

Flanked by Rudolf and Alexander, Prince Yuri walked out the door a few minutes later. His mouth curled in an infuriating smirk. "What do you want, Kazanov?"

Drako grabbed his cravat and yanked him closer, warning, "Do not approach my fiancee again."

"I saw no ring on the contessa's finger," Yuri replied, "nor did I read any betrothal announcement."

"Leave Kat alone," Drako said, "and keep your mouth shut."

"Or what?"

"I may drop a word to the *Times* reporter that Anya was the disguised woman seen leaving a prince's house," Drako told him, "or I may kill you this time around."

Alexander stepped between the princes. "Yuri is not worth the trip to the gallows."

"You do not frighten me," Yuri said, ignoring Alexander. "The sight of blood sickens you."

"Heed my cousin's warning," Rudolf spoke up, "or the Kazanov clan will ruin you."

"Kazanov clan?" Yuri rounded on Rudolf. "I heard you are no true Kazanov but some nobleman's bastard. Your English mother was a—"

Without warning, Rudolf slugged the other prince. His fist connected with the other man's face dead-center.

"Yadrona mysh' syn," Yuri shrieked, blood running down his face. "The bastard broke my nose."

"You will live," Rudolf drawled.

"What did Yuri say?" Alexander asked.

"He said *son of a mousefucker*," Drako interpreted. "The bastard broke—"

"I understood the English."

Chapter Seventeen

"How was the wedding?"

With his arms folded across his chest, Alexander Blake leaned against the window sill in Amadeus Black's office inside the Central Criminal Court Building. "The bride glowed and the groom beamed." He looked at the constable and shrugged. "Drako was upset because Yuri accused the Contessa de Salerno of being the woman seen leaving a prince's residence."

"Yuri is fishing for information." Constable Black cocked a dark brow at him. "Did the groom beam lasciviously at the bride?"

"I doubt it." Alexander smiled. "Raven told me the bride already carries the groom's heir."

Amadeus chuckled at that, a rare sound very few ever heard. "How lucky for the bride that the groom was an honorable man."

"Mikhail Kazanov is the lucky one," Alexander told him. "He had been trying to convince Belle Flambeau to marry him."

"Raven gave you the insider gossip?"

"My sweet betroth possesses a wealth of useless information," Alexander answered. "Do not tell her I said that."

The door swung open.

Barney walked into the office and sat in the chair in front of the constable's desk. "The runners stalking Scratchy and Itchy tell me the prince has passed several late nights at the countess's residence, leaving the brothers standing in Trevor Square until the wee hours of the morning." Barney chuckled. "Those idiots don't realize they're being watched."

"I'll be damned," Alexander exclaimed.

Amadeus looked at him. "Are you thinking what I am?"

"What are you thinking?" Barney asked.

"I will let you know if it proves true," Amadeus told him. "I would not wish to slander an innocent man."

"Should we question Prince Yuri?" Alexander asked.

"I will decide after we speak with the baron," Amadeus answered.

"There hasn't been another assassination attempt," Alexander remarked.

"Calm before the storm," Barney spoke up. "The assassin wants us to relax our guard before he tries again."

"That is most logical," Amadeus said.

Barney grinned. "Thank you, Boss."

"If Eddie refuses to talk," Amadeus said, turning to Alexander, "pick a fight and steal something of his for Raven to read."

"We cannot use her psychic reading in court," Alexander said, surprised. "Why should we bother?"

"Her reading can do no harm," Amadeus answered, "and we might use it as leverage to coax the baron into revealing what he knows."

Someone knocked on the door, and Amadeus called, "Enter."

Prince Yuri walked into the office. He wore a large bandage across his nose and sported two blackened eyes.

Alexander looked away to keep from laughing. He

hoped this prince had learned his lesson about insulting another man's mother.

Amadeus stood when the prince entered. "Your Highness, how may I help you?"

"I want to press charges against certain individuals."

"Wait outside, Barney," Amadeus instructed his man. "Escort our witness here when he arrives." He looked at the prince and gestured to the chair. "Make yourself comfortable, Your Highness, and tell me your story."

Yuri sat in the chair vacated by Barney. "I am surprised your associate did not tell you," he said, tossing the associate a sullen look.

Amadeus sat at his desk. "Suppose you tell me whom to press charges against and the reason."

"I want attempted murder charges against Princes Rudolf and Drako Kazanov as well as the Contessa de Salerno," Yuri announced.

Standing near the window, Alexander smothered his laughter but not very well. Yuri sent him an angry look while Amadeus cocked a brow at him.

"Those are serious charges," Amadeus said, his tone concerned.

"The Marquis of Basildon—your associate laughing at my injury—was their accomplice."

"A witness is never considered an accomplice," Alexander informed the prince.

"You did nothing to help."

"I was invited to the wedding as a guest, not as security patrol."

"Your Highness, please tell me what happened," Amadeus said.

"Katerina Garibaldi threatened my life and later Drako Kazanov did the same," Yuri said. "Rudolf Kazanov struck me and caused these injuries. The bastard broke my nose."

"What did you expect?" Alexander said. "You insulted Rudolf's mother."

"If you provoked Kazanov by insulting his mother," Amadeus told him, "then you must shoulder the blame. No jury will convict a man defending his mother."

"And the two death threats?"

"Death threats are merely words," Amadeus explained, "and I can do nothing unless the threats are acted upon."

"Do you mean I can press charges after they murder me?" Yuri challenged him.

Amadeus shrugged. "The law is the law, Your Highness."

Prince Yuri's face mottled with anger. "What kind of justice is that?"

"English justice," Amadeus answered, looking him straight in the eye. "We English do not arrest people because a nobleman says so."

Yuri stood. "This is outrageous."

"No, Your Highness, this is English fair play," Amadeus said, standing when the other man did. "Any foreigner who dislikes our system is free to return to his homeland."

"I am a prince."

"Every man is equal under English law."

"You are merely a constable," Yuri said. "My uncle will appeal to the king."

"Even the king may not bend the law to suit a whim," Amadeus told him. "Leave my office and do not return until someone tries to kill you."

Yuri whirled away, but the door opened unexpectedly. Barney and Baron Shores walked into the room.

"Boss, our witness has arrived," Barney said.

"So I see."

Alexander watched the prince's expression when he recognized Crazy Eddie. Yuri looked surprised, his complexion paling. Then his aristocratic bland expression fell into place, but Alexander had seen the prince's dismayed recognition.

"Baron Shores, please be seated," Amadeus was saying. "Prince Yuri is leaving."

The prince walked out, slamming the door behind him.

"I thought nothing unusual happened yesterday," Amadeus said.

Alexander shrugged. "Arguments at weddings are not unusual."

"Baron Shores, I told you to sit," Amadeus said, his voice stern.

Alexander squelched the urge to grin, unable to decide if the constable was irritated with the prince, the baron, or himself. He knew one thing for certain. The Russian prince was a squealing little weasel.

"What happened to Yuri?" Crazy Eddie asked, gesturing toward the door. "Is he in trouble?"

"I will ask the questions," Amadeus told the baron. "What do you know about those assassination attempts?"

The baron's expression became mulish. "I know nothing."

"You are involved somehow," Alexander spoke up. "Tell us the truth."

"I swear I know nothing."

Amadeus folded his arms across his chest. Glancing at Alexander, he said, "Tell me again what Eddie said at the golf match."

Alexander stared at the baron. "He said the stupid bastard hit him."

"Which implies you"—the constable looked at the baron—"know who the shooters are. What do you say to that?"

"I say I know nothing," Eddie repeated, "and you cannot prove otherwise."

Alexander closed the distance between them in three

steps. Reaching out with both hands, he lifted the baron out of the chair and shoved him against the wall.

"We know your activities." Alexander yanked a diamond and gold cufflink from the baron's exposed sleeve, ripping the shirt in the movement. He held the jeweled cufflink in front of the baron's face. "Your father gambled, and your insubstantial inheritance could not have covered the price of this quality."

"If the baron knows nothing," Amadeus said, "beating him won't help."

Alexander released Eddie and walked away, pocketing the jeweled cufflink.

"You may leave now," the constable told the baron.

Crazy Eddie straightened his waistcoat and jacket. "My cufflink, please."

Alexander whirled around, a growl in his throat and a sneer on his face. "I am keeping it as a reminder of your lies."

"One of my runners will return the cufflink as soon as Alex calms himself," Amadeus assured the baron.

"He tore my shirt," Eddie complained.

"We will reimburse you," Amadeus added.

"See that you do." Eddie walked out the door, grumbling about the need to return home to make himself presentable.

When the door clicked shut behind him, Amadeus looked at Barney. "Do not let the runners lose him."

"I understand, Boss." Barney left the office in a hurry.

Amadeus looked at Alexander. "Excellent job. If the marquis business fails, you have a future as a pugilist."

Alexander smiled. "I'll go see Raven now."

Sitting inside his grandfather's coach, Alexander relaxed on a seat made in the softest leather money could buy. The jaunt to the enclave of the wealthy across town would waste thirty minutes in snarled weekday traffic.

Alexander closed his eyes, his thoughts drifting to Raven. The constable's confidence in her psychic ability would please her.

Conjuring her image in his mind's eye, Alexander saw a tranquil picture of serene femininity sitting in the idyllic setting of the duke's garden on this glorious summer's day. She would be wearing a virginal white morning gown and, perhaps, holding freshly cut blossoms in her hands. He would pass her the cufflink, explaining that the constable requested it, and she would gift him with a sweet smile.

"My lord?"

Alexander opened his eyes and saw his driver standing at the coach's open door. He had arrived at Inverary House.

"Good afternoon, Tinker," Alexander said when the majordomo opened the door. "I hope Raven is home."

"Good day to you, my lord." Tinker stepped aside to allow him entrance. "Miss Raven is in the garden."

"I know the way."

Alexander walked down the corridor toward the rear of the mansion, smiling that the image he had conjured was proving true. Opening the garden door, he heard two female voices raised in anger. Raven and Blaze stood facing each other while Puddles the mastiff conducted his business against the duchess's rosebush. Not precisely the scene he had envisioned.

"No blond friends today, traitor girl?" Blaze was asking.

"The gruesome sight of your revolting red hair sickened them," Raven countered, "or perhaps they feared catching your freckles."

"Why, you—" Blaze pushed her.

Raven fell backwards into the mastiff's mess. "Oh, this gown is ruined." She leaped up and tossed a clump of grass and dirt at her sister.

"Good afternoon, ladies," Alexander called, preventing

further combat, and sauntered toward them. "I use the term loosely, of course."

"If I were you," Blaze said, passing him on her way inside, "I would reconsider marrying my sister."

"Thank you for the advice, Freckles."

Alexander crossed the garden to Raven, who had dropped onto a stone bench. "You smell sweet," he teased her. "Are you wearing a new fragrance?"

"Essence of Puddles." Raven looked at him, her eyes brimming with tears. "When will this be finished?"

"Very soon."

"How do you know?"

"I know because I know," Alexander echoed the words she spoke whenever he questioned her alleged psychic ability.

"Are you making fun of me?"

"Would I do that?"

"Yes."

"Calm yourself, Brat." Alexander reached into his pocket. "The constable requests a reading on this cufflink."

With a satisfied smile, Raven reached for the cufflink and cupped it in her hands on her lap. She closed her eyes and breathed deeply.

Alexander studied her lovely face. Perfectly arched eyebrows. A small nose slightly tilted up at its tip. Irresistible courtesan lips. Stubbornly etched chin.

"What do you feel?" he asked.

"I feel you staring at me," she answered.

Alexander smiled at that. "I meant, what feeling do you get from the cufflink?"

"Its owner knows and relishes other people's secrets and weaknesses," Raven told him.

"Does the owner have knowledge of the assassination attempts against the prince and the contessa?"

"Murder for hire," Raven answered. "The owner ordered a halt to more attempts for reasons I cannot glean."

"Where did he purchase the cufflink," Alexander teased her.

Raven opened her eyes and looked at him. "He won the cufflinks dicing."

Your son will not thank you for tossing his birthright away.

Sitting in her studio, Katerina pondered her brother's words instead of focusing on the task in front of her, the Flambeau girl's betrothal ring. Hektor had been correct about many things lately, especially his warning about dragons breathing fire. How had she dared to think of outsmarting Drako? The prince did know her better than she knew herself.

Katerina knew she needed to tell Drako about the child she was carrying. Sooner rather than later. How long could she wait on the off-chance that he would reveal the identity of the man who had destroyed her family? She could not live with a guilty conscience if she ruined her own child's future. On the other hand, could she live with her conscience if she failed to keep her graveside promise?

Telling the prince about the baby could buy her time, discouraging his pursuit of more suitable society ladies. How humiliating and scandalous to be caught by pregnancy. Once she revealed her condition, the prince would hold the upper hand in their relationship. Or had he already gained the upper hand when she bedded him?

If only she had an older female relative like the duchess. She was no sophisticated widow and shockingly inexperienced handling gentlemen, the reason she had always remained aloof.

Katerina heard Viveka giggling in the courtyard and

smiled. She could not love the little girl more even had she given birth to her. What would Viveka think about a baby brother or sister? What would she say when Viveka began asking questions about her own father? She did not relish the idea of telling Viveka about her shadowy origins. Perhaps she could keep the lie alive that Viveka's father had died. No one needed to know the truth, not even Viveka.

Other voices in the courtyard penetrated her thoughts. Masculine voices.

Rising from her workbench, Katerina peered out the window. Hektor and Drako stood together while men piled lumber on one section of lawn.

Lumber?

Clapping her hands in glee, Viveka gamboled around and around. Her two nannies tried to keep the little girl out of harm's way.

Katerina removed her leather apron and fingerless gloves, tossing them aside. She marched out of the studio and down the stairs, intending to discover what was happening. Crossing the courtyard in their direction, Katerina saw her brother whisper to the prince.

Drako turned to smile at her. "Good afternoon, my lady."

Katerina did not return his cordial greeting. She had the impression that her brother and the prince were conspiring against her, and she did not need psychic ability to tell her so.

"What is happening here?" she demanded.

"I am building Viveka's tree house," Drako answered, gesturing at the lumber.

"I do not recall asking you to do that," she said.

"Hektor wanted to build a tree house," Drako told her, "and I offered my services."

"So Hektor wanted to build a tree house," Katerina echoed, staring at her brother. "Hektor cannot bother to clean the studio when he finishes working and expects me to clean his mess."

Her brother grinned at her apt description, irritating her even more. This was her home because she paid the bills, yet her brother had invited the prince here and was forcing her to confront her own untenable position.

There was nothing she could do now. Her daughter was standing a few feet away and listening to their conversation.

Drako held a rolled parchment. "Do you want to see my plans?"

"No, thank you."

Looking uncertain, Viveka sidled up to her and tugged on her skirt. "Mummy Zia, prince building me tree house. What fun!"

"What fun, indeed." Katerina managed a smile for her daughter and then looked at her brother. "Watch that Viveka does not get injured."

"Sister, I am no idiot."

"You could have fooled me." Cursing in Russian, Katerina walked toward her studio and, disappearing inside, slammed the door behind.

She knew her behavior was churlish, but she felt tired and cranky and queasy. Carrying your lover's child was not as wonderfully romantic as society matrons implied. Most likely, they lied because no maidens would marry if they knew the truth.

Sitting at her workbench, Katerina willed herself to forget the prince in her courtyard, but the sounds of sawing and hammering and her daughter's giggles ruined her concentration. At this rate, Raven Flambeau will have been married for many years before her betrothal ring was delivered.

Katerina surrendered to the inevitable. She stowed her materials away and retreated to her bedchamber.

Without bothering to remove her gown, Katerina lay across her bed. She could not allow the prince to steal her focus. Since tree houses could not be built in a day, Drako would be working in her courtyard for a week or two or more.

Katerina decided to ignore his presence until she was ready to tell him about the baby. Her avoidance could encourage him to reveal what she needed to know.

After her customary sickness the following morning, Katerina dressed with care in the unlikely event she saw the prince. She enjoyed a late breakfast alone and went to her studio to work on the Flambeau betrothal ring.

The courtyard was silent. Katerina wondered if Drako had given up the idea of building the tree house. Viveka would be devastated if he did.

And then Katerina heard the masculine voice in the courtyard. Doubting the prince made her feel guilty. She should have known he would never disappoint her daughter.

The sounds of sawing and hammering comforted her today. During lulls in work, she could hear her daughter's conversation—asking questions, telling little girl stories, giggling. The scene seemed so . . . so *domestic*.

A knock on the door drew her attention, and Dudley walked into the studio. "My lady, His Highness wondered if you would care to survey their progress and enjoy a picnic with them."

"No, thank you."

"May I bring you anything?" the majordomo asked. "Tea, perhaps?"

"No, thank you, Dudley."

Katerina wanted to join the building party but had decided to avoid the prince. She refused to weaken now.

Resuming her work, Katerina discovered that focusing

proved impossible. She rose from her workbench and wandered to the window.

Hand in hand, Drako and Viveka were walking together and deep in conversation. Wearing an expression of adoration, Viveka appeared enthralled by whatever Drako was saying.

Katerina felt a wrenching tug on her heartstrings. She had not realized how much her daughter needed a father. Though she knew other children had daddies, Viveka had accepted without question that her own daddy had died. In fact, Katerina knew she had discouraged her daughter asking those unanswerable questions.

Unexpectedly, Viveka glanced at the window and called, "Mummy Zia, come and play with us."

Katerina suffered the irrational urge to duck. She did not want the prince to think she had been watching him.

"I am working, darling," Katerina called, waving to her. "I will see you later." She returned to her workbench, feeling that she had lost something.

Windswept rain beating against the window awakened Katerina the following morning. No one would be working in the courtyard that day, much to her relief, giving her space to ponder her problem and her next move.

Katerina felt certain that Drako would call upon her that afternoon. She was wrong. The prince did not visit, nor did he send her a note.

The following day dawned rainy, too. She missed the prince and was beginning to dislike the rain that kept him away from her courtyard.

At breakfast, Katerina did something she had never done before. Dragging the *Times* closer, she read the society gossip column for any mention of Drako. There was nothing.

Katerina wondered where he was and what he was doing. Most important, with whom was he doing it?

Again, the prince did not visit or send her a note. That stole her concentration more than the sawing and hammering. With a heavy heart, Katerina retired early to her bedchamber that night and suffered through a troubled sleep.

Sunshine streaming into the bedchamber window awakened Drako and heartened him. Only his immense willpower had kept him away from Katerina as her brother had advised him. He doubted he would have had the strength to ignore her existence another day.

Hektor's rainy day reports had told him his sister seemed at loose ends. He had even caught her reading the society gossip column, which she never did.

She had missed him. Well, of course, she had missed him. He was a handsome, wealthy prince, blessed with a sparkling sense of humor and a quick wit. If his future wife needed to change him, she could work on his arrogant conceit.

Drako dressed, ate a leisurely breakfast, and then climbed into his coach for the short ride to Trevor Square. He imagined her racing into his arms when he arrived to work on the tree house. Then he realized she was not the racing-into-any-man's-arms type of woman.

The closer the coach got to Trevor Square, the more his confidence waned. Katerina was carrying his baby but had not informed him. *Yet.* His child must be born within the bonds of marriage.

If she did not accept his proposal soon, he would abduct her to Gretna Green and force her—gently, of course—into marriage. A prince needed a legitimate heir, and he had no desire to marry elsewhere.

The coach halted in front of the Lancelot Place mansion. Drako climbed out without waiting for his driver to open the door and banged the knocker.

"Good morning, Your Highness," the majordomo greeted him, stepping aside to allow him entrance.

"Good morning, Dudley."

"Your Highness, my lady wishes to speak with you in the parlor."

Drako climbed the stairs to the second floor. Was this good news or bad? Was she going to tell him about the baby or send him away permanently? Had missing him these past few days opened her mind to the possibilities of marrying for love?

And she *did* love him. Love did not always cause pain. Many couples married and remained loving and caring and faithful for their entire lives.

Drako walked into the parlor, a surprising sight greeting him. Katerina sat on the settee, a pair of knitting needles in her hands.

She looked up and smiled at him. "Good morning."

"The sun shining makes this a glorious morning," Drako said, sauntering across the parlor.

A private conversation, a warm smile, and a cordial greeting boded well. Apparently, she *had* missed him.

Drako gestured to the settee. "May I join you?"

"Yes, of course." Katerina pointed at the completed knitting projects on the table. "What do you think?"

Sitting beside her, Drako studied the uneven stitches. One was a frog's sock and the other would have fit a thoroughbred.

"Interesting shade of blue," Drako said. "What are they?"

"Baby booties," Katerina answered. "I admit my stitching and sizing are a tad off."

Drako stared at the booties. The woman who created incredibly exquisite jewels had knitted these?

"Who is having a baby?"

Katerina hesitated and then looked him straight in the eye. "*We* are having a baby."

Drako dropped his mouth open in surprise, hoping his expression seemed genuine. Lifting the knitting out of her hands, he set it on the table and drew her into his arms.

"Will you marry me, Kat?"

She dropped her gaze to his chest. "No."

"Marry me, Kat."

"No."

"You love me," he said, "and I love you."

Unshed tears glistened in her eyes. "You love me?"

"Madly."

That brought a wobbly smile to her lips. And then the tears slid down her cheeks.

"My loyalties are tearing me into pieces," Katerina told him. "I promised my father I would avenge his death, but my baby needs my protection. Life would be easier if you would tell me the villain's name."

Drako recalled the rivers of tears his mother had shed during her many pregnancies. Now, he emulated his father's gentleness.

"*Our* baby," Drako corrected her. "I dare not reveal his name, but I promise we will work this out together."

"I need comforting," Katerina said, resting her head against his shoulder. "Let us retire to my bedchamber."

"We will not share a bed again until we are husband and wife."

Katerina drew back and looked at him. "That is blackmail."

"Consider it a bribe," Drako said, smiling. "May I escort you and Viveka to the tea party tomorrow?"

"Viveka and I will enjoy your company."

Drako stood then and drew her to her feet. "Take a nap," he suggested, "and join us later for our picnic lunch in the courtyard."

"I must work on Raven Flambeau's betrothal ring," she told him. "I am almost finished."

"And so you will work on the ring after our picnic."

"I will nap later," Katerina said, shaking her head. "The baby puts me to sleep after eating."

"Very well, work now," Drako agreed, "and then we will enjoy a leisurely courtyard picnic with Viveka."

"I cannot believe my brother is actually building a tree house," Katerina said, before turning to walk down the annex hallway to her studio.

Drako winked at her. "Hektor prefers watching more than building."

Chapter Eighteen

"Do I look like a princess?" Viveka asked, touching the tiara on her blond head.

"See for yourself." Katerina took her daughter's hand and led her across the room to the cheval mirror.

The five year old smiled at her own reflection. An awed expression appeared on her face, entranced by the way she looked in her glittering tiara accompanied by her white dress with pink, embroidered flowers.

Her daughter's excitement tugged on Katerina's heartstrings. She had been remiss in seeking companions for the little girl, who desperately needed to socialize with girls her own age.

"I do look like a princess."

"Trust me, Viveka. You *are* a princess." Katerina looked away when a gust of wind rattled the windows. "Let me secure the tiara with clips."

"Princesses do not wear clips," Viveka told her. Her daughter needed everything to be perfect on her coming out day. "The prince is waiting," Katerina said. "Do you want to go to the tea party or admire yourself all day?"

Viveka giggled. "I want the tea party." She paused long

enough to wave good-bye to her reflection, making her mother smile.

With her daughter's hand in hers, Katerina left the bedchamber and walked down the hallway to the top of the stairs. "A lady always makes a grand entrance."

Viveka looked at her. "What is that?"

"We pause on the last landing and wait for the gentlemen to see us," Katerina explained. "Then we walk down the stairs gracefully while the gents admire our beauty."

Mother and daughter descended the stairs to the last landing within sight of the foyer. With their backs to the stairs, Drako and Hektor spoke together while Dudley stood near the door.

"Look at us gents," Viveka called. "We make grand—?"

"Entrance," Katerina whispered.

"Entrance," Viveka finished.

Drako, Hektor, and Dudley turned toward the stairs. All three were smiling.

"Walk slowly," Katerina instructed her daughter, "so the gentlemen can admire us."

"You look beautiful," Drako said, waiting at the bottom of the stairs.

Viveka smiled. "I know."

"When a gentleman says you look pretty," Hektor said, crouching in front of his niece, "you must thank him for noticing. Can you remember that?"

Viveka nodded.

Drako gazed into Katerina's dark eyes. "You look beautiful, too."

"Thank you for noticing."

The majordomo opened the door. "Enjoy your tea party."

"Thank you, Dudley," Viveka answered.

Drako and Katerina exchanged smiles, and then he

escorted them outside. The sun shone, the sky was a vibrant blue, but a strong breeze marred the idyllic day.

"My crown," Viveka cried, a sudden gust of wind taking her tiara.

Drako rescued the prized tiara before it rolled into the street. After helping them into the coach, he wiped the tiara and crowned the little girl.

"I should have clipped the tiara," Katerina said.

"I don't want clips," Viveka whined.

"Too much excitement makes the little ones cranky," Drako said.

Viveka pointed at the packages on the seat beside him. "What is that?"

Drako glanced at the boxes. "That, princess, is a surprise."

"I love surprises." Viveka clapped her hands. "Do you love surprises, Mummy Zia?"

Katerina put her arm around her daughter. "I adore surprises."

The ride to Grosvenor Square was relatively short, no congested downtown traffic to navigate. When the coach halted in front of a mansion, the prince climbed out first and then assisted the ladies. Holding the two boxes in one arm, Drako lifted the lion's head knocker with his free hand and banged it against the door.

"Good afternoon, Your Highness," the majordomo greeted them.

"Good day to you, Boomer," Drako returned the greeting.

"Princess Belle has moved the tea party into the parlor," Boomer told them.

Waving the majordomo away, Drako led them from an outer foyer through French doors to an inner, reception foyer. In the middle of the foyer stood a sculpture of Atlas, holding the world up. A circular staircase rose on one side of the reception foyer.

Belle Flambeau crossed the parlor to greet them. "Welcome to our home."

"Thank you for inviting us," Katerina said.

Belle turned to Drako. "Mikhail has taken refuge at Rudolf's if you would like to join them."

"I prefer the tea party."

Five little girls, ranging in age from four to six, sat watching them from a round table positioned in front of a white marble hearth. There were two empty chairs and place settings awaiting invited guests.

Belle gestured a footman to begin serving and held her hand out to lead Viveka to the table. "Princess Roxanne, this is Viveka. Will you introduce her to the girls?"

"It is *my* tea party," one girl said.

"The eldest, namely *me*, takes precedence over the hostess," Roxanne told her cousin.

"What is *press-see-dents*?" another girl asked in a loud whisper.

"Sister, that means I am in charge," Roxanne answered, and cast her new aunt a smile. "After Princess Belle, of course." Then she began the introductions, pointing to each girl in turn. "These are my sisters, Natasha and Lily. Cousin Bess is our hostess, and here is Cousin Sally. Everyone, this is Viveka."

"We know her name," four-year-old Lily said, rolling her eyes at her eldest sister.

"*Princess* Viveka."

"We are all princesses," Roxanne said, "so we don't bother with titles."

Viveka touched her tiara. "See my crown."

"I don't have a crown," Lily said.

"You *do* have a crown," Drako announced, opening his first package. "I commissioned tiaras for all my little princesses."

The five princesses clapped their hands in pleasure.

"What is commissioned?" Lily asked.

"I don't know," Bess answered.

"Commissioned means made for you," Drako told her.

"Why don't you say *made*?" Lily asked.

He crouched beside her chair, explaining, "Big people use big words so little people will think they are smarter."

The princesses giggled at that.

Deferring to the pecking order, Drako placed a tiara on Roxanne's head first. "Thank you, Uncle Drako." While he circled the table and crowned each princess, Roxanne told Viveka, "Uncle Drako is our cousin, but we call him uncle because he is so old."

"Thank you, Princess Roxanne," Drako said.

"You are welcome, Uncle."

Drako looked at Katerina and winked at her. She smiled, pleased by his behavior. The prince would make an excellent father for their child.

Caught between duty and desire, Katerina regretted her graveside promise. If only she had known this man would walk into her life one day.

A footman served each princess a selection of cookies from a tray and then set the tray in the middle of the table. There were angel cookies with cinnamon and nuts, stuffed meringues, and shortbread hugs and kisses cookies. Another footman poured glasses of lemon barley water. Carrying a tray with tea and accoutrements, the majordomo entered the parlor and set it on the table near the sofas and chairs.

"We will serve ourselves," Belle said. "Thank you, Boomer."

"Mummy Belle baked these cookies," Bess told Viveka.

"Mummy Belle is nice," Viveka said. "My mummy—"

"Your mummy brought *medoviya prianiki*," Drako interrupted, serving each girl from his second box.

"What is it, Uncle?" Roxanne asked.

"*Medoviya prianiki* are honey cookies," he answered. "Russian guests always bring *medoviya prianiki* when they visit."

Five-year-old Natasha took a big bite. "I like honey," she said, her mouth full of cookie.

Four-year-old Lily gave him a flirtatious smile. "I *love* honey."

"Me, too," added five-year-old Sally.

Silence reigned as the princesses ate their cookies. The adults sat nearby and drank their tea.

Wearing a concerned expression, Katerina kept glancing at Viveka. She wanted her daughter to make friends and worried that she had isolated her too much.

"Do not fret," Belle said, as if reading her thoughts. "Making friends requires more than five minutes in each other's company."

"Viveka will do just fine," Drako assured her. Then he raised his voice, calling, "Bess, Viveka likes honey. Do you like honey?"

Bess nodded. "I like candy, too."

"I *love* candy," Viveka exclaimed.

The other princesses loved candy, too. Eating candy was common ground. The six girls began a lively discussion about which candies each of them loved best.

"You see," Drako said, turning to Katerina. "I solved the problem. You can relax and enjoy the visit, too."

"Princess Viveka, do you have sisters?" Roxanne asked, once the candy conversation died away.

Viveka shook her head. "No."

"I wish I didn't," Lily whispered to Bess, earning frowns from Roxanne and Natasha.

"Do you have any nasty brothers?" Natasha asked her. "No."

"Cousins?" Sally asked.

"No."

"Do you have any friends?" four-year-old Lily asked.

"I have one uncle, two aunts, and a fairy godfather," Viveka told them, "but I have no friends."

"Who is your fairy godfather?" Bess asked.

"His name is Dudley and he guards the door."

Six-year-old Roxanne stared at her. "Why don't you have friends?"

Viveka shrugged. "Mummy never takes me to tea parties."

Bess touched her hand, saying, "I will be your friend."

"Will you?" That perked Viveka up. "You are my first friend."

Princess Roxanne, their undisputed queen, took charge of the situation by gesturing around the table. "We are your friends, too."

Viveka laughed. "I like friends."

Watching them, Katerina felt tears brimming in her eyes. She could not quite control herself, though, and droplets streamed down her cheeks.

"Do not weep," Drako whispered, leaning close to wipe the tears from her cheeks. "You will upset her."

Viveka pointed at the empty chair beside her. "Who sits there?"

"I do."

"Uncle Stepan," the five princesses cried.

Prince Stepan Kazanov crossed the parlor, nodding at the three adults before he joined his nieces. He sat in the empty chair beside Viveka's, asking, "Who is this beautiful young lady?"

"Thank you for noticing," Viveka said, making her mother and Drako smile.

"Uncle, meet Princess Viveka," Roxanne introduced them.

"The pleasure is mine, Princess Viveka." Stepan feigned disappointment. "I do not have a crown."

"You can borrow mine." Viveka placed her crown on his head.

"Thank you, Viveka." Stepan placed a sample of cookies on his plate. "Mmm, I love *medoviya prianiki*."

"Mummy brought them," Viveka said.

"Good cookies, Countess Kat and Mummy Belle," Stepan called over his shoulder. "I wish my wife could bake like you."

Belle laughed. "Stepan, you are incorrigible."

"What is that?" four-year-old Bess asked.

"Incorrigible means naughty." Stepan looked at six-year-old Roxanne. "Speaking of naughty, what is the latest gossip?"

"Well . . ." Roxanne waited until everyone's attention fixed on her. "Lord Naughty and Lady Begood danced *five* times at the ball."

"How scandalous," Stepan said, illiciting giggles from his nieces. "Do you know any gossip, Sally?"

The five year old nodded. "The Earl of Goodness offered for Princess Sunshine."

"Did Sunshine accept?"

"Who would refuse an earl?" five-year-old Natasha asked, sounding like her great-aunt, the Duchess of Inverary. "Goodness and Sunshine are an item."

"Bess, do you know any gossip?" Stepan asked the tea party hostess.

"Viveka is my new friend."

"That *is* exciting." The prince turned to his last niece. "Lily?"

"Nana Nasty went to the Earl of Rotten's funeral," Lily told him. "She wanted to be certain he was really dead."

Stepan laughed, and the little girls laughed with him. "Who told you that gossip?"

"Daddy."

"Princess Viveka," Stepan said, turning to the five-year-old, "do you know any gossip?"

Katerina smiled when her daughter blushed beneath the prince's attention.

Viveka pointed at Drako. "That man is my new daddy."

Katerina coughed, her own blush darker than her daughter's. Drako chuckled at her reaction.

"Tell me more," Stepan said.

"Prince is going to marry my mummy."

Stepan nodded. "Then Prince will be your daddy."

"And . . ." Blossoming beneath the attention, Viveka mimicked Roxanne's dramatic flair. "Mummy is giving me a baby sister or brother."

All the princesses clapped at that.

Stepan glanced over his shoulder, saying, "Welcome to the family and congratulations on the newest addition."

Katerina was mortified, her face hot, her complexion scarlet. She glared at Drako, who had spoken to her daughter without her permission.

"Oops," Viveka said. "It was a secret."

Too long without attention on herself, Princess Roxanne assured her, "We can keep a secret."

"Lily cannot keep secrets," Natasha reminded her older sister.

"I want to tell Daddy," Lily said.

"If you tell Daddy," Natasha said, "I will tell Mummy."

Prince Stepan rose from his chair and set the tiara on Viveka's head. Then he ended his visit in his usual manner, circling the table to give each niece a peck on the cheek, saying, "I love you and you and you and you and you."

Reaching Viveka, Stepan bowed over her hand. "Thank you for the gossip, Princess Viveka. I love you, too, because you are so pretty."

"Thank you for noticing."

Silence descended after Prince Stepan departed. The six little girls resumed eating their cookies.

"Nothing will leave this house," Belle assured Katerina. "The Kazanovs can keep a secret."

"What happened to your old daddy?" Roxanne was asking Viveka.

She shrugged and looked over her shoulder at her mother. "Mummy, what happened to my old daddy?"

"He stopped breathing." That seemed to satisfy the princesses.

Katerina could not contain her annoyance a moment longer. "You should not have discussed marriage and babies with my daughter unless I was present."

Drako gave her a charming smile. "Kat dear, this is neither the time nor the place."

At the tea party's end, Drako held Viveka's hand as they descended the stairs to the foyer. Frowning with displeasure, Katerina walked beside them.

"Mummy Zia, are you angry with me?" Viveka asked.

Katerina managed a smile for her daughter. "No, darling, I could never become angry with you."

Viveka gave her a worried look. "I told a big secret."

"The secret slipped out by accident," Katerina told her, as they reached the sidewalk. She gave the prince an arch look. "Telling secrets on purpose is naughty."

In growing irritation, Drako turned to her. "Can this wait until we return home?"

"You should not have shared our secret with anyone, especially my daughter," Katerina said. "Furthermore, I do not need you to pretend I baked those cookies."

"I lied for me," Drako told her, "because I do not want my cousins to know I enjoy baking and cooking."

"Viveka, no." Katerina brushed past him.

Drako whirled around to see Viveka chasing her windblown tiara into the street.

A coach, driven at breakneck speed, careened down the road toward her. Even as he began moving, Drako realized he could not reach the child or the mother in time to prevent a tragedy.

Two hulking bodies materialized from nowhere. One grabbed the child out of harm's way while the other hooked his arm around the mother at the last possible second and yanked her back. All four landed in the dirt.

Sitting on the side of the road, Katerina pulled Viveka into her arms and clutched her against her chest. She rocked her weeping daughter back and forth and wept with her.

Watching them, Drako felt an insistent tugging on his heartstrings. He had almost lost his most precious possessions, the mother and the daughter.

"I lost my crown," Viveka sobbed.

A beefy hand offered her the tiara. "No, baby girl, here's ya crown."

Drako helped Katerina stand and lifted Viveka out of her arms. Then he turned to the two men. "Thank you, sirs, for risking your lives to save my ladies."

"Ya very welcome, Ya Highness," one of them said, and the other nodded.

"You know who I am?" Drako asked, surprised.

"These miscreants know you well," said a familiar voice. "They have been watching you for weeks."

Drako whirled around in surprise.

"Cuff them," Alexander Blake was ordering the constable's runners.

"I do not understand," Drako said. "What are you doing here?"

Alexander Blake glanced at Katerina. "Put your ladies in the coach, Kazanov, and then we will speak."

"Are you certain you are well?" Drako asked, escorting Katerina to the coach.

"I have been badly frightened," she answered, "but

otherwise I am well." When he dropped his gaze to her mid-section, she added, "*We* are well."

When Drako returned to his side, Alexander told him, "That near-miss was no accident, and I am bringing those two downtown for questioning."

"I insist on witnessing that," Drako said.

"Take the countess home," Alexander told him. "The constable and I will wait until you arrive."

An hour later, a grim-faced Drako sat inside his coach en route to the Central Criminal Court Building. He had ordered Katerina not to move, but she was so shaken, he doubted she would ever leave her house again.

Opposite him sat Hektor, who would not be denied accompanying him. He could not fault the younger man for that.

Arriving at the Central Criminal Court Building, Drako knocked on the constable's office door and then entered without waiting for permission. Hektor walked two steps behind him.

"Thank you for allowing me to be present," Drako said, shaking the constable's hand. "Meet the countess's brother Hektor."

Looking uncomfortable, the brothers sat in chairs placed in front of the constable's desk. They appeared too frightened to move.

Alexander Blake leaned against the window sill, his arms folded across his chest. Beside him stood Barney, the constable's man in charge of the runners.

"Before the questioning begins," Drako said, turning to the brothers, "I want to thank you again for saving the countess and her daughter."

Both men nodded, acknowledging his gratitude. Neither spoke, though, apparently frightened by the famous constable and their surroundings.

"Scratchy, tell us about the assassination attempts," Amadeus Black said.

"I doan know nuthin', guv," the man answered.

"What do you have to say, Itchy?" Alexander asked.

"We saved the baby girl's life," the brother answered, "but I doan know nuthin' neither about t'other."

"The constable's runners have been watching you," Alexander said, "while you have been watching the prince and the countess."

"We din touch 'em," Scratchy said. "Watchin' ain't a crime."

Itchy nodded. "He tole us jus' watch, no touchin'."

Scratchy scowled at his brother. "Nobody likes a snitch."

"I ain't a snitch."

"Who is *he*?" Amadeus asked.

Both brothers remained stubbornly silent.

"*He* may be regretting his involvement," Drako said. "If you tell us his identity, the constable can persuade him to share his knowledge. Consider it saving little Viveka from an untimely death another day."

"Well, we doan want ta see baby girl hurt," Scratchy said. "Do us, brother?"

Itchy shook his head. "I like bein' a hero."

"'Twas Baron Shores what hired us," Scratchy told them.

Constable Black looked at Barney. "Find Crazy Eddie and bring him here."

"Thank you for telling us," Drako said.

"You will not regret saving my sister's and my niece's lives," Hektor added.

An hour later, Barney returned with Baron Shores. Crazy Eddie stopped short when he saw the brothers. "Ah, shit," he swore.

"Get a couple of runners to guard Scratchy and Itchy in another room," Constable Black instructed Barney. "Sit here, Baron Shores." He gestured to the chair vacated by

Scratchy. "I know you hired the brothers. Tell me who hired you."

Eddie shifted uncomfortably in his chair. "Snitching is bad for my businesses."

"Murder for hire is not one of your usual ventures," Amadeus remarked. "Tell me everything, or it will go worse for you."

"I cannot say precisely who hired me." When Drako growled and stepped toward him, Eddie held his hand up and continued, "However, I did report to this bloke every week at The Guinea on Bruton Place. Curiosity got the better of me so I followed him one night. As it turns out, this bloke is the Russian ambassador's majordomo."

Amadeus Black looked at his assistant. "Alex, fetch the ambassador's majordomo."

"Wait," Drako stopped him. "We must discuss something before you do that. *Privately*. Only Alex and Hektor can hear this."

Amadeus stared at him for a long moment, and Drako felt relieved that he had not committed any crime. Finally, the constable nodded, saying, "Barney, escort Eddie to another office and guard him."

Alexander reached into his pocket and then passed Eddie his cufflink. "By the way, where did you purchase the cufflinks?"

"I won them dicing," Eddie said, and walked out the door.

Alexander dropped his mouth open in surprise. "I thought she was joking."

"Who was joking about what?" Amadeus asked him.

"I asked Raven where Eddie purchased the cufflinks," Alexander answered. "She said he had won them dicing."

Constable Black arched a brow at him. "Are you prepared to drop your skeptical attitude?"

"Hell, no." Alexander grinned. "I enjoy tormenting her with my skepticism."

"Your Highness," Amadeus Black said, "what do you want to discuss?"

"Yuri and Anya, as well as her blond friends, are involved," Drako said, "which is the reason both Kat and I were threatened." He paused, wondering how much he needed to reveal in order to persuade the constable to agree to his plan.

"And?" Amadeus prodded him.

Drako sat in one of the vacant chairs and gestured Hektor into the other. "Five years ago in Moscow, a certain person caused the deaths of the countess's father, sister, and brother. Since then, she has been waiting for revenge."

Hektor chuckled. "Kat thought Drako was the villain and had planned on killing him."

Drako looked from the constable to Alexander to Hektor. "Prince Yuri is the guilty party."

"Yuri?" Hektor echoed.

Drako ignored him. "Blake, we can resolve both situations if Raven and you can overlook a bit of chaos at your betrothal party."

Alexander shrugged. "I don't mind, and Raven wants this ended as soon as possible."

"Thank you." Drako looked at the constable. "Is it possible to keep Eddie and the brothers in custody until the party and wait until that day to interrogate the majordomo?"

"I can do anything," Amadeus answered. "No one will dare question London's famous constable."

"Thank you again," Drako said. "I want all parties involved in both situations brought together at the ball."

"Do you want me to unload Kat's pistol?" Hektor asked.

The constable frowned. "The countess shoots a pistol?"

"I have never seen her shoot," Hektor answered, "but she does own a pistol."

"Unloading the pistol will arouse her suspicions." Drako looked at the constable. "I guarantee Kat will kill no one."

"This is risky business," Amadeus said. "How can you guarantee she won't pull the trigger?"

"Kat will not endanger the baby."

"What baby?"

"*Our* baby." Drako grinned at the other man. "I am going to be a father."

Chapter Nineteen

"I do not like this."

"Neither do I."

Drako looked at his brothers, Lykos and Gunter, sitting opposite him in their coach. Tomorrow was the Flambeau-Blake betrothal ball, and he worried that the Blond Brigade would decide not to attend. After all, Raven was the third Flambeau sister to catch a title this season, and no gentleman had shown more than a passing interest in the blondes.

His plan would fail if the blondes preferred to remain home instead of facing another loss. Only Lykos and Gunter could provide the right incentive for the blondes to attend the Inverary ball, but he did not want his brothers to appear less than sincere and arouse the blondes' suspicions. The fewer who knew the plan, the better the plan would work.

"I understand your reticence," Drako said, "but I need your assistance."

"I dislike lying to females," Lykos said.

Drako cocked a dark brow at his brother. "Are you implying you have never lied to a female?"

"Well," Lykos hedged, "I dislike lying but did not mean I had never done it."

"I dislike lying, too," Drako agreed, "but sometimes it is necessary."

"Why are we doing this?" Gunter asked.

"You will understand at the ball," Drako answered, and ignored their grimaces.

"I had planned to invite Blaze Flambeau to go down to supper with me," Lykos said.

"I promise you will not need to sup with Lavinia Smythe," Drako told him. "You need only ask her to supper."

"You miss the point," Gunter said, smiling. "Lykos cannot ask two ladies to supper, and by the time he can invite Blaze, Ross MacArthur will already have invited her."

"Eating supper together is not a lifetime commitment," Drako said. "There will be other suppers. I need your help."

"You can count on me," Lykos said, reluctance etched across his features.

"If Lykos is inviting Lavinia Smythe to supper," Gunter said, "and I am inviting Cynthia Clarke, who will entice Princess Anya to attend?"

"I will take care of the princess," Drako answered.

Both brothers looked surprised. "That will not please the countess," Lykos said.

"Kat will never know," Drako told him. "She will be focusing her attention on enticing Yuri to attend."

Drako glanced out the coach window when it halted in front of a town mansion. "We have arrived."

Lykos climbed out of the coach. He felt like the wolf for which he was named, hunting a delicate blonde but preferring a red-haired, freckled hellion. That sneaky Scotsman would get to her before him, and he dare not ask two ladies to supper lest they speak. Though there was little chance of that happening because Blaze despised the blondes. Besides, his brother would make him suffer if his plans went awry.

Glancing over his shoulder, Lykos saw his brothers watching him. He nodded and reached for the doorknocker.

The door opened to reveal the Smythe majordomo, who paused for a moment and then stepped aside, allowing entrance to the mansion. "Good afternoon, my lord," the majordomo greeted him, his tone haughty. "Whom did you wish to see?"

Walking into the foyer, Lykos stared at the servant for a long moment. He disliked arrogant servants, who usually served the most plebian masters.

"Your Highness."

"I beg your pardon?" the man said.

"I am Your Highness," Lykos said, passing the man his calling card.

Appearing confused, the majordomo looked from Lykos to the calling card and then blanched. "Please forgive me, Your Highness."

Lykos gave the man his most insincere smile. "Of course, I forgive you."

"Thank you, Your Highness."

"I want to speak with Lavinia Smythe."

"I am sorry, Your Highness," the majordomo said, "but Lady Lavinia is visiting friends this afternoon."

What ill luck. Lykos could not return to the coach without issuing the invitation. "May I speak with Lady Smythe?"

"Please follow me, Your Highness."

Walking down the corridor, Lykos prayed the mother was not entertaining any society hens who would spread the gossip about his visit. He entered the drawing room and found the elder Smythe alone.

Lady Smythe's expression brightened when she saw him. "Welcome to my home, Your Highness." She gestured to a chair. "Join me, please."

The woman glanced at the majordomo, but Lykos anticipated the woman's next move. "No refreshments for me," he told her. "I am on my way to a business meeting."

"What a wonderful surprise," Lady Smythe said, as the

majordomo exited the drawing room. "Lavinia will be disappointed to have missed your visit."

"To tell you the truth," Lykos said, "I was hoping to speak with Lady Lavinia."

Lady Smythe smiled. "Oh?"

"I admire Lady Lavinia," Lykos said, hoping he sounded sincere. "I was intending to ask her to go down to supper with me at the Inverary ball tomorrow night."

"A mother knows her daughter better than anyone," Lady Smythe said, beaming with pleasure. "On her behalf, I accept your invitation."

Lykos felt guilty about lying. "You are certain she will accept?"

"I have no doubts."

Standing to leave, Lykos managed a pleased smile. "Thank you, Lady Smythe. I will be looking forward to tomorrow night."

Lykos flustered the older woman by bowing over her hand. He descended the stairs to the foyer and nodded at the uppity majordomo on his way out. Climbing into the coach, Lykos leaned back against the seat.

"Lavinia was out visiting friends," Lykos told his brothers as the coach eased into traffic. "Her mother accepted on her behalf."

"I suppose you charmed the old lady," Drako said with a smile. "Your smooth sophistication works every time."

"My title did the work this time," Lykos said. "I cannot understand the reason titles impress people. I did nothing to earn it."

"As the Duchess of Inverary says," Drako told him, "immense wealth and a high ranking title makes for a powerful aphrodisiac."

"I wonder how many maidens married a wealthy title and lived to regret it," Gunter said.

Lykos turned his head to look at his younger brother. "You are extraordinarily deep . . . for an idiot."

Drako smiled and looked at the idiot. "You do understand what I want?"

"Of course, I understand," Gunter replied, giving Lykos a sidelong glance. "I am *not* an idiot."

The coach halted in front of the Clarke residence. Gunter hesitated for a moment, giving both brothers a long look. Feeling as if he were going to the gallows, he opened the door and climbed down. He turned to close the door, his gaze meeting his eldest brother's. When Drako made a shooing gesture, Gunter nodded and walked toward the front door.

If his brother's plan failed for any reason, Gunter thought, he would be supping with Cynthia Clarke. The blonde was a pinhead, whose mother would try to trap him into marriage.

Before lifting the knocker, Gunter glanced over his shoulder again. Both Drako and Lykos shooed him into action.

The front door opened, revealing the Clarke majordomo. The man stepped aside, asking, "With whom do you wish to speak, my lord?"

Gunter passed him his calling card. "Please tell Lady Cynthia that Prince Gunter wishes to speak with her."

"I am certain the lady will speak with you, Your Highness," the majordomo said. "Lady Clarke and her daughter are communing in the drawing room. Please follow me."

"I am not going to the Inverary ball!"

Uh-oh. The Clarke girl did not want to attend the ball.

"Sweetheart, you said you liked Raven," Gunter heard the mother reply.

"I do like Raven," Cynthia said, "but I cannot face another Flambeau bastard from nowhere catching a title while I have none."

"You listen to me, you little witch," the mother told her daughter. "Those Flambeau bastards came from an influential duke. You will attend the ball, smile at the Inverarys, and show respect for each of the Flambeau bastards. Do you understand?"

The Clarke majordomo looked at Gunter and rolled his eyes. Gunter smiled and shrugged.

"Excuse me, my lady," the majordomo said, slipping into the drawing room. "Lady Cynthia has a caller."

"I do not want to see anyone," the girl told him.

"I believe you will want to see *this* caller." The man's tone was dry.

Gunter struggled against the urge to laugh. This majordomo was too good for the Clarkes. Perhaps he would hire the man one day.

"Who is asking for Cynthia?"

"Prince Gunter Kazanov."

"A prince is visiting me?" Cynthia exclaimed.

"Please show the prince here."

The mother sounded like the cat who ate the canary. If he wasn't mistaken, *he* was the canary.

The majordomo stepped into the hallway and whispered, "Are you sure you want to visit Lady Cynthia?"

Gunter did laugh, then. "There is no need to announce me."

Mother and daughter wore beaming smiles. Gunter did not know if their flushed complexions were the result of arguing or his unexpected arrival.

"Good afternoon, Your Highness," Cynthia greeted him, a hungry look in her gaze.

"Please be seated," Lady Clarke said.

"Thank you, but I cannot stay," Gunter said, and noted the girl's expression droop. "I am on my way to a business meeting, and my brothers are waiting in the coach."

"I see." Lady Clarke wore an insincere smile. "How may we help you?"

Gunter cleared his throat and looked at the younger woman. "I wondered, Lady Cynthia, if you would do me the honor of going down to supper with me at the Inverary ball. If you are not otherwise engaged, of course."

The droop disappeared. "I would enjoy supping with you, Your Highness."

"Please, call me Gunter."

"Thank you, Your . . ." Cynthia blushed. "I mean Gunter. You may call me Cynthia."

"I will look forward to our supper, Cynthia." Gunter smiled at both women and left the drawing room.

In the foyer, the majordomo opened the door for him, saying, "Good luck, Your Highness, I pray you do not get indigestion."

Gunter burst out laughing. "I am made of stronger stuff than that, my good man."

"I hope so."

Outside, Gunter climbed into the coach and leaned back against the leather cushion. He closed his eyes, took a deep breath, and then opened them again when his brothers chuckled.

"Well?" Drako asked.

"Mission accomplished," Gunter told him. "You were correct, though. I overheard Cynthia telling her mother she refused to attend the Inverary ball. My invitation changed her mind."

"Thank you, brothers," Drako said. "I will drop you at White's after I speak with Anya."

"I need a vodka," Gunter said.

"Drop us before you speak to Anya," Lykos said.

"I do not want to be in her company longer than necessary," Drako said, shaking his head. "Your waiting in the coach gives me an excuse to leave."

When their coach halted in front of the Russian ambassador's home, Lykos asked, "What will you do if you see Yuri?"

"I will ignore him," Drako answered. "Yuri's reckoning for past deeds is scheduled for tomorrow night."

Exiting the coach, Drako marched up the stairs to the front door and banged the knocker. He smiled at the majordomo's surprised expression and, without waiting for an invitation, brushed past the man.

"I want to speak with Princess Anya," Drako said, unnecessarily passing the man his calling card.

The majordomo did not bother to pretend ignorance of Drako's identity. "The princess is in the garden," he said. "Please follow me, Your Highness."

"No."

The majordomo looked confused. "I beg your pardon?"

"I will not follow you," Drako said, assuming his most imperious tone. "Fetch the princess to me."

"Yes, Your Highness." The man hurried down the corridor.

Within mere minutes, Princess Anya arrived in the foyer. "Your Highness, this is an unexpected surprise." Her smile was gracious and thoroughly insincere.

"If you are not otherwise engaged," Drako said without preamble, "I would like you to go down to supper with me at the Inverary ball."

Anya narrowed her blue gaze on him, her suspicions apparent. "What about the Contessa de Salerno?"

"Katerina Garibaldi?" Drako frowned. "What about her?"

"Your defection may annoy the contessa," Anya said.

"Ah, you misunderstand our relationship," Drako said, his expression clearing. "The contessa and I are friends and business associates."

She arched a blond brow at him. "Business associates?"

"The contessa is a jeweler," Drako reminded her, "and I own several gem companies and mines."

That answer satisfied the princess. Her expression

cleared, her smile sincere. "I had forgotten," she said. "In that case, I will accept your supper invitation."

"Thank you, princess." Drako bowed over her hand, giving her his best smoldering look. "I look forward to our supper."

"Would you care to stay for tea?" Anya invited him.

"I would like nothing better," Drako answered. "However, I and my brothers—waiting in the coach—are late for a business meeting."

Returning to the coach, Drako looked at his brothers. "That went well. Now I only need Kat to take action, and all will be set for tomorrow night."

Drako dropped his brothers at White's and went directly to Trevor Square. Baiting Katerina into his trap was his final task of the day. Drako prayed he had not misjudged her, thinking she would choose their baby and him over deadly retaliation. He would worry until she showed her mettle on the following night.

"Good afternoon," Drako greeted the majordomo.

"Good afternoon, Your Highness." Dudley passed him a sealed missive. "Your arrival has saved my courier a trip to Grosvenor Square."

Drako stared at the note in his hand, almost reluctant to open it. Breaking the seal, he read the short message and smiled.

"Good news, Your Highness?"

"No news, Dudley. The countess wants to speak to me."

"Her Ladyship is in the parlor."

Drako took the stairs two at a time. His lady had something on her mind. Was it a good something? Or bad?

Pausing in the doorway, Drako smiled at her expression of consternation. She was trying to knit those damn baby booties again.

Katerina looked up and smiled when he started to cross the parlor toward her. "Sit here," she invited, patting the upholstered sofa.

Drako dropped down beside her. "How do you feel?"

"I feel fine," Katerina answered. "The sickness strikes me in the morning."

Slipping his arm around her shoulders, Drako drew her against his muscular frame, pausing to plant a chaste kiss on her mouth. "You wanted to speak to me?"

"I have made a decision about us," Katerina said, gazing into his blue eyes. "I will marry you."

Holding her close, Drako dipped his head to kiss her, whispering, "Thank you, Kat, for making me the happiest man in England."

"Thank you for making me a happy woman," she returned the compliment.

"I reached a decision, too," he told her. "Prince Yuri is the man who destroyed your family."

"Yuri?"

Drako nodded. "Speak truthfully, Kat, can you live without your revenge?"

Katerina stared at him for a long moment. "A cautious gentleman would have asked that question before revealing the man's identity."

Uh-oh. Did she suspect his ploy?

"Love makes me careless."

That made her smile. "I love you and our baby enough not to kill him."

"Thank you, sweetheart."

Drako suppressed the urge to laugh. His lady was so wonderfully predictable. Technically, she had not answered his specific question, precluding his naming her a liar when she acted upon the information.

"What do you think of my knitting now?" Katerina asked, changing the subject.

Drako glanced at the uneven stitches. "I think we will honeymoon on Bond Street to purchase whatever our baby needs."

"That bad, huh?"

"Do not give up your jewelry design business," Drako teased her. He stood then, saying, "I must leave to meet my brothers at White's. By the way, I will be attending a business meeting at Inverary's before the ball, but I will leave early to escort you."

"Do not bother about that," Katerina said. "My coachman will drive me, and you can bring me home."

"Until tomorrow evening." Drako quit the parlor and retraced his steps to the foyer where he paused to speak with Dudley. "The countess will be ordering a courier to deliver a note to Prince Yuri. If she fails to do that, send me a note in the morning."

"You can depend upon me, Your Highness."

"By the way, I bought the mansion next door and plan to make a ballroom there, the grandest ballroom in London."

Dudley smiled. "Oh, happy day."

"Good evening, Tinker."

"Good evening, my lady." The Inverary majordomo greeted her, his gaze touching her violet silk gown and the hundreds of diamonds she wore on her ears, wrists, fingers, and in her hair. "Forgive my boldness, but you are the most spectacularly beautiful lady in attendance tonight."

"Thank you for noticing," Katerina echoed her daughter's words. "You could say I dressed to kill."

"I daresay you will break many hearts tonight."

"Tinker, I consider you a national treasure."

"Thank you for noticing." The majordomo winked at her and then turned to announce her arrival. "The Contessa de Salerno."

Revenge will not breathe life into the dead, Katerina reminded herself, pausing at the top of the stairs. *Setting limits is the road to winning all.*

Katerina scanned the ballroom before joining the elite throng. Drako was waltzing with Princess Anya, Lykos was partnering Lavinia Smythe, and Gunter was stepping onto the dance floor with Cynthia Clarke.

How interesting. Something was definitely amiss here, but she needed to go forward with her plan.

Spying her quarry at the far end of the enormous chamber, Katerina walked into the crush of guests and circled the dance floor. She ignored the greetings from friends and acquaintances, her focus on the blond gentleman.

"Your Highness."

Prince Yuri whirled around, his expression a mingling of relief and irritation. "Good evening, my lady." He bowed over her hand in exaggerated courtly manner. "I despaired of seeing you this evening."

"Tonight is ours," she said, her voice a seductive purr. "I brought you a gift."

His irritation vanished. "One of your priceless gems, my lady?"

Katerina reached into her reticule. In a flash of movement, she drew her pistol and pointed it at his head.

Several women screamed, drawing the crowd's attention. Guests began backing away out of the line of fire.

"What are you doing?" Yuri demanded, his expression of fear at odds with his harsh tone.

"Pulling this trigger will separate your royal head from your royal body," Katerina answered, her smile serene. She could not quite keep her hand from shaking like the palsy.

"What have I ever done to—?"

"My name is Katerina *Pavlova* Garibaldi." She noted his stunned recognition. "Justice has been delayed too long."

"You do not understand," he whined.

"Die like a man instead of a weasel."

Without warning, a masculine hand materialized from

behind her, covering her hand on the pistol, but did not snatch it away. "Well-mannered ladies do not point pistols, darling."

Drako.

"The coward deserves to die for his crimes against my family," Katerina said, without turning to look at him.

"His Highness does deserve punishment," Drako agreed, "but death by pistol is too quick and so messy."

"My fingers itch to finish what he started five years ago," Katerina said.

"Do you love me enough to listen before executing the weasel?" Drako whispered against her ear.

"Speak."

"Do you trust me enough to lower the pistol while I speak?"

"No, duty before desire." Katerina tightened her grip on the pistol, her finger on the trigger. "I will handle this myself, darling."

Silent indecision.

Katerina could feel her beloved's tension, his hand remaining on hers. And then his hand lifted up and away, proving his trust in her.

"Do not move," Drako warned the other prince, "or I will kill you myself. Kat darling, do what you will."

"Kazanov, do not let her shoot me."

"Tell these lovely people about Alina," Katerina ordered him.

Yuri stared at her for a long moment and then mumbled, "I dishonored her sister."

"Louder."

"I dishonored her sister." His voice carried to the far corners of the silent ballroom.

"My sister died because of you," she said. "Now tell them about Ilya."

"Her brother challenged me to a duel," Yuri told the listening guests, "and I killed him."

"You shot my brother in the back," Katerina accused him.

"Yes I did," Yuri admitted.

Shocked gasps rippled through the assembly. Pockets of masculine murmurs broke out here and there.

"Losing two children in one day killed my father," Katerina said, once the murmurs faded. "Did you know that?"

"I–I had left Moscow."

"You are a spineless coward who preys on unsuspecting women and shoots boys in the back," Katerina said. "I will give you the choice you denied my brother. Shall I shoot you in the face or the back?"

"Kazanov, stop her."

Drako remained silent.

"Are you afraid to die?" Katerina asked him. "Why do you not kneel and plead for your life?"

"Do not shoot me," Yuri said, dropping to his knees.

"I can find no mercy in my heart for you," Katerina told him, moving the pistol to keep it trained on his face.

"Kazanov, stop her. *Please.*"

"Think before you pull the trigger," Drako said, his tension apparent in his voice. "Consider what you will gain and lose."

"I have considered nothing else since yesterday. Which is the reason"—Katerina pulled the trigger and *click*—"I did not load the pistol."

Drako shouted with laughter as did the other guests. For the first time since entering the ballroom, Katerina tore her gaze from Yuri to smile at her beloved.

"Bitch." Yuri lunged at her.

Drako leaped in front of her, his arm already raised. His fist connected with the other prince's mouth, sending him sprawling on the floor.

"Damn you, Kazanov," Yuri groaned, his hand covering his mouth. "You knocked my other front tooth out."

Chapter Twenty

"Come with me, Your Highness." Alexander Blake yanked Yuri to his feet and handed him a handkerchief to cover his bleeding mouth.

"I want to press charges against—"

"Constable Black is waiting to speak with you in His Grace's office," Alexander interrupted, escorting him from the ballroom.

Drako put his arm around Katerina and lifted the pistol out of her hand. "You look pale," he said. "Retire to one of the bedchambers to rest."

"I will see this through to the end," she told him.

"I knew you would say that." Drako glanced around and nodded at his brothers and cousins who began to move discreetly toward the Russian ambassador, Princess Lieven, Lady Smythe, and Lady Clarke. Then he ushered Katerina out of the ballroom, the guests parting for them as they made their way through the crowd.

Drako led Katerina past the constable's runners, milling in the corridor, and then into the duke's office. He sat beside her on an upholstered sofa and held her hand.

Constable Amadeus Black and Alexander Blake stood

together in front of the duke's desk. With their arms folded across their chests, both men looked forbidding.

The Duke of Inverary stood near the door, barring entrance to all but the invited. Scratchy, Itchy, Baron Shores, and the Russian ambassador's majordomo sat in chairs positioned on one side of the office where Barney guarded them. Looking unhappy, Prince Yuri stood alone on the opposite side of the office, still holding the marquis's handkerchief against his mouth.

When someone knocked, the Duke of Inverary opened the door a crack and said, "The three young ladies will come inside now, but the adults will wait until summoned."

Princess Anya, Lavinia Smythe, and Cynthia Clarke walked into the room. All three paled when they spied the majordomo.

"I want to be with my daughter," Lady Clarke was telling the duke.

"We demand to know what is happening," Lady Smythe added.

"You will know all soon enough," Inverary told them.

"I protest this treatment," said Princess Lieven, the ambassador's wife.

"Protest all you want, Lieven." The Duke of Inverary shut the door in her face and locked it.

Constable Black looked at the brothers. "Scratchy, tell us your tale."

"The baron hired me and me brother to ass-ass-murder that prince over there and his lady," Scratchy said. "Then the baron says watch'em but doan touch."

"Thank you." Amadeus looked at Crazy Eddie. "Baron Shores?"

"Jeez, I knew this was bad business."

"Delete the editorial," Amadeus ordered, "and tell us the facts."

"This bloke offered me fifty thousand pounds to get

rid of Kazanov and the countess," Crazy Eddie said, gesturing to the majordomo. "One night I followed him and discovered he was the ambassador's majordomo. I told the brothers to watch without touching because I worried the Russians could claim diplomatic immunity once the deed was done, and I would hang on the gallows." He shrugged and smiled. "Fifty thousand pounds means nothing to a dead man."

"Thank you, Baron Shores." Amadeus Black looked at the majordomo. "Boris, tell us your story."

"Prince Yuri ordered me to hire Baron Shores to kill Prince Drako and—"

"How could you do that?" Princess Anya screamed, rounding on her brother. "You knew I wanted to marry him."

"Princess, be quiet." Amadeus gestured to the majordomo.

"Before I could make the connection," Boris said, "Princess Anya ordered me to get someone to murder the countess."

"That is a lie," Anya screeched.

Someone pounded on the door. "I demand to know what is happening."

"Behave yourself, Lieven," the Duke of Inverary called, "or I will order you tossed out of my house for disturbing the peace."

"Did you hear that?" Princess Lieven screeched like her niece.

"For once in your life, keep that mouth shut," the Russian ambassador shouted at his wife, "or I will shut it for you."

"Cynthia and Lavinia made me do it," Anya told the constable.

Lavinia Smythe started to weep, but Cynthia Clarke rounded on the princess. "You hired the murderers, not me."

"The whole affair was your idea," Anya countered.

"My idea was to frighten the countess, not kill her."

"You and Lavinia gave me money to pay the assassins," Anya argued.

"We paid to *frighten* her."

"Enough, ladies." Amadeus Black looked at the duke. "Your Grace, you may invite the others inside."

The Duke of Inverary unlocked the door and beckoned the parents into his office. "You will listen to the constable without interrupting," he warned them, "or you will leave."

"I refuse to listen to anything with those"—Princess Lieven pointed at Scratchy and Itchy—"those filthy beggars in the room."

Amadeus looked at Barney. "Tell the runners to take them away."

Katerina leaned close to Drako, whispering, "I want them to stay."

"The filthy beggars stay," Drako told the constable. "If Lieven does not want to remain in the same room, she can leave and her husband will tell her what transpired."

Princess Lieven rounded on Drako, her face contorted with anger. "I do not want—"

"We do not give a damn what you want," Drako interrupted. "Make up your mind, go or stay."

"I will stay."

Amadeus Black gestured to the four sitting in a row. "These men and your children have confessed to conspiracy to commit murder."

"My Lavinia would never do that," Lady Smythe said, her arm around her weeping daughter.

"Neither would my Cynthia," Lady Clarke said.

"This is a horrible misunderstanding," Princess Lieven insisted.

"There is no mistake," Amadeus Black told them. "Using Boris as a go-between, your children hired those men to assassinate Prince Drako and the Contessa de Salerno."

"I heard their confessions," the Duke of Inverary said. "However, since no lasting harm has been done, Constable Black and the intended victims are amenable to preventing a scandal of epic proportions."

"How do we do that?" the Russian ambassador asked.

"Prince Yuri and Boris will be deported to Moscow," Inverary answered.

"That is no punishment," Katerina whispered.

Drako patted her hand. "Wait and listen."

"A letter has already been sent to the czar informing him that Yuri confessed to murdering the contessa's brother," the duke added. "Letters were also sent to Yuri's creditors announcing that he will soon be returning to Moscow. Anya, Lavinia, and Cynthia will rusticate in the country for one year. Hopefully, the isolation will enable them to ponder the seriousness of their crimes."

"I do not want to rusticate," Anya cried.

"Neither do I," Lavinia agreed.

"How will we find husbands?" Cynthia asked.

"Rusticate in the country for one year," the constable said, "or rusticate in Newgate. The choice is yours."

"The ladies will not correspond with each other," Alexander Blake added. "Newgate awaits those who break the rules."

"You may take these criminals away," the Duke of Inverary told them. "The runners are waiting to escort you to your homes via my back door."

The duke opened the door and beckoned someone. Several runners came into the room to escort the families out.

"What about the newspapers?" the ambassador asked.

"Yuri's murder of the contessa's brother will be reported," the duke answered, "but the conspiracy plot will be squelched."

"How do you know?"

The Duke of Inverary smiled. "My influence extends to the *Times*."

Once the families had gone, Amadeus gestured to the three still sitting in their chairs. "Barney, escort these felons to Newgate."

"You will not send them to Newgate," Katerina said, her commoner roots protesting the law's unfairness.

Amadeus shifted his gaze to her. "I beg your pardon?"

"The aristocrats rusticate in the country while the commoners pay the price?"

"I am not common," Crazy Eddie said, sounding offended.

Katerina looked at him. "I meant, the little people."

"I am a baron, not one of the little people."

"You are one of the stupid people to disagree with a woman trying to keep you out of Newgate."

Crazy Eddie nodded. "You could be correct about that."

"What do you suggest we do with these felons?" the constable asked her.

Katerina looked at Eddie before answering. "How much were you being paid for your services?"

"Fifty thousand pounds."

"The baron must give you one hundred thousand pounds which you will donate to charity," Katerina told the constable. "Do not trust him to pay you later."

"Barney, escort Baron Shores to his residence so he can pay you," Amadeus said. "Take a few runners for protection."

"The banks are closed at this hour," Eddie reminded him.

"The money you make from gambling and other businesses are not deposited in a bank," Alexander said. "Pay the money or go to Newgate."

"I will pay the money." Crazy Eddie left the office with Barney.

Katerina looked at the brothers. "What are your names?"

"I'm Scratchy."

"And I'm Itchy."

"What are your real names?"

"Mum named me Ezekiel," Scratchy answered, looking embarrassed. "She named me brother Ignatius."

"You are much better at saving lives than taking them for which I am grateful," Katerina said. "Would you accept honest employment that gives you a decent salary, a place to live, and good food?"

Both men nodded. Paradise loomed before them instead of prison.

"With the constable's and my fiance's approval," Katerina said, "I would hire you as my daughter's bodyguards."

"Baby girl what we saved?" Scratchy asked.

"Viveka is her name."

"A pretty name for a pretty baby girl," Itchy said.

Katerina looked at Constable Black who glanced at Alexander. Both men shrugged their acceptance. Next Katerina looked at Drako who was smiling at her.

"There are conditions to the employment," Katerina told the brothers. "You must be cleaned and, if necessary, deloused. You will be called by your real names, but Zeke and Iggy will suffice. No drinking, no gambling, no women."

"Kat." Drako's tone told her the last three conditions were impossible to expect.

"Except on your days off, of course," she amended.

"We accept, Ya Ladyship," Scratchy said.

"No Newgate?" Itchy whispered, and smiled when his brother shook his head.

The Duke of Inverary opened the door and beckoned to someone. The Kazanov princes walked into the office.

"Take Ezekiel and Ignatius to the countess's residence," Drako said, gesturing to the brothers. "They must be washed and, if necessary, deloused. A shave would not hurt either. Tell Dudley to feed them, and Hektor will find them a perch for the night. Kat and I will follow in a little while."

Once they had gone, Constable Black asked Katerina, "Will there be anything else, my lady?"

"I want the duchess and the Flambeau sisters brought here," she answered.

A few minutes later, the Duchess of Inverary led her charges into the office. "Thank you, Kat darling," the duchess gushed, "for making this betrothal ball one for the history books."

"You are not angry?"

"Darling, this night perpetuates the fact that *I* hostess the most exciting events."

Katerina turned to the Flambeau sisters. "Raven accepted Alexander's request to spy for him by befriending the Blond Brigade and, at his insistence, kept it a secret from you. I apologize for creating discord between sisters."

The surprised horror on Blaze Flambeau's face was almost comical. "Sister, I am sorry for the ugly things I've said."

"I forgive you." Raven turned to Alexander. "Can we dance now?"

"Of course." Alexander offered his arm and escorted her from the office.

"You cannot forgive me so easily," Blaze complained, following them out. "I cannot live with my conscience unless I make it up to you."

"You don't need to do that," Raven said. "I forgive you."

"You must get even with me . . ." Their voices faded away down the hallway.

The Flambeau sisters giggled, and the duchess gestured them to leave.

"Your Grace, may I impose upon you to help me plan my wedding?" Katerina asked.

"I would love to plan your wedding," the duchess answered. "Magnus and I will host the reception at Inverary House."

Drako cleared his throat. "We want to marry as quickly as possible."

"What do you say, Magnus?" the duchess asked her husband. "Meet on Beltane, marry on Lammas, parents on—?" She looked at the prince. "Parents on Beltane?"

Drako shook his head, and Katerina blushed.

The duchess's dimpled smile appeared. "Parents on St. George's Day?"

Again, Drako shook his head.

"The vernal equinox?"

Drako shrugged. "Thereabouts."

"You have been busy, Your Highness." The Duchess of Inverary looked at her husband. "You ordered me to leave them alone and let nature take its course."

The Duke of Inverary looped his wife's hand through his arm to escort her from the room. "Roxie, nature did take its course."

Drako stood and offered the constable his hand. "Thank you for all your help."

"I hope you are still grateful when you receive my bill," Amadeus said, shaking his hand.

Once the constable had gone, Drako sat beside Katerina on the sofa and slipped his arm around her. The two sat in silence for a time, content within the security of the other's nearness.

"You knew I would bring my pistol."

"I trusted you not to use it."

"Admit you worried I would pull the trigger," she teased him.

"I dislike the sight of blood and feared I would embarrass myself by puking if you blew Yuri's head off," Drako told her.

Katerina giggled at that.

"I need to set the record straight about one additional thing," Drako said. "Yuri and I were always at odds, and he used my absence from Moscow to seduce my former fiancee, driving Raisa to suicide."

"Why did you not force him to admit it?" Katerina asked. "That would have ruined his reputation, prince or no prince."

"I could not increase her family's anguish by allowing her indiscretion to become public knowledge," Drako said. "I paupered him instead, forcing him to live off his family's largesse like a beggar."

"Prolonging his torment, I suppose."

"You are beginning to learn the fine art of subtlety."

Drako dipped his head, his mouth covering hers in a lingering kiss that melted into another. And then another.

"Let us go home to bed," he suggested.

Katerina gave him a feline smile. "You said you would not visit my bed until we were husband and wife."

"I changed my mind."

One Year Later

Katerina sat on a stone bench in the shade beneath the elm tree in her garden. In her arms slept her four-month-old son, Prince Adam Konstantin Kazanov. Drako sat beside her, his arms around her shoulders.

With his coattails flapping, Dudley raced across the courtyard from their main residence to the refurbished town mansion that housed their grand ballroom. Three minutes later, the majordomo retraced his path to their main residence, his pace even faster on the return trip.

"With those coattails flapping, Dudley reminds me of a strange bird," Drako remarked. "He is making me tired."

"Our first anniversary celebrated with our first ball in our grand ballroom," Katerina said. "I fear Dudley may expire from excitement."

"I caught him in the foyer practicing his announcing of guests," Drako told her, his gaze following hers to the six little girls sitting around a table in the gazebo. "Why is Viveka hostessing her tea party in the gazebo instead of the tree house?"

"Ezekiel and Ignatius are providing today's entertainment," Katerina said, "and they dislike high places."

"Let me hold Adam." Drako lifted his son out of her arms and cradled the infant against his chest. "You should have designed a setting for the Sancy and worn it tonight."

"*Le Grand Sancy* is too rare to cut into pieces," Katerina said. "Someone of importance should wear the diamond."

"You are the most important person to me."

"You say the sweetest things, darling."

"What shall we do with the Sancy?" Drako asked. "Keeping it locked away seems a crime."

"I suggest we have my brother present the diamond to the king," Katerina answered. "Hektor may win a title for his generosity."

"You scheming little witch," Drako said, smiling. "I like the idea. Let us run it by the Duke of Inverary tonight."

The two lapsed into silence, listening to the little girls conversing between courses of cookies and lemon barley water. All six wore their tiaras, Viveka's lopsided like a drunken princess.

"My bodyguards will perform tricks for us," Viveka was saying.

"What is a bodyguard?" Lily asked her.

Princess Roxanne answered her youngest sister, "A bodyguard guards your body from harm."

"My daddy says"—Viveka smiled in Drako's direction—"princesses need bodyguards."

"I do not have a bodyguard," Bess said.

"Neither do I," Lily said.

"None of us have bodyguards," Roxanne said, her expression deeply concerned. "How remiss of Daddy not to buy us bodyguards."

"You can borrow mine to take you home," Viveka said, "and tell your daddies to get you one tomorrow."

"Do we buy them on Bond Street?" Lily asked.

Viveka shrugged, calling to Drako, "Daddy, did you buy my bodyguards on Bond Street?"

"Newgate," Drako answered.

Katerina giggled and glanced at her son who gave her a toothless smile. "Adam thinks his daddy is silly."

"Here come my bodyguards now," Viveka cried.

Zeke and Iggy, formerly known as Scratchy and Itchy, crossed the courtyard to the gazebo. "Hello, baby girls," Zeke greeted them.

"We are big girls," Lily said.

"Princesses," Roxanne added.

"Hello, big baby-girl princesses," Iggy said, making them giggle.

"Zeke, will you do the trick?" Viveka asked.

"Watch my head." Standing perfectly still, Zeke performed the death-defying task of wiggling his ears.

The princesses clapped their approval.

Meanwhile, Iggy rolled his shirt sleeve up to his shoulder. "Watch this." He hummed a tune, his arm muscles dancing up and down to the rhythm.

Again, the princesses clapped.

"Watch this." Zeke looked at Iggy, asking, "Are you ready, brother?"

Both men stood still. Their tongues slipped out from between their lips and touched the tips of their noses.

"I can do all three tricks," Hektor called, crossing the courtyard. "At the same time."

"Do it, Uncle Hektor."

"I am joking, sweetheart."

Dudley appeared in the mansion's doorway, calling, "Ezekiel and Ignatius, I need you here."

Hektor walked across the garden to his sister and his brother-in-law. "Adam wants to attend the tea party," he said, lifting his nephew into his arms. "I caught Dudley practicing his announcing. Perhaps you should practice your waltz for tonight."

With the princesses giggling in the background, Drako rose from the bench and bowed. "My dearest wife, may I have this waltz?"

"My darling husband," Katerina said, dropping him a curtsey, "*all* my waltzes belong to you."

Humming a tune only she could hear, Drako swirled Katerina around and around the garden. He pulled her against his body, his face inching closer to steal a kiss. And the—

"Oops."

"Mummy, Baby Adam puked on Uncle Hektor."

"Tell Uncle Hektor to wipe it off," Katerina called.

Drako's lips touched hers. "I love you, wife."

"And I love you, husband."

Please turn the page for an exciting sneak peak of
Patricia Grasso's
DESIRING THE HIGHLANDER,
coming soon from Zebra Books.

Chapter One

The duchess was giving her grief.

Blaze Flambeau crossed the bedchamber to the window overlooking the gardens. Her lips quirked in grudging admiration for her stepmother, a woman determined to reach her goals, not unlike herself.

After persuading the duke to acknowledge his seven Flambeau daughters, the duchess had decided to find them advantageous matches from the ranks of society's elite. Her Grace had managed to marry the two eldest Flambeaus to Russian princes, and the youngest was betrothed to a marquis. That left four unattached sisters, including herself, an astonishing piece of matchmaking accomplished in one year.

Her meddling stepmother refused to accept that she planned never to marry, and discussing the situation with her father had not helped. He had shrugged at her complaint and explained that his dearest Roxie wanted everyone to marry and live as happily as she. Of course, as the duke's second wife, the present duchess had not been abandoned at home while her husband sired seven daughters on his long-time lover.

Blaze knew she would not feel differently once she had met—as her father insisted—the right man, her true love. What had love given her mother except heartache and seven daughters?

Scanning the world outside her window, Blaze spotted the gardeners performing their daily chores. She would need to wait before slipping outside to complete her task.

Blaze leaned against the windowsill, willing the gardeners to hurry, when the first stirrings of dread seeped into her consciousness. Her stepmother had invited several bachelors to dine with the family that evening, and nobody refused an invitation from the Duke and Duchess of Inverary.

Snoring from the bed intruded on her thoughts, drawing her attention. Puddles was lying in the middle of her bed, all four limbs out-stretched. The brindled mastiff looked like he was sleeping off a seven-day drunk.

Blaze wandered across the room to the cheval mirror. Studying her reflection, she wondered how she appeared to gentlemen.

Gawd, she hated her freckles, and her red hair accentuated the sprinkling of dots across the bridge of her nose. Blushing diminished the tiny flaws, but she could not blush every minute of every day for the remainder of her life.

If only she had inherited the Flambeau black hair and flawless complexion. A Scots ancestor—Aunt Bedelia Campbell, her father said—had sent the riotous red hair and freckles through time and space to land on her, making her the cuckoo in the nest. The classic Flambeau beauty had even touched her own twin, who looked nothing like her.

What sane gentleman would offer for a redhaired, freckled-face monkey? Blaze asked herself.

A blind man, came her honest answer, *or a man desiring a close connection with the influential Duke of Inverary*.

She supposed her freckles did not matter, though. Attracting a husband did not appear on her list of priorities. Winning the thoroughbred races that season would give her the money to reach her goal. At least, set her plan into motion.

And yet . . . A smile touched her lips when she recalled the handsome gentleman who had requested a dance at her eldest sister's wedding the previous year. Waltzing with the Marquis of Somewhere-Or-Other had made her feel almost pretty. At least for the dance's duration. The marquis had then proceeded to dance with every female guest, no matter her age or appearance. The fond memory disappeared as quickly as it had come. Men were untrustworthy in affairs of the heart, the bane of women's existence.

Gazing out the window again, Blaze noted the gardeners had gone. She grabbed the bulging sack stowed beside her bed.

"Outside, Puddles," she called, heading for the door.

Awakened by the word *out*, the black-masked mastiff bolted off the bed. He trotted beside her down the corridor.

Blaze stopped at the next door and peered into her twin's bedchamber. Her sister was sitting at a table near the window and working on ledgers.

"Bliss?"

"I'm too busy at the moment," her sister said, without looking up. "Ask someone else."

Blaze closed the door. Her twin was always busy when she needed her assistance.

Continuing down the hall, Blaze paused at her sister Serena's bedchamber and pressed her ear to the door. The sound of muted voices in conversation reached her. She opened the door. Apparently, Serena was posing for Sophia, her artistic identical twin.

Blaze cleared her throat. "Sisters?"

Both twins looked at her, their gazes dropping to the sack in her hands. "No," they said simultaneously, and then giggled.

Blaze closed the door and walked the length of the corridor to her youngest sibling's door. She raised her fist to knock but heard her sister's voice.

"Come inside, Blaze."

That made her smile. Raven always knew things in advance. She wondered if her sister could tell her how successful the thoroughbred racing season would prove.

Blaze stepped into her sister's chamber. "Will you—?"

"I've been waiting for you," Raven interrupted, crossing the chamber, "but I am not digging."

"I will bury the deceased."

Raven laughed at that. "What if Her Grace catches you?"

"I'll say I was simply playing an April Fool's joke on her," she answered.

"You are sneaky."

Blaze gave her a sunshine smile. "Thank you for the compliment, sister."

"Do you have a shovel?" Raven asked, following her into the hallway.

"I borrowed one of the gardener's and hid it behind the gazebo." Blaze started to walk down the corridor to the main staircase.

Raven touched her arm. "Using the servants' stairs will be more discreet."

Blaze nodded and retraced her steps in the opposite direction. "You are almost as sneaky as I am."

"Thank you for the compliment, sister." Raven threw her arm across her shoulders in camaraderie. "Sneakiness must run in our family."

Blaze gave her a sidelong glance. "Did we inherit our sneakiness from the Flambeaus or the Campbells?"

"Both, probably."

Hurrying down the back stairs to the garden door, Blaze and Raven stepped into an unseasonably warm April afternoon. They walked through the formal gardens and passed the maze's clipped hedges. Ahead of them stretched an expanse of manicured lawns and then the woodland, the white gazebo standing guard between the two.

Birdsong wafted through the air, catching Blaze's attention. She looked up at the sky. High, thin clouds diluted its blue brilliance, a hawk was gliding on a breeze while searching for its next meal.

Walking around the gazebo, Blaze grabbed the shovel and returned to where Raven sat on the structure's top step. Puddles dashed around, enjoying his freedom like a felon released from Newgate.

With her right foot on the shovel, Blaze used her weight to lift the grassy top layer of grass and gently set it aside. She repeated this again and again until she had the width and the length of the hole she wanted to dig.

"Life seems different with Fancy and Belle married," Blaze said as she worked. "In a few months, you will be gone, too."

"I may need to postpone the wedding," Raven told her.

Blaze stopped digging. "Why is that?"

Raven shrugged. "Among other things, I feel one of my sisters may need to use the wedding plans for herself."

"Which sister?" Blaze asked, her blue gaze narrowing.

"I don't know everything," Raven said. "Why are you setting the grass aside?"

"Once the hole is filled," she answered, "I will replace the grass, and no one will notice the grave."

"That *is* sneaky," Raven said. "Alex will be arriving in Newmarket this afternoon."

"Are he and the constable investigating that jockey's murder?" Blaze asked, glancing at her.

"I suppose so," her sister answered, "but Alex will be staying at his grandfather's estate. He will be following the thoroughbreds when they leave Newmarket."

Blaze fixed her thoughts on her own thoroughbred, a gift from her father, and their success during the racing season. She wanted to ask her sister if Pegasus would win but feared the answer.

"You will experience joy, sadness, and surprise," Raven said, her smile ambiguous.

"Do you mean Pegasus will win?" Her digging forgotten for the moment, Blaze sat on the stair beside her sister.

"Your filly will beat the others," Raven answered, "but she must overcome a slight problem first."

Her comment surprised Blaze. "What is the problem?"

"I don't know, but you will find the solution to it."

Blaze smiled at the encouraging words. "Pegasus loves running."

"Doesn't winning require strategy, too?"

Blaze considered the question. She hadn't thought about strategy in terms of horseracing. "I will speak to Rooney," she said, referring to her jockey.

"Wait until he's sober," Raven advised her.

"Rooney does enjoy his spirits." Blaze grinned and, rising from her perch, resumed digging. "Her Grace invited several bachelors to dinner this evening."

"Stepmama has invited three bachelors," Raven told her.

"That takes care of Bliss, Serena, and Sophia," Blaze said, her mood brightening. For the first time in her life, she felt happy being overlooked. "Perhaps the duchess has accepted my preference for remaining unmarried."

"If I were you," Raven said, "I wouldn't wager on that. Why don't you want to marry?"

Blaze tossed a shovelful of dirt aside and then looked her sister in the eye. "Testicles cause trouble."

Raven laughed. "Sister, all three bachelors have been invited to meet you."

"Me?" Blaze stopped digging to brush a wisp of fiery hair away from her face. "That woman will not rest until she marries me off. I don't think she likes me."

"Stepmama is giving you a choice," Raven told her. "That means she likes you best."

"What if I don't want anyone?"

"That is *not* one of your choices." Raven smiled, adding, "Her Grace possesses a wealth of knowledge for living with troublesome testicles."

"Have you been following her advice?"

Raven nodded. "I am becoming adept at confounding Alex."

"I should speak to Her Grace before the Jockey Club Ball," Blaze said, and then a disturbing thought stepped from the shadows of her mind. "What if none of those bachelors interests me? What if I don't interest them? What if one interests me, but I do not interest him?"

"You think too much," Raven said. "Relax and enjoy the competition for your affections."

"Humph, Bliss says I do not think at all." Blaze tossed another shovelful of dirt aside. "The man I marry should love me even if I were not the Duke of Inverary's daughter, but how will I know which gentleman is sincere?"

"You will know in your heart."

"Gawd, you sound like Papa."

"Miss Raven."

Both sisters turned at the call and spied Tinker, the duke's majordomo, hurrying toward them.

"The Marquis of Basildon has arrived," Tinker announced, reaching them. "Her Grace sent me to find you."

"Thank you, Tinker." Raven rose from her perch on the stair. "Tell the marquis I will be along shortly."

"Yes, Miss Raven." Tinker turned to walk away but paused, his gaze shifting from Blaze to the shovel in her hand and the hole.

"You did not see me digging this hole," she said.

The man's lips twitched. "I have not seen you all afternoon, Miss Blaze."

"Thank you, Tinker."

"You are very welcome." The majordomo started across the lawn toward the mansion.

Blaze looked at her sister. "How will you confound Alex today?"

"I will take the long way round," Raven answered. "Walking slowly, of course. I believe that will set the tone for his visit. I would never want him to think I had been waiting for him."

"Were you waiting for him?"

"Yes, I have been anticipating his visit." With that, Raven walked away.

Alone, Blaze patted her dog's massive head. "Good boy, Puddles." Then she resumed her digging, pressing the shovel into the dirt with her foot before scooping it up and tossing it aside.

A sudden chill danced down her spine, and an uncanny feeling of being watched seeped into her senses. She could almost feel someone's gaze on her.

Blaze stilled, her gaze drifting to the mastiff lying relaxed in the sunshine. Which meant there was no imminent danger.

Nevertheless, Blaze could not shake the feeling. She scanned the woodland behind the gazebo but saw nothing. Then she whirled around to scan the lawns and formal garden. No one was lurking about.

Blaze lifted her gaze to the mansion's windows and

caught movement in one of the second-floor rooms. That would be her father's office.

Damn, damn, damn. Trouble had found her again.

Blaze knew she would be getting another lecture from her father and stepmother on proper deportment. Digging in the dirt would never be considered a ladylike pursuit.

And then she smiled. Thank God for those bachelors. If they arrived early, the bachelors could save her from a dressing down.

What the hell is she doing?

Ross MacArthur, the Marquis of Awe, stood at the duke's office window and watched the petite redhead digging in his kinsman's manicured lawns. He'd never seen a gardening girl, never mind one bent on ruining a fine lawn.

The marquis admired the girl's fiery hair glinting in the afternoon's sun. A smile touched his lips when she bent over to scoop another shovelful of dirt, offering him the sight of her backside's delightful form in the light gown she wore.

When the girl stopped working to look over her shoulder, Ross scanned the area. He wanted to see what had distracted her, but the gardens appeared deserted.

Resuming her task, the gardening girl tossed another shovelful of dirt. A moment later, she paused again, this time facing the mansion.

Ross guessed the girl felt watched. She stood motionless, staring at the mansion, and he knew her gaze was traveling from window to window.

"Come here, Ross," the Duke of Inverary beckoned him. "I want to test your whisky knowledge."

"Ye pour the whisky into a glass and drink it," Ross

said, turning away from the window, his dark gaze on his kinsman. "What more do I need to know?"

Ross smiled at the duke's irritated expression. Heavily invested in the business, the duke and his own father believed whisky akin to chalice wine, the symbolic blood of Christ.

"Never joke about whisky or horses," the Duke of Inverary warned him. "That would be sacrilegious."

Sauntering across the office, Ross dropped into a chair in front of the desk. Five chunky glasses, each containing a measure of whisky, stood in a line on the desk.

Ross wondered the reason he'd been summoned. Inverary was as wily as his own father, and Ross knew damn well that he hadn't been invited here for the purpose of tasting whisky.

"Isna investin' in Campbell whisky enough?" Ross managed to appear relaxed in the leather chair. "What scheme are ye and my father hatchin'?"

"I need to decide if you're worthy," the duke told him.

His dark gaze narrowed on the older man. "Worthy for what?"

The Duke of Inverary smiled. "I will tell you by and by."

The duke's inscrutable smile meant trouble. His own father wore that same expression when he wanted something.

Ross slid his gaze to the Jockey Club's Triple Crown trophy, which the Inverary stables had won the previous year, reminding him of his perpetual second place finishes. He planned to win the coveted trophy this year, or at the very least prevent his kinsman from taking it home again, the same horse needing to win the three main classic races.

"Verra well, Yer Grace." Ross lifted the first glass and sipped the whisky, holding it in his mouth, letting the warmth of his tongue release its flavors. "Full-bodied, muscular, and bold." He set the glass on the desk. "Highland whisky, of course."

The duke smiled at the correct answer. "How is your father?"

"Da and the Feathered Flock will be arrivin' in Newmarket before the Jockey Club Ball," Ross answered.

"What is the Feathered Flock?"

"My sister Mairi will be bringin' Drucilla Gordon, Felicia Burns, and Catriona Calder," Ross told him. "I called them the Feathered Flock because they're constantly preenin' and twitterin' like canaries."

"All women preen and twitter, especially wives and daughters of aristocrats," Inverary said. "I recall your father was hoping for a match between you and the Gordon girl."

"I've no inclination to marry one of my sister's friends," Ross said, reaching for the second glass of whisky. He kept the liquid in his mouth a moment before swallowing. "Elegant and floral. Lowland whisky, no doubt."

The Duke of Inverary nodded at his answer. "I never hear your name attached to any ladies."

"I dinna trifle with maidens or marrieds."

"Do you keep a mistress?"

The question gave Ross an unexpected jolt, putting him on guard. "Why do you ask?"

Inverary shrugged, his inscrutable smile appearing again. "Simple idle curiosity while passing time with my favorite cousin's son."

Idle curiosity, my arse, Ross thought. He smelled a trap. He'd never known Inverary to be prone to idle curiosity. The man's duchess was another matter, though.

"Where has Douglas Gordon been hiding himself lately?" Inverary asked, changing the subject.

Ross relaxed again. "Dougie's been delayed in London,

confounded by this Seven Doves Company undercuttin' his prices, but he'll arrive in Newmarket before the Jockey Ball."

"I suppose you'll be stayin' with Gordon once this Feathered Flock perches at your home," the duke said.

Ross smiled at that. "I keep rooms at the Rowley Lodge to escape the preenin' twitterers."

"Did you hear what happened to Charlie?"

"I heard he'd been stabbed in a drunken brawl, God rest his soul," Ross said, reaching for the third whisky glass.

"Horseracing's best jockey would never have been involved in a brawl two weeks before the first race," the duke said. "I've given Harry the nod to ride Thor."

"Perhaps, Charlie was reluctantly drawn into the brawl."

"Charlie was murdered to prevent his winning me the Crown again this year," Inverary said. "Alexander Blake is arriving today for the races and helping Constable Black investigate the murder. Hiring London's most famous constable is costing me a fortune."

"You can afford it." Ross sipped the whisky. "This spicy taste screams Campbeltown whisky."

The Duke of Inverary chuckled. "You are three for three, lad."

"What's this I heard aboot a monkey livin' with ye?" Ross asked, resting his tongue before continuing the whisky tasting.

"My daughter Blaze acquired a Capuchin monkey," Inverary said, rolling his eyes. "Blaze inherited my Aunt Bedelia's affinity with animals. Did your father ever tell you stories of Aunt Bedelia and her husband?"

"Ye mean the witch?" Ross asked, reaching for the fourth glass of whisky.

"Bedelia was no witch," the duke said, "but she did possess several unusual gifts, one of which was communing with animals."

Ross sipped the whisky, savoring its flavor. "Speyside whisky, soft and lovely but no Lowland lady."

"Correct again, lad." Inverary continued his story, "Anyway, Blaze acquired Miss Giggles, but Roxie insisted the monkey needed to go."

"Why?" Ross's lips quirked in a barely suppressed smile at the duke's predicament. "Monkeys are such wee, cute creatures."

"Do you know how a monkey expresses displeasure?" Ross shook his head.

"The monkey tosses its feces," the duke told him, "and Miss Giggles took an instant dislike to my wife's good friend, Lady Althorpe."

Ross chuckled. "I wish I could've seen that."

"I needed to lose the monkey," Inverary said, gesturing to the fifth glass of whisky, "or I would lose my wife. On the other hand, I'd lose my daughter if I used my pistol on it."

"How did ye solve the problem?" Ross sipped the whisky, the warmth of his tongue releasing its distinctive taste. "Peaty and smoky, this Islay has been aged better than fifteen years, I'd say."

Smiling his approval, the Duke of Inverary nodded and then continued his story, "I sat Blaze down and explained that Giggles, being an adult female, needed a husband. Though it broke her heart, my daughter saw the sense in that and agreed to give Miss Giggles to the Tower Menagerie. I bought the monkey a husband—Chuckles—and the two recently became proud parents. Problem solved."

"Good thinkin' on yer part," Ross said. "Now, tell me what I'm worthy of."

"You are worthy to marry one of my daughters," Inverary answered.

Ross coughed and reached for a glass of whisky. He gulped a healthy swig and shuddered as the potent liquid burned a path to his stomach.

"Russian princes are all very well," the duke was saying, "but I aim for some of my girls to wed sturdy Scotsmen."

"I'm honored," Ross hedged, "but our families dinna need another connection, ye and my father bein' cousins and all."

"My wife has decided," Inverary said, his gaze narrowing on the younger man. "Accept your fate, Ross. After all, you need to marry someone."

"Which daughter does the duchess have in mind?"

"Blaze."

"The animal communicator?"

"You breed and race horses," the duke said, "and my Blaze added to the Inverary coffers by picking last year's winners."

Ross slid his gaze to the Triple Crown trophy. "Did she ever pick a loser?"

"I don't believe so."

Ross knew he'd been hooked neater than any fish. "How does she do it?"

"You will need to ask her."

"I will certainly enjoy meetin' Blaze," Ross hedged, trying to sound casual.

"There are two minor problems," Inverary warned him. "The first is Blaze doesn't want to marry. She intends to win enough money this racing season—*I gave her a filly*—to open a farm for unwanted horses, dogs, and cats. Naturally, Roxie worries the chit will end a spinster."

"Yer daughter has ambition," Ross said. "Which filly did ye give her?"

"I gave her Pegasus," the duke answered, "and Rooney will jockey her."

"Pegasus balks at goin' through holes," Ross said, "and Rooney is a drunkard. Ye've set yer daughter up for failure."

"Blaze needs to learn that horseracing can be a difficult and heartbreaking business," the duke replied.

"I dinna ken the reason ye keep Rooney on yer payroll," Ross added.

"My grandfather was his great-grandfather," Inverary answered, "though Rooney hails from the illegitimate branch of the family." The duke chuckled, adding, "Rooney got Aunt Bedelia's red hair, too, and could pass as my daughter's brother. I thought you could become acquainted under the guise of helping her."

"Mind ye, I amna agreein' to marriage at this verra moment," Ross said, "but I'm curious to know if yer plannin' to force the lass down the aisle."

"Roxie insists on giving this daughter a choice," the duke told him, "but she does favor you."

Ross loved nothing more than a challenge. "Who's my competition?"

"Prince Lykos Kazanov and the Earl of Boston have been invited to dine with us tonight."

"Dirk Stanley is a compulsive gambler."

"We don't expect Blaze to choose the earl."

"I'll be lookin' forward to meetin' the lass and my competition," Ross said, stretching his long legs out in front of him. This racing season could prove interesting as well as lucrative.

"You'll like her," Inverary said. "My Blaze has a big heart along with a hot temper to match her fiery hair, which she also inherited from Bedelia Campbell."

Ross stood, crossing the office to the window, and gestured outside. "Is that Blaze?"

The Duke of Inverary joined him there. "That is she. What is she doing to my garden?"

Blaze dropped the shovel and, opening a sack, pulled out a fur. Shaking her head, she folded the fur and placed it in the hole. Then she reached into the sack again, producing another fur.

"Good God, she's burying my wife's fur coats."

Ross shouted with laughter, and the Duke of Inverary chuckled. Neither heard the door opening.

"My lord, you were able to join us," a woman said, by way of a greeting.

Both men whirled around at the sound of the duchess's voice. They stood with their backs against the window to block the duchess's view.

"You gentlemen look guilty," Roxie teased them, crossing the chamber. "What are you hiding?" The duchess peered out the window through the space between their bodies, the girl's red hair catching her attention. "What is Blaze doing?"

"I believe she's buryin' yer furs."

"Oh, dear God." The duchess swooned at his words.

Ross caught her before she dropped to the floor and, with the duke's help, carried her to the sofa in front of the hearth. Inverary dropped on his knees beside his wife.

"Send a maid to fetch hartshorn," the duke instructed him, "and then go outside and save my wife's furs."

Ross started for the door but paused half-way across the chamber. "Yer Grace, I'll take the lass," he said, smiling, and turned to leave. "If she's agreeable to the match, that is."

"MacArthur wants to marry Blaze?" he heard the duchess exclaim. "Even though, the little witch is burying my furs?"

"I daresay the lad wants to marry her *because* she's burying your furs."

The door clicked shut behind Ross, but he'd heard the laughter in his kinsman's voice. His conniving father must have told the duke how to pique his interest.

Ross decided he would play along. After all, he was competing against a prince and an earl, a foreigner and a gambler. He enjoyed winning, and the earl was inferior competition. The prince might give him a bit of trouble but that would make winning so much sweeter.

The lass would not prove a problem, but her dog was a monster. Wheedling a few cookies from the cook would suit his purpose in keeping the dog sweet.

Once armed with the dog's favorite cinnamon cookies, Ross strolled across the duke's lawns in the direction of the gazebo, his gaze fixed on the petite redhead's backside as she bent over. His future bride had herself a fetching arse. True, she was no bigger than a mite, the perfect size for a jockey had she been born male.

Lucky for him, the lass had been born female. That glorious red hair positively screamed stubborn determination. Life with her would never bore him.

Ross recalled the dance they had shared at her sister's wedding. Her small, perfectly proportioned breasts had enticed him. The fine sprinkling of freckles across the bridge of her delicate nose had intrigued him, and he'd wondered if she sported freckles anywhere else on her body.

He'd been tempted to seduce her that night, but no sane man trifled with Inverary's daughters. Besides, seducing maidens and marrieds was dangerous in the extreme.

Apparently, both Inverary and his own father wanted him to marry her. He would demolish the other two contenders and win the lass's hand in marriage. By fair means or foul.

Ross glanced at the mastiff, wagging its tail at his approach. No protection for her there.

Standing with his hands on his hips, Ross willed her to turn around. She was muttering to the dog about the slaughter of animals and remained oblivious to his presence.

"Drop the fur, lass."

GREAT BOOKS, GREAT SAVINGS!

When You Visit Our Website:
www.kensingtonbooks.com
You Can Save Money Off The Retail Price
Of Any Book You Purchase!

- **All Your Favorite Kensington Authors**
- **New Releases & Timeless Classics**
- **Overnight Shipping Available**
- **eBooks Available For Many Titles**
- **All Major Credit Cards Accepted**

Visit Us Today To Start Saving!
www.kensingtonbooks.com

All Orders Are Subject To Availability.
Shipping and Handling Charges Apply.
Offers and Prices Subject To Change Without Notice.